Praise for
RAGE IN CHUPADERA

"A stem-winder of a story."
—Douglas C. Jones, author of *The Barefoot Brigade*

"An every-way worthy successor to *Passage to Quivira* and Zollinger's other fine chronicles ... Truly a stunning picture of New Mexico in the roaring days before it achieved statehood. Once again Zollinger has retrieved the legendary past as it lived in the sun-drenched mesas of the mountain desert."
—R.D. Brown, author of *Hazzard*

"A fascinating panorama of Territorial New Mexico."
—Jeanne Williams, author of *The Unplowed Sky*

"In *Rage in Chupadera*, Zollinger firmly establishes himself as the master of the western saga.... Readers may rest assured that they are in the capable hands of authority."
—William J. Buchanan, author of *A Shining Season*

Forge books by Norman Zollinger

Chapultepec *
Corey Lane
Not of War Only
Passage to Quivira
Rage in Chupadera
Riders to Cibola

*forthcoming

RAGE IN CHUPADERA

NORMAN ZOLLINGER

A TOM DOHERTY ASSOCIATES BOOK
NEW YORK

RAGE IN CHUPADERA

Copyright © 1991 by Norman Zollinger

A Forge Book
Published by Tom Doherty Associates, Inc.
175 Fifth Avenue
New York, NY 10010

Forge® is a registered trademark of Tom Doherty Associates, Inc.

ISBN: 0-812-54843-4

First Forge edition: April 1996

Printed in the United States of America

0 9 8 7 6 5 4 3 2 1

*For
all my
Anns and Annes*

1

A thousand feet above Nogal, up where the big timber begins, the May morning air was as still as the pause between movements of a symphony, and the first rays of the sun felt warm and cheery on Corey's face.

He had begun the ride up to the Mescalero Apache reservation before dawn, when everyone except the bunkhouse cook at the X-Bar-7 was still sound asleep. Cookie had packed him a second breakfast to eat on the trail—beans and jerky, probably, he hadn't looked—and he planned to stop at the big rocks that framed Cuchillo Peak, nineteen miles back across the wide valley of the Rio Concho. From the rocks, where the trail forked upward and over the ridge toward Blazer's Mill and the Mescalero, the timbered side of Cuchillo would swell against the northern sky, making a view not as dramatic as the one from deep in the basin, but softer in its contours and friendlier, and even after spending all his life in the Ojos Negros Basin he had never tired of looking at it. In his sometimes solitary boyhood this particular look at the mountain had given his spirits a never-failing lift, had become a need. After Cuba and the war with Spain and in the years that stretched ahead of him, it might be an even greater need.

But just before he reached the rocks, a rifle shot cracked in the dry air and his horse reared.

It took a few moments to get the animal gentled down, and a few more to restore his own calm. He took a deep, easy breath. Hell, no one could be shooting at him here. He wasn't riding armed, and this sure wasn't Cuba. It was probably a hunter taking a mule deer out of season.

The sun had cleared the twin summits of Sierra Blanca, but the rocks and the trail were still half in shadow. Fifty yards ahead of him an Indian wearing the cotton leggings, the *tl'aakal* kirtle, and blood-red headband of a Mimbreño Apache, a warrior of the Red Paint People, had stepped into the trail. Long black hair fell to his shoulders. He cradled a rifle in his arms, without a doubt the one whose report had shattered the morning quiet. In spite of a lingering feeling of wariness, Corey smiled. The man on the trail was a throwback to another time in these mountains; he could have been an illustration for the book Corey was working on and not making a lot of headway with these days.

He assured himself again that the Red Paint man posed no threat, eased his mount up toward him and the rocks, and when he reached them reined up and slid from the saddle. He hoped Cookie had packed enough grub for two.

The Apache spoke first. "Been watching you for more than twenty minutes, *mage'edu*." He pushed the rifle barrel forward an inch or two with the crook of his left elbow. "Could have killed you in any of the last five."

"For Pete's sake, Harold! I wasn't exactly *sneaking* up here. And what's that *mage'edu* stuff? You know damned well I'm no more a cowboy than you are anymore."

Even though he had expected to see Harold Bishop in another hour at the most, he hadn't recognized his friend until he spoke. The last time he had seen him, long before Corey had gone off to the war, the young Mimbreño's hair had been trimmed well above his ears, and he had been wearing a blue serge suit, the one Corey's mother, Virgie, had bought for him at Stafford's down in Black Springs, before Corey and Virgie, along with Jim McPherson, publisher of the *Chupadera County News*, put him on the train for Pennsylvania and Carlisle Indian School.

Corey had never expected to see Harold dressed like this again. It was, of course, the way he had dressed when they first knew each other, when Harold had been about the only soul in Chupadera County to breach Corey's solitude.

Harold leaned the rifle against the nearest rock, smiled the lopsided smile he had so often smiled as a boy when he yanked a trout from the Rio Bonito with more eagerness than art, then rushed to Corey and flung his slim arms around him. It was a long embrace.

"Thanks for coming, Corey," Harold said as he stepped back. "I've been expecting you for a week."

"Would have come sooner. First time I was in town to pick up mail was yesterday—and I would have come without your note, anyway. You know that."

"Sure, but I couldn't wait much longer. How was your war, Junior?"

"Hot. Boring when I wasn't scared spitless." Harold wouldn't pry about the war. He knew Corey too well for that. Funny. It was surprisingly pleasant to be called Junior again after all these years. He didn't bridle at it as he had so many times when Harold and he were growing up together, riding the high pastures of the X-Bar-7, camping and fishing in the giant timber of the Mescalero, and racing over the ridge to the store at Blazer's Mill to see if a shipment of horehound candy had come in from the Martin Dawson Company in Chicago. He wondered if the young Apache facing him still

had that incredibly hollow sweet tooth. He pointed to the rifle. "What do you mean you could have killed me? You never
could hit the wall of an outhouse with a Winchester, even
from inside it."

"I'm better. Honest Injun, Corey. Been getting in a lot of
target practice lately. Hit *two* outhouses just last week—out of
five tries."

"Has that got anything to do with the *chihende* getup? You
look like you're going on the warpath."

Unless Corey was mistaken, Harold's look turned a little
dark at the last remark, but of course Corey hadn't seen him
since he went off to school. Perhaps college had turned his
happy-go-lucky friend into a more serious man all the way
around. The two-week-old message waiting for Corey in the
X-Bar-7 post office box in Black Springs had been serious
enough, come to think of it. *Come up to the Mescalero pronto,
Corey. Important.*

"What's up, Harold? What did you want me up here for?"

"It can wait a bit, Corey. Ana said to haul you to the house
even before we talk."

Ana Bishop! Corey felt a surge of homecoming as powerful
as the one that overwhelmed him when he came back to the
X-Bar-7 from the war. Harold took more after Ana than he
did after the father who was killed accidentally in his sawmill
three months ago, while Corey was still doing occupation
duty in Havana. Tony's death was something Corey would
have to talk about with Harold now, little as he wanted to.

Tony Bishop had been just about the last of the Red Paint
People led by old Nana in that dangerous summer of '81 and,
Corey could bet, was still an unrepentant Mimbreño to the
core until the day he died. Virgie had written Corey about
Tony's death, and Corey had sent a long letter to Ana and
her family. Tony had ridden against—and, at the end, with—
Corey's father. He had been there the day the elder Corey
died. Tony and Corey had never spoken about it when Corey

was a frequent guest in the Bishop home. Too bad. Tony's memories of those days would have helped bring more life and surely some much-needed honesty to the history Corey was now writing. No point in lamenting it, though. Tony never had been a talker. Even had he been, Corey might not have listened. Now only the mountain spirits could listen to Tony, and they wouldn't pass his stories on to the living.

"Lucy's looking for you, too," Harold said. "She made something special for your birthday. What will you be next week, twenty-eight?"

Lucy Bishop must be nineteen now. In the Apache view she had been a woman for six years or more, but she had still seemed a child the last time Corey had seen her, at the ceremonial dances three years ago, just another pretty, costumed Indian girl with bright black eyes and a figure like a boy's. Good people, the Bishops—even Tony, for all his sometime sullenness. Corey suddenly missed the old warrior terribly, something he hadn't had time to do in Cuba.

"Sorry about Tony, Harold."

"I know you are." Harold merely shrugged, but the dark look came again, and to Corey's eyes it held something stronger than sorrow. Apaches might well have inured themselves against physical pain to the point of indifference; but they had no more defenses than Corey had against torments of the soul. He had been right to dread bringing up the subject of Tony's death, but he could never have avoided it, or even delayed it for very long. He started to ask more, then thought better of it when Harold went on, "Thanks for the letter, Corey. I had such a miserable slow time getting back here it beat me home by a week. Meant a lot to Ana and Lucy."

"Where's your horse?"

"In the rocks." The smile was back again, absolutely dazzling now. What a quicksilver young man Harold Bishop was. "You know us Apache savages only ride *to* the battle, Junior. We do our real fighting strictly on foot. Incidentally, *you* may not be a cowboy now, but I still put in my time with the council's herd. Mount up. I'll get my pony and race you to the house."

"How much of a start do you want?"

Harold laughed. He had every right. It would be a race Corey stood little chance of winning. Even three years at Carlisle couldn't have made Harold Bishop forget how to coax speed from the most reluctant mount. Corey couldn't remember a single race he had ever won against his friend, and there must have been three a week through all those halcyon summers. Harold picked up the rifle and disappeared in the nearest rocks. The years in the East hadn't robbed him of his ability to move like a bobcat in the mountains, either.

The hoofs of the horse Harold was riding were already clattering from behind the rocks by the time Corey had swung into the saddle, and perhaps it was the sharp hoofbeats and their echoes that kept him from hearing the riders coming up the trail he had just come up himself. At any rate the first he realized he and Harold were no longer alone was when the Apache eased a spotted pony through a gap in the rocks and stared back over Corey's shoulder. Something had clouded his good-natured face again, turned it almost black.

When Corey turned he saw two mounted men leading a string of black mules. The mules plodded along under diamond-hitch packs as big as the rocks which had hidden Harold's pony.

The rider in front looked vaguely familiar to Corey, although Corey couldn't have put a name to him. He had a thin, foxlike face with three days' growth of beard, and with his greasy wide-brimmed hat and well-worn chaps he looked like any local saddle tramp, one of the layabouts from Black Springs or the ranches.

The second rider wore a campaign hat much like the one Corey had worn in Cuba, and a khaki tunic above military-style riding breeches. His horse seemed to be giving him a difficult time.

The small train turned toward San Isidro, not toward Harold and Corey. The lead rider glanced up once toward the rocks and down again; the man in the campaign hat, too busy trying to manage his mount, didn't so much as turn their way. The men apparently weren't even going to hail Harold and Corey—odd for this big, all too often lonely country.

As the last mule in the string turned on the San Isidro trail, Corey saw it wasn't loaded the same as the others were. A freight saddle was piled high with leather cases, and on top of these was a surveyor's transit. The pack train moved on and out of sight in the ponderosas.

Behind Corey, Harold muttered something Corey didn't catch, then spat another word out like venom. *"Gu'uchi!"*

Corey wasn't sure—his Apache had suffered some during his time in Cuba—but it seemed that Harold had said "pig," or "pigs." The Mimbreño's face under the red headband was still as black as a Jornada storm. The young Red Paint man might take after his mother in every other respect, but at this moment he had suddenly become his father, Tony.

"All right, Harold. Something's gnawing at you. Are you sure what you wanted me up here for can wait till we reach the house? Your note said 'important.' Do those men have anything to do with it, or have you just turned sour on general principles?"

A slight wind breathed through the rocks behind them, and from somewhere—hard to tell distance or direction—a raven cried an off-key, mocking cry. For a moment Corey feared that these were the only replies that would come his way today. Perhaps he had been too direct, too abrupt. Harold Bishop didn't always answer questions, even when he was in a lighter mood than he appeared to be right now.

Then Harold spoke. "What do you know about how Tony died, Corey?"

"What Virgie wrote me—and what I read in the *Chupadera County News* she sent me.*" He hoped Harold didn't mean for him to spell it out—the newspaper account had been brutally graphic—and he sure hoped Harold wouldn't want to recite all the gruesome details for *him*, either.

"And how did the *News* say it happened?"

"That Tony was working the mill alone and apparently slipped and fell into the roughing saw."

Harold turned his pony and squared it up with the trail. He was staring hard at where the pack train had disappeared, and all Corey could see was his slim back until he turned. The Indian's face had become a dull bronze mask. "My father's death was no accident, Corey." Then the mask slipped away, leaving only the impish countenance that had laughed its way through the sweaty, grimy, backbreaking work of more than half a dozen roundups and brandings at the X-Bar-7. "Now—how about that race?"

Harold and the spotted pony were ten yards up the trail toward the reservation before Corey could so much as set his spurs.

The Mimbreño's words were still ringing in his head. *My father's death was no accident, Corey.*

Corey lashed his horse with the free end of the reins.

Homecoming? It might not be one, after all.

2

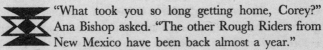"What took you so long getting home, Corey?" Ana Bishop asked. "The other Rough Riders from New Mexico have been back almost a year."

"I was transferred to General Miles's command right after the fighting stopped, Ana. We stayed on doing some occupying and relief work. I didn't mind. I hadn't even *seen* Cuba until then."

"Nelson Miles? Star Chief Miles?" She pursed her lips.

He nodded. Yes, the mention of the man who had taken the Chiricahua's final, pitiful surrender in '86 still brought uneasy memories, even though Tony Bishop himself had never surrendered.

"Well . . ." she said, "I suppose Miles wasn't the worst of them. Not as good as Gray Wolf Crook, but who of the soldiers was? Tony always said Miles never *meant* to lie to us."

Ana's thick black hair, like Virgie's, was graying a little now, and there were just a few more pounds on her than three years ago, but they were firm-looking, even becoming. He had been more than half in love with her when he was fifteen, and he remembered amused looks from Tony—when Tony wasn't brooding—who had recognized how smitten he was. Ana Bishop had been the most beautiful woman in Lincoln or Chupadera County—anglo, Mex, or Indian—if he didn't count Virgie. They had always been a lot alike, his mother and this earthy mountain woman. They had the same steady, fearless look, the quick, dark, intelligent eyes, the same black hair, of course . . . and the same fierce honesty. Yes, like sisters, except that in a reversal of what you might expect—knowing Apache women and the ranch wives of the basin—it was Virgie who was quiet and reserved, withdrawn almost, Ana who had always been the quick-to-laughter, outgoing one.

Except now. Sure, she had burst through the door of the little house Tony had built with lumber from the sawmill he had run on contract for the Mescalero tribal council, meeting Corey in the front yard with a boisterous greeting, a wide, gleaming smile, and outspread arms, but it was apparent even before they sat down to eat that this was still a sorrowing and strangely tormented lady. Talking about Tony's death with Harold had been hard; with Ana it would be even worse. As with Harold, though, he would eventually have to do it.

Did she share Harold's suspicions, whatever they might be? He couldn't ask. If Harold hadn't told his mother what he was thinking, Corey certainly didn't want it to come secondhand—from him. Harold—the fugitive little weasel—had been no help at all. He had indeed beaten Corey to the house in the high, pine-ringed meadow that hung above Cow Camp Creek—by more than fifteen minutes, it turned out—but he had made himself scarce since then. "Chores," he had muttered when Corey tried once to get him alone.

Well, until Corey could corner him, he had to play this whole thing with caution. "That was a great dinner, Ana.

Thank you," he said, looking down at the wreckage on his plate. It certainly had been: a saddle of venison with wild spinach, and for dessert the *ba'n likani'* with black walnuts he had loved so much as a boy. He had wolfed it all down as greedily as a boy, too, since he hadn't touched Cookie's second breakfast still moldering in his saddlebag, and it was amazing how comfortable he felt here, eating and laughing with Ana and Lucy, when his mind was still ticking away with what Harold had said back on the trail. He wondered how Ana knew he was coming up to the Mescalero today of all days; Harold obviously hadn't. You didn't fix a feed like this for unexpected visitors. Then he remembered the second sight she always claimed she had. Might be something to it.

"*Thought* you liked it. Didn't they feed you in the army or since you got back to the X-Bar-7? You're like Harold—too thin." She chuckled, reached over and squeezed his arm, and the touch of her hand was like the warmth of a soft woolen sweater on a January day.

Ana had mentioned Tony several times during the course of the meal, not with any easily discernible grief, but with sadness, certainly. Her and Tony's marriage had been a real love affair. It relieved Corey to know that she could talk about Tony, and that he could, too, if he had to.

Still, there was something odd in the way she looked at Harold from time to time, and something even odder in the way he didn't seem to notice her glances. He was avoiding his mother as much as he was avoiding Corey.

There was something else at the table that tangled Corey's thoughts—or rather, someone else.

As much as he loved Ana, as fond as he was of Harold—who was truly a *k'is 'ilndi' naaghan*, a brother—and as much as the specter of Tony seemed to sit with them because of what Harold had said, it was Lucy who claimed his attention more and more as they ate. She looked so like the Ana of twelve or thirteen years ago she could have been her mother's twin, and yet she had something so especially her own even the most myopic man could never confuse the two of them. This certainly wasn't the Lucy Bishop he remembered from the dances three years ago, or the Lucy of three years before that, at the midsummer puberty rites that marked her passage into womanhood. He had total recall of that earnest little face when she made her trips around the four ceremonial baskets, and the shy, secretly proud smile she cast in the direction of Ana, Harold, and Tony when she rounded the third one, the one that told the world of the mountain gods that Lucy Bishop had become a woman.

Actually, Lucy was the only one of the three Bishops at the table now whose manner seemed completely normal, but Corey couldn't be sure of that, either. What was normal for Lucy? No, this was definitely not the child he remembered.

"About the dinner . . ." Ana was saying now, "Lucy did everything. Even with all the time they spent on that catechism stuff the sisters at the mission school teach, she did learn *something* useful. Lucy is now *niiji'te'e' dadziiya'*, Corey." He almost choked on the last of the black walnut muffin before she made the translation he didn't need. "Marriage age."

Lucy's head snapped up. "Stop that, Ana Bishop. You talk about my cooking and sewing to every young man who comes to the house. They can see right through you. They know you're afraid I'll be an old maid. That's why they never come back—well, almost never." She tried to scowl, but it didn't quite come off when a smile broke through.

"You're already an old maid; you'll be twenty soon," Ana said.

Lucy laughed. "Twenty makes me an old maid?"

Corey laughed, too. Then he sobered. If the young men "almost never" came back, it wasn't what they saw that kept them away. Lucy herself must not have wanted them. It hit him then that he felt good about it.

But he knew he had to get his mind off Lucy. It wasn't

good Apache manners to stare at an unmarried girl the way he feared he might have been doing, second family though the Bishops were. "Harold," he said. "There's something I just have to ask."

Harold looked up from his coffee. The only sound he made was something marvelously like a grunt. His eyes darted from Corey to Ana to Lucy and back to Corey. Corey had been dead right before in not telling Ana about the brief exchange back on the trail. Harold was terrified he was going to spill the beans.

"Your hair," Corey said. "How did it get so long in the three months you've been back from Pennsylvania?"

The grin of pure relief that came was as bright as the noonday Mescalero sun streaming through the windows.

"I started letting it grow a year ago. I got tired of being an imitation *ind'aa.*"

"Didn't the school kick up a fuss?"

"Sure. But there were other things about me they liked even less. They probably would have kicked me out if I hadn't left for home when I did."

"Will you go back and finish?"

Harold shook his head hard enough that the long black locks lifted from his shoulders. "Three years was more than plenty, Corey."

"What were the other things? Grades?"

"No. My grades were good. Hell, I loved my classes, loved studying. It was the little stuff. That old bastard Pratt has more damned rules than your army has. There was a lot I couldn't get away with, but since most of the teachers and the staff never really look at the Indians they see all day, my hair was down over my ears before they even noticed. They sure raised hell when they did."

"But any school has rules, Harold."

"Sure. All the same, I'll bet that fancy place in Massachusetts you went to—Amherst?—didn't make you cut the grass and pass inspection and force you to listen to missionaries every day, or trot you out for the politicians to see how peaceable you'd become—or check your room every night to see that you were on your knees saying the Lord's Prayer." He didn't sound bitter. On the contrary, his voice was light and gay, probably because Corey had just let him off the hook about what he had said about Tony's death. But he wouldn't have complained if he *had* been bitter. No Apache Corey had ever met, for instance, had ever even mentioned all the children who died at Carlisle in those first years Geronimo was held at Fort Marion in Florida, nor did they come down too hard on Pratt, the Carlisle superintendent, who from all accounts certainly deserved it. Harold went on. "I was never openly rebellious, but I suppose I was a bad influence on the younger kids."

Ana broke in. "Tell him he's *got* to go back and finish, Corey."

"Ma!" Harold's grin had disappeared. "I thought we had forgotten about that."

"*You've* forgotten, you stubborn *ja'e*. I haven't!"

This, from the wicked sharpness of the volley, was apparently a bone of some contention—and a frequently worried bone. An awkward, heavy silence followed, and Corey was grateful when Lucy suddenly entered the conversation again, her voice as soft as corn silk. Something told him it wasn't the first time Lucy Bishop had made peace on this tender subject.

"Speaking of studies and things like that, Corey," she said, "how is your book coming? When will we get to read it?"

It startled him. "How did you even know about it, Lucy?" He felt gratitude again. Her interrupting meant he could look straight at her for a bit without another breach of etiquette.

"Your mother told me—when she came up here for the funeral."

Virgie up on the Mescalero? Of course. She would have insisted on coming up here for Tony's last rites. Probably had dragooned Jim McPherson into bringing her, not that that would have required a great deal of effort. Jim would have wanted to come. And anyway, Jim would have undergone far worse things than funerals to be with Virgie Lane, had done so often enough in the past. As he had done periodically since adolescence—hell, long before that—Corey wondered now why Jim and Virgie had never married. Then he wondered why he wondered. He knew. Those memories of the first Corey Lane . . .

"Don't know why you would ever want to read what I'm writing, Lucy. History, at least the way I write it, isn't always too absorbing."

"The story of my people would have no trouble absorbing me," she said.

"I suppose that's so. Actually, it's going better than I have any right to expect. Cuba put me at the right distance from what I'm writing about, and I turned out a respectable amount of material in the months I was in Havana. Our military duties weren't too demanding, and the work habits I developed during my stay there seem to have carried over—" He stopped. He sounded pedantic, not at all the way he suddenly wanted to sound to this glowing girl. Not girl—woman.

"Well, you're the only author I've ever met," Lucy said. "Wait. I forgot. Emerson Hough came down from White Oaks to St. Joseph's School a couple of years ago to talk to our classes, and I helped the sisters with a reception they gave for him afterward. Nice man." She smiled. "I do want to read what you're doing, Corey, when you'll let me. I need a good history of Apachería for my classes. There's hardly anything."

"You're teaching at St. Joe's? Tell me about it."

"Maybe later. Right now I've got to get started on these dishes."

She pushed her chair back, stood up, and began to clear the table, carrying the platter that had held the venison to the wooden sink with the little iron pump. She moved with the deceptively swift grace of a fawn. He had to force his eyes to leave her.

He looked around the room. It was the first time he had been in Ana's house. When he was up here last the Bishops were still in the tar paper shack near the sawmill. Tony had built a fine, sturdy home for his family here above Cow Camp Creek. He must have learned to handle carpenter's tools as well as he handled a pony or a Winchester back in bloodier days. Bloodier? Nothing could be much bloodier than the way he had died in the sawmill, accident or whatever Harold thought it was.

Harold had been quiet since the rapid-fire exchange with Ana, not sulky—Corey had never seen Harold Bishop sulk—but subdued.

Now he, too, got up from the table.

"I'm going out to look to the stock."

"I'll give you a hand," Corey said. It would be his first chance to be alone with Harold.

"No!" It was little too emphatic. "Stay and talk with Ma and Lucy. The three of you have a lot of catching up to do."

As if you and I haven't? Corey almost said it aloud, but if he had, Harold wouldn't have heard him; he was almost through the door before Corey completed the thought. *Damn it, Harold. If you don't want to talk to me, all right, but why the hell did you send me that note? And why did you even bother to tell me your thoughts about Tony's death?*

While Lucy and Ana finished the kitchen chores, Corey wandered to a wall covered with yellowed newspaper clippings pasted down on bristol board, and framed photographs—daguerreotypes for the most part, but some of them the newer Eastman process prints.

There they all were, the sepia and silver masks of this peculiarly American tragedy: Geronimo and Naiche with General Miles at Fort McKenzie; Gatewood; next to him the rest of the Chiricahuas who had surrendered with the two chiefs and who were now rotting at Fort Sill after rotting first in the tropical, disease-laden, humid air of Florida and then at Mount Vernon Barracks in Alabama—not appreciably better for men used to the high, dry climate of their desert and mountain homeland.

Chief Juh and confused, betrayed old Eskiminzin of the Lipans, and many, many more Corey didn't recognize, looked out from the wall with wintry eyes. He let his gaze linger longest on the famous photograph of Nana, taken, if memory served him right, well before the long, desperate summer of '85. Nana was old even then, ancient. Incredible to think of the chase he had led the army on with what was left of Victorio's Mimbreños after Tres Castillos: wives, mourning women widowed by Terrazas's soldiers, children, half-grown boys, with only a handful of real warriors to raid for food and horses, and those way past their fighting prime.

"Tony loved Nana." It was Ana at his elbow. "Nana was his uncle, or rather great-uncle, you know. They fought together for five years. You like my picture wall, Corey? Tony would never let me put them up. Too sad, he said. He wanted to remember all of them as they were in what he called the good old days. I guess he was right. All of them are dead or prisoners now. Maybe I should pack them all away again."

"Tell me something, Ana. Maybe it's something I should know, but I don't. How did Tony manage to escape being sent east with Geronimo and the others?"

She was silent for a moment.

"The reason you don't know is that Tony would never talk about it or let me talk about it. He always felt—not ashamed, really—but a little funny that he wasn't imprisoned with them. He shouldn't have. Nobody ever blamed him, no one in the family or on the Mescalero."

It still amazed Corey how well this largely untutored woman—by white standards, anyway—had mastered English.

She spoke it without a hint of accent. Her Spanish, he remembered, was as flawless, and she had passed her special genius for language straight down to Harold and Lucy, too. Half the people in the basin didn't speak their respective English and Spanish as well as this family did. Half the people on the reservation probably didn't speak Apache as well, either.

"Anyway," she continued, "when the *chihende* Mimbreños were penned up with the Chiricahuas at San Carlos after Geronimo surrendered the first time, I wasn't with Tony. My mother was dying, and I had already brought Harold here to the Mescalero to see her before she went to *Ussén*, or wherever it is Mescaleros go. Lucy wasn't born yet. That was the bad summer of '81. In '85, when Nana, Naiche, and Geronimo decided to go out again and down into the Sierra Madres in Mexico that last terrible time, Nana made Tony stay with Chato at San Carlos. It nearly broke Tony's heart, but Nana knew how it all would end. Tony was the only one of them who could read and write English. Oh, what a time I had teaching him. He never did get good at it." She laughed, but there was a little choke in the laugh. "Nana thought that might someday be useful to the *chihende*. Staying at San Carlos still wouldn't have saved Tony, but he had a big fight with Chato. He had promised Nana he wouldn't follow him to Mexico, so he decided to come here to us. A warrior named Robert Bear had died at San Carlos from the lung sickness, and Tony put his own tags and bracelets on Robert Bear's body and ran away, slipped out of Chato's *ranchería* one night and crossed the Gila, the Rio, and the Jornada—unarmed and on foot. He knew the Buffalo Soldiers wouldn't worry too much about one missing Indian, but a rifle and a horse? . . . that would make a difference. The whites marked my Tony as dead. They didn't know him as Tony Bishop, but by his *chihende* name. Of course, we heard up here he was dead, too. I've lost him twice, in a way.

"Hiding, starving, with no way to hunt, it took him more than nine months to reach us. After he got here he was lucky. Russell, the agent then, accepted him as another Mescalero, although I think he knew Tony wasn't one, and my people up here vouched for him whenever the army checked for fugitive hostiles. It didn't hurt that I was Mescalero, either. I used to laugh about the way we fooled the army, but he'd still be alive if they had known about him."

Lucy had joined them. For the first time Corey noticed she was taller than her mother, almost as tall as Harold. Ana smiled at her and went on. "We had a good life, Corey, but you know that. The Mescaleros are fine people. They fought hard in their time, too, but except for the few who rode with Victorio and Nana, most of their fighting was done with long before even Mangas's time, so they didn't have to turn themselves in when the others did. This is a good place, as reservations go. At least it's not San Carlos. When Tony finally realized that all the wars were over for the Red Paint People, he settled down. Oh, he wasn't happy for a while—he couldn't stand farming—but when he took up lumbering and found that his hands could be used for something besides holding a Henry or a Winchester, life turned really good for us."

Tears welled in her eyes, and now her body shook with soundless sobs. Lucy put a hand on her mother's shoulder, and the touch of it seemed to calm the older woman in an instant.

"Mama," Lucy said, her voice just above a whisper, "did you forget we promised to walk over to Sinuoso Creek and see Emily Takai's new baby? I think it would do you good."

Ana pulled a handkerchief from inside her blouse and blew her nose.

Lucy looked at Corey. "You'll stay the night, won't you? You'll have to bunk with Harold, of course." Her eyes were so large and liquid he felt he could drown in them. "Please say yes."

"Well, if I won't be any trouble." He hadn't intended to stay when he left the X-Bar-7 this morning, nor until this moment, but he remembered now that the walk the two women would make to Sinuoso Creek and back was about four miles long. If they spent any time at all with the Takais, it would give him the opportunity to corner Harold. That *was* the only reason he suddenly wanted to stay, wasn't it?

"Corey," Ana said. She seemed in complete control of herself again, although he detected a new look on her fine face, not a sorrowful one this time, but worried. "When you talk with Harold while Lucy and I are gone, get him to go back to school. If not Carlisle, *somewhere*."

"Don't make Corey do the things we should do ourselves, Mama," Lucy said.

"He won't listen to me, Lucy!" There was a trace of hysteria in her voice, something he had never heard from Ana before. "Corey's the only one he'll listen to."

There was something else at work here besides a mother wanting her son to get an education.

"I'll do my best, Ana," he said.

3

Corey watched Ana and Lucy until they vanished where the meadow dipped down toward Cow Camp Creek, then he looked at Harold Bishop standing with his elbows on the fence of the piñon-post corral seventy-five yards away, absolutely motionless, gazing down to where the long hanging valley lush with spring galleta grass opened on the Ojos Negros Basin. The afternoon breeze was up and Harold's black hair blew back over his shoulders. He looked like something out of a Remington engraving in *Harper's Monthly*. Again, as Corey had thought on the trail, something out of place and time.

I'm going out to look to the stock, Harold had said, but there wasn't an animal in the corral and none in sight, except for the two horses Corey and Harold had ridden, and they had been "looked to" a mere two hours earlier. Corey *could* sashay down there and collar him, but that probably wouldn't work.

He knew from long experience that Harold wouldn't talk until he was damned good and ready.

The gusts were turning the air a bit chilly. Corey went back in the house, put on his hat and jacket, took a chair from the table Lucy had cleared, and carried it outside. He tipped the chair against the wall facing the corral and settled into it. *I'll do my best,* he had told Ana. Unless his best consisted of doing nothing, it was a lie. He had no intention of doing anything. Harold was a grown man—wasn't he?—capable of making his own decisions.

He pulled his hat brim down over his eyes. This might take time. Talkative and lighthearted as he remembered Harold from their boyhood together, he also recalled times when his friend had gone into long sessions of almost catatonic silence. The first came right after Corey met him more than a dozen years ago, when he was fourteen and Harold a year younger, when Tony brought him down the mountain and asked Virgie to put him on as a hand. "He don't know nothing, Mrs. Lane. Won't learn lumber work, and there ain't nothing else for him up on the Mescalero yet except making baskets. That ain't no job for a Mimbreño." Tony, who could read and write English, as Ana had reminded Corey, never did bring the remarkable gifts Ana possessed to the speaking of it. "The council wants to start running cattle pretty god-damn quick. I think maybe he learn that. He can't be dumber than a cow."

Even that low assessment of Harold's intelligence had seemed too generous his first half day on the ranch. He didn't utter a word, even at the dinner Virgie fed him—which he had at the outset refused with a shake of his head, no words. He had finally bolted it down so fast it looked as if it might have been the first meal he had ever had, or the last he ever expected to get. He went to bed in the bunkhouse as mute as when he had arrived.

The next morning a different Apache reported to the corral for work, an effervescent elf, quick to learn, good in the saddle, and with the traces of the teasing imp he would become already showing in everything he did. Harold never explained this chameleon change, and Corey never asked about it. He and the young Apache rode together four summers when Corey came home from Hotchkiss to Chupadera County each May, and encouraged by Virgie, they spent a lot of their nonworking hours up on the reservation. Tony and Ana were something quite different from Corey's schoolmasters and fellow students, and different too from the people in the basin. Lucy, at six, began calling Corey "brother" before that first summer season passed. That was probably still the way she thought of him, if she thought of him at all.

Now Corey stared at the Mimbreño's rigid back down by the corral. *Patience, Lane, patience. When he's ready, he'll talk an arm off you, like anyone else in Ana Bishop's family.*

He closed his eyes and tried to think about his book. Some of the manuscript was nestled in the same saddlebag with Cookie's second breakfast. He had told Lucy it was going well, but this was only partly true. He was turning out enormous chunks of work in Grandfather Jason's old study, but the results seemed labored and overwritten compared to the chapters he had done in Cuba. The section on Mangas Coloradas was giving him problems. He hadn't even begun to do that great old chieftain justice. How then would he ever be able to deal with Victorio and his own father's part in the raging, cruel events that followed? The detached view of the historian was easy to talk about—devilishly hard to come by. He needed a visit to Gideon Bainbridge's library and a talk with the owner of Tres Piedras before going on, and he had hoped to circle over toward Gideon's ranch before he headed back to the X-Bar-7 to resume his work. His heart leaped at the thought of seeing Gideon again. This thing about Tony wouldn't help, particularly if Harold was right.

But none of this was what he wanted to think about right

now, nor was what Harold had said back on the trail. What he wanted to think about above all else was Lucy. The thoughts that came were unsettling in a way, but not unpleasant.

"Corey!"

He must have dozed off. Harold stood in front of him, holding the reins of his and Corey's horses, both saddled. "I want you to ride to the sawmill with me while there's still light."

It was a silent ride, and it was a silent inspection they made of the mill. There didn't seem to be any one thing in particular that Harold wanted to show him about the scene of Tony's death, nothing for him to learn. There wasn't a visible trace of the horror that had visited Tony here three months ago, no sign of blood or violence, nothing but the idle machinery looking like relics of the distant past. The roughing room where Tony had died was immaculate, except for a sifting of pine sawdust that covered everything, some of the particles catching the sun slanting through the wide doors and reflecting it the way mica does.

Outside, mounted again, Corey said, "Well . . ."

"Just wanted you to get the feel of it."

"I didn't feel anything but bad, Harold." He still did. He would have preferred not to talk at all, but he suddenly sensed that this might be his only chance, and reluctant or not he had to take it. "Harold, why did you avoid me the way you did most of the afternoon after saying what you did?"

"Ana was mad at me when she found out about the note I sent you. That's why she's so strong about me going back to school. I spent this afternoon wondering if I was right to ask you to come up and see me. She doesn't think I should do *anything*.

"Doesn't she agree with you about Tony's death?"

"Sure she does, but she won't admit it."

"Have you considered that maybe she *doesn't* agree with you?"

"Corey, my father was murdered!"

"Nothing I saw tells me that—and who on the Mescalero would want to kill him!"

"It wasn't anybody on the reservation."

"You're telling me that maybe someone down in the basin—"

"Yes."

"But *why?*"

"I don't know that yet. All I know is that there have been some funny things going on up here. Stock fences cut, wells turning bad all of a sudden, more fires than we usually have. Maybe Tony knew something."

"And you think white men—"

Harold nodded. Corey burned with more questions, but Harold spun the spotted pony around and shouted over his shoulder, "Come on. Let's go home by way of Sinuoso Creek. Maybe we can catch up with Ana and Lucy."

They had ridden as far as the Baptist Mission School when they found the two women. They hoisted them up and rode double, Ana behind Corey. The unpainted wooden school across the creek was where Harold had received his first imprinting from white society. Apache children were playing in the school yard, little girls down on their knees in the caliche, with jacks, apparently, half a dozen boys busy at something that looked like baseball, probably One Old Cat or Piggy-Move-Up. One of the girls, a sober, brown little acorn, waved to Ana.

"I sent Lucy to the padres and Harold here to the Baptists," Ana said to Corey as she returned the wave. "Seemed a good idea to get a foot in both white camps."

Corey couldn't decide for a bit whether he was more disappointed or relieved that Lucy was posted behind Harold. In the end he was relieved. Ana's arms around his waist weren't as troublesome as they might once have been, and not as troublesome by half as Lucy's slender ones most assuredly would be. He was relieved, too, that Ana didn't speak of Harold's returning to school during the ride. He needed more time alone with Harold before that subject came up again. If he worked on Harold too soon about what Ana said she wanted, the Mimbreño might sink into one of those moody silences again. Damn it!

The time is out of joint. Oh, cursed spite that ever I was born to set it right.

But—as he more or less feared—he didn't get any more time alone with Harold as soon as he would have liked. After a fairly light supper, for the Bishop table, Harold started a fire in the wood stove and Corey played dominoes with Ana as he had a dozen years before, and her keen joy in beating him was not keener than the pleasure he took in seeing her forget for the moment the things which had beset her since he had ridden into the yard a poor second in his race with Harold. She had always beaten him easily in the old days because he couldn't get his thoughts from her lovely face. She beat him just as easily now because he couldn't get his mind off her daughter's.

Lucy had settled into a chair across the room and directly behind Ana, reading—he couldn't see the title of the book, and he wondered if ever his writing could hold her attention half as much. Once in a while, when Ana's glee at winning brought cries from her, Lucy would glance up, and once or twice her eyes and his met.

When the domino game ended Corey wandered to the wall of pictures again to check something. He had been right the first time. Among all the pictures of soldiers and Apaches, there wasn't a single one of his father, although there was a print of the one known photograph of Victorio. Good.

Harold had busied himself with some leatherwork, tooling *chihende* designs into a wide belt. He, too, looked at Corey and caught his eyes from time to time, but they were different looks from the ones Corey got from Lucy. *Bide your time, Corey,* Harold's eyes seemed to say.

At last Ana announced that she was tired and ready to go to bed.

"I'm ready, too," Lucy said. "My children graduate in less than two weeks, Corey. These are busy days." She put her book down, blew out the lamp on the table beside her. "It's so good to have you back again, *chu'uune'.*" She took three steps to him and kissed him on the cheek. He couldn't quite see her eyes now in the half-light from where he and Ana had played their games. She left the room.

Chu'unne'. Friend. Well, at least she hadn't called him "brother"!

"I think White Painted Woman would like my Lucy, Corey," Ana said.

"She *is* White Painted Woman," Corey said.

There was a warm laugh. "That's a little disrespectful. Never say that in front of the Old Ones. But I kind of agree with you."

From his cot in Harold's room, Corey couldn't see the full moon that had lighted his way to the outhouse and back, but its beams were marking out a sharp-edged, opalescent rectangle on the pine-plank floor. The sacred woman of the Apaches, the white painted one Ana and he had invoked, could have danced in that magic space. So could Lucy.

After fifteen minutes without a sound from the other cot, he gave up any hope of Harold talking to him tonight, but just as he closed his eyes, Harold's voice came through the half darkness.

"Asleep yet, Corey?"

"Not quite." Not quite? He was wide awake. Something in Harold's voice remembered from long ago told him that his friend would now let it all come rushing out. Corey waited.

"From what the Old Ones tell me," Harold said, "my father was a reckless fighter back before the surrender, but you remember what a careful man he was in everyday life. Methodical. Almost a plodder. Never once saw him stub his toe. I was the one who was always in a hurry and a little careless. Get it from Ana, I expect. I can trip over a string, but Tony was as surefooted as an *'idui*, a mountain cat. You remember. The reason I didn't say anything when we were inside the sawmill was that I wanted you to see the layout for yourself—without me giving you ideas. Now—can you picture the roughing saw and what's around it?"

"There's a wooden platform about two feet above the saw table and running parallel to it. Two or three steps lead up to this deck or whatever it's called."

"What else?"

"There's a guardrail separating it from the saw."

"How far away are the steps from the blade?"

"A dozen feet or so."

"You said you read Tom Hendry's story in the *News*?"

"Yes."

There was a moment when he thought Harold might not say anything more, after all. Then . . .

"Where did it say my mother's uncle, Pete Jandeezi, found him?"

He knew Harold didn't expect an answer to this last question. He didn't need one. And he knew suddenly that Harold was absolutely right. Tony's death had been no accident. His mangled body, according to Hendry, had been in the center of the table. Someone had to have held him against that saw, or knocked him out and fed him into it. Corey shuddered, then took hold again. He could speculate about a heart attack or a stroke bringing down any of a number of people he knew—but Tony? That didn't seem any more right to him now than it obviously must have seemed to Harold when Pete Jandeezi had told him about the "accident." Tony had been only forty-five or so, and as fit as any twenty-year-old on the entire Mescalero, and the odds against him climbing on the roughing table with the saw running and having some strange seizure at exactly that same moment were astronomical. Tom Hendry wouldn't have given it a thought, of course. No reason to, from a newsman's point of view. He hadn't known Tony as Tony's son had, and Tony's son had been away at school. Pete Jandeezi wouldn't have been able, or perhaps wouldn't even have wanted, to steer Tom toward the truth even if he suspected something. He didn't much care for jawing with white men about anything.

"None of this ties it to *white* men in particular, though," Corey said.

"Who else is there? No Mescalero would have laid a hand on Tony. Remember my saying he might have known something? Did you know, for instance, that my father kept a journal? It's missing—gone. But all the sawmill records he stored in his desk with it are still there. And then there's all the other strange stuff I told you has been going on up here."

"Look, Harold. Even if you're right—and I'm not saying you're wrong, mind you—maybe somebody was just trying to rob Tony, some drifter, a white man, sure, but not necessarily one from the basin. You're talking about conspiracy. I just don't buy that. Wells go bad and fires break out, and funny things happen in this country all the time."

Harold snorted. "Remember those two men we saw on the trail? I don't know the one in the fancy engineer's outfit, but the other one is a local. Don't know his name or exactly where he's from, but he's been spending a lot of time poking around the edges of the reservation the past few months—a hell of a lot of time. I do know he was seen up here in the high country the day Tony died. Uncle Pete saw him right before it happened. He was up here, too, when Sadie and Joe Ditsa's cabin burned. If he's got business up here none of the *nüt'ahende* I've talked to know about it."

The white rectangle on the floor had shifted several inches. Corey knew what was coming next.

"Corey . . ."

"Yes?"

"I need your help."

There was a long silence before Harold went on. "Someone's got to do some digging down in Black Springs and the basin. I can't do it. Can you see an Apache playing detective in Chupadera County? They would run me out of there before I so much as asked one question. You're my only way into certain parts of the white man's world."

Harold was right. There probably hadn't been an Apache in the streets of Black Springs since the great raid of '79.

"Harold, have you discussed this with the tribal council?"

"First thing I did. No help. With so many of our people still prisoners at Fort Sill they're afraid to make a move. Hell, I can't blame them, although I wish I could."

"How about the Indian agent?"

"The agent we've got now is the very last *ind'aa* I would ask. He's no Sam Russell. Will you help me, Corey?"

The white rectangle had started its climb up the side of Corey's cot. He would have to answer Harold before the moonlight showed his face, particularly as neither of them would be satisfied with the answer.

"I can't promise, Harold." There was nothing from the other bed. All he could hope for now was that Harold would understand. But why should he? Corey didn't fully understand his evasiveness himself.

4

Jim McPherson leaped from his swivel chair in the office of the *Chupadera County News*.

"Corey!" He dropped the sheaf of galleys he had been reading and waved Corey into the chair at the side of his rolltop desk. "How's your mother?" It wasn't the ordinary polite question people ask only to ignore the answer—it would never be from Jim McPherson. He never let Virgie Lane stray half a thought away.

Corey smiled. "You can see how she is for yourself, Jim. We rode in to Black Springs together, and she's shopping at Stafford's. I told her we would meet her at the Sacramento House later on."

"Well, let's go, then." Jim walked to a hall tree and grabbed a hat.

"Not so fast." Corey laughed. "She'll be a while. Something I want to talk to you about first."

He could see Jim win the battle with his impatience, just

barely. Looking at the tall, almost frail McPherson, it would have been impossible for anyone not familiar with the history of Chupadera County to see in the publisher the man who had saved Black Springs from destruction twenty-two years ago. Jim was in his fifties now, but he couldn't have been a much more imposing figure back in those bloody days than he was now—not physically. He still had that slight cough which brought him to the Ojos Negros country back in '76, and still had that eastern scholar air about him. He also, among those who remembered his part in the war of '80, served as the conscience of the town, and not just in the editorial columns of the *News*.

"What's up, Corey?" he said now.

"I went up to see the Bishops on the Mescalero two days ago."

"Glad you did. Losing Tony was terrible for them. How are they?"

"That's what I want to talk with you about. But . . . I don't quite know how to start." This was going to be hard. He hadn't committed himself to Harold two nights earlier. Would he now be committing himself to McPherson? Well, he could at least ask the questions he had grudgingly told Harold he would ask. He could relay the answers to the Mimbreño and perhaps forget about it. "Jim . . . is there something I don't know about going on down here in Black Springs? Something to do with the reservation?"

Jim looked as blank as his inquiring nature would ever let him. "Not that I know of. Why?"

"Well, according to Harold Bishop there have been some peculiar happenings up in the big timber in the northwestern part of the Mescalero lately, things that don't exactly square with neighborliness."

With that he told Jim about Harold's thoughts on the death of Tony, the fires Harold was convinced were being set, the fences ripped up and the stock run off, and the poisoned.

wells. He told him, too, about the two men on the trail when he met Harold, and described the "local" as best he could. "Of course, I was at some distance from him, but I'm sure I'd know him if I saw him. I think I've seen him before."

"I can't place him, Corey. From your description he could be any of a dozen hangers-on here in town. As for the other man, he sounds like a professional of some sort. There have been a number like him in and out of here since we became a section point on the Southern Pacific: geologists, civil engineers, land law types, and such. There've been some squabbles over right-of-way boundary lines down toward Three Rivers and Tularosa. Some of it has touched on the Mescalero, but it's all been aboveboard and in the open, and certainly none of it nasty enough to provoke the kind of things Harold described. No violence or other funny stuff that I've heard about." He paused. "Corey—do you think Harold is right, that Tony Bishop really was murdered?" He didn't wait for an answer. "Funny Tom Hendry didn't tumble to anything out of the way. Let's get him in here."

He went to his door and called out to the main office of the *News*. "Copy boy!" It was a hoary joke.

Tom Hendry had been considerably more then a copy boy for all the years Corey had known him, first as a reporter, then as editor of the *News*, an editor who still wrote the more important stories himself. Corey didn't particularly want to see Hendry now, much as he liked the man. Little as there might be to Harold Bishop's suspicions, Tom would go after the story like a ferret.

In his usual rumpled suit, too big for him, really, and with his hair looking as if he had combed it with a towel, Hendry entered Jim's office.

Corey had seen a lot of Tom in the not too distant past, but not here in the basin. They had been in Cuba together, Tom as a war correspondent. With so many men from the Territory in general and Chupadera County in particular

serving with Colonel Roosevelt, Jim had somehow found the
wherewithal for the *News* to have its own man on the scene.
Tom had been in on some of the heaviest fighting Corey had
seen, without shrinking from the lethal fire of those brilliant
Spanish snipers with their Mauser rifles. His dispatches hadn't
always gone down well with T.R.'s staff: too brutally honest,
pointing out that only the overwhelming weight of men and
matériel had beaten the tough soldiers from Iberia, not the in-
herent superiority of Americans the Hearst people regularly
described in the drumbeat, jingoist stories they filed from can-
tinas well away from combat. Someone had noticed Tom's
work. Jim had been able to syndicate his report on San Juan
Hill to the *New York Sun*.

"Tell Tom what you just told me, Corey," Jim said.

Well, in for a dime, in for a dollar. Corey went through it
all once more, watching Tom's bright blue eyes cloud a little
toward the end.

"I'm ashamed of myself, Corey. I took things at face value,
I guess. I should have asked a few more questions. And it's no
excuse that I don't speak much Apache and that old Pete
Jandeezi's English leaves something to be desired. Ana Bishop
was there, interpreting. I sure as hell should have gone to the
sawmill."

"Then you didn't see where it happened?"

"No. I talked with Pete at Ana's. Look, I'll go right from
here to Orrin Langley's office and see if our lazy sheriff knows
anything, and then I'll start for the sawmill this afternoon.
You've already talked to the Ditsas, I expect—and Pete. He's
Ana's uncle, isn't he?"

Corey nodded. "Sadie and Joe Ditsa really couldn't tell me
much. Luckily they and the rest of the family were visiting
relatives down toward Three Rivers at the time the cabin
burned. I didn't get to talk with Pete. Don't be too hard on
yourself, Tom. Pete's pretty well past it now. And he always
was sort of a dreamer, anyway."

"Well, in my own feeble defense, I will say that Pete seemed to think it was an accident. Now that I think about it, so did Ana. I'll see all three of them, and I'll certainly talk to Harold. My memory of Harold is that he was always a pretty clear thinker, for all that he had a tendency to kid around."

"Why did you cover the story, anyway, Tom? An accident up there with just an Indian getting killed wouldn't excite your readers."

"Well, for openers, I felt the death of one of Nana's warriors certainly rated some mention, even if there was no public demand for it here in Black Springs. He was part of our history. Not an entirely glorious part, for our side. I'm one of the few who are uneasy that we've got Geronimo and the others in that Oklahoma pokey fifteen years after the Apache troubles have all been over with. They're prisoners of war, for Christ's sake—not criminals!"

"You knew Tony rode with Nana?"

"Sure. My dad told me. He fought the old coot."

"And you've never said anything about it in print?"

"I knew Tony. Liked him. I didn't want to have him on my conscience if they shipped him off to Fort Sill, too."

"One other thing, Tom. Have *you* heard anything down here in the basin that would justify Harold's other suspicions?"

"Not a thing. But maybe I've been as blind to that as I obviously was about Tony. Don't much like the sound of those fires and the bad wells. I'll sniff around town when I come back down the mountain. I'll get back to you. And if I find anything, you'll read about it, too. It may take a few days, though, Corey."

He was gone. Corey realized that Tom might just be taking Harold's dark thoughts seriously.

Jim McPherson's face had turned as gray as his hair while Tom and Corey talked. "Maybe Tom can get you off the hook, Corey," he said. You didn't have to spell things out letter by painful letter for Jim McPherson. No one in town knew better than Jim the way Black Springs had felt about the Lanes while Corey was growing up, and how a good part of it still felt about them.

"I'm not exactly *on* the hook, Jim. I'm really not."

Jim looked surprised. Yes, he would be. Jim would have put himself squarely on any hook dangled in front of him, baited or not, if people he knew and liked were in any kind of trouble.

"I only promised Harold I'd ask some questions. Tony was a friend, and Harold and Ana still are friends." And Lucy? Was she a "friend"? She had given him another feathery kiss—on the cheek again—the morning he had left the Mescalero.

"Whatever you decide to do," Jim was saying now, "be careful. This can still be dangerous country. Particularly when you have no idea where the danger might be coming from."

Good Lord! Was Jim, like Tom, giving credence to Harold's notions? Would *he* have to now?

"I'll be careful. But I've kept you here long enough. Let's find Virgie."

When they stepped into Estancia Street in front of Jim's building, the sound of a motor car popping away as it rounded the corner of Frontera half a block away echoed from the storefronts across the way.

"God, I hate those things," Jim muttered. "Of course, I suppose it's because I'm getting old and tend to think all technology should have stopped with the invention of the typewriter—well, maybe the rotogravure. Hey! It's Gideon. That's the Duryea that came in on a flatcar a week ago. He had to grade out seven miles of new road at Tres Piedras for the damned thing."

The man driving the ungainly vehicle now bearing down on Jim and Corey had disdained the goggles most motorists fancied, although he was tricked out in the customary duster.

He was wearing a soft gray fedora, not even as western a hat as the one Jim had taken from the hall tree, and knowing Territorial Senator Gideon Bainbridge as he did, Corey would have bet the label would read BORSALINO. Nothing but the best would do for the stylish senator. There was no one in Chupadera County—except for Jim—whom Corey admired more.

And it wasn't only admiration he felt. He owed Gideon for a lot of things.

Corey's first memory of Gideon was of when he was ten, when three young Latino toughs had caught him passing the Café Roja in Mex Town on his way to the adobe of Isabel Flores with a birthday gift from Virgie. What began with the usual taunts about his father had ended up with the three of them beating him up and finally pinning him down on the street, one prying open his mouth with a knife and then cramming it with handfuls of caliche dust. Out of nowhere Gideon Bainbridge had appeared—on horseback then—and his riding quirt had flashed across the arms and faces of Corey's assailants like the wrath of God. Corey never learned what an anglo gentleman such as Gideon had been doing in the meaner part of Mex Town at that particular moment. This had happened a long time before Gideon would have been canvassing this section of Black Springs for votes. Corey still had a tiny scar at the corner of his mouth from the knife.

Then, during his school years, he had gotten to know Gideon fairly well, and after graduation from Amherst even better. Corey liked the man more every time he saw him.

Gideon was not a talker, but when he did speak his words were carefully chosen, given out in a cultivated accent which owed little to the Ojos Negros Basin, although from what people said, he had been born on the big, showplace ranch in the Arroyo Concho where he lived now.

Except in his political speeches he never talked about himself, and if it hadn't been for Jim, Corey might never have discovered that Gideon had ridden with Corey's father against Cochise and the Chiricahuas in the Battle of Apache Pass—as a fifteen-year-old. Had fought marvelously well there, too. There had been two young tigers on those blood-stained slopes that day. That, of course, was long before the first Corey Lane turned renegade. And it was from Jim that Corey learned that Gideon had once called a local merchant to account on Corey's behalf after the merchant had passed a remark about Corey and his antecedents. "The sins of the fathers are *not* visited on the sons," Gideon had said. "If you insist on trying to visit them on *this* particular son, sir, I'm afraid you might have to pay for it." The merchant, no hero, had recanted in a hurry. A bolder man might well have done so; that had been ten or twelve years ago, when men still walked the streets of Black Springs armed, and Gideon's reputation as a sure hand with a gun would have made the most hotheaded local man think twice.

It was a well-earned reputation, as Corey himself had seen firsthand. Late one summer, just before Corey went back for his senior year in Massachusetts, Gideon had invited him out for a wild turkey shoot. With his light sporting rifle the man was incredible. He had dropped two of the birds, more elusive game than most people thought, at a distance of eighty or ninety yards with just two casual shots. Gideon had worn a Norfolk jacket on the hunt, surely the only garment of its kind in Chupadera County then or now.

There was a lot more to their relationship than Gideon's rescue of Corey and the later defense of him with the Black Springs storekeeper, though. On one of his early visits Corey discovered the library of Tres Piedras, Gideon's fourteen-room ranch home in the Arroyo Concho. More than a library, it was an archive, loaded with original source material from all over the Territory: photographs, letters from and to the early settlers, mining and cattle industry records, and the memoirs of three famous Indian agents, including those of the revered S.E. Russell up on the Mescalero during the time of the first Corey Lane and whom Ana and Harold had talked about. Even Santa Fe and Albuquerque couldn't claim a finer collection. Gideon, when Corey told him about his first attempts at writing, had made it his to use when and as he pleased.

The senator had displayed also a vast firsthand knowledge of the events Corey was even then thinking about someday putting in a book, and it was Gideon who first urged him to write a study of the people his father had fought against and then with. In spite of the fact that Gideon had fought the Apaches, too, his affection for the desert and mountain people was genuine and boundless.

After college Corey mined a lode from the library in the big house at Tres Piedras, and he owed in large part what he now knew about Cochise and the early stages of the careers of Delgadito and Mangas Coloradas to what he found in its carefully kept files. That he didn't mine as much from Gideon himself was his fault, not Gideon's. Corey had shied away from asking too many questions. As clearly sympathetic as Gideon was to Corey's bitter legacy, Corey didn't want any offhand revelations about his father, not then. But perhaps now, once this thing about Tony had been taken care of. . . .

The Duryea skidded to a stop on the rock-hard caliche in front of Jim and Corey, raising a choking yellow cloud of dust.

"Corey! Didn't realize you were back from Cuba. Your last letter didn't even mention your coming home," Gideon shouted over the rattles and bangs of the automobile. Even shouting, there was something admirably controlled and courtly about him. He reached out, took Corey's extended hand in both of his, and squeezed hard.

"When I wrote I didn't know myself that the army was through with me, Gideon. And I was too busy closing my apartment in Havana to write again before the ship sailed."

"No matter. What counts is that you're here. Forgive me if I don't turn this contraption off. There's sometimes hell to pay to get it started." He dropped Corey's hand and turned to Jim. "How are you, McPherson?"

"Couldn't be better, Senator." Had the answer stuck in Jim's throat? Corey had expected that it might. He almost laughed. Jim was Gideon's friend, respected him unstintingly, and got along with him extremely well—except when Corey was with them. Mild jealousy, he supposed. He had been the protégé of Jim long before his first trips to Tres Piedras—still was, even if the publisher no longer realized it. He owed both these men more than he would ever be able to repay.

"I hope seeing you and Corey together means you're trying to persuade him to stand for Territorial office someday soon."

"Don't either of you start that again," Corey said. "I'm content to be just a bookish drudge. You both know that." He had fought such overtures from both these men ever since he first came home from college.

"We'll see about that, won't we, McPherson?"

Jim answered with a polite nod, nothing more.

Gideon, tall to begin with, looked even taller in the high seat of the touring car. Under the brim of the hat full side-burns showed touches of iron gray, as did the mustache, and his hawk features bore the tan of an outdoorsman. Handsome man. Still a bachelor, to the secret delight and yearnings of even some very young women in Black Springs. He and Jim McPherson were each what the other one was not. Corey needed them both as friends—as more than friends.

"Now, Corey," Gideon was saying, "tell me how you really are. You never got sick or wounded, did you?"

"Not a scratch and not even a touch of fever. I'm just fine, really," Corey said.

"Come out to Tres Piedras," Gideon said. "Make it soon. I want to hear firsthand about your war. I've missed you. The book room has missed you, too." It was like Gideon to call that immense library of his a "book room."

"I've missed it, too, sir. And thank you. I will impose on you again. I find I'm going to need a lot more background on Mangas's death. but I won't be ready for another month."

"Anytime. If I shouldn't be there, Pedro will unlock things for you." He pulled a watch from inside the duster. "Sorry to rush away, but I have a meeting to attend."

He touched his fingers to the brim of his hat, showing as he did a huge diamond ring, and then reached down and pushed forward a lever under the dashboard of the car. It moved off down Estancia.

Corey looked around to see if any listeners had heard him shouting the name of Mangas. No one but Jim was within earshot. Good. No point in offending his neighbors, and his screaming the name of the old Apache at the top of his lungs could do it. Apaches had once killed people on this street.

As Jim and Corey angled across to where the Sacramento House gleamed beneath a new coat of twentieth century celebratory paint, Jim said, "Might not be a bad idea to tell Gideon about the peculiar aspects of Tony's death. The upper sections of Tres Piedras border the Mescalero timber, and he or his people up there might have seen something." It cost Jim McPherson a little something to come out with that, but it was in character. Personal pique would never stop him from saying anything which should be said, or could help.

"Good Lord, Jim. Can't we get on firmer ground before we go shooting off our mouths? Let's keep this the way it is, with only Tom, you, and me in the know, for the time being."

"I suppose we should. I take it, then, that you haven't told Virgie any of this?"

"Not yet. I want more to go on. There's still the chance there's nothing really to it." Typical of Jim. Somehow or other he judged almost everything by the effect it might have on Virgie Lane.

Virgie met them in the lobby. It flashed through Corey's mind that he would still be hard put to decide whether his mother or Ana Bishop was the most beautiful woman in the basin, or the Territory. Except for the tiny streaks of gray in the glossy black hair, she didn't look anywhere near her forty-seven years.

"Jim!" Virgie flew to the publisher and embraced him.

"It's been nearly three weeks, Virgie." Jim sounded as if it had been a lifetime. Nothing warmed Corey more than seeing these two together, nor turned him colder than the thought of how his father, dead for more than twenty years, was still somehow keeping them apart.

But before he was quite awash in the acids of bitterness, a man descending the stairway from the second-floor rooms caught his eye.

Not dead sure for a second, he then realized it was the man from the trail in the pines above Nogal, not the khaki-clad professional type, but the other one. He wasn't wearing his cowpoke getup now, though. He was dressed in a sober business suit, and he looked as if he had just come from the barber shop, clean-shaven and with slicked-down hair. This was a burly, strong-looking man. The thin face had fooled Corey that day with Harold. He walked to the desk, tossed a key on it, and headed for the door Corey and Jim had just come through. He glanced at Corey with a look that said he had seen Corey somewhere before, but couldn't remember where.

Virgie and Jim had just finished their embrace. Corey touched the publisher on the elbow.

"Look quick, Jim," he whispered. "Do you know that man just going through the door?"

Jim turned around.

"Sure. Matt Kessler. Used to be a sutler to Fort Stanton. Has an office in San Isidro in the upper Concho about ten miles past Gideon's place and one here in Black Springs. Land sales and mining claims."

"I should have remembered him. Harold should have, too. But he wore a full beard when we were kids. He brought beef allotments into the Mescalero a few years back."

Through the glass of the door Corey could see the man was walking directly across the street toward the law offices of Gideon Bainbridge, where the Duryea was parked. At Gideon's door he turned and walked with sure steps the length of the boardwalk and out of Corey's sight.

"That's the man I saw with Harold upon the Mescalero that morning," Corey said. "The saddle tramp."

"Are you sure, Corey? Kessler's anything but a saddle tramp. He's pretty well connected up in Santa Fe, from what I hear. Can't picture him bushwhacking in the timber."

"Just the same, that's the man I saw. And that's the man Harold says was on the Mescalero the day Tony died."

5

Corey pushed himself away from the old desk in Grandfather Jason's study, where he had tried writing the chapter on Mangas Coloradas half a dozen different ways, only to find that none of them worked. He knew why.

The coffee in the cup on the desk had grown dead cold, and he started for the kitchen, changed his mind, and went out on the back patio that gave a clear view of Cuchillo Peak. He sank into the old rocker he had pretended was a cow pony when Mike Calico played reluctant nursemaid to him as a child, before Mike put him up on real horses. Corey's make-believe in those lost days brought the laconic Zuñi as close to impatience as he ever came. Mike couldn't abide pretending. He wouldn't abide what Corey was going through now. At twenty-eight, Caminito—Little Lane—as Mike called him then, was too old to pretend.

Harold was right about everything. Tom Hendry had

known it in an instant. Jim had known it. So, he realized now, had he.

The mountain, big and dominant as ever, but somehow bland and lacking character under the early afternoon sun, wasn't quite as appealing as he had hoped, or as it had been in the morning when the shadows were deeper; nor was it as luminous and lovely as it would be later on, when the sky darkened behind it and a fading orange sun touched its front. He looked to the southeast, to where Sierra Blanca's twin summits, still snow clad, hung regally above the Mescalero. From here he couldn't see the meadow that bordered Cow Camp Creek, of course, but he could make out the ridge it hid behind. Not much solace from that direction, either.

It wasn't too strange that he had thought about Mike Calico more than once in the past few days. Mike had died in violence even as Tony Bishop had, but there had never been any doubt about the identity of the little wrangler's killers. Apaches, Mimbreños, as a matter of fact, Tony's own Red Paint People. Perhaps Tony had even been one of them. Corey would have to ask Jim McPherson—who had tried to outrun Victorio's warriors with little Mike that day—if he remembered. But that had been war, not murder.

It had hurt a little when Jim McPherson had expressed surprise at Corey's reluctance at helping Harold, not that Jim would ever make a judgment. Corey would have to put that surprise out of mind. He had at least done what he had told Harold he would do. He had asked questions.

He had gone back to the office of the *News* with Jim after the lunch with Virgie at the Sacramento, sought Tom Hendry out again, and told him about his identification of Matt Kessler. Tom had let out a low whistle and then said he would check on Kessler, too, when he came back down the mountain.

Damn the whole ugly mess! It wasn't as if he hadn't enough other things to do. He had to go on with the book.

Roundup and branding would be on them in another month, and Virgie was counting on him. Except as an extra hand, he hadn't been involved in the X-Bar-7's cattle business since college, but Virgie would need him when the spring work began; every rider was precious then, even such a sorry cowboy as he had become. Virgie didn't have an easy time of it keeping a reliable crew. Local anglos still shied away from the X-Bar-7's range as if it were a pesthole. More than one had turned down a chance to work for the X-Bar-7 by stating flatly that they would starve rather than ride with Indians. Jim had gently tried once to get Virgie to stop hiring Mescaleros from the reservation: "It isn't as if they needed the work, Virgie. The tribe's own beef operation is big enough now they could keep busy up in the pastures above Three Rivers full time all spring and summer."

"They stay on my payroll, Jim," she replied. "The Mescaleros came down the mountain and helped me put this place back into something resembling a stock ranch when no one else around here would do it for love or money. They're the best hands I've got. Besides, even if I put on riders from down here in the basin exclusively, when we join with the Mescalero herd for the drive up to Corona the same problem would come up again. I'd rather go into it shorthanded to begin with than have men quit on me halfway there."

Jim's eyes had shone with pride at Virgie's loyalty to her Apaches, and no more was said.

Yes, Corey had to get on with the book, finish up the part on Mangas before branding started or before Tom came up with something he might have to act on even if he didn't want to. Harold, busy with his own riding up on the Mescalero, would just have to wait on things a bit. Roundup was a legitimate enough excuse that Corey wouldn't have to go up to Cow Camp Creek and explain why he wasn't doing something he just plain didn't want to do. It settled his mind a little—not much but a little—that until roundup was over he wouldn't have to face Ana's doubts about Harold stirring things up, doubts he was afraid he still secretly wanted to share.

It meant, of course, that he wouldn't be riding up the mountain to do the other thing, the thing he desperately *wanted* to do. See Lucy.

It wasn't that he was thinking of her all the time; Harold's problem—and damn it, it *was* Harold's problem, not his—held too much threatening immediacy for that. But she was on his mind almost every moment he hadn't spent reflecting on Tony's death or on the book.

Corey rubbed the cheek she had kissed when he left the Mescalero that morning a week ago.

Women—young, beautiful women, at least—hadn't played a big part in his life, but there had been a few of them. There had been the girl in the library in Havana and before that those he had known in college. One—not the first, but close to it—the New York cousin of his Amherst roommate, had opened his still innocent psyche in a way he decided ultimately was a fair trade all around.

Fannie Duquette had been as circumspect and decorous as any of the college and finishing-school girls who had arrived on the trains from Boston, New York, and Philadelphia for the homecoming weekend parties, a pleasant dancing partner and little more, but when he got away to Manhattan two weeks later she had taken his breath away with her boldness. A minor socialite and by day a volunteer nurse in a teeming hospital on the Lower East Side, Fannie was two years older than Corey, a gap that had seemed at the time as wide as an entire generation, particularly given her intimate knowledge of the things which could go on between a man and a woman, things it turned out Fannie was far from averse to trying herself. Corey's first sense of shock faded in the delirium of their encounters, and for twenty-four hours he thought he was in the grip of a total and undying love, before he suddenly recognized that this seemingly grand passion was purely physical—on both sides.

No spiritual blood had been drawn, but he, at any rate, felt some small sharp pangs of regret. He knew that he wanted someday to fall truly in love. Someday he would have to face the consequences. Would want to. Would he face them with Lucy? If that happened, it would be just another of the secret things which had tugged him back to the country he loved.

And he did love it. Jim and Virgie might wonder why. Growing up here under the long shadow of the first Corey Lane had been anything but easy, and they had watched him try.

It might have been easier if he had inherited Virgie's ability—no, courage—to shrug off the censure of Chupadera County. She had lived with the awareness of what his father had done to all of them far longer than he had and still had managed to find an exquisite balance for her life. Running the X-Bar-7 was something she had been totally unprepared for, having grown up in Kansas City, but she was running it as if she were born to it. He smiled. If the inhabitants of this hard, unforgiving country hadn't looked askance at him because of the memory of his renegade father, or because of his fascination with the Apaches, they probably would have harbored doubts about him anyway. Able-bodied men of twenty-eight didn't bury themselves in books and let their womenfolk operate cattle ranches. He had brought the subject up with Virgie once. "I like what I'm doing, Corey," she had said, "and you like what you're doing. We're both getting good at what we do. Let's just keep on doing it. We can help each other from time to time, although I'm sure you'll be of more help to me than I could ever be to you."

Yes, he loved this country. After Cuba he could have lived out his life here contentedly if not joyously. He still could. But to do so required a quick settlement of the thing about Tony—by Tom and Jim, not him—and probably a resolute forgetfulness about Lucy. Did he really want either? He honestly didn't know.

What he did know was that his book was more important than ever now. Just working on it since his trip into Black Springs had—until today, at least—brought him at least some of the peace of mind he needed to cool the white-hot memories of the fighting he had seen in Cuba.

Virgie had doubted that she could help him. She meant with his work, of course. But without her help years ago there wouldn't have been a chance in hell that he could have even started the history. The help she had given him—he had thought it unwitting at the time but knew better now—was still something he feared he couldn't discuss easily with her, if at all.

After his father's death Virgie and he had been gypsies in Europe for a year. The long trip abroad had been a kaleidoscope, impossible for a boy of seven to profit by completely, but a whirling, wonderful, phantasmagoric experience he still remembered in astonishing detail. It had washed some ugly things from his memory.

But when they returned to the basin—in a tearing rush, it seemed to his child's mind after their meeting with Jim McPherson in New York, when it had appeared that *Jim* would never come back to Chupadera County—the dreams began.

They never varied. He, Virgie, and Grandmother Alicia rode again through the high meadow on the mesa south of Black Springs, straight into the great war party of Apaches that the first Corey had gathered to attack the town. Those hard, cruel, dark faces would press in on him in the dream and he would awaken to find himself trying to scream, but with never a sound issuing from a throat so dry and constricted he feared he could never take another breath. Even today he didn't doubt that if the dreams had come every night he would have died.

He hated the basin then, looked at its sand, rocks, grass, and wickedly barbed plants with burning, narrowed eyes. But he never said a word about the dreams to Virgie, nor to Grandmother Alicia in the five years before she died when he was twelve, when she sat every afternoon staring at the Chiricahua shield and the long Spanish lance that hung above the fireplace in the sitting room, the silence around her as impenetrable as a wall.

Once, when Corey was eight, he begged Virgie to take him away from the X-Bar-7 and Chupadera County—forever.

"I'm sorry, Corey. We belong here. You, I think, even more than I." Her eyes had been troubled as she said it, but even at eight years old he could see how granite hard her determination was. He never asked her to take him away again.

When the Mescaleros began coming down from the reservation and hiring on to reshape the X-Bar-7 to Virgie's liking, the dreams came more frequently, particularly whenever he saw an Indian dressed in the old way, as if for war. There wasn't anywhere to hide, but he knew he would have done so if he could.

Then Tony Bishop showed up with his son, Harold, the two of them riding double.

Tony hadn't looked as much like Corey's idea of Apaches as like one of the Mexican farmers of the upper Rio Concho, across the valley from Gideon Bainbridge's magnificent Tres Piedras, but he was an Indian all the same, and likely as savage as any in the dreams. His lithe, sinewy son, naked to the waist when they arrived and looking every inch an apprentice cutthroat warrior, seemed right out of the dreams even after Virgie dressed Harold like the other hands, although in pants and shirts way too large for him. After Tony went back up the mountain—leaving his saddle (an ancient McClellan that Corey told himself Tony had probably lifted from some dead cavalryman's remount) with an at first disconsolate Harold, and riding bareback as he left the X-Bar-7—Corey watched every move Harold made that first afternoon and the next morning with the skittish alertness of a pronghorn at a water hole who knows a lion has come down out of the rocks during the night. He realized he was being foolish, but the young Mimbreño, harmless as he now looked, and half Corey's size, wasn't going to take him by surprise.

But Harold did take him by surprise. He made him laugh, and Corey found it impossible to maintain even a silent hostility toward people who made him laugh.

Then, and it puzzled Corey that she would do it with so much fence to ride and other work to do at the X-Bar-7, Virgie began insisting, almost demanding, that he and Harold visit the Bishops up on the Mescalero every weekend. "I don't want Harold getting homesick, Corey," she had said.

In those days Tony, Ana, and Lucy lived in a two-family, board-and-batting, former army supply building much closer to tribal headquarters than either the shack near the sawmill—their next home on the reservation—or the new house Tony eventually built for his family, the one that now stood in comfortable isolation in the meadow above Cow Camp Creek. They had neighbors then, dozens of them. Harold— and consequently Corey—was warmly welcomed by them all. Most spoke English after a fashion, but an occasional family only had Apache and a little Spanish; Corey had to make do with an argot composed of two and sometimes all three languages.

After half a dozen such weekends in the cool pines the dreams stopped—at night, at any rate. Waking was another matter.

It began to come to Corey even then that, for all its surface sun-drenched openness, the basin, with the lofty peaks that ringed it, was sometimes a closed, dark place, as gothic in some unfathomable way as the thick forests southeast of Heidelberg he had tramped through during his summer "grand tour" of Europe his first year out of Amherst.

And its people . . .

Open, generous, friendly to the casual eye, there was still something secretly dark and closed about them, too, at times. It was as if the three races couldn't share this land if they talked to one another, particularly about the black past. That must be it. Too much blood had rushed through these now bone dry arroyos, too much savagery had raged across the alkali wastes and the gypsum flats. The gloss of civilization that now covered towns like Black Springs, La Luz, and Mescalero itself to only a slightly lesser degree, was in large part a sham. In mute agreement the three peoples who grubbed for an existence here—it wasn't easy even for *los ricos*—seemed to have decided that if they didn't talk about the past, perhaps none of it had ever happened.

Corey's reasons for turning to history as a way of life as well as a profession seemed more valid than ever now. And he had Gideon Bainbridge to thank for that. Perhaps somewhere in the as yet unmasked past there were answers—even hope, if he could avoid looking too *hard* for the answers or the hope. He couldn't write history before it revealed itself, couldn't, above all, be an advocate for a world he wished for. That wasn't the role of the historian, even though Thucydides himself on occasion—to modern readers, at least—fell into predetermined postures, to say nothing of the lapses of Prescott and the sainted Gibbon. One thing he did know. If he was looking for fault and guilt, he was looking for it everywhere, in the hearts of the Apaches he wrote about as well as in the hearts and minds of his neighbors, Spanish and "American." For all he knew, he might find it in the mountain rocks and the basin's grama grass. Maybe in the bright, dry, heady air itself; it might indeed be something everybody in this country pulled into their lungs all their lives, something they never could have escaped, even supposing they had ever tried.

Yes, he owed a great deal to Gideon Bainbridge for this

stasis he had reached. The senator was a good amateur historian himself, with the instincts and habits of a scholar. More even than Jim, he had pushed Corey toward his studies of the Apaches. Perhaps Gideon was doing it for the same therapeutic reasons Virgie had had when she sent Corey up the mountain with Harold Bishop, but the end result had been to give direction and meaning to Corey's life in a way few other things had done to date. In the process Gideon had become a good deal more than a friend. Perhaps that was why Corey had rebelled at Jim's suggestion that they bring the senator into the Tony Bishop thing. You didn't burden people that close to you with your own particular agonies.

He took one more brief glance at big Cuchillo and returned to the study, where he shuffled through the papers on his desk and read his notes. Before he finished the section he was working on he would have to make another try at locating Daniel Conner, the miner who had served with the California Column and who had witnessed the alleged torture and death of Mangas on the night of January 18, 1863. By all accounts Conner would be far and away the most reliable witness to the old chief's murder. Murder? *Careful, historian.* It surely wasn't murder until all the facts were in and weighed in the balance of scholarly judgment.

General West's report had completely exonerated the two privates who had guarded Mangas and who had shot him to death while he "was trying to escape." Although West came off badly in accounts of the way he had followed Carleton's genocidal orders right up to and including that ugly night, it was still possible that the officer was telling the truth, but it was hard to have much faith in a military man who had permitted his troops to scalp the dead Mangas, and who hadn't apparently lifted a finger when Mangas's mighty head was hacked from his body and dumped in a pot so the meat could be boiled away, and who had made no remonstrances whatsoever when the skull was sold to Orson Squire Fowler, the phrenologist, who used it in demonstrations as evidence to support his cockeyed racial theories for almost twenty years on the lecture circuits of the East. The skull had disappeared when Fowler died in 1887, and letters to his family in Connecticut had produced no word of its whereabouts. Tony Bishop could never mention the missing skull of Mangas without getting a wild, crazed gleam in his black eyes. "The head must be put back with the rest of Mangas even if someone must die to get it there," he had said once. Corey had written more letters to no avail, had contacted historical societies in every city and town where the phrenologist had displayed it.

Strange that he could throw himself into detective work with such dedication about an Indian the world largely considered an inconsequential savage, one he hadn't known, one dead thirty-seven years and all but forgotten by his killers and everybody else, and yet he couldn't stir himself for a friend, and the father of that friend. Was he afraid? Yes. But not in any physical way, certainly not the way he had been often enough in Cuba. This was a far deeper kind of cowardice, the cowardice of the soul. Someone else, long ago, had put it into words with sublime devastation.

Who calls me coward? breaks my pate across, plucks off my beard and blows it in my face? 'Swounds and I should take it. For it cannot be but I am pigeon livered and lack gall. . . .

Overstatement? Sure. But this troubling thought was something he would sooner or later have to deal with.

6

"Pete Jandeezi wants to see us," Tom Hendry said when he picked Corey up at the X-Bar-7 the Monday morning after Corey and Virgie's trip to town. "Sent word to me by way of Daisy Juh, the girl who works for the agent. When I talked with Pete after I saw you in the office he said he remembered something he hadn't told me the first time, right after Tony was killed. In point of fact he hadn't told me anything then, but all during this second talk with him he sounded spooked. Ana Bishop wasn't with me this time, and believe me, it was tough going."

"I can guess, but go on."

"Well, he let on that somebody made several visits to Tony at the sawmill in the weeks before his death."

"Kessler?"

"No. He said he knows Kessler, and it wasn't him. He said he knew this other man, too. Then he backtracked and said he didn't. Then, for Pete's sake, he did another flip. I think he figures it will knock the socks off us when he tells us who this mystery hombre is, and that if he stunts around like this we'll fall all over ourselves getting it out of him." Tom chuckled. "And he let me know that whoever it was he saw didn't see *him*. He was pretty smug about it."

"I can believe it. Old Pete is probably getting close to senility, but if he didn't want this man to see him, the man sure as hell *wouldn't* have seen him. The rest of his behavior is in character, too. Pete Jandeezi has made a life's work out of secrecy—to a point. When he finally *wants* to tell you something he'll beat you damned near to death with it. Chances are he's dramatizing the whole thing. Five will get you ten that whoever he saw had a perfect right to be there. Legitimate lumber business, most likely. But look, Tom. Do you really need me on this trip?"

"You bet. When I saw Pete last he hinted that if he decided to talk he'd only tell *you* who the man was. Pretty clear he didn't quite trust me."

"All right. Let's get up there. We'll stop at Cow Camp Creek and pick up Harold." Yes, Harold should be in on this. And as much as Corey disliked the thought of getting involved any deeper, it would be good to see old Pete again.

He was almost beginning to look forward to the ride up the mountain when Tom said something that unsettled him all over again.

"Taking Harold with us might present a problem."

"How so?"

"I got the notion Pete didn't want Harold in on this."

Strange. Pete had always been damned fond of Harold, and his fondness had been even more than that of one family member for another. Harold might turn awkward about being excluded, whether he still wanted Corey's help or not.

"Maybe *I'd* better not go, then. If Pete gets me, he gets Harold, too."

"Suit yourself, Corey, but this might be our first real break.

Now—my other news. Matt Kessler, it turns out, is the front man for some sort of development consortium."

"Development of what?"

"Haven't found that out yet. And I haven't been able to find out who his principals are, either. Oh, one thing. He gets regular mail from a big wood products company in Missouri, and a hell of a lot of mail from members of the legislature. Now, don't ask me how I found that out." Tom grinned again.

"You're hinting that there's a connection with Tony's death, aren't you?"

"I sure as hell am."

Corey felt a tremor in his belly. Things were moving in on him. Well, the only thing he could do would be to move right out and face them. "Give me ten minutes to saddle up and have Porfirio put your buggy away and get a horse for you. While I'm doing that, would you mind telling Cookie we'll need some grub?"

They stopped to eat at the rocks where Harold had barred Corey's way that first day. Corey had pushed pretty hard for Tom, no horseman, and he wondered exactly why he was in such a hurry. There hadn't been much talk. His thoughts strayed to the old Indian they were on their way to see.

A gangling, aged wood sprite who never looked straight at you when you spoke, but gazed over your shoulder as if he were listening to other, more important voices, Pete was incredibly tall for an Apache—as Mangas had been, if the descriptions of the dead chief in Gideon's old newspaper files were accurate. Pete had contributed in no small measure to the warmth of the weekend stays Corey had made in the Bishop home back when Virgie more or less forced Harold and him to play truant from their cowboying at the X-Bar-7. Corey had liked Pete from the start, even though Pete always dressed in the old way, something that should have made Corey shrink away as he did from the dreams.

The rickety old Mescalero still lived in an honest-to-God wickiup with a bark roof instead of the cabin Tony had offered to build for him, and he never entered Ana's house without carting in armloads of pine greenery to spread around, to Ana's joy, and opening every window wide, to her dismay, even when the wind had peeled off a five-inch layer of the basin itself and was hurling it up the canyons. Pete was a practical joker of some accomplishment, too, almost like the trickster gods of the Apaches. High good humor ran like a prairie fire through Ana's side of the family, and Pete's waggishness was typical of that of all of her relatives with the exception of quiet Lucy. Unlike so many of Ana's older kin, Pete had never, by his own statements, been a warrior. "Never been a husband, either!" he said once, seeming to imply that war and wedlock were the same.

Pete was an incurable gossip, too. Little that went on up here on the Mescalero escaped him, and he loved to share it with the family, and sometimes with anyone else who cared to listen.

What Corey had learned about Mescalero lore and beliefs he had leaned from Pete, who often seemed as much a supernatural being as any of the *gah'n* he chanted about when the mood seized him and his eyes glazed. It was by way of Pete that Corey became acquainted with the legends of White Painted Woman. He suspected that most of Harold's grounding in his tribal heritage had come from Pete, too. Ana was, for the most part, too modern and pragmatic to link herself totally to the ancient Apache ways. There were times when she seemed to Corey less Indian than Virgie was. Harold hadn't learned about the Apaches' spirit world from Tony, either; in his second life as a lumberman, Tony Bishop had been as single-minded as he must have been in his first as a desert raider and lieutenant to the likes of Nana, Naiche, and Victorio. Theology, to Tony, would have been for those who didn't fight or work.

Not that he hadn't taught the hard physical world of the Red Paint People to his son; Corey still remembered Harold telling him of the excursions he and his father made to Little Round Mountain before he was ten years old, when Tony would give him a sip of water from a gourd, tell him not to swallow, and have him run to the top of the steep small peak and down again, always under a blazing sun. If, after the run, there wasn't enough water left in Harold's mouth for him to spit it out, a thrashing with a cane cholla branch would make sure there was the next time. The sweat baths Tony had insisted on and that Harold had described to Corey didn't sound like larks, either, nor did the trips out into the alkali flats, where Tony would leave the youngster to make his way back to the piñon line on foot, often a distance of twenty miles. It all made the easy tasks Mike Calico had set for Corey, which had seemed Satanic sadism to him then, seem like play.

Old Pete, bless him, had been as easy and gentle as Tony had been hard. Ana looked after him as if he were another child.

When Tom and Corey rode into the yard of the Bishop house, Harold was sitting on the front stoop at his leatherwork again, and Ana was hanging a wash.

She greeted Corey with the same affection as she had a week ago, but she fell silent, almost brooding, when she saw Tom—and when Corey told her of their planned visit to her uncle. Corey looked over her shoulder, wondering if Lucy was at home and berating himself that he didn't have the nerve—or whatever it took—to ask.

Ana must have read his mind. "It's graduation today at St. Joe's. Lucy has to be with her pupils until after supper." Whatever had been bothering her when she looked at Tom had disappeared for the moment. She was smiling again— eager. Easy to see where Harold came by those swift mood changes of his. "You and your friend will come back and eat with Harold and me, won't you, Corey?"

"Don't know if we can, Ana. Don't know how long we'll be with Pete."

Her black eyes darted from Corey to Tom to Harold, who had left the stoop after saying hello, and who was now heading for the corral to get his pony, and back to Corey again. "What do you want to talk with Pete for?" Her face had gone a nasty gray , with suspicion, it seemed. And it wasn't just suspicion Corey read in her features—but rather a fright, a quick moment of something close to terror. Then she apparently got a tight grip on herself. "Come inside the house. I've got some dried meat and some other stuff you can take to Pete for me."

Corey slid from the saddle and handed the reins to Tom. The newspaperman was watching Ana with heightened interest and clearly hadn't missed these sudden, subtle changes in her. Hard to get anything past Tom. Corey followed Ana into the little house as Harold led his pony out of the corral gate. He must have had it saddled all the time, almost as if he had been expecting them.

"What do you want to talk with Pete for?" Ana said again when they were inside. She was more composed now than when she had asked the question earlier, but there was still the same inquisitorial air about her.

"Tom wants to, Ana."

"Maybe I'd better come, too. You'll need an interpreter."

"Harold can interpret for us."

"But I still don't see what you—Tom wants from Pete."

"Just a couple of details about the accident he'd like to get straight."

"That was more than three months ago, Corey. Can't we forget about it? Uncle Pete wasn't too clear about things at the time it happened, and he sure won't remember anything now." Corey got the funny notion that she was deliberately willing such an outcome. She turned away from him and moved to the kitchen side of the room, stopped in front of the wooden sink, and looked out into the yard. Through the window he got a glimpse of Harold, mounted and facing the newspaperman, and Tom shaking his head while Harold talked to him with considerable animation.

"Ana," Corey said. "Let's you and I level with each other. I know you know what Harold thinks about Tony's death. What do *you* think?"

Without turning to face him she shrugged. Or was it a shudder? "What difference does it make what I think? And what difference does it make how it happened? Tony's dead."

"He was your husband. I would think it would be terribly important to you how it happened."

"What's *likely* to happen is far more important."

Ana turned to face him, her features as placid suddenly as he had ever seen them, but her eyes fearless and brimming with determination. Formidable woman. He knew even before she spoke that she was going to change the subject and that it would be useless for him to try to go on.

"You and Mr. Hendry come back for supper, Corey. Lucy will be back from the school before dark. I know how much she wants to see you. I know how much you want to see her, too. Now—if you must bother Uncle Pete, you'd best get going. I've got work to do."

As they rode out across the meadow, Corey looked back at the house. Ana was in the yard, too far away for him to actually see that she was still watching them, but he knew she was.

"This little spread isn't technically *on* the reservation, is it, Corey?" Tom pointed to a corral and a tack shed they were riding past on the trail that would eventually lead them through the timber to the sawmill and then past it to Pete Jandeezi's wickiup, which was up in a glade of aspen seven miles east and a mile south of where Corey and Harold had seen Kessler and his mule train.

"I don't know," Corey said. "I think you'd better ask Harold." He turned to his friend, who sat the spotted pony alongside them. "Harold?"

There was no answer. Harold was suddenly acting as sullen as Tony ever had. Usually his periods of silence were more trancelike; something was eating at him today, something new.

Tom motioned Corey to drop back with him and in a low voice said, "His nose is a little out of joint. I told him Pete said he only wanted to talk to you."

Sure. That accounted for Harold's moody silence. Perhaps they had heard the last from him today.

Then, to Corey's surprise, Harold answered Tom's question. "That's part of Lincoln Kanseah's little operation. Might as well be on reservation land, even if it isn't officially. I don't think anyone up here really knows exactly where the boundaries are in some places. Mescalero and other Apache families been living out this way for more than fifty years. Nobody but us ever wanted this land. You can't grow anything on it, and it's only been the past few years that lumber got to be much in the way of a reliable cash crop."

"Have your people proved up on these holdings just to be on the safe side?"

"Come on, Tom! White government has never let Indians homestead in the Territory. At least that's what the agents have always told us. Of course they maybe just said that because they wanted us living closer in to the agency, where they could keep an eye on us. Besides, if we did try to prove up, wouldn't we be admitting it isn't ours? You tell *me*. I'm no lawyer."

"Makes two of us. I'll admit I don't know what the law is on that. The agents may damned well have been telling the truth."

Corey broke in. "Indians aren't citizens, Tom. They don't fall under the Homestead Act." The talk of the reservation's boundary lines rang a tiny bell in his head. He silenced it at once. He had better hold fast to the idea he had put to Harold that night of the full moon. If Tony's death hadn't been an accident as everyone had supposed at first, it surely had come about from something as simple and easy to understand as a robbery attempt that had somehow gone awry. Had to be. Nothing "funny" had gone on; tragic, yes, a wanton killing always is, but not necessarily sinister.

Still, the ideas of the boundary lines, together with Tom's talk about the outlying Apache families "proving up," wouldn't leave him. An image of a map he had seen somewhere, a map of the high country the three of them were riding through at the moment, kept coming into his mind. There had been a well-established line of demarcation of most of this northwestern section of the Mescalero on it, plotting out all the adjoining terrain and the big timber tracts that rolled splendidly down to the Rio Concho. He recalled that line clearly, but where had he seen the map itself? Jim McPherson's office? The Chupadera County Courthouse in Black Springs? Perhaps in Santa Fe in the office Eloy Montoya kept just off the plaza when he held the Territorial Senate post now filled by Gideon Bainbridge. Yes, there had been an old map there. Maybe, Corey thought, he had made some mention of its whereabouts somewhere in his own notes. He should have, were he to consider himself a scholar.

They had left all the pastureland behind them and were now entering the aspen glades that had sprung up to replace the giant ponderosas destroyed in the terrible burns of the 1870s. Later, in the eighties, probably, Pete had carved Apache symbols and stick-figure animals and birds into the white bark of the trees for a mile or so around his wickiup, and the carvings had now scarred over, the symbols themselves standing away from the trunks like welts.

Strange country. The sunlight coming down through the delicate new leaves underwent a peculiar sort of diffusion, looking as though it were coming up from the ground as much as coming down through the yellowing canopy above. The odd light lent everything a look of spectral eeriness, as of something not quite real. The big fires of twenty-five years ago had completely burned away the pine duff and all the other material of the forest floor, leaving in their place delicate, pale green grasses and here and there fungi even a botanist might think alien to this dry upland country. The foliage and the soft, spongy trail muffled sound, even the hoofbeats of the three horses, and it seemed that the piñon jays and ravens, usually a noisy lot, were reluctant to break the silence.

It wasn't too intolerable today with his two companions riding with him, but Corey remembered once—he was about seventeen and it had been in October—when he had been hunting this particular stretch of second-growth wilderness with Harold and had become separated from the young Mimbreño, feeling at first the quiet thrill you sometimes get when you suddenly, unexpectedly, find yourself alone with beauty, even beauty as unearthly as that of the aspen glade. Then, just as suddenly, he *hadn't* been alone, and whatever beauty he had felt was gone. He was lost. That, in itself wasn't something to worry him—he had been lost in the high country before and knew he could handle it—but now something unseen had come into the woods, something which bore him an ill will he could feel as palpably as if someone had poured ice water down his spine. Pete Jandeezi's *gah'n?* Nonsense—when he thought about it now at twenty-eight— laughable; it hadn't seemed so then. He had spurred his horse back toward the open rocks to look for Harold in a cold-sweat panic, only to come across another hunter—Gideon. The meeting with his friend made things right at once.

He hadn't mentioned his clammy fright to either Harold or

Gideon that day, but he was sure Gideon had guessed at it, and he had developed a new respect for Pete; it took hard, flinty nerve to live in this spooky place.

On the right-hand side of the trail and a bit ahead of them, he spotted the deer carving on the trunk of an uncharacteristically twisted aspen that told him they were just a half mile short of Pete's wickiup.

It was just as they passed the carved tree that he got his first whiff of the stale smoke of an old fire.

For an almost delirious moment he thought perhaps it was the aftersmell of the blaze of more than two decades earlier.

Harold reined in the spotted pony and Tom and Corey pulled up their horses, too.

"Been a fire up here. Yesterday, I'd guess," Harold said. "Damned funny. It's been too wet and green for anything to burn. Campfire, maybe."

"Pete's?" Tom asked.

"Nope. Pete only starts a fire in the winter. Eats his food raw or cold. And he would never let anybody build a fire within a mile of here. Says fire scares away his spirit friends."

Then Harold's slim back stiffened. His mouth opened, and a low moan began deep in his throat.

He reached down to the saddle holster, and the Winchester leaped into his hand. He beat the pony with the free end of the reins and the startled animal shot forward down the trail so swiftly it set Tom's bigger mount to tossing its head, wild-eyed.

Corey got under way next.

Almost as if one of the *gah'n* had whispered it, he knew exactly what had gone through Harold's mind and what he and Tom would find when they caught up with the Mimbreño.

The wickiup was gone. In the center of the clearing where it had stood a few wisps of smoke swirled above its ashes, stirred to motion by the rush of Harold's pony. The odor of burned wood and plant matter was stronger here, mixed with another disgusting, sickly smell. When Tom and Corey reached Harold he had already dismounted and was looking down at what remained of his great-uncle Pete.

"My God!" Tom Hendry whispered to Corey. "*This* wasn't robbery."

"No, it wasn't, Tom."

7

It was a ghastly trip back to Cow Camp Creek, first from Pete's smoldering wickiup by way of tribal headquarters just east of Blazer's Mill to alert Mescalero Chief of Police Sam Naaki to what they had found in the aspen glade, then back to the scene of the murder again with the policeman—and with it the forced second look at the old Mescalero's corpse, now crawling with insects, but with the ashes of the wickiup around it still too hot for buzzards or other big scavengers to make their greedy visits. Naaki clearly recognized Harold's unspoken worries about this and silently began the unsavory task of wrapping Pete in a tarp and strapping him across the packhorse he had trailed behind him to the aspen glade, refusing the halfhearted offers of help from Tom and Corey, motioning to them to take Harold off some distance while he worked.

"Whoever killed Pete probably thought the body would be burned up clean," the Apache officer said, "but the rain last night held the fire back. Must have been a hell of a fire. That rain was a hard one. Too damn bad. I got some of the best trackers in the Territory, but they won't cut sign now. Looks like it was done with a shotgun, and from real close. Maybe I got to do some more thinking about what Harold claims happened to Tony."

Corey looked at Harold to see if he took any satisfaction from this remark, but Harold was simply staring into the charred space where Pete's body had lain.

"Do you actually have jurisdiction here, Sam?" Tom asked when they had started back toward tribal headquarters.

"If I don't, I don't know who does. White lawmen don't come up here ever."

Jurisdiction! Yes. The question of the real boundaries of the reservation began to worm at Corey again. He searched his memory for the whereabouts of that vaguely remembered map—to no avail this time, either—and he tried, also without success, to decide why he was beginning to feel in his bones that that particular map and no other would tell them something they needed to know.

He would have stayed with this line of thinking, but it soon became apparent he would have to do considerably more and even harder thinking about Harold. At the burned wickiup, during the ride to the agency, and afterward, Harold hadn't uttered a word. It was one of his patented trances again, but in spades. He was almost catatonic, his face as blank as one of the fresh sheets of paper on Grandfather Jason's desk each morning when Corey settled in to work, and as silently threatening.

In the house at Cow Camp Creek, Ana, too, after a first barely audible, suffering cry at learning about Pete, fell silent, but with a difference: in some strange fashion she seemed resigned, perhaps even relieved. Corey took himself to task for these well-nigh accusing thoughts. But then he thought back to the early afternoon, before he, Tom, and Harold had started for Pete's. There had been, after the initial fuss about them going to see her uncle at all, a look of resignation and relief about her then, too—at the end, anyway, when she realized that the three of them would ride to Pete's wickiup without her and with or without her blessing.

"You and Mr. Hendry will stay the night, won't you, Corey?" was all she said when she finally spoke.

He said they would. Tom looked doubtful, but agreed after he pulled his watch from his vest and decided it was far too late to get down the mountain and into Black Springs before nightfall.

Ana turned, went to a cupboard, and began carrying dishes to the table. After she had set four places Corey remembered that Lucy wasn't expected back until after the evening meal.

She then went to the cookstove and built a fire. When she had set a match to it, she turned back to Corey. "Maybe Uncle Pete was lucky. Maybe he didn't even see it coming." She shook her head then, her face grim. "No. Pete would have seen it. He saw everything. He would have seen whoever was going to kill him." The latter observation, for some odd reason, seemed to give her comfort, although why it should baffled Corey.

It wasn't the only thing that puzzled him. An unreal air drifted about the house and the two Bishops. At a glance the look of things was nothing out of the ordinary. Ana busily straightened up the living room, dusted, plumped up cushions on the couch, and hummed as she did it. Harold had gotten out the belt he had been tooling when Tom and Corey arrived earlier today, but now it lay untouched across his lap where he sat in a corner of the living room. He stared at it as if in hopes it might have answers. His head moved up and down in time to the rhythm of Ana's hummed notes.

Neither the young Mimbreño nor his mother had so much as embraced or looked at each other since Corey broke the bitter news. Yes, it had been Corey who told Ana; Harold hadn't roused himself from his funk even for that.

Apaches didn't register grief in the usual way, and the thought wasn't just some kind of racial generalization; these people, this family, had been through too much. Death was an old acquaintance, an all too frequent unbidden visitor. They were grieving now in their own particular manner, not in the way expected of them, but they were grieving—deeply. The strain Ana hummed as she worked and that Harold kept time to was an Apache death chant.

Corey had heard it before on the Mescalero, but it wouldn't sound like what it was to Tom, and he prayed silently that the newsman wouldn't think less of the Bishops for this display. He would have to explain it to the newspaperman as soon as they were alone.

"We've got to ask Sam Naaki to keep a watch here, Ana," he said.

"No!" It was almost a scream.

Harold actually snarled.

Corey knew he should have remembered the Apache pride they both had. He didn't press the matter. It wasn't the right time for pressure. He would have to bring it up later, when they had thought it over.

It turned out that Ana wasn't the last person Corey had to tell about Uncle Pete.

She looked at him from the stove again. "Corey. Would you mind riding to St. Joe's to bring Lucy home?"

As he neared the mission he found Lucy had already started to walk to Cow Camp Creek. She waved as he rode toward her with Tom's X-Bar-7 horse on a lead behind him. The sun slanting toward them from the far Oscuras had turned her face an even richer bronze, and the sight of her brought a sweet ache to his throat—swiftly replaced by a choke when he remembered it was up to him to break the news about Uncle Pete. When he reached her he reined up, left the saddle, and held the head of Tom's horse to help her mount.

"Hello, Corey. This is such a nice surprise." She laughed and put her hands down to the sides of her long, full skirt. "I'm not exactly dressed for riding. If I'd known you were bringing me a mount, I'd have worn pants, or at least *chihende* leggings."

Then she did something that delighted him, made him forget for a moment the awkward task facing him. She bent from the waist, reached between her legs, and, grasping the back hem of her skirt with both her hands, pulled it forward and above her waist and stuffed the gathered cotton tightly under the silver concho belt she was wearing. Her slender brown legs, now exposed, caught the dying sun. With any other woman it might have been an ungainly, even comic thing to do; with Lucy it was all grace and beauty.

She looked up into his eyes. He had heard of "smiling" eyes, but this was the first time he truly remembered seeing them. *She knows*, he thought. *She knows exactly how I feel*. He looked back down at her, holding his breath and wishing he could hold the moment as easily forever.

She lifted a foot to a stirrup and he eased his hand under her elbow. His touch seemed to float her up into the saddle, and the feathery, buoyant lightness it seemed to lend her gladdened him, until he realized that she would have risen magically like that with or without his help. She hadn't needed him for that. Maybe she would never need him for anything. She needed him least of all for what he had to do now.

"Lucy," he said, tightening his hold on the bridle of the horse, "I've got to tell you something."

She took the news with the same low moan and the same silence as had Ana. She simply turned the horse, once he had let go of its head, and moved slowly up the trail toward the house in the meadow. When he mounted and caught up with her, she reined to a stop and turned to him.

"Corey, did you know that Joe Ditsa is Ana's cousin? Or that Robert Walksnice was best man at my parents' wedding? Robert's well was the first one poisoned. Now there's Uncle Pete. Is Harold right about what he thinks happened to my father?"

Although she controlled it well, the fear in her voice hit him and hit him hard. It hit him, too, what a smug, walled-in fool he had been. Until now the danger the Bishops faced—not only Harold, but Ana and Lucy, too—had been purely a hypothetical exercise, a historian's intellectual outing. Lucy and her mother and brother were verging on mortal peril—and Corey Lane hadn't even gotten serious about it.

"I don't know exactly what to think now, but my guess is that yes, he's right," he said.

"Let's get home to Mama and Harold, Corey! I've got to be with them."

She moved off smartly on the big horse, but for all her sureness in the saddle she suddenly looked fragile.

He couldn't allow anything to happen to her. He had to see Sam Naaki in the morning and make sure the policeman arranged a guard for this family that was as much his as anyone's, whether Ana and Harold liked the idea or not.

When they reached the house they found Ana silhouetted in the doorway. Something told Corey she had been standing there for a long time. Lucy slid from the back of the horse and ran to her mother, who took her in her arms and folded her to her with a tightness that must have taken the younger woman's breath away. Busy securing the reins of Lucy's mount to take it to the corral, Corey saw no more of this part of the encounter, didn't want to; the two Bishop women needed at least this brief moment alone together in the wake of their newest loss.

When he unsaddled the two horses, turned them into the

corral, and stowed the tack in the shed, he started toward the house. He was almost there before he realized he hadn't seen Harold's spotted pony nor either of the two utility animals that usually stood dozing in the far corner near the water trough.

Tom met him just outside the door of the house.

"Harold's gone," he said.

"When?"

"Half an hour ago. Fifteen or twenty minutes after you went to bring Lucy home."

"Did he say where?"

"Didn't say anything. But at least he looked conscious again. He stayed in that damned silent Indian shell until just before he left. packed saddlebags, rolled his bedding, and piled enough ammo on that Appaloosa and one of the pack-horses for a three-month hunt—or a war."

"Ana try to stop him?"

"Not so's you'd notice. She loaded him down with grub. You going after him, Corey?"

"Not unless Ana knows where he's headed. And will tell us. I'd never find Harold Bishop in these mountains if I didn't know where to look, particularly with the start he's got."

"You know what he's got in mind, don't you? And what it will mean for us?"

"Sure, Tom. Kessler. I guess we'll have to warn the man, whether he's involved in these killings or not, and whether or not he deserves it. We can't just assume he killed Pete and Tony."

Tom looked thoughtful. "I know you're right. But damn it! I've been pretty circumspect in my snooping around. Now Kessler will know that we're looking at him. Until now he hasn't had pressing reason to cover any trail he might have left."

"You're dead right, but so am I." Something occurred to Corey then. "Look, Tom. Let *me* see Kessler. I think it might be smart now for you to shift your aim a little. Don't ask me what or why, but something has been running through my mind the past few days." He wouldn't mention the map tickling his memory, not yet, not until he pinned down where he might have seen it. He might have dreamed the whole thing. "I've got this hunch you might find out more in Santa Fe than you would in Black Springs. You could check those connections in the capital Jim says Kessler has. I'll tackle him tomorrow. No need for me to rush. If I know Harold, he'll wait for Kessler somewhere up here. He couldn't get very close to him down in white man's country. The main thing is, you get up to Santa Fe. Anything that has to do with what's going on will end up there, anyway—or in Washington, since Indians are involved."

"All right," Tom said. "I'll head up there pronto. If it gets big enough, maybe Jim will pop for a trip back East, too."

"Before you go up there," Corey said, "See Gideon Bainbridge if you can. I told Jim I didn't want anyone but the three of us in on this, least of all Gideon, but I guess it's time. I can't think of anyone who could be of more help digging into things in Santa Fe." He paused. "Forgive me, Tom. I kind of forgot you already know your way around up there pretty well."

"No offense, Corey. I always take all the help I can get. Bainbridge is up in Santa Fe right now, by the way. The governor has called a special session of the legislature on some land reform stuff Lattner is interested in."

"Horace Lattner?"

"Thought that might perk you up."

"What land reform stuff?"

"Over by Silver City."

"Nothing in our neck of the woods?"

"Not that I know of. Why?"

"Just curiosity, Tom. Now, do you happen to know where I can find Kessler?"

"I expect he'll be at his office in San Isidro. He left Black Springs yesterday—with his mail." The infectious grin came again. "How much are you going to tell him?"

"I haven't really got a good answer for that. I suppose I'll tell him as little as I have to. Just that Harold has been acting a little funny, I guess. That's true enough."

"Well, I hope Kessler isn't already somewhere out there." Tom waved his arm in the general direction of the forest beyond the meadow. "Be damned careful, Corey. It's hearsay, of course, but I understand Kessler brought a mean reputation with him when he came down here from the Dakotas."

Corey had felt a little shiver when Tom had said *somewhere out there,* but he shrugged it away. "Hell, Tom. I don't think he'd be too rough on a man who's there to warn him that he might be in some kind of danger."

"In any event, I don't envy you, having to tip him off about your friend, even for your friend's own good."

Yes, there was that to consider, too. Perhaps he could get to Harold after he saw Kessler and explain to him why he had to see the ex-sutler and then somehow dissuade him from whatever foolhardy undertaking Harold had in mind. He could only do that, though, if Ana knew where Harold was and would let him in on it.

And that led to the next nasty chore. Talking to her. With Lucy listening.

"I want to tell you, Corey, but I can't. I promised!"

There was nothing to be gained by insisting. Except for the few tears she had shed at the picture wall his first night back on the Mescalero, it was the first time he had ever seen Ana Bishop cry, and of course he didn't dare look at Lucy. Tom sat in the chair against the wall that Harold had been sitting in earlier. If looks meant anything he was more embarrassed than Corey and seemed, against all his good reporter's instincts, as reluctant to force the issue as Corey was himself.

"Mama," Lucy said. "Maybe you had better tell Corey. You know Harold. He'll end up doing something we'll all be sorry for."

Ana shook her head. It wasn't stubbornness. There was genuine regret in her voice when she spoke. "I'm sorry. A promise is a promise. Harold would never forgive me if I said something that took away his chance to be a man—and a warrior. Look. I don't like this any more than any of the rest of you."

Mixed with the sense of dread when Ana said *and a warrior*, Corey felt a wave of relief wash over him that Lucy at least saw things somewhat the way he did, not that it would have made a particle of difference had it been she instead of Ana who had given Harold the promise. Under those circumstances she wouldn't have told him where Harold was headed, either.

"All right," he said. "I guess this is as far as we can go tonight. I'm going to see Sam Naaki first thing in the morning. He'll get his trackers out here, and with any kind of luck they'll tell me where our brother has gotten to."

What he didn't want to say to the two women, and wouldn't, even though Lucy had become an ally of sorts, was that when he left tribal headquarters he would ride straight for San Isidro and Kessler. Even these two fair-minded women might think that was carrying things a bit far even in the interests of civilized behavior. He wouldn't tell Sam, either.

The policeman looked pretty much the law-and-order type, no different basically for any other conscientious peace officer, white or Indian, but you never knew. Sam would fully understand what was driving Harold, might even approve, or at the very least sympathize. He wouldn't refuse his and his people's help to keep Harold from doing something rash, but he might balk were he to think that Corey was giving Kessler an undeserved edge by alerting him. It wouldn't surprise

Corey if Sam turned out at bottom more Mescalero than policeman. Hell, Orrin Langley down in Black Springs was far
more an anglo politician than he ever had been a sheriff.
Harold's leaving had made one thing easier. Naaki, with his
trackers rooting around, could set up a watch over Cow
Camp Creek without alarming the two women. He wouldn't
even have to mention the guard he would ask for.

Tom spoke up from his corner. "If I'm going to make it in
to Black Springs tomorrow in time to write a story and still
catch the afternoon coach for Santa Fe, I'd better hit the
hay."

"Go straight into town from here in the morning, Tom,"
Corey said. "Don't go by way of the X-Bar-7. Just drop the
horse at Kelly's livery stable. They'll keep it for me, and I'll
get your buggy back to you."

"Thanks, Corey. You coming to bed, too?"

"Not for a bit. You go on ahead. I want to check on the
horses before I turn in."

Corey's last remark to Tom has been something of a fib,
like Harold's *I've got to look to the stock* that first day, and as
Harold had that day, he walked down to the corral to be
alone.

The moon had waned a good bit, but up here in the thin
air of the Sierra Blanca highlands it still bathed the meadow's
grasses in silent platinum. The stands of ponderosa to the
north and west of Cow Camp Creek were even blacker and
more impenetrable by contrast. That was the rub. The things
happening up here where Corey had spent so many happy
hours as a boy and as a younger man were as impenetrable
as the forest wall and, despite the weak moonlight that fell
and shattered on the meadow, every bit as black.

Who was the man Pete Jandeezi had decided to tell them
about? From what Tom had said about the effect Pete
thought it would produce, it might be someone Corey knew,

or knew of. But not Kessler. Tom had been fairly well convinced it hadn't been him the dead Mescalero had wanted to talk about. Perhaps it was one of the "principals" the former sutler was fronting for, and maybe a name would surface either in his meeting tomorrow with Kessler—if it came about—or when Tom made his inquiries in Santa Fe.

There was now in Corey's mind no doubt at all about the primary reason *why* all these things were happening. That took no amount of insight. Kessler, and whoever the unknown people behind him were, wanted the timberlands Tony and his people were beginning to make a little money on. Tony must have known it. But did these shadowy intruders feel it was necessary to kill and terrorize to get it? Apparently. That much was easy. But what else would they do to further the plans they had?

The fact that Tom had not found any answers in Black Springs only went to prove how good this mystery "development consortium" was, how well organized. Secrets were difficult to keep in this wide-open country. Wait a bit. Wide open? Hadn't Corey just two days ago come to the reluctant conclusion that even when the Ojos Negros sun was at its brightest, the basin, clasped in its mountain rim, might be a closed, dark place, as closed as that looming forest there? He had to recognize that it could be both.

Something nagged at him: Tom's remark about the "land reform stuff Horace Lattner is interested in." The name did indeed catch Corey's interest. Senator Horace Lattner of Santa Fe had been the major of volunteers who had fought with Corey's father in the first punitive expedition against Victorio, before the elder Lane had turned renegade and joined the Mimbreño chief. Corey had found Lattner's account of that action in Gideon's archives, and a copy of it was now in his own files in his grandfather's study.

The memoir was a strangely impassioned document, seething with mixed admiration and hatred for the first Corey

Lane, a fair reflection of almost all the attitudes toward his "pathologically proud" forebear (as Lattner characterized him) Corey had faced all his life here in Chupadera County. The former military man had written it just three years ago, the better part of two decades after the event, but Lattner was clearly a man who could lug a grudge over time and distance.

Corey had taken Lattner's account to Gideon when he discovered it and Gideon had laughed. "Your father gave Horace Lattner a lesson in soldiering in that first battle against Victorio, Corey," he had said. "It was a valuable gift, but the kind a man never gets much thanks for giving. If I were you I wouldn't ever cross Horace Lattner, as long as such restraint is consistent with honor. He's a powerful man, shrewd and ruthless."

Apparently the warning didn't apply to Gideon himself. In the last two sessions of the legislature he had tangled with Lattner repeatedly—who on the record still bore a raging hatred of Apaches because of a leg lost fighting them at Hillsboro—on issues that touched on Indian affairs, and beaten him every time, earning love and respect on the Mescalero, and the unstinted support of Jim McPherson's newspaper.

Was it too much of a leap of imagination to speculate that there might be some tenuous connection between Lattner's "land reform stuff" and the terror here on the reservation?

Corey would have to mull that over in the morning. Tomorrow would be a grueling day.

"Corey . . ." It was Lucy. The skirt and blouse had given way to a nightgown and a robe. She had loosened her black hair, and it cascaded over her shoulders. "I just came out to say good night—and to thank you."

"Nothing to thank me for, Lucy."

"Yes, there is, Corey. Even if Ana and Harold don't know what this has cost you, and how much more it's liable to cost you, I do. Oh, I think they *do* know, but Harold's so intent on whatever it is he's doing, and Ana too frightened for him because of it, to think straight."

If she had been bronze in the late afternoon sun, she now gleamed pure silver in the moonlight. White Painted Woman, but real and human. She turned toward the house, turned back to him.

"It's been more than six years since I made that trip around the third basket, Corey."

For a second he didn't grasp what she was saying. Then he remembered. The rites at the dances. She was reminding him that she was a woman now.

Something strange happened in his chest.

He stepped to her, took her in his arms—and they kissed. He couldn't tell where he ended and she began.

8

"Señor Mateo Kessler?" the boy playing in the churchyard in San Isidro said. *"Sí, señor. Venga conmigo, por favor."* He didn't look at Corey.

The youngster, six years old, perhaps, led him to a wagon trace at the northwest edge of the tiny hamlet, stopped where a NO TRESPASSING sign had been nailed to a tree, and pointed down the road, curiosity written all over his cheerful brown face but held in check by the *cortesía* that had been drilled into him since birth.

"Gracias," Corey said. He dug in his pocket, found a dime, tossed it to the boy, and rode on past the sign. *Was* he trespassing? If he was, was it on Kessler's domain or Harold's rights?

He found Matt Kessler's office building in a grove of dusty cottonwoods by the Rio Concho. It was a sprawling place with mammoth cedar vigas forming a *portál* as imposing as that of the the old Murphy-Dolan store at Lincoln, one valley

over. The sun had faded a sign on the Territorial-style adobe
almost to illegibility, but through the heat shimmer he could
still make out:

MATTHEW KESSLER
Sutler—Outfitter

He tied off the reins of his horse at the hitch rail and
looked around.

The place seemed more coach stop than it did office. It
was as silent as the churchyard where he had found the boy.
From the powdery gray of the leaves of the cottonwoods it
seemed the storm that had belted the high country the night
Pete died had bypassed San Isidro. The place could use a
rain now.

He walked to the *portál* and tried the door. Locked. Alongside the door a new sign with sharp black letters read:

SIERRA DEVELOPMENT COMPANY
Matthew Kessler, Gen. Mgr.

Then he noticed the handwritten note tacked up inside the
glass.

> Back after dinner and siesta
> —KESSLER

It was a crude, infantile scrawl that didn't speak of too
much schooling, but the signature had been struck off with
something like arrogance, the K a huge block letter that
brought the scruffy bum Corey had seen on the trail a week
ago and the barbered Kessler of the Sacramento House
swiftly to mind. Somehow it seemed in character for both.
Corey pulled his watch—his father's watch, actually—from
the pocket of his vest. Eleven forty-five. There was no telling

how long Kessler took for his noon meal, and the siesta might be a lengthy one in this heat, but little as the prospect appealed to him Corey would have to wait. He could eat the lunch Lucy had packed for him. A mistake, that—letting her fix it. It was going to be hard enough keeping her out of his mind after last night in the meadow, and he mustn't even think of her for a second now.

He shouldn't be in any hurry to eat, anyway. Supper would be a problem. If he didn't leave San Isidro by two, he couldn't possibly make it back to the X-Bar-7 or even Black Springs until long after darkness came.

He tried to peer through the glass around the note. A thick coating of grime obscured almost everything inside, but in the unlit cavern behind the door he managed to make out a desk, a pair of file cabinets, what appeared to be a gun cabinet, and in a far corner an unmade bed. A dozen or so big wooden crates with legends stenciled on them that he couldn't read in the gloom had been stacked against the far wall. It was a big room to hold such scant furnishings.

His little Mexican guide was peeking at him from behind a tree back on the wagon road, only his black shining hair and two huge eyes visible. Corey smiled and waved to the youngster. The dark head disappeared.

He left the *portál* and rounded the corner of the building. He was looking for something, he didn't know what—perhaps something that would give him a clue as to just how he could approach the man he was waiting for, if Kessler showed. The haphazard manner in which Corey was going about the errand he was on, like a rookie Pinkerton man on an unfamiliar prowl, was growing more ridiculous to him by the minute. No, not ridiculous. Grotesque, perhaps.

What *was* laughable was that an unarmed scholar, a bookish type (and he sure as hell was bookish, no matter what he might have proved to himself in Cuba) was here at all. He had pressed Tom Hendry before they parted this morning about the "mean reputation" Kessler had reportedly brought with him from the Dakotas.

"Might be nothing to it, Corey, but he's supposed to have killed a man in a poker argument in Fargo. I guess it was a dozen years ago." Tom had laughed. "Hard to imagine gunfights in this day and age."

Remembering the man on the trail, it wasn't all that hard for Corey at the moment. One consolation. It generally took at least two guns to make a gunfight.

The note was welcome in one important way. Kessler wasn't up on the mountain where Harold could try something harebrained with him, not this morning, anyway. And for the moment he wasn't up on the mountain where he could pose any threat to Ana and Lucy. Corey had every confidence that Sam Naaki would do what he could to look after the Bishop women, but would Sam's watchful eye be enough? A lot could turn on Kessler's response to the warning Corey intended giving him. Kessler, warned and perhaps turning panicky, might try for some kind of preemptive strike against the three Bishops. Corey would have to be very, very careful in his talk with the man.

He realized with a sense of foreboding that on the ride down from the Mescalero to San Isidro he had negotiated an even greater distance than just the geographical one between the reservation and the somnolent little town. He had now come all the way to a genuine commitment to finding out what or who was behind the campaign of terror up in the ponderosas, a longer journey by far than this morning's ride. If Sam could only find Harold for him, Corey would tell his friend that he had at last truly come in for a dollar, not just a measly dime like the one he had tossed the Mexican boy. Perhaps then, together, and with the help of Tom Hendry, they could do some rational thinking about how to stop it.

First, though, he had to see Kessler. There would be precious little change coming from the dollar of Corey's commitment if Harold went berserk.

Behind the building Corey found a rambling corral whose east and west fences straddled the Rio Concho, only a dozen feet wide here, boulder-strewn and swift-running, the only lively thing in this whole backwater community, it seemed.

From the look of it there had been a large number of animals in the corral, and recently. Strange. Why would Kessler be quartering a horse herd of any size?

As far as Corey knew there was no longer a market for any great number of remounts at Fort Stanton or any of the other army posts within striking distance; except for the units stationed at Fort Bliss the cavalry had cantered into history ten years ago—even he and the Rough Riders had fought on foot in Cuba, like Apaches—and the Chupadera and Lincoln County ranches had always filled their working remudas with home-bred stock. Virgie did, and so did Gideon Bainbridge, and theirs were the only cattle operations big enough and near enough to the upper Concho to even consider buying horses here in any quantity.

But a lot of horses had beaten down the earth here at Kessler's, and so, Corey now discovered, had rolling stock. A large gate opened into the corral and tracks dimpled and creased the caliche in a broad path in front of it. When Corey bent to examine them he saw ruts from iron-wheeled wagons and hundreds of hoofprints. The ruts were deep; the wagons must have been freighters, and loaded to the tops of the sideboards, and the hoofprints certainly weren't those of cow ponies or cavalry horses. Draft animals had pressed these prints into the rock-hard dirt. What goods had been hauled in and out of here so many times? He could have used Sam Naaki's trackers now. They could read these signs as easily as he read the *Chupadera County News*, could have told him to within an hour when almost every vehicle and animal had gone in and out—and probably fairly accurately what each of them had carried.

There was one set of tracks he didn't need Sam's Apaches for.

Leading from the side of the building opposite the end he had circled, Corey discovered two pairs of wheeled tracks quite unlike any of the others. These hadn't been made by freight wagons or buckboards. It was a moment before he realized exactly what he was looking at. A dark stain in the caliche where the tracks stopped gave him the answer. Oil. One of those automobiles Jim McPherson disdained so had rolled in and out of the compound. Did Kessler own one? If he did, it surely was the only one in San Isidro.

Well, there was nothing more for him to learn out here before Kessler showed up; he might as well go back to the *portál* and eat.

When he got there, he knew at once that his little amigo spy was still lurking in the cottonwoods, although he didn't see him this time. Maybe there would be a sweet or something in the food Lucy had stuffed into his saddlebag that could lure the boy out of hiding.

When he sat down on the weather-grayed deacon's bench under the *portál* and unwrapped the cheesecloth, Corey knew he was defeated. Every bite would make him think of her.

There hadn't been anything more than the one embrace and the one kiss before she turned and ran lightly back to the house, but the kiss and the embrace had been enough—for the moment. Corey wasn't a "friend" or a "brother" any longer. Her mouth, tender and soft at first, had in the end replied to his so fiercely it dizzied him.

Why did their world have to be so utterly out of kilter? Not *think* of her? He should, after that electric moment last night, have to think of nothing else—not of Harold, stolen stock, Pete Jandeezi, Kessler, bad wells and fires, secret men on hidden, wicked business—nothing. Only Lucy . . .

He bolted down the two bacon and chili sandwiches he found and one of the two *ba'n likani* that nestled with them. Better to get it over with. He was about to start on the second muffin when he caught sight of the boy again. He put the muffin down on the end of the bench and went back to the horse. Perhaps his little friend would come and get it while Corey took the animal to the stream and then fed it. He waved into the woods and pointed to the *ba'n likani*, untied the horse, and led it off.

This time—it struck him it would be easier to reach the Concho this way—Corey circled the other side of the building, the side the automobile tire tracks had led from.

As he rounded the corner something greeted him that stopped him cold.

An immense, open-sided shed had been tacked onto the old adobe, and under the shed roof lay a mountain of equipment: pumps, well parts, enough farm tile stacked in orderly piles to drain every one of the lower Concho's two hundred or more beanfields, and drill bits by the score.

It wasn't a sight to have occasioned much surprise had he stumbled on it fifteen miles down the Concho Valley. Up here at the nine-thousand-foot level it made no sense. San Isidro was kind of a last outpost. No one farmed the higher ground beyond it; that was sheep country. Customers for this welter of material would have to be found much farther down the canyon toward Black Springs. Why haul it up the rocky road so many hard miles *past* all the small Mexican freeholds? The Mescaleros wouldn't draw on these supplies, either. Ninety-five percent of the reservation was situated three mighty ridges away from San Isidro, and Tony and Ana Bishop's kin and friends and neighbors, those who didn't subsist entirely on government issue, did almost all their purchasing and out-fitting down in Three Rivers, near the badlands.

Corey's horse was smelling the water now and snorting a little, and he moved on down in front of the shed. There was another, separate stack of stuff near the back. This second lot, however, did make a certain kind of threatening sense.

Two-man saws and gleaming double-bladed axes, dozens of them, lay cheek-by-jowl with peavey poles and cant hooks. Under a tied-down tarp almost at the far reaches of the shed he saw three brand-new donkey engines. Kessler's Sierra Development Company was getting set to embark on a logging operation—an impressive one, judging by the amount and heft of the equipment here.

Suddenly Corey had a powerful feeling he had seen something like all this once before, and it was a moment before he figured out where. In Cuba he had marched his company past a huge arms and ammunition dump two days before San Juan Hill. It, too, had been half hidden under shed roofs jerry-built on old buildings, and it had looked remarkably like this. He couldn't rid himself of the sense that what he was seeing now wasn't only for a logging operation; not in the ultimate—it was meant for war.

When he returned to the front of the building to resume his wait for Kessler, Corey found that the black walnut muffin he had left on the bench was gone. Good boy! It was a small thing, but it made the hot day more tolerable.

Improbable as it seemed, with so much to rile his mind, all the time Corey had spent wandering the compound under the early afternoon sun had made him drowsy. He sat down on the bench again. There could be no harm in closing his eyes for a few moments, anyway.

Before he could, he caught sight of a horse and rider on the wagon road. Kessler!

When the rider reined up alongside Corey's horse at the hitch rail he looked as unkempt as he had that day when Corey met Harold near the rocks. He must have missed his last three regular shaves. Corey recognized again how wrong he had been that first time in thinking him small and thin. It must have been because of the slanting view of him from high above and possibly the size of the horse he had ridden then. He seemed even bigger now than he had in the lobby of the Sacramento House. After Tom had related the rumor about the killing in the Dakotas this morning, Corey had half expected to find Kessler armed, but he wasn't wearing a weapon now, not even a sheath knife, and the saddle boot that might have held a rifle was empty, too.

When Kessler slid from the back of the big horse he hit the caliche with surprising lightness for a man his size. He tied off the reins at the rail, his big hands quick and sure. Then he looked at Corey—for the first time, it seemed.

Corey had seen cornflowers with more color than Kessler's eyes, but they were steady, hard. Fixed on Corey as they were, he still knew they weren't missing anything else around them. Perhaps in the mountains or on the desert Harold Bishop could deal with such a man, but never where Kessler had staked out a territory for himself. Corey saw something else. Kessler, who hadn't shown a flicker of recognition in the Sacramento House, had placed Corey now. On this one point Corey could read his mind. It was almost as if Kessler had said, *You were on the trail with that Indian.*

There went any chance of keeping the intended warning general, one that wouldn't single out Harold but would keep Kessler out of the high country for the time being, at least.

"Matt Kessler?" he said.

"Yeah. Who the hell are you?"

"My name's Corey Lane."

Kessler's pale eyes widened. "Not the son of—"

"Yes."

"Guess that answers why you ride with Apaches, don't it?"

Corey felt the heat in his face more than that of the sun. In that instant he almost reached the decision that this sutler, developer, killer, whatever he was, didn't deserve a warning.

"Mr. Kessler, I'm sure you're aware of the trouble some-body is causing up on the Mescalero reservation."

Kessler's eyes narrowed now. "Ain't aware of nothing. Why don't you let me in on it?"

"Fires, stock run off and perhaps stolen, wells that have gone bad under peculiar circumstances." Should he say "kill-ings"? Perhaps Kessler didn't think they had figured out that Tony's death hadn't been an accident, didn't even know they had found Pete Jandeezi's burned body.

"What's it got to do with me?" It wasn't a denial, and Corey knew it wasn't meant to be one.

"Nothing, maybe. I hope that's so. I'm afraid my Apache friend thinks otherwise."

Kessler grunted. It wasn't a pleasant sound. "And the little varmint's going to come gunning for me. That's what you're telling me, ain't it?"

"I don't know if it would come to that. I do think it advis-able that you don't spend any more time than absolutely nec-essary up in the Mescalero timber."

"You threatening me, Lane? Get one thing straight. I don't hold still for threats."

"It's not a threat, Mr. Kessler. Just a caution."

"I don't get run off any place I got business by any runt In-dian."

"Then you have business on Indian lands?"

"Yeah. You could check up in Santa Fe with—" He broke off. Kessler's face showed he had been at the point of saying too much. He looked less sure of himself than he had a mo-ment earlier. It was time for Corey to take a chance.

"Do you know who killed Tony Bishop, Kessler?"

Rage flooded the pale eyes. Kessler clenched his huge fists, and for a moment Corey was certain he would attack, but the flare-up died quickly. Something about the question, which should have left this brute looking stricken, had restored his confidence. Would Corey's next question bolster it even more?

"Did *you* kill him?"

Kessler's eyes narrowed again. "Get off my place, Lane. Get off my place pronto—and never show up here again." It was hardly more than a breathy whisper, but it reached right into Corey's bones.

No doubt lingered now. Matt Kessler was Tony Bishop's killer. Corey untied his horse and mounted. "One more thing," he said. "Did you kill Pete Jandeezi?"

"Who?"

The suddenly quite curious expression on Kessler's face settled that question, too. The man in front of Corey might well be a consummate liar for his own purposes, but he surely didn't have the subtlety to fake the look of blank surprise he was giving Corey. A different murderer had come to the wickiup in the aspen glade.

As Corey rode out on the wagon road the boy moved out from behind a tree.

"*Adiós, señor, y muchas gracias,*" he said. "*Vaya con Dios.*"

9

Darkness would come early today. From where he rode, high on the eastern rim of the Ojos Negros Basin, Corey watched the clouds build up like a tidal wave in a retributive sea, ready to thunder ashore and crush everything the lightning of the night before last hadn't scarred or mutilated. It would be good to hole up in a line shack somewhere and revel in this atmospheric theater, but he still had more than a five-hour ride to the X-Bar-7 and one of almost four to Black Springs.

The storm broke as he reached the short back road to Tres Piedras, and any notion he harbored of trying for either of his original destinations was quickly pelted out of him. Gideon had said that Corey was welcome anytime, whether he was there or not, had said it often enough that Corey could believe he truly meant it. Corey certainly wanted to believe him now.

The rain had soaked Corey to the skin, and after the superheated day the plummeting temperature left him chilled to the marrow by the time he dug his slicker from the bedroll behind his saddle. Across the feeder valley of the Rio Concho hail was turning Cuchillo Peak a dirty gray. The gray inched fitfully down toward the *río* as if giant hands were tugging a monstrous blanket down the far slope, then jerking it up the near side to where he rode. When the hail reached him it hit hard. One egg-sized chunk of black ice struck him on the wrist and raised a painful welt. He set his spurs and turned onto the road to Tres Piedras.

Gideon's majordomo, Pedro Chavez, answered the dull clang of the lion-headed knocker on the great mahogany door.

"Señor Lane! Come in, *señor*, come in, *por favor!*"

Corey must have looked terrible to the fastidious little Mexican. He pointed at the priceless Navajo rug in the hallway behind Pedro. "Not the way I'm dripping, Pedro. I just wondered if I could spend the night in the bunkhouse with the hands, or in a tack room or stable if they don't have room."

"*No, señor! Que un pensamiento.* Señor Gideon would boil me in oil if I allowed that. Already I have kept you outside long enough to deserve a whipping. Come, come, *por favor.*" Corey feared the little man might actually pull him through the doorway if he held back a second longer, and he stepped inside.

As a boy he had felt as if he were being spirited to some magical kingdom he had no right to visit whenever he entered this graceful hall, and even after all the visits over the years it was always several minutes before he was completely at his ease. He felt that way now, and coupled with that feeling was his reluctance to enter it in his present state: soaking wet, grimy, his boots coated with caliche gumbo, nearly as unshaven as Kessler, and probably smelling to high heaven as well. He hadn't had time for more than a perfunctory washing up before Tom and he had ridden off from Cow Camp Creek in the predawn dark, and he had been bathed in sweat until washed by the storm. Tom, at least, going down through Nogal, would have made it in to Black Springs and a bath before this weather hit, probably was already on his way to Santa Fe to meet with the master of this house.

Pedro helped him out of his slicker and ushered him to a room off the central patio, where the leaves on the hanging plants were wet and glistening from the still-falling rain.

"Let me draw you a tub *por un baño*, Señor Lane. Señor Gideon will never forgive me if I let you catch cold. Then I must see to your *caballo*."

Nice man, Pedro. Gideon had surrounded himself with others like him, not only here at Tres Piedras but in Black Springs, too, and in the office in the capital, all of them capable and fiercely loyal to him. It would be futile to protest against Pedro's ministrations, and anyway Corey didn't really want to. Ten minutes later, shaved with a razor Pedro provided, he sank gratefully into a steaming tub.

When he had dried himself with a warmed Turkish towel as thick as a buffalo robe, Corey found his clothes gone, and in their place gleaming fresh linen, a pair of pants, and a fine cambric shirt—Gideon's, presumably; Corey and the senator were of a size—and his derelict boots had been somehow miraculously cleaned and dried. Pedro had placed a decanter of amontillado and a crystal glass on a dressing table. He dressed in front of a full-length mirror with a carved gilt frame, feeling for the moment every inch a sybarite. Strange. He hadn't once thought of Kessler since he knocked at the massive door of Tres Piedras.

Out in the *portál* that surrounded the patio again, he found the torrent had ceased. Through the foliage of the hanging plants, luxuriant, almost tropical, and still dripping, he could see patches of cloudy sky, irregular and featured now, not the solid pewter it had been all through the rain and hail. The storm was nearly over. Perhaps his own storm would abate now for a while.

"Señor Lane."

Pedro's plump, handsome wife, Juanita, cook and house-keeper for Gideon, stood in a doorway on the far side of the patio.

"Yes, Juanita?"

"Supper will not be ready for another hour, *señor*. I am very sorry. If only we had known."

"I hope you aren't going to any trouble just for me."

"It is our pleasure, Señor Lane." She disappeared.

An hour. It wasn't that he was especially hungry—the fatigue and chill and then the hot bath with the perfumed salts Pedro had poured into it had left him more drowsy than ravenous—but he would have welcomed the meal immediately just for something to do instead of the probability of thinking willy-nilly about the meeting with Kessler, the whereabouts of Harold Bishop, the possible threats to the safety of Ana and Lucy—and about Lucy in particular. He had kept them all out of his mind since his arrival at Tres Piedras, hadn't he?

A sudden desire to visit Gideon's library took hold of him, but he discarded the notion as quickly as it came, feeling a sharp stab of guilt that he could be so callous as to want to indulge his own petty desires when his friends had so much more at risk right now.

He wandered to the big living room, which had windows on either side of a huge marble fireplace looking out over the Concho Valley.

Tres Piedras sat atop a pine-clad swell in the shoulder of the mountain. Gideon had cut out most of the timber to the west, leaving a broad vista framed in green that gave a breathtaking view of the Ojos Negros. From this height and distance Corey couldn't make out Black Springs, and the X-Bar-7, eighteen miles away, was hidden behind the Rincon

Ridge, but the black lava *malpais* that streaked the desert floor was clearly visible, looking from here like a frozen black river of perdition. Beyond the lava flow the Oscuras welled up like painful bruises.

Unlike the X-Bar-7, or the Shelby place that nestled up against he side of Cuchillo Peak, or any of the other big ranches in the basin, Tres Piedras in its grove of ponderosas didn't gather its outbuildings close to it. A stable looking more like a Massachusetts carriage house than an Ojos Negros ranch building was the only other structure in this manicured compound with its improbable—for this mountain-desert country—sweeping lawns and fantastically shaped ornamental shrubbery. The working corrals, equipment sheds, and the bunk and pump houses, were all a quarter of a mile down the ranch road and around a curve, completely hidden from the main house by design. Most Chupadera stockmen liked their workshops close at hand, two short jumps away every morning. Not Gideon. The main compound of Tres Piedras was a park, and the house itself a "stately pleasure dome," set in the mountainside like a precious stone.

Edging up close to the left-hand window and looking hard to the side beyond the pecan and lime trees brought the tennis court into view. As far as Corey knew, it was the only court in Chupadera County, packed caliche, of course, not the close-cropped emerald grass of the courts he had known at Cambridge or New Haven. He had played on this one twice with Gideon, losing both times in close matches. He was younger and faster than the senator and had a stronger serve, but Gideon had shown marvelous court sense and boundless patience, passing Corey at the net with surgical precision on most of the important points.

Jim McPherson had laughed when Corey described the sessions to him.

"Sounds just like the way Gideon plays politics. He can wait forever on an issue, then skewer the opposition so neatly they hardly feel it. I don't think he's ever forgotten a thing that's happened to him in public life. And he never lets go of anything, never forgets a friend, or an enemy."

Gideon's sitting room, as was the case with every room Corey had seen in the fourteen-room Tres Piedras, had a character all its own. While the patio was prototypically southwestern with its forest of plants, ancient Mimbres pottery, snugly fitted giant vigas and corbeled columns, and a profusion of Navajo rugs both on the tiled floors and as wall hangings, the sitting room with its paintings, brocaded divans, and chairs that probably were Chippendale could have been transported magically from the college president's home at Amherst where the obligatory faculty teas had been held. The room was larger than the lobby of the Sacramento House and more opulent by far. The breakfront, and indeed every delicate end table, held treasures: freshly cut flowers from the solarium-greenhouse nodding gracefully in Sevres vases, Dresden figurines, incredibly worked Florentine lace table scarves, and gold-framed miniature oils whose provenance was surely the France of the ancien régime.

Strange that Gideon had never taken a wife, a consort, a queen to share all this. Any number of eligible Chupadera County women would have pawned their souls to become the chatelaine of Tres Piedras, and there must be scores more beyond the county's borders—or the Territory's, for that matter—every whit as willing.

All Corey would ever be able to offer Lucy would be the X-Bar-7: no hovel, of course, but still fortresslike, dimly forbidding, and reflecting the hot pride and stern, cold passion of his father in spite of all Virgie's efforts over the years to soften and humanize it.

Corey went to the window again. The sun was just breaking the last chain of cirrocumulus clouds stretched above the far Magdalenas, gathering itself for its last plunge into the distant mountains. He stared into the rich, deep colors of the dying day for longer than he knew, thinking nothing.

Juanita had to call him twice before he heard her. "Señor Lane, supper is ready." Where had that hour gone?

Pedro served the meal. Aromatic slices of *cabrito* steamed on a silver salver big enough to feed a branding crew or a rifle squad. As Corey took his seat at the end of the long, dark, polished table—where he had sat opposite Gideon Bainbridge on the one other occasion he had broken bread here—and found in the candlelight only one place set, he asked Pedro if he and Juanita weren't going to join him.

"Certainly not, *señor!*" It seemed a mild rebuke, but with no resentment in it. "That would not be *bien parecido*, not *protocolo*."

Not protocol? Then Gideon must dine in solitude every evening he was in residence at Tres Piedras. Surely there must be guests from time to time, but when he thought about it, Corey could remember no one in Chupadera County save himself who had ever been here for an evening meal, not Jim nor Virgie, no one in the ranks of official Black Springs, not even the more important members of Gideon's Democratic party.

The thought of Gideon Bainbridge sitting alone in his customary place at the far end of this long table night after night, gazing down its length even as Corey did now, was somehow sad, even tragic for some unfathomable reason. Corey hadn't seen or heard from Juanita since she called him to the dining room, and Pedro had come and gone in utter silence, pouring the wine with such a careful hand it didn't make a sound. He wanted to think that when Gideon was the solitary diner there was conversation, banter at least, between master and man, but he couldn't force himself all the way to that conclusion. Something about the sure, swift, practiced manner of the majordomo told Corey that this was the way it always was. Aristocracy carried a steep price, no matter how willingly one paid it.

When Pedro cleared the table and brought coffee and cognac and a canister of cigars giving off an aroma Corey hadn't known since Havana, he at last broke the silence.

"Did you wish to use the library tonight, Señor Lane? Señor Gideon would be pleased. *Verdad.*"

"I don't think so, Pedro, I—" With nothing to do before he went to bed, and with his fervent wish to keep from thinking about all the things he couldn't do anything about tonight, perhaps it wouldn't be a matter of such shameful self-indulgence, after all. At the very least he could find something to read before he closed his eyes. "Yes, on second thought, I believe I would, *gracias.*"

After Pedro twisted the key in the heavy lock and pushed open the oak door, he turned back to Corey.

"There will be dust on everything, *señor.* Juanita and I only clean in here when the senator tells us to. I don't think the door has been opened since Señor Gideon worked here a month ago. Let me go first and light the lamps."

As the glow of the lamps swelled in the huge room a strangled low lament came from Pedro. "*Dios!* This is not like the senator. He did not put away any of the *escrituras* he was working with." One of the two tables where Corey had often worked himself was piled with loose papers and what appeared from the door to be journal pages. "He must not have expected anyone."

Corey laughed. "He certainly didn't expect me, Pedro. He didn't even know I was back from Cuba until I saw him in Black Springs a few days ago, and at the time I told him I wouldn't come to Tres Piedras for a month. Look, would you feel better if I didn't use the library tonight?"

"Oh, no, *señor!* If I didn't permit you in here that would be much worse. I trust you. . . ." The poor man coughed his embarrassment. "*Perdón*. It is not for me to say anything like that."

"No offense, Pedro—and thank you. I'll be very careful not to disturb the senator's work."

"*Gracias*, Señor Lane." With that the little man left the room, actually bowing as he backed out.

The library was another room with its own special character. Gideon had indeed created a small *world* here at Tres Piedras, not just a home. No two rooms were alike; each, it seemed, reflected just one facet of its owner's complex nature. Above an antique escritoire hung a photograph of Gideon in his fencing costume at Princeton and on either side of it certificates for rifle and pistol marksmanship won in competitions in Gideon's student days at the eastern college.

Rich as the paneling of the library was, and sumptuous as were its appointments—the monstrous globe with its four spiraled legs holding the giant gimbaled equatorial ring, the ladders on wheels that reached to the topmost shelves, the leather-upholstered easy chairs—this was a working room. Except for Grandfather Jason's study, Gideon's library was the spot Corey loved best in all the Ojos Negros country, or had until just last night at the house on Cow Camp Creek. It was in this room that Gideon Bainbridge had urged him with genuine sincerity along the path his life should take.

Corey crossed the room to the table next to the one with the piles of papers and settled into one of the leather-covered chairs. There were penholders and inkwells on the table, but there was no blank paper of any kind. A check of the drawer in the table revealed none there, either. He left his chair and went to the supply closet behind one of the freestanding stacks, opened the door, and once his eyes had adjusted to the dimmer light found reams of paper, notepads, more pens, ledger-type binders, and all manner of stationery neatly laid out on shelves at the back of the closet. One of the smaller notebooks would do just fine after he pulled out Gideon's records on old Mangas. Lord, but it would be good to lose himself in work again, if only for this one pleasant evening.

Then, as he left the closet, he saw the map that had plagued his memory the past two days fastened to the back of the door.

It didn't surprise him, now, that he had forgotten it; he had never really looked at it in the half dozen times or so he had opened and closed this door. Now that he had come across it again, and despite yesterday's certainty, he doubted that it would have anything to tell him, but he brought a lamp from the table where he had intended working.

The map was an original, not a print, and it took but a second for him to find Gideon's initials and the date, 3 July 1898, in the lower right-hand corner. It was a meticulous piece of work, with full credit for the data given to a U.S. government surveyor named J. J. Carswell. Just as Corey had supposed, it didn't answer any questions, at least not the ones about the exact boundaries of the Mescalero Tom had asked of Harold on the ride to the aspen glade.

The limits of the reservation where it abutted Lincoln County were definite enough, but the dividing line between Indian land and that of Chupadera County wasn't clear at all. As a matter of fact, Gideon, if he really had drawn the map, had written *Area at issue* across an orange-tinted section south of his own holdings at Tres Piedras. From the scale of the map, this "area at issue" comprised something slightly over three hundred square miles, almost all of it timberland, and all of it on the side of the watershed that broke down toward Three Rivers, not the Rio Concho.

No, the map didn't answer any questions; it raised some.

Gideon—it must have been Gideon—had stuck a number of pins with colored heads into the map, four blue ones into the orange section and two more into the part that was undeniably part of the reservation, and half a dozen yellow ones right on the north edge of the "area at issue," near the village of San Isidro. Corey couldn't remember the pins being there on whatever occasion or occasions he had previously seen the map. Good Lord! That had been before Cuba. He moved in closer to look at them.

One of the blue pins was jabbed into a feathery line indicating a small stream. Cow Camp Creek! It didn't take him long to figure out that the three blue-headed markers nearby were the sawmill, Joe Ditsa's tiny spread, and the Robert Walksnice place, but it was several seconds before he divined the meaning of the other pair. They were the first two homes of Ana and Tony Bishop.

Corey had no guess as to the meaning of the yellow pins, but it seemed clear that Gideon must have been following the happenings up on the Mescalero with at least a minimum of interest. It made sense; even though the reservation held no part of Gideon's legislative constituency, it abutted it. The fact that he apparently kept himself informed should make Tom's attempts to secure his help all the easier, even if Gideon hadn't yet learned about Pete Jandeezi. Good. It would make Tom's job of telling Gideon about Harold Bishop's thoughts about his father's death that much easier.

As Corey walked back toward the stacks holding the boxes where he would find the records he needed to work with, he brushed against the table holding the loose material, and several pages fluttered to the floor. He bent and picked them up, trying not to look at them, but as he tapped the pages together on the tabletop, he couldn't help himself.

They looked as if they had been torn from a ledger binder such as the ones in the storeroom and were dense with writing done a long time ago; the ink had faded from its original black to a sepia almost as light as the color of straw. On the top page he read:

. . . and nott as menny of us now. Nacho Second dyed late last night and today Longnose Martinez and her

son Clava stade behind at Snake Spring. She says thay
will go up to the white mountain. Nana says she is loco.
Blucotes are waching all the trales and water holes up
thatt way. We must rade soon. Food allmost gone . . .

He read to the bottom of the page, but his eye kept flicking
back to "Nana." This had to be the journal of someone who
had ridden with the superannuated Red Paint chief in that
last, desperate foray. Valuable material, utterly beyond price
if it turned out to be anything like a full account of the old
warrior's movements up and down the Territory in the flaming summer of '81. How had Gideon acquired it?

Then Corey's heart turned to stone.

It was as if Ana Bishop's voice were really and truly
echoing here in the silent library of Tres Piedras: *Tony was the
only one of them who could read and write English. What a time I had
teaching him.*

With fingers that trembled as if he had palsy, Corey ruffled
through the other pages in his hands and then went to the
stack on the table. There was one smaller than the rest, of a
different kind of paper and written in a completely different
hand. He had seen this script before. Today, in San Isidro.

Is this the stuff you said we might find in the sawmill office? Think you ought to burn it.

K.

He fell into the chair behind him as if he had been pole-
axed. His stomach was doing something desperate, and for an
awful moment he was certain he would vomit.

Five minutes passed before he could force himself to go on
with his perusal of the journal pages. Then he read for the
better part of an hour. The record of Tony's time with Nana
was complete, sure enough, and so was his account of all the
years that followed—to a point. Tony had been a diarist of

single-minded dedication and of no small accomplishment, despite the deplorable spelling and the tortured syntax that under other circumstances would have been comic, but the entries—there was at least one a week for the entire nineteen years encompassed—ended with the twenty-eighth of February, 1900, three weeks and two days before he died. Would Tony have stopped of his own accord keeping a journal that seemed almost an obsession? No. The clue was in the note from Kessler: "Think you ought to burn it."

But only the last entries had been destroyed; Gideon the painstaking collector simply hadn't been able to bring himself to get rid of all of them.

Corey, even in his state of almost paralytic shock, felt a sick understanding of that reluctance.

The lamp on the table flickered, the flame bending as if a cold draft had been loosed in the room, and then sputtering out. The other lamp might soon run out of fuel as well. Whatever he decided to do tonight had better be decided quickly.

He couldn't take the journal, or the map, or Kessler's note. Evidence they might well be, but would they all hold up as such coming from him, with no proof other than his word about where he had discovered them? Probably not. Could a judge be found in the Territory who would issue a warrant against Gideon Bainbridge at the request of a Corey Lane? Not likely either. Perhaps if he left everything as he had found it and got someone like Tom Hendry in to look at it . . .

Tom!

He had sent Tom to Santa Fe to see Gideon!

Now he would have to get up there himself—fast. He would have to bury his fears for Lucy and Ana, and for Harold, too, try to forget about them for a while.

He looked at the portrait photograph of Gideon in his fencing garb. Corey had never noticed before, but there was no button on the foil Gideon held. The tip was naked.

10

"I'm sorry as hell, Corey. I can guess what it must have done to you," Tom Hendry said when the waitress brought his second cup of coffee. "But it does come a mite closer to answering some of the questions I've asked myself since I got here, even though it doesn't tell me *why*. Not in the case of Gideon Bainbridge. For most of the others the answer is what it usually is. With Gideon? I don't know."

Corey hadn't intended to tell Tom of his discoveries at Tres Piedras, had promised himself that he wouldn't, but when the earnest newspaperman met him at the coach station in Santa Fe and Corey learned how wholeheartedly Tom had thrown himself at Harold's problem, he knew he had to come across. He trusted Tom, and there could be no secrets between allies. Tom's reaction, though, had baffled him at first.

"Why is Gideon different from the others, Tom?" When he

heard his own question he heard the hope in it. Was there a way to let Gideon off the hook?

"For one thing, he's too rich. I decided pretty early that somebody was after the Mescalero timber, but yesterday when I checked with the Department of the Interior's office here, they told me the total value of the lumber crop from the reservation has averaged about a hundred and fifty thousand dollars a year. Although that's more money than I expect to make in my entire life, it isn't a whole hell of a lot when you consider there are more than twenty people to divvy it up, and even if they plan to rape those forests and accelerate the take with clear-cut harvests, it won't add up to a great deal more. Now, some of the men who make up Sierra Development, even the other senators, are small-time operators and could get pretty excited about such a payday, but Gideon could spill his share of any possible loot from this affair and never miss it—if he's getting a share."

"Lattner's rich. Why would he involve himself in such a petty scheme?"

"I knew Lattner wasn't in it for the money from the start. He just plain hates Indians. The reason I'm so mystified about Gideon is that, so far as I know, he doesn't. Do you know different?"

"No. Until now I would have sworn he was the best white friend the Mescaleros ever had, including Agent Russell. And he's always wanted all the Indians in the Territory to get a fair shake, too—not just Apaches, but the Pueblos and Navajos, too." He knew Tom was right in trying to pin down Gideon's part in whatever was going on, but it hurt deep inside when either of them spoke Gideon's name. "Have you learned anything more about Kessler?" Yes, it was better for his peace of mind at the moment to get the talk off Gideon.

"Not really, Corey. Kessler's apparently just what he appears to be: a front, the company's resident professional, listed in their prospectus as general manager, although Lattner is chairman of the board. Kessler is dangerous, maybe, but not as dangerous in the long term as the politicians. He's got a history of doing the dirty work in anything he's been connected with, but not of masterminding things. Rumor, sure, but from rumormongers I can trust. That's another funny thing. I can't for the life of me picture Gideon Bainbridge in league with a dog-robber like Matt Kessler, or even getting in bed with Lattner, for that matter. He's been on the opposite side of almost every political fence from Lattner since he first came up here—not just about Indians, either. Siding with Lattner is a real switch for Gideon. He wasn't listed anywhere in the Sierra prospectus, but you can bet your life that Lattner and his cronies would never in a million years make a move on anything in Chupadera County or on the Mescalero, or any other place in Gideon Bainbridge's backyard, without clearing it with him first. He's just too damned powerful. Our senator is in this up to his neck even if we can't figure out why or prove it for the moment."

Again the hurt, sharper now, along with something like guilt. He felt like an informer. Why? His reason told him Gideon was a killer. Was part of him still holding belief at arm's length? "Tom," he said, "dig out that list of Sierra's shareholders. Let's go through the names again and see if they tell us anything this time."

Tom reached inside his jacket and brought out a notebook.

"All right, there's Lattner from here in Santa Fe, of course, and Smith from Hidalgo County. Bradford of that big spread near Dulce. Henderson and King from Gallup and Reserve. All Territorial senators. The rest, from Terrell Jones through Aston and Whitman, are businessmen of no particular reputation, good or bad, but all from the towns and counties the senators represent. I suppose it's a pattern, whatever it might mean."

It surprised Corey to find that dinner and the talk with

Tom had lifted his depression a little. "Let's get over to the Senate building first thing in the morning."

"You know there's no general legislative session tomorrow, don't you? Just committee hearings."

"Doesn't matter. It's the hearings I'd like to hit. Will they let us in?"

"Depends on the committee and who's chairman. Which one are you interested in?"

"Didn't you say the governor convened this meeting of the legislature to look into some land reform matters?"

"Yes."

"What particular kind of reforms?"

"Freeing up more public lands for homesteading. Doesn't sound sinister. I guess it needs doing."

"Who initiated it?"

"Lattner. Then Gideon got involved, for reasons that weren't clear to me at the time."

"Lattner again? Is he chairman?"

"I think so. Hey! You look like you're getting your teeth into something. Spill it."

"It probably has nothing to do with any of this, Tom, but twenty-two years ago Horace Lattner was a major with the Territorial Volunteers. He fought Victorio with my father. Then he fought the Apaches when my father was riding *with* them. That leg he's missing was taken off after a wound he got at Hillsboro turned gangrenous, and he's been vindictive about Indians ever since. His fights with Gideon have mostly been about Indian policy, but I guess you know that. Anyway, I want to see how far outside Chupadera County this thing might reach. The Mescaleros aren't the only Indians in the Territory—and Horace Lattner isn't the only politician who hates them."

"Maybe you ought to be the newspaperman, Corey. I'd forgotten all about Lattner and your father. And I was old enough at the time that I ought to have remembered it pretty well." Tom looked thoughtful. "Are you going to confront Gideon on this trip?"

At Tom's remark depression bent Corey's spirits once again. The thought of facing Gideon, as he knew he eventually must, was what had brought it on. It had begun, of course, even before he had left Tres Piedras, and it had ridden him like a harpy all the way up the long valley of the Rio Grande. Tom would return to the subject every chance he got. Why on earth shouldn't he? Gideon Bainbridge would be the making of his story.

"Depends on what we find out tomorrow," Corey said. "I know I won't tell him what I found at Tres Piedras. There's no reason for Pedro Chavez to go to a lot of trouble getting a message up here just to tell Gideon I stopped by to get in out of the rain, and if we're lucky, he won't. Gideon could get rid of all the stuff I saw. I'd like it to stay right where it is for the moment."

"Gideon Bainbridge. I still find it a little hard to swallow," Tom said. "Is there any chance he could explain this away?"

"I've hoped so since I was at Tres Piedras, but I'm afraid not. That note from Kessler; no chance he could explain that."

"It hurts, and I can guess what kind of hell it is for you."

"It's been worse for a lot of other people. I'm tired now. Let's get back to our room and get some sleep. We've got a full day ahead of us."

They left the restaurant and walked up San Francisco Street toward the cathedral and the Loretto Chapel, then cut over to Palace Avenue and Sena Plaza. Some of the old buildings in the plaza still had bunting up from what must have been wild, boisterous brand-new-century celebrations back in January, lending a festive look that still hadn't quite subsided, tattered as some of the decorations were. Even in the darkened streets, empty this long after the regular dinner hour except for a few stray dogs, the capital still proclaimed

"Manifest Destiny" in some subtle way from every newly painted storefront and public building. Indeed, when Corey arrived on the late afternoon coach, the town had been bustling, exuberant, cocksure in the way many conquered cities become when they finally join the conquerors and sign on for the conquerors' dream, buckboards and buggies jamming the streets, and with confident men in confident clothing bent on seemingly important errands.

Corey had shared the coach up from Albuquerque with two likable drummers—one in hardware, little more than a boy, the other, with the mien of a friendly undertaker, in pharmaceuticals—and an embryo investment banker late of San Francisco and now of the capital who regaled his three listeners with his views on the Territory's future. The money man in his gaudy plaid suit looked and sounded more like an itinerant card sharp than a financier.

"This is the land of tomorrow, gents," he had said. "Opportunity everywhere. Silver and copper and cows in the south, farmlands in the high plains, coal nearly all over the place, and a handful of ignorant Mexicans and land-poor dumb ex-Texans who never learned how to make the most of any of it. The Indians don't matter more than a fiddler's fart. A sharp operator can make a fortune overnight. Men like me will bring money in, that's all this Territory needs, that and the Yankee brainpower already coming in from the East and the Coast. New Mexico's just got to finish its siesta—been sleeping long enough. 'Course the Territory will be a state someday soon, I expect, so a smart man will have to get a move on. When that happens it won't be such easy pickings as it is under the loose rein Washington keeps on the place."

At the time, weighed down by thoughts of his discoveries in the library at Tres Piedras, Corey had only half listened, dismissing the speaker's words as harmless bombast, no worse than the homegrown boosterism heard more and more often in backwaters like his own Black Springs, and Alamogordo,

Las Cruces, and any number of other dusty, windblown cow and railroad towns. Now, after his talk with Tom, he reconsidered the arrogance of the remarks. What kind of forces were at work in the Territory if men like this could sound off with such confidence and braggadocio? He had grieved a little as they topped La Bajada, the rift that lifted them to the capital's mesa. Predators more greedy than Crook's men, the tough miners he had known since boyhood, the raiders of Victorio and Cochise, or even the conquistadores of three centuries earlier, were circling the political and economic skies of his homeland, waiting for the carcass of the Territory to ripen sufficiently before they gorged themselves. And it sure as hell wasn't limited to outsiders; he had learned that the past two days. Too bad it wasn't.

"Tom," he said now. "I asked you to see Gideon, and then I came up here so defeated by what I found at Tres Piedras I never did hear how your meeting with him turned out."

"It was weird. Now—with what you've told me—it's all clear as crystal, but I was mystified by his attitude at the time, surprised that he didn't even argue once that Tony's death was accidental, the way my own paper said it was. He didn't offer help, of course, but I think now he was trying to have me believe it would be forthcoming. Perhaps he's as shrewd a man as I've ever met. He only let his emotions out once, and then not by very much. That was when I told him you were on your way to see Kessler. He went pale. In the light of what you discovered I suppose he was afraid of what Kessler might spill but at the time I thought it was genuine concern for your safety."

They had reached the door of the boardinghouse on Palace Avenue where they shared a room. A light from the sitting room lit Tom's features. His face was alive with thought. "Damn it! Even though we know he's in this to the hilt, I *still* think he was worried about you. Before I told him why I'd come to see him he was singing your praises like a campaign manager. Yes, that's apt, by golly! He even dropped a remark that someday you should run for public office, maybe for his senate seat." Tom paused again. "He's right, you know. I'll confess it had never occurred to me because you've posed as such a recluse, but he's right as rain."

"Thanks. I don't see myself that way." Corey drew a breath. "My father ran for that seat twenty-one years ago."

"I remember."

Corey tried the door. It was unlocked, and they stepped inside to find their hostess, an imperious-looking lady he judged to be seventy or thereabouts and whose every gesture let you know she hadn't always had to run a boardinghouse, reading by the light of a coal-oil lamp.

"Good evening, Mrs. Copeland," Tom said. "Did you wait up for us?"

"As a matter of fact I did, Mr. Hendry. A Mr. Eloy Montoya, a *Mexican*, came to call." The stress on the word "Mexican" left little doubt about Mrs. Copeland's feelings about some of her fellow citizens—so little doubt, in fact, that Corey could be sure Eloy hadn't gotten one inch inside this dingily ornate room that, like its owner, smacked of better days.

"Did he leave a message, ma'am?" Tom asked.

"Yes, he did. He wants you to come to his *office* tomorrow morning." Again the stress. If Mrs. Copeland had been a teamster instead of a "lady," she probably would have followed her remark up with a question: *What right has a greaser like him to have an office?* She went on. "His exact words were, 'Tell them to come to my office before they see anybody else.'" There was a challenge in the look she gave Tom and Corey now. Were they going to go trotting off to some Mexican's "office" on his *command*? "I'll retire now, gentlemen. Breakfast is at six-thirty sharp. Copeland House doesn't serve after six thirty-five."

Corey wondered for a second what Eloy might want with

them. Perhaps it was only Tom he wanted. The man from the Rio Concho was probably one of Tom's sources of intelligence here in the capital.

Corey forgot about him until they reached the room they shared, when Tom said, "What's gone wrong with me? Why didn't *I* think of Eloy? If we can't get Gideon's help, and obviously we can't, we sure as hell can count on Eloy. You don't really know him, do you, Corey?"

"No. He had resettled here in Santa Fe before I was old enough to pay any attention to politics. I know Jim McPherson and my mother think the world of him, though, even though he was the man who beat my father in that senatorial election."

"Eloy was a fine senator, Corey. It was a loss to the county when he decided to retire. But he's been able to help his fellow Mexican Americans even more as a lobbyist and consultant than he did as a politician. His health isn't the best now, but he still puts in long, hard days. Yes, Eloy will help us." Tom settled his eyes hard on Corey. "But you look a little doubtful. What's troubling you?"

"I'm not sure it's a good idea to bring him into this, Tom. Perhaps because of Gideon it's a case of once bitten, twice shy, but you know how Hispanics feel about Apaches, don't you? Wouldn't Eloy lose credibility with his own people if he lines up with them and us?"

Tom laughed. "No, I guess you really *don't* know him. Eloy Montoya doesn't pander to anybody. When he sees who's right and wrong on this, he'll go the whole mile for us. He's interested in things all over the Territory now, but I know for a fact that his big love is still Chupadera County and the entire Ojos Negros Basin. You need this lamp anymore?" Corey said no, and Tom blew it out.

Corey lay in the darkness waiting for the sleep he knew he needed, but now wasn't sure he wanted. The bed they occupied wasn't exactly a kingly double, and he tried to lie as still as possible, for Tom's sake. In Cuba he had yearned to be back at the X-Bar-7 and under the same covers every night, and now he had stretched himself out on four different beds in as many nights, six nights in all away from the ranch in the last fourteen.

Would he someday talk to Lucy in a darkened bedroom—afterward? That was one part of what he knew would someday come to pass between them he hadn't let himself think too much about, but he wanted her that way, yes; he wasn't putting her on a pedestal, White Painted Woman notwithstanding. Her kiss had made promises his hopes had swallowed up. But it would be the "afterward" that really mattered. That was what lifted this, made it a thing apart. Decent as Fannie and the others had been, and as affectionate as he had felt toward them at the time, there had been no such thing in all those times.

Tonight he had better push Lucy away from him, if he could. There were enough worries facing him here in Santa Fe without his having to speculate in the dark of night on how well Sam Naaki was looking after her and Ana.

"Can't sleep, Corey?" came from the other side of the bed. He must have turned and tossed in spite of his efforts not to.

"No," he said.

"Me neither. Mind if I light a smoke?"

"Not at all."

Tom struggled from the bed, and in a few seconds his face was orange in the flame of the Lucifer held to the long panatela between his teeth.

"First time I've seen you smoke, Tom."

"Don't very often. I have to run across one of these before I want to. One of two or three expensive habits I picked up in Cuba. I smoked like a chimney when we were there. Partly nerves, I guess—or cold fear."

Tom nervous and afraid? As Corey had been? It hardly seemed possible. The odor of Tom's smoke reached him now.

Pure, rich Havana. He had smoked regularly in Cuba, too, and like Tom might still if he could find cigars as good as that. "That's a Corona-Corona, isn't it? Where did you find it?"

There was a moment's silence as the glow around Tom's face faded.

"Will you forgive me, Corey? Gideon gave it to me in his office."

Corey would have bet he never could have laughed this loud tonight.

"I have to forgive you. I smoked one exactly like it at Tres Piedras the other night."

11

The combined home and office of former Territorial Senator Eloy Montoya sat in a small grove of cottonwoods on Calle San Fidel, a dirt lane that twisted away from the Alameda. With Mrs. Copeland's sausages and buckwheat cakes still weighting them, Corey and Tom set out on foot. The sun was up, but it hadn't cleared the tops of the Sangre de Cristos. Tom was eager. Corey still fought the misgivings of last night.

He hadn't seen Eloy for a dozen years, not since the dinner party at the X-Bar-7 when the then senator had announced to Virgie and Jim McPherson that he would not seek reelection that fall. Corey hadn't paid it much mind at the time, but now, with all that had happened near Montoya's old home on the upper Concho, he remembered how his mother and the publisher had appeared actually stricken, and when they recovered had begged Eloy to reconsider.

"No, no, amigos," the Concho man had said. "Muchas gracias

for thinking so well of me, but it is time for me to become a farmer again, and only a farmer. It is not as if there weren't others to represent Chupadera County. The *abogado* Bainbridge is interested in going to the capital. He is a fine man and more capable than I ever was."

Eloy had gone on at even greater length about what a paragon Gideon was. Corey's memories of the regard in which Eloy had held the present senator—and probably still did— didn't help with the worries he now had about enlisting Montoya's support. But Tom had been a steamroller at breakfast, and Corey might as well try to make the best of it. Was he lumping Gideon and Eloy together in some way because of that dozen-year-old endorsement? He tried to dredge up his feelings the night of that dinner party.

If at sixteen Corey had had any regrets of his own about Eloy's retirement, they faded at his mention of Gideon's name in connection with the Senate seat. Gideon's rescue of him in Mex Town had still been fresh in his memory at the time of the dinner; his hero worship of the owner of Tres Piedras had already gotten well under way.

He had scarcely kept himself aware of the things that happened to Eloy Montoya in the succeeding years: Eloy's loss of his wife three years after he went back to the bean farm on the Concho a few miles down the road from San Isidro, the arthritis that had left him a semi-invalid, and his reluctant decision to leave the land again for the capital, become a lobbyist, and advocate for his people's interests.

"Don't know how he keeps that derelict old body and that great soul together these days, Corey," Tom said as they reached an adobe wall with a faded sign that read ELOY MONTOYA in neat, modest letters. "Half the people he helps can't afford to pay him a *centavo*, and those who can don't have much actual cash; I think he exists on bartered goods, for the most part."

"What do you suppose he wants to see you about?"

"Beats me. Maybe—from the way he said, 'before you see anybody else'—he really knows something about our problem. He can't know what we know, of course. Anyway, I don't particularly care why he wants to see me. We need to see him."

"Do we? Look, I don't wish to appear cynical or ungrateful, Tom, but I don't see *why* we need him. It could even be risky. After all, there's a good chance he might decide to fight us. As I mentioned last night, Eloy's people and the Apaches have been enemies too long. It goes back far longer than any troubles the anglos in the Territory ever had with Indians, two centuries and more. Fair-minded as you say he is, he won't want to remember that Spanish settlers brought a good deal of the killing on themselves, both here and in *old* Mexico. Didn't he lose relatives in '78 when my—when the Mimbreños, attacked Black Springs?"

"Yes. His two sons. All the children he had. But trust me, Corey. One way or another I've never failed to get something good out of a talk with Eloy." Tom fell silent and stayed that way for the rest of the walk.

The morning sun was burning through the leaves of the trees shading the small adobe, but in the shadows the Santa Fe air was still brisk and biting. The faint smell of breakfast fires of piñon and mountain oak worked its way through the ancient trees on the Calle San Fidel, and a thin, gauzy pall of blue smoke drifted slowly across the road. Somewhere a rooster crowed.

When they reached Eloy's little house, Tom finally spoke again. "Will you at least tell him what you found at Tres Piedras, Corey?"

"No! As damning as it looks on the face of it, we still haven't given Gideon a chance to explain. I'd like to see how we do at the hearings today before I tell anyone anything. At the moment there doesn't seem to be any connection between Gideon and the Sierra crowd."

"Kessler's obviously working for Gideon. Isn't that a connection?"

"Not necessarily. San Isidro's just a stone's throw from Tres Piedras. Gideon and Kessler are neighbors. It may be no more than that." A glance at Tom's face revealed that the newspaperman was as close to sulking as Corey had ever seen him. He would have to look for a way to square things with him. Even should the visit to the former senator prove to be the waste of time he was sure it would be—or, much worse, the setback—it wouldn't do to thwart Tom. Corey needed him too much.

As confident as he was in following a trail through historical records and moldy, moth-eaten old documents, up here in the unfamiliar hallways of Territorial power Corey was a babe in the woods. Tom had worked these precincts until it was second nature to him. The innocent, boyish face that belied the fact that he was ten years older than Corey masked a probing intelligence and mental toughness Corey envied. He had marveled at Tom's tenacity and savvy when they were both in Cuba.

Now he wondered exactly why he was resisting enrolling Montoya. Was it really for his stated reasons? Or was it because he still had some tiny hope that Gideon's part in things could be explained away?

When Tom knocked at the nail-studded wooden door of Eloy's office-home a voice from inside called out. "*Venga, por favor.* If you speak only English, please come in." It was a weak, thin, reedy voice, an old man's voice. Corey did some lightning mental arithmetic. If he remembered rightly, Eloy Montoya had been about the same age as the first Corey Lane when they had faced each other in that election in '79. He couldn't be more than fifty-three or fifty-four, but the voice Corey had just heard had been that of a much older person, with none of the clarity and vigor of other men that

age Corey knew, men like Jim McPherson and, face it—
Gideon Bainbridge.

Tom pushed the door open and Corey followed him in.

The way Eloy Montoya looked shocked him more than the
voice had.

The first word that came to mind was "wizened." Eloy had
never been a big man, but he had been strong, supple as
oiled leather, and always with a bright look about him, for all
his quietness. Only the dark, lively eyes were the same. Or
were they? Not quite. They showed a different darkness now,
the darkness of pain. The little man seated in the cane arm-
chair at a table in the center of the room must not draw a
single breath that didn't hurt. How could this old man help
them, even supposing he wanted to? Even Tom must see how
inadequate he would be.

"*Hola, señores.* Will you have breakfast with me? It is only
frijoles and *churros,* but *mi casa es su casa.*"

"Thanks, Eloy. We've already eaten," Tom said, "but I
sure could use another cup of coffee."

Eloy looked at Corey. "*Cómo está,* Señor Lane? It has been
a long time."

"A dozen years, I think, Mr. Montoya."

The little man nodded and motioned toward a couple of
rickety chairs. "Would you help with the coffee, Tom? This
back of mine doesn't work too good before noon."

No, Corey thought, *and not too well after that, either.*

As he poured the coffee, Tom said, "You wanted to see us,
Eloy."

"*Sí.* Drink your coffee and have a smoke first, Tom. There
is no hurry." He turned back to Corey. "You favor your
mother very much, Señor Lane."

More than his father? Yes, the implications was plain. Eloy
was holding his gaze on Corey, and for a moment the dis-
comfort was almost more than he could bear. When he had
first looked at the former senator he had wondered how this

forlorn, shriveled wraith of a man could possibly have ever beaten the first Corey Lane in *anything*, regardless of the circumstances, or how he could possibly be the help Tom claimed he could be against a titan like Gideon Bainbridge. It still remained to be seen, but perhaps the answer lay in those eyes. They burned. No amount of suffering, no disaster, could quench the will behind them.

"How did you know I was in town, Eloy?" Tom asked.

Eloy shifted that burning gaze to the newspaperman. "Santa Fe may be the capital, Tom, but it is still a small town. People I have been connected with in the past are still kind enough to bring me news, now that I don't get out as often as I once did. Señor Lane's presence is a surprise, though."

Tom smiled. "Don't fault your informants, Eloy. He just got in late yesterday. I suppose you also know why we're here in Santa Fe."

"A little, *sí*. I know you saw Senator Bainbridge yesterday morning, Tom, and the news has reached me about the terrible things going on at the reservation. The senator will come to your assistance, no?"

"There's some doubt about that, Eloy."

Eloy blinked, but said nothing.

Something about the way Eloy had said "terrible things" didn't mesh with Corey's guarded feelings about him. He also had been grateful for the split second when the Concho man had closed his eyes and the pain wasn't visible.

Eloy went on. "How did your meeting with the senator go?"

"We can come to that later." Tom shot Corey a look that clearly implored him to take Eloy into their confidence without waiting a second longer. Then he sighed and began again. "First things first, Eloy. What did you want to see me—us—about?"

Eloy struggled to his feet and hobbled to an old Spanish secretary-style desk against the far wall. He shuffled through a pile of papers, held up what from where Corey sat looked like a piece of newsprint, and turned back to them. He handed the one he had culled from the pile to Tom, but his eyes were fastened on Corey again.

"Read this. Read it aloud so Señor Lane can hear. It is from a newspaper published in Illinois, the *Chicago Polish-American*. A *primo hermano* of mine, a cousin who is the *alcalde* of San Isidro, found it on the wagon road that leads into town from the east."

Tom looked down at the paper and his eyes popped. He cleared his throat and read aloud.

HOMESTEADERS WANTED

HAVE you dreamed of starting a new life in the glorious West, the land of Golden Opportunity, only to despair of having the dream come true because of the expense of moving? Don't let a lack of funds keep you from joining the Great Adventure of the brand new Century.

THE Sierra Development Company will stake selected, enterprising Polish families at absolutely no interest, in their desire to become landowners in the Territory of New Mexico.

If interested, reply in writing to Box 332,
c/o The *Chicago Polish-American*,
Chicago, Illinois.

Take part in History!

When Tom finished reading, he lifted his eyes to the top of the page. "The date is January 5, 1900." He glanced down again. "What appears to be the same advertisement is here in what I guess is Polish, too."

"It was only found by my *primo* a few weeks ago," Eloy said. "If anyone else had found it, it might have gone unnoticed. Luís is perhaps the only man in San Isidro who could have read it. Not too many people in the village read very well at all, and none but Luís can read English. He is also an *hombre* of wonderful Montoya curiosity."

"He followed up on this and found out more?"

"*Sí.*"

"And . . . ?"

"He asked a sheepherder—another Montoya and another cousin, it is a big *familia*—to keep a lookout in the high country east of the village. This sheepherder *primo* found an encampment way up on the headwaters of the Concho, at what remains of the old Harris ranch: six wagons, six families."

The six yellow pins on Gideon's map!

Eloy continued. "Luís visited the camp. None among these six families spoke any Spanish, and only a few of the younger ones had even as much English as Luís has, so he's not sure how much of what he *thinks* he discovered is really true. He came up here to the capital to see if I could find out for him."

"What does he think he discovered, Eloy?"

"These Polish 'anglos' all have contracts with this Sierra Development Company. In return for the money they got to come to the Territory, they have ceded to the company all timber and mineral rights on any homesteads they establish. *Los immigrantes* were waiting in their camp until a Sierra man named Mateo Kessler gave them instructions on where their claims would be."

"That's almost the whole damn thing!" Tom said. "Sierra wants to frighten the Mescaleros out of the timber and move people they control in. Polacks! Sure. They wouldn't know a thing about this country."

Corey hadn't spoken at all, and throughout the recital and

Tom's outburst Eloy had looked only at him, as if it were solely Corey's reaction he had wanted to see, as if he were going to judge him by it in some way. In a sense they were both playing the same game.

"Mr. Montoya," Corey said, "how well do you know Senator Bainbridge?"

If Corey had expected surprise at his bringing Gideon's name up at this moment, he didn't find it.

"As a public man I know him very well indeed. Whatever other man he might be . . ." Eloy shrugged, "that one I don't know at all. How well do *you* know him, Señor Lane?"

"Until two days ago I thought I knew him as well as I know anyone in Chupadera County—but now . . ." It was Corey's turn to shrug. "Matthew Kessler?" The banked fire in the dark, steady eyes glowed a bit brighter.

"I sold him a crop of beans once when he was a sutler to Fort Stanton. I don't know *all* about him, but I know he is a hard man to deal with."

"How about Horace Lattner?"

The name seemed to almost douse the small fire that had flickered in Eloy's eyes when Corey mentioned Gideon and Kessler.

"There is no difference between the public and the private man in Senator Lattner's case. These two Horace Lattners are both dangerous hombres, men to be feared." The little man closed his eyes again. "I find it very interesting that you should ask me about Señor Kessler and Señor Lattner at the same time you ask about Gideon Bainbridge. It seems to me that you have somehow put the senator from Chupadera County in strange company."

Corey looked at Tom and found again exactly what he expected. The newspaperman was still pleading with him silently. Oh, hell! If Eloy couldn't help, he might not hurt, and he had just now provided them with fairly valuable intelligence. And one thing Corey could count on, no matter what

Eloy's feelings about their struggle turned out to be: He was honorable. Jim McPherson had once called him the most honorable man in Chupadera County. How had Jim put it? "Eloy Montoya is the soul of probity." He wouldn't pass information on if they asked him not to. Corey turned back to him.

"I have some things to tell you, sir," he said. Tom blurted out a small cry of pleasure. He must have guessed everything running through Corey's mind. "This will all be in utter confidence, of course."

"Of course, *señor*."

It took fifteen minutes. Tom came in for a word from time to time, voicing again to Eloy the wonderment he had voiced to Corey, that a man as rich as Gideon would involve himself in what at best could only turn out to be a moderately lucrative piece of graft. Eloy had nodded his agreement rapidly at this, agreeing with the newspaperman. When they finished there was a great silence in the little room. At last Eloy broke it.

"I cannot tell you how it grieves me to hear these things about Señor Bainbridge." It wasn't an idle, pro forma statement. "You want my help."

"Yes, sir," Corey said.

Eloy fixed Corey with eyes as sharp as black diamonds. "And you aren't even going to ask how I feel about Apaches."

"No, sir." Shrewd little man. He had divined Corey's doubts as surely as if Corey had spoken them.

"It is eleven years since I served on a committee of the Senate, and five since I so much as testified. My work here has consisted of little things: presenting petitions, seeing that San Isidro and other small communities like it do not get left behind when the appropriations are made. I may no longer be up to this."

"No matter, Eloy," Tom said. "Without Gideon we have no one here."

"And you are sure about me, Señor Lane?"

"Yes, sir."

Eloy looked from Corey to Tom and back to Corey again.

"Then I will give you whatever help is within my poor powers to give, *señores*. It may not be much. And it will be a risky undertaking, with more chance of failure than success. You know that, don't you?"

Then they talked and planned, and as they did a remarkable change took place in Eloy Montoya. He seemed to grow and straighten as Corey watched, and his voice, while still not strong, became firmer, if soft and gentle, with only one lapse. "No, no!" he said to Tom with some slight heat when the *Chupadera County News* reporter-editor told him of his and Corey's plan to take in today's Lattner Committee hearing and present their case. "At all costs you must *not* speak at the hearings. Not today. Later, perhaps, but not today. You should know better, Tom—not Señor Lane, of course, but you should. You are an old hand up here!" He stopped then. Corey couldn't detect a blush in the dark features, but he was sure one had come. It was that same Spanish *cortesía* he had noticed in the youngster at San Isidro, impeccable personal decency, but not obsequiousness or servility by a long shot. "*Perdón, señores, por favor.* Politicians like Señor Bainbridge and Señor Lattner are professionals, they are killers on their own ground. They would turn every other senator in Santa Fe against you before the day was out. They know how to play on all the old fears that have plagued the Territory, and they know how to play on them so that it seems they are only trying to help *my* people. You would lose *los Hispanos* who sit with them on their committees, and you would lose later on the floor."

Corey had to admit that at the very least Eloy sounded competent.

"What can we do, then, Eloy?" Tom asked.

"Today we can listen."

"We? You're going with us?"

"*Sí*. If you will indulge me in a buggy."

"Absolutely!" Tom sounded as if he had been given a prize.

Corey broke in. "Perhaps I'd better make an appointment with Gideon while we're there."

"To tell him about your discoveries at Tres Piedras?"

"Yes."

"*Por favor*, Señor Lane, I would rather you did not do that. I do not think it wise to let him know what we know until we know much more." His tone was gentle, almost apologetic.

"But don't I owe it to him? We go back a long way. He should be given the chance to defend himself."

"At the moment that is not necessary, *señor*. If we are right, you owe him nothing. If we are wrong, our silence now is his best protection against false accusation."

"Just how should we proceed, Eloy?" Tom asked.

"Today, as I said, we listen—and learn. Decisions on matters such as this aren't made in these committees, they are made in Washington, no matter how much the senators try to delude themselves. They have much influence, *sí*, but no real power except what they have always had, the control of treasure and, unfortunately, guns. We have time. Luís will keep us informed about any movement at the encampment at the Harris ranch. When we are sure of what we know, we will see the governor. It is vital that he sees things our way. And he will not be swayed by the emotions in their arguments as the Senate would."

"All right," Tom said. "I guess I'd better take a hike and find a buggy."

"Could you wait here with me, Señor Lane?"

"Certainly, sir."

When Tom left, an awkward silence hung in the air for a minute, an almost palpable silence. Eloy gestured toward the coffeepot once, but Corey shook his head. At last the former senator spoke.

"I should have mentioned it to Tom, but I forgot. I think it would be wise to see if Señor McPherson could come up to Santa Fe and go with us when we see the governor. This governor is deeply in his debt. Señor McPherson sent his newspaper's support for his appointment all the way to the president. Miguel Otero pays his debts."

"I'm sure Jim would gladly come, sir." For a second Corey thought of saying something to ease the formality with which they had addressed each other since Tom and he had arrived, but then he thought better of it. To do away with it might not, in the long run, ease things at all. Tom's bonhomie and Eloy's genial familiarity with the newspaperman in return not withstanding, something told Corey that Eloy had probably had to deal with anglos from the self-imposed, relatively safe confines of rigid protocol all through his public life and was comfortable doing so, rather in the way wise old regular-army sergeants Corey had soldiered with during the war had handled officers, paying almost laughable heed to the requirements of military courtesy, particularly when they had to tell those same officers things they didn't want to hear.

"How is your mother?"

"Just fine, sir. Disturbed by all of this, of course, doubly so with roundup getting close. The Mescaleros ride for her, you know."

"*Sí.* Your family is well thought of up on the Mescalero. *Verdad*—on the Concho, too."

Should he rise to this? Yes. "Not all of my family, I'm afraid."

"I fear that is true, too. But the Concho people dwell only partly in the unfortunate past. They do not forget that in '93 when the diphtheria struck so hard, your mother and Señor McPherson came up our valley with food and medicine and help like *los angeles de Dios.* That *muchacho* that you met in San Isidro is my grandnephew Pepe. He would not be alive without them. *I* do not forget."

Corey had forgotten. He had still been at Amherst that winter, and Jim and Virgie had never talked about it. Strange. Gideon had. If recollection served, Gideon had thrown his and Tres Piedras's considerable resources into the rescue mission, too, but when he recounted to Corey the heroic efforts made to save some of the deathly ill children of the bean farmers, he had generously given all the credit to the owner of the X-Bar-7 and the publisher of the *News*. This unassuming reticence had been just one more thing to add to the long list of things Corey had admired, hell, loved him for. Did Eloy remember Gideon's part in it? Sure he remembered. This keen little man would forget nothing that turned on his valley, wouldn't forget the diphtheria mission, either, particularly since he had been stuck here in Santa Fe at the time and unable to come to his neighbors' aid himself.

Still, there would be no escaping the shadow of Corey's father with Eloy. How much it might darken this struggle they were now embarked on was anybody's guess. But the silence had settled in again, covering them like a shroud. After thirty seconds of it, Corey knew it would become unbearable. He had to start a conversation some way. But about what? He knew to a certainty that small talk, the everyday inanities most people made do with, wouldn't be acceptable to Eloy Montoya. And any other sort of discourse might become wounding swordplay.

Then he realized how wise—or perhaps just lucky—he had been when he had decided to keep to the excessively formal patterns of speech that the man from the Concho seemed to prefer. It would indeed make it easier to bring up weighty matters. Language could be a shield as well as a sword. Had he in his wishful thinking been too quick to judge Eloy a man of genuine good will?

"Mr. Montoya . . ."

"*Sí, señor?*"

"You commented before, sir, that I didn't ask your feelings

about Apaches. I mean no disrespect, sir, but the reason I didn't ask was that I thought I already knew what they were. Perhaps you guessed that, too. I assume that you share your people's hatred of them. If I'm wrong I would appreciate it if you would disabuse me of the idea. I must in all candor caution you that it will take more than mere assurances."

Eloy's eyes narrowed, and for a moment his lips pressed together until his mouth was a razor-thin red line. Then, suddenly, he smiled. It was a strange smile, almost sardonic.

"You are perceptive, Señor Lane. *Bueno!* That perception will stand us in good stead when we go to the hearing, and in all the other things we may have to do here in the capital. But this compliment is not an answer, is it?"

"No, sir."

"So. Do I hate Apaches? *Quién sabe?* They once caused me great loss." Then Eloy touched two fingers of a hand tortured by arthritis to his temples. "Up here—and you must simply take my word for this—I have no hatred of Apaches or any other people. But here . . ." his hand covered his left breast, "and here . . ." the hand slid down his waistcoat and settled on his stomach, "I am not so sure. In these places my hatred for my enemies—no matter that the padres tell us we must love them as ourselves—may be as strong as ever. You spoke just now 'in all candor,' as I believe you said. I must respectfully insist that you continue in that vein. How do Apaches feel about *my* people now? Are they still *my* enemies?"

It would take more than mere assurances for Eloy, too. Fair enough.

"I honestly don't know, sir. Sometimes, I'm afraid, they think all society save their own is the enemy, and the history of this Territory provides some justification for this point of view. We Europeans moved in here three hundred fifty years ago and imposed a new order on them, one they didn't understand, didn't want, and for which we gave them no preparation."

"I know that, Señor Lane. But some of us have been on this soil long enough to take root. We cannot now pull up those roots and go back where we came from, can we?"

"I suppose not."

"I think we understand each other, Señor Lane."

It had been no "victory," there hadn't been a struggle of any kind, no real enemy, and yet Corey, while they waited for Tom to return with the buggy, experienced from time to time an unexpected sense that he had won something in this drab little house on the Calle San Fidel. Not the least of it was that it appeared to be a triumph of sorts over himself.

12

"The Senate clerk told me that it's an open meeting today, but he didn't exactly volunteer that information," Tom said when he returned to the bench in the hall of the Senate building where he had left Eloy and Corey. "I had to pry it out of him. He did come across with passes for us, but I got the feeling that, although the public is permitted, it sure as hell isn't welcome. Not today."

"Bueno!" Eloy smiled and chuckled.

Corey was puzzled by the Concho man's elation. "That's *good*, Mr. Montoya?"

"Sí. It means that what they intend to discuss today is important and that they *have* to talk about it. If it was of no consequence they would try to round people up to come and listen to them. They are politicos; they like an audience—unless something questionable is going on."

"Why don't they just close the session if it's something questionable?"

"Some bills of recommendation to the Congress must have public hearings, of course. This may be one of them. Sometimes you call more attention to things by deliberately keeping the citizens out." He looked at the pass Tom had handed him. "This is the smallest of the three rooms where we— they—hold hearings. That, too, is deliberate, I think. *Sí*. It is an unusually large committee and ordinarily they would want the big room on the street side."

"Could have been an even bigger bunch if all the senators we think are in this thing were on the committee," Tom said. "Not all of those listed as shareholders in Sierra Development are members, for instance, although most of them are. Gideon, although not on the Sierra list, *is* a member of the committee. No sign of him in the cloakroom or the halls, though." At this last he had given Corey a searching look.

Eloy pulled a watch from his vest pocket. "It is still early, but with this small room we had better find seats pronto, amigos." He stood up and leaned on the thick dark cane he carried. He had accepted Tom's and Corey's help in getting from his adobe to the buggy and its swaybacked horse earlier and then into the entrance hall here with apparent gratitude and no sign of embarrassment, but now, when Corey tried to take his arm, he pulled it away. "Forgive me, Señor Lane. *Muchas gracias, pero no.* I have always gone my own way in these corridors. I still must do so."

The journey down the hall seemed almost as painful to Corey as it must have been for Eloy. It was an agonizingly slow processional, with Tom and Corey a discreet step behind the little man, and with Eloy halting from time to time to look at something, something remembered from his own time in these surroundings, a framed photograph or a plaque, but they finally reached the committee room, an airless chamber that reeked of stale cigar smoke, not from Havanas like Gideon's, but of the poisonous Mexican *cigarros* that were the common smoke of the Territory, the acrid smell mixing unpleasantly with that of days-old food.

Not all the food smells were old; two men, one in rough outdoor woolens that looked uncomfortably hot for today's weather and one dressed in a cotton twill jacket, were sitting at a narrow table by the one wall of windows, eating what appeared to be some kind of stew. A pitcher of beer sweated between them. The man in the woolen suit was belted with a revolver in a fringed buckskin holster. Corey hadn't seen a buckskin holster since he was a child. Mike Calico had worn one.

Tom must have caught Corey's look at the pair. "The one with the sidearm is Jed Buckner, sergeant-at-arms for the Senate," he whispered. "The other dude was in Gideon's reception room when I came out from my meeting with him yesterday. Don't know his name or function, but I got the notion he worked for Gideon."

Eloy's whisper followed close on Tom's. "Let us find a place near the back. We cannot hide in this *pequeña sala*, but there is no point in attracting attention, either."

They had scarcely settled into seats against the back wall before the committee room began to fill. The first arrivals weren't the senators or other spectators like themselves, but clerks or aides who carried file folders and leather cases and who began taking seats in front of a long table on a raised platform that ran along a wall cocked at a right angle to the windows overlooking the patio. The patio was a leafy, shady space with a tiny fountain that appeared more and more inviting as the stuffy air in the room seemed to thicken—to darken, too; half a dozen smokes were already alight, with the promise of more to come.

Tom waved to a knot of men with notebooks sitting against the inside wall and drew three or four waves in reply. Other reporters, Corey guessed. One of them reached inside his jacket, pulled out a white-metal flask, and held it out toward Tom, who shook his head. The man smiled, uncapped it, and after taking a long pull held it out to Tom again. When Tom responded with another shake of his head the man opened his mouth as if to say something, shrugged, capped the flask, and turned to face the front. The others must have had their own supplies of booze; he didn't offer the flask around. Two of the men sitting with the drinker asked him something and then turned and looked at Tom, quizzical expressions on their faces. Tom was blushing a deep, flaming red.

"Perhaps you ought to accept, Tom," Corey whispered. "Eloy doesn't want us to be conspicuous." His lighthearted remark amazed him. It was nothing short of astonishing that he could suddenly find humor in their situation after the deadening brown mood that had enveloped him most of his waking moments since Tres Piedras.

"Look, Corey," Tom said. "I don't drink with them every time I'm up here."

But this hearing *was* different, and if the preliminaries had not been exciting so far, they were at least mildly riveting. In his junior year at Amherst Corey had gone to Cambridge to use Harvard's library and had taken in a session of the Massachusetts legislature with a fraternity brother majoring in political philosophy. It had presented a proper, prim, purely Bostonian face, and he had been bored out of countenance. By comparison this hearing in Santa Fe gave early promise of turning into something like a bearbaiting or a bullfight. New century or not, the frontier, or some part of it, still lived in the Territory.

A young woman in a long skirt and wearing a white blouse that looked very much like a man's shirt entered and walked briskly to a chair at the end of the table on the platform. She carried a large stenographer's pad. A mutter began in the room, which had pretty well filled by now, and above the mutter rose a low, drawn-out, suggestive whistle. The young woman didn't seem to hear it. She smoothed the back of her skirt as she sat down, and without looking out at the spectators she flipped the board top of her pad over to the back and sat looking at the pad as if it held some secret message. The whistle came again, and again she paid no notice. She had been through this before, sure enough, and she was putting on a wondrous show of calm, but something about the rigid set of her back told Corey that inner voices were urging her to run and hide.

The few working women he had seen in Black Springs other than the waitresses at the Sacramento House—Ellen Stafford, assistant editor at the *Chupadera County News*, whom he had taken to dinner a couple of times at the Sacramento; Hattie Spletter at the library; and the handsome, new-in-town Easterner in Dr. Colvin's office—didn't have to contend with this. He supposed the difference was that there was always an out-of-town element here in the capital, men who felt no neighborly pressure to comport themselves like gentlemen.

Since they had taken their seats Eloy hadn't spoken. The cane was straight up between his legs and his hands were cupped on top of it with his chin resting on them. His eyes seemed closed, but when Corey leaned forward a bit to check and make sure, he saw that they were merely narrowed. The Concho man wasn't missing anything. But it did seem as if he was barely alive.

It came as a shock when he whispered, "I had hoped that we would see the senator." He didn't have to say which senator. He meant Gideon. Corey didn't know what *he* had hoped.

Three men who obviously *were* senators and members of the committee had by now mounted the platform that held the long table and were taking seats. Others followed. Tom began to announce them sotto voce. "Sam Bradford . . . Smith of Hidalgo . . . Henderson . . . Joe-Bob King . . . that's just about the whole Sierra Development bunch except Bainbridge . . . the saintly-looking character on the end is Seth Turner of Taos, but he's not with Sierra. Neither are Mintern of Farmington or the old geezer from Las Cruces, Archuleta. Don't let the fact that Turner looks like he's already asleep fool you. He's like Eloy in that respect. A little like him politically, too. He's bright—and honest. Could be the next governor if Lattner doesn't brazen his way into El Palacio ahead of him."

The way Tom said "already asleep" told Corey that the newspaperman wasn't expecting fireworks any more than Turner apparently was.

Tom didn't have to announce the last senator to mount the platform, Horace Lattner of Santa Fe, who hopped up fairly nimbly for a man with a wooden leg. Corey knew him in an instant, although the only other time he had seen him in his life was when he was six years old, when Grandmother Alicia had taken him to the bivouac outside Black Springs to say good-bye to his father before the elder Lane rode out on the punitive expedition against the Apaches who had left the agency at Fort Tularosa. Lattner, a major then, had brought a company of volunteers down from the capital to serve with the Ojos Negros cattlemen under the command of Corey senior in that first battle against Victorio, long before the great Mimbreño's last breakout ended in his death at Tres Castillos. Gideon had been in that bivouac, too, but Corey couldn't remember seeing him.

The only surprise today was that Lattner, still as erect and ramrod straight as Corey remembered him, seemed so big a man, so poised and autocratic, so very much in control of himself and everything around him. Corey didn't recall him being quite that way twenty-two years ago. Who, though, would have looked in command in any camp that held the first Corey Lane? At any rate, he was impressive enough now, even with the clumsy walk, as tall as Gideon, and with the look of an eagle about him. No. Under the circumstances it was more the look of a buzzard.

Lattner took the chair at the center of the long table and reached for a gavel lying there. He had the gavel raised and ready to fall when the man Tom had said he had seen in Gideon's office hurried to him and bent over, his mouth to Lattner's ear. Lattner turned his head and gazed straight at Eloy. His eyes flicked once to Tom and then back to the Concho man. A momentary irritation clouded the stern features and then disappeared. He didn't so much as glance at Corey.

Eloy grunted. It sounded like pure satisfaction.

Lattner looked down the table, left and right, and the gavel fell. "These proceedings are called to order!" His voice still carried the ringing notes of the parade ground. He looked at the young woman. "Are you ready, Miss Bailey?" Corey didn't hear an answer. Perhaps the girl was too cowed and there hadn't been one.

"This hearing concerns the matter of certain public lands to be redesignated as subject to the Homestead Act," Lattner began. He went on to spell out the Territorial government's desire—and his, he added, his voice even stronger on this—to open more land for settlement.

It sounded pretty good, pretty noble, in fact, if you thought of those lands as vacant, fallow, worthless, and just waiting for the honest, hardworking pioneer plow, lands whose true value couldn't be realized without the Bible-toting presence of men in Levi's and women in gingham and poke bonnets and with flocks of towheaded children underfoot, white children, of course, the message was clear.

After this preamble Lattner called for the clerk to read the legal descriptions of the public lands under consideration. This took some time. Some land in the Territory, particularly that parceled out after the advent of the railroads two decades earlier, carried "legals" written in the new fashion, the precise, sterile combinations like "Block six, section eleven, township seven, range four west of the third principal meridian . . ." but all of those parcels from the old royal Spanish grants were still geographically fixed by the ancient, graceful, at times almost poetic "metes and bounds" descriptions, with passages such as, "the south boundary line running to the brown-veined marker stone in the northeast corner of the El Paradiso pasture of Don Juan de Bautista and thence to an iron stake on the near bank of the third bend of the Rio de las Moscas south of its confluence with the Rio Caballo . . ."

Corey, the historian in him suddenly rising, much preferred the latter.

But at the moment, anxious for things to get moving, he would have preferred a lot less of either. What was all that stuff he had given himself about how exciting this session would be compared with the staid rites in Boston? This might prove every bit as dull and its pace deadly slow—"glacial" would be the word if it weren't already getting too warm in here. The close air in the chamber—gradually turning blue with the smoke of *cigarros*—and the drone of the clerk's voice were superb ingredients for drowsiness, no matter that these "proceedings," as Lattner had called them, held high portent for Eloy, Tom, and Corey—and peril for some who couldn't be here.

Corey willed himself to attentiveness. If the Mescalero timberland was on this list they couldn't afford to miss it.

He needn't have worried. Halfway through the clerk's reading Eloy lifted his chin, removed one hand from the cane, and touched Corey on the elbow just in time for him to catch the words ". . . from the ring in the well at Tres Piedras thence to the graveyard of the Iglesia de San Isidro, thence to the southern bank of the Rio Concho at the Perdido rocks . . ." The ball wasn't quite in their court yet. This particular legal description didn't apply to the huge tract

Gideon had labeled *Area at issue* on his map, but it was getting close to it.

But then things dragged again: seemingly endless paragraphs in murky legislative jargon read by the clerk; motions on procedure offered, seconded, and passed—between the yawns of even the more lively-looking members of the committee. Once or twice one of the senators Tom had said was involved with Sierra tried to ask questions, but to no avail. Lattner just tapped his gavel on the square of mahogany in front of him, and the questioner subsided into silence. The progress of the hearing was indeed turning dull, but perhaps the senator from Santa Fe intended it that way, as a soporific. At any rate, the Mescalero lands didn't come in the reading of the first sections of the bill of recommendation.

"Little more will happen this morning," Eloy said.

Tom growled. "No wonder the voters get so disgusted with the process."

"Have we wasted our time, Mr. Montoya?" Corey asked.

"By no means. We have already learned something."

We have? Corey thought. "Exactly what, sir?"

"This committee is not one big hard rock. There are cracks in it, no matter that Señor Lattner seems to be running it with a sure hand. He is *muy buéno* as a chairman. And when I said little more will happen, I did not mean that 'little' would be of *importance*. Señor Lattner will call a recess before the important part comes up."

As if it had been a cue, Lattner did just that. "We shall reconvene in half an hour," he added just before he rapped his gavel smartly on the mahogany square. There was a rush for the door.

Eloy chuckled. His watch was out of his vest pocket. "Eleven oh five," he said. "He is clever, is our Señor Lattner. Half of the spectators will go right to lunch. By the time they return, if they do, this session will be in the record."

Horace Lattner left the platform and headed straight for

where the three of them sat in the back of the room, striding with uncommon vigor for a man with an artificial leg. When he reached Eloy he put out his hand.

"Good to see you, Senator," he said. "What brings you to our small affair?"

"*Cómo está, señor.* I had a desire to visit the old place. These kind friends made it possible. I believe you know Tom Hendry. This gentleman is Corey Lane."

Lattner stared at Corey. "Was your father—"

"Yes, sir."

"I knew him, Mr. Lane." He kept his eyes on Corey for another second, then turned to Tom. "Does the *Chupadera County News* have an interest in my committee, Tom?"

"The *News* has an interest in everything that happens up here, Senator." Tom kept it light.

The senator turned back to Eloy.

"And you, Eloy? I hope that at last you feel that things are in good hands here. Did anything this morning not square with your conscience or your scruples?"

"Not thus far, Senator."

"Good. This hearing, although the press has not remarked much on it"—he shot a glance at Tom—"is very important to the Territory. I would hate to see someone try to derail its work at this late hour. Well, if you will excuse me, gentlemen." He turned and left. It hadn't been exactly a military about-face, but it was close to it. When he had made his way through the hearing-room door it was as if the whole place sagged.

What exactly had been said by the four of them that Corey now felt a sudden heightening of tension? The words had only been pedestrian, everyday greetings—and an introduction. Civilized. And yet . . .

"Señor Lattner has just fired a warning shot, amigos," Eloy said. "We did our best to look innocent, but we didn't fool him. He will brook no interference under pain of all-out war."

"We didn't think it was going to be easy, Eloy," Tom said. "Now, would you two like me to see if I can rustle up some coffee or something else to wet our whistles?"

"I think not, Tom. Things will move very fast indeed when the senator reconvenes his hearing. I would give it no more than an hour before all these homestead matters are put to the vote. At the moment he is very confident that it will all be concluded to his satisfaction, but he takes no chances. He will not waste time."

"Is there nothing we can do to stop it or slow things down?" Corey asked the purely academic question. From what he had seen, Lattner was rolling things along with all the power of a juggernaut, although a quiet one.

"Perhaps, Señor Lane," Eloy said. "If I can get a few minutes alone with Senator Turner of Taos County."

"By God, you're right, Eloy!" Tom erupted. "I thought I saw Turner perk up at something there, too. I was so busy following the reading, listening for anything touching on the Mescalero, that I guess I forgot about it."

What had Corey missed that was the cause of Tom's sudden high excitement? Even listening must be an art in these hearings. The two veteran campaigners sitting with him could still teach him a great deal about Territorial politics.

"Turner?" he whispered to Tom. "What about him?"

"Well, Seth Turner and Lattner are probably the two most likely men to be the next Territorial governor, Corey—or state governor, if the Congress decides to let us in. One of those big tracts in the bill is up near Taos. That hill country where Blue Lake is."

"The sacred lake of the Taoseños?"

"Yeah. It's apparently not just the Apaches that Sierra is trying to steal land from."

"And Eloy thinks Turner will fight it?"

"I guess so. If Turner decides he's not alone. He hasn't beaten Horace on anything of substance lately. I think that's what Eloy wants to talk to Seth about, getting him some other votes from this committee. Eloy was pretty close to Mintern and Archuleta when he was in the Senate, and that's where the support might come from. There are a couple of others who might want to stretch things out, too, rather than just ramrod it through. Jeremy Gray of Farmington has made noises that lead some people to believe he's in Turner's camp."

"Will there be time?"

"Who knows? Maybe Eloy can make time. He probably can if the people we aren't sure about haven't gone on Sierra's payroll."

Eloy hadn't looked as if he was listening to them, but by now Corey knew that the little man missed nothing. Eloy lifted his head at this point and said, "Tom, please see if Senator Turner will see me, and find out if we can talk in that office your newspaper friends use. With the recess I don't think they will be in there."

"Sure, Eloy." Tom hurried off.

Eloy turned to Corey. "Your friend is not always the completely impartial journalist, is he?"

"No, sir. He feels things too deeply for that. I think Chupadera County is lucky he's the way he is."

Senator Seth Turner of Taos listened with attentiveness as Eloy told him everything they knew except the implication of Gideon Bainbridge in the killings on the Mescalero, but Turner said nothing even after the Concho man had finished. It didn't take any long-time experience of how things worked here in the capital for Corey to see that Turner was reluctant to take on Horace Lattner without some solid assurance that he stood a chance of winning. Could Eloy give him such assurance?

"Manuel Archuleta and his people will in all likelihood line up behind you, Señor Turner," Eloy said.

The Taos senator wrinkled his brow. "Maybe. Even should they, I'm not sure that will be enough, Eloy. Not to be too blunt about it, but if I can't get help from at least some of the more important gringos, I'm not sure I want to rock Horace Lattner's personal boat, which I don't need to remind you he most often looks upon as the Ship of state."

"I know all too well," Eloy said ruefully.

"How about your boss, Tom?" Turner said. "Will the *News* come in on our side?" Well, the *our* side was a hopeful sign— barely.

"I can't talk for Jim until I see him, Seth, but I'm pretty damned sure, knowing him."

"I can't overstress the importance of that. Jim McPherson's opinion on anything carries great weight in the Territory. I might feel a mite less shaky on this limb you're asking me to shinny out on if McPherson was under me with his paper as a net."

Once or twice during the discussion Turner had fixed Corey with a quizzical look, as if to say, *What are you doing here?* It was a question —or one very close to it—that he had been asking himself all morning, or at least ever since he had agreed with Tom and asked Eloy's help. The newspaperman and the former senator were paramount to this effort. He, on the other hand, felt unnecessary, almost helpless.

Now the senator from Taos looked at Corey again, and this time there was no question in his eyes. Whatever it was, it looked more like challenge.

"Mr. Lane," he said, "there's no way you would have of knowing this, but I rode with Horace Lattner against Victorio and your father. I've never regretted taking part in that. That's where I first met McPherson. Eloy and Tom, I'm sure, didn't know that either until now. What exactly is *your* interest in this matter? Justice? Some desire to do something for the

Apaches? Or are you just plain opposed to what the settlers of the past hundred years have tried to accomplish in this country? Are you an uncritical apologist for Indians, as I've heard all the Lanes of Chupadera County are?"

He meant Virgie, too. What was Corey to say? That he was only looking out for personal friends? Or that there was indeed something larger at issue here? Turner's question was a valid one. What exactly *was* his stake in all of this?

"I don't quite know how to answer you, Senator Turner. It's risky for me, I suppose, to noise it around that I'm close to the people up on the Mescalero, but I have to admit it's the plain, unvarnished truth. Some of them have died already and others have suffered damage, and yes, I do want justice for them. But I'm certainly not opposed to the other people who live in the Ojos Negros. My family is one of those of the 'past hundred years.' We all have a right to our share of the Territory—or no right at all; none of us, not even the Apaches, are natives here if you look back far enough."

"That's just about what I thought you would say, Mr. Lane. I wanted to hear the way you said it." He turned to Eloy again. "Let's suppose we manage to block Lattner. That won't end things. And I've got one other question. Speaking of important gringos—why isn't Gideon Bainbridge sitting here with the three of you?"

"There is grave doubt," Eloy said, "that Senator Bainbridge sees things quite the way we do."

Turner seemed to weigh Eloy's remark very carefully. "What you're saying is that I'd be bucking Gideon, too, as well as Lattner." Whatever else he was, Seth Turner of Taos was quick enough. Corey could see why Eloy judged him so necessary to them.

"*Sí, señor,*" the little man said next. "We cannot in good conscience tell you otherwise."

Turner's face set like granite. "And I can't tell *you* in

good conscience that the prospect of opposing Gideon Bainbridge pleases me."

Was Turner lost to them only seconds after Corey thought Eloy had him?

"Senator," Eloy said. His voice was even lower than before. "*I* will oppose him if I must—and I assure you it pleases me no more than it pleases you."

Then came a long moment when the tension in the small pressroom was heavier than the tobacco smoke or the smell of whiskey. Finally the Taos man spoke again.

"All right, Eloy. You're putting me to a test. I don't know if it will get me a passing mark, but I'll give you a maybe. Right now you've got to line up your other senators, and line them up solid. If you get them—and by my reckoning you've only got about fifteen minutes to do so—I'll consider a move to table any motions on Lattner's bill. That's only a delaying action, though, while you and your friends get ready to see the governor. Good day, gentlemen."

When Turner told Eloy he had about fifteen minutes to organize his senatorial opposition to Lattner, Corey's heart sank. Montoya couldn't possibly persuade the five men he needed to turn their votes against the chairman in that short span of time, could he? He asked him.

"It is not a matter of persuasion at the moment, Señor Lane. I hold what you anglos call IOUs, I believe. I will call them in. Bear in mind, though, that by my doing so, we shall use up a good part of our political capital. I can only call them once."

The deus ex machina once again. But at least it was Eloy who extracted the god from his contraption. Eloy scribbled notes on pages torn from Tom's notebook, and Tom delivered them almost as fast as they were written.

The first of Eloy's predictions was right on target. When Lattner reconvened his hearing the room held perhaps only a fifth as many spectators as it had before, and none of the newsmen were among the smaller crowd. Two of the committee members, Bradford and Smith, Corey thought, were among the missing, too. Lattner didn't seem troubled by their absence; obviously he felt he still had the votes he needed.

The clerk wasn't five minutes into the reading of the rest of the legal descriptions when Gideon's "Area at issue" came up. As he finished ". . . and in addition to the foresaid, all the land not heretofore described, but which is known as Cow Camp Meadow," Seth Turner called to the chair from his place at the end of the table.

"Mr. Chairman!"

Lattner recognized him.

"Mr. Chairman, ain't these changes you want a vote on today a much larger business than we were led to believe when the chair talked about it the other day? Seems like the whole damned Territory has suddenly come up for grabs."

Lattner didn't answer for a moment. He seemed to keep his eyes steady on Turner, but it took little to discern that he was assessing the rest of his committee, counting heads. "Why does the senator from Taos bring this up now? He has had almost a week to register any objection."

"It's been a busy session, Senator."

Lattner faced the room. His eyes settled on Montoya. "It seems to have gotten considerably busier this morning."

Turner broke in again. "I just think we're being rushed a little. I won't say stampeded, but it's felt like that a time or two today. Would there be any great harm done if we take a second or so to roll a smoke, kick off our boots, and chew this over before we send it to the governor and then the Congress? It ain't as if we got a herd of homesteaders rampaging on the Territory's borders just waiting to get at all this free land. Seems like we ought to put off any hard and fast decision for just a bit." He leaned back and laced his fingers behind his head. "Wouldn't it be a crying shame to have all the chair's fine work go down the drain with a hurry-up vote that could very well go against it? Tabling it until there's more chance to take a square look at things might save this worthwhile project."

There was muttering up and down the long table, but not from the Sierra men. They turned to Lattner and waited.

The Santa Fe man's face betrayed no emotion of any kind, but his back stiffened just enough for Corey to notice. When he spoke again, his voice, though, carried the hiss of a branding iron.

"The chair will entertain a motion to table this bill of recommondation until Friday when we meet again."

If Corey hadn't guessed so before, Lattner's disinclination to argue at this point clearly demonstrated what a hard-bitten realist the ex-soldier was.

He took the motions for tabling and then for adjournment by quick flicks of his eyes. The gavel didn't tap now, it banged.

"Today's proceedings are adjourned!" Again the clear, crisp, drillground voice. He looked at Eloy, Tom, and Corey as he spoke.

"Hot damn!" Tom said. "I know it's not victory, but we sure avoided a licking today. Nice work, Eloy."

"*Gracias*, Tom." There was no exulting in the little Concho man's voice. "Make no mistake. Senator Lattner has just declared war."

When the committee broke from the table, Seth Turner stopped where the three of them were sitting.

"I had no idea I was going to go as far as I did, Eloy. You're good. But I couldn't help thinking while I was sitting there that success, ultimately, is going to ride on who you get to go up against Gideon Bainbridge."

13

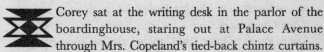Corey sat at the writing desk in the parlor of the boardinghouse, staring out at Palace Avenue through Mrs. Copeland's tied-back chintz curtains.

There was an entire afternoon and evening to kill. It staggered him that so much of the day was left. Since awakening this morning he had lived a complicated lifetime or two of decisions and impressions with Eloy Montoya, Tom Hendry, and the forbidding figure of Horace Lattner, and it was only two o'clock.

Now he had to force himself to an entirely different mode of thinking.

He slipped a sheet of stationery from his leather writing case, dipped the pen Mrs. Copeland had provided into the square crystal inkwell in its filigreed brass holder, and inscribed the day and date at the top of the page, and then underneath that, "Dearest Lucy . . .

He smiled. Then the smile fled. He was beginning the first real love letter he had ever written.

How to go about it? Oh, the first part of it surely wouldn't prove too difficult; he would bring Lucy and, when she read it to her, Ana, up to date on the things he and Tom had had been able to do here in the capital, the things which bore so heavily on their predicament and on that of their family and friends on the Mescalero. Perhaps Harold had returned to Cow Camp Creek and he, too, would learn of the way things seemed to be bending ever so slightly their way. After that would come the hard part, perhaps something quite beyond him. He put his pen to the paper again.

So many things to tell you, Lucy. It goes as well here in Santa Fe as I had any right to expect. We—Tom Hendry, Eloy Montoya, and I—spent the morning at a hearing in the Territorial Senate. Nothing has been concluded as yet, but it would seem that we have made some small gains. Mr. Montoya is the former senator from Chupadera County, a man from the village of San Isidro on the upper Rio Concho. He has been invaluable, more to me, of course, than to Tom, who knows his way through the labyrinth of the capital pretty well from his years of sending news dispatches back to Black Springs.

Yes, that part had been easy. He went on at great speed, telling Lucy of his visit to the Sierra Development headquarters at San Isidro and his inconclusive meeting with Kessler, about the Polish homesteaders quartered on the Concho, and of the emerging strategy of Eloy Montoya, the planned trip to press their case with Governor Otero, and the seemingly staunch ally they might have unearthed in the Taos senator, Seth Turner. What he held back for the moment were the things he had found during is overnight stay at Tres Piedras.

It troubled him that he couldn't bring himself to tell her. Was he still holding some secret, hidden brief for Gideon?

Not so troubling was that he penned none of the fear and apprehension he had for Harold, who was still, as far as he knew, brooding and perhaps plotting in some remote mountain camp. Corey only asked Lucy if she, Ana, or Sam Naaki had had word from his Mimbreño friend. Sam's name, of course, had only been dropped in to see if Lucy—in any reply she might make, and if it arrived while he was still in Santa Fe—might mention the Apache officer, let slip in some way confirmation of his hope that the policeman was staying close to the two Bishop women. When he finished this letter he would send a separate one to Naaki and make sure he was.

But now the hard part was at hand.

Mrs. Copeland's pen was a scratchy one, and the squeaks from the paper as he wrote seemed to echo in the parlor like plaintive cries.

We didn't get to talk the morning after my last night at Cow Camp Creek, Lucy, but I feel sure you must have guessed what I, at least, would have said. I love you. There is nothing more I could possibly add. Words are the means by which I have built my life so far, but beyond that simple statement they fail me utterly now. I hope and pray that I will hear those few words from you when we meet again. I will write them one more time.

I love you.
Corey

He read the paragraph over. It was weak, thin, and carried but a fraction of the things within his heart, but it would have to do. He sealed the envelope and hurried through a note to Sam Naaki. When that was done, he got his hat, left the house without a good-bye to Mrs. Copeland, and headed for the plaza. If he didn't post Lucy's letter before the doubts—not about what he felt, but about how it might strike Lucy—began to haunt him, he might never send it.

When he dropped the letters in the slot at the Territorial post office on San Francisco Street, his hand trembled. He wondered if it would stop before he saw Lucy Bishop again.

With the letter gone, beyond calling back, he suddenly felt as lonely as only that man can whose self has been stripped away. He missed Tom, and he missed Eloy, too, even though he had only really known the Concho man since morning.

After they had left the hearing, the newspaperman had announced that he was going to the Western Union office to wire Jim McPherson to see if the publisher could get to the capital on an early coach and join them in their visit to the governor.

"I'll take Mr. Montoya back to his house, then, Tom," Corey had said. He turned to Eloy. "Unless you would like to join us for dinner, sir."

"*Gracias, no,*" Eloy had said. "There are some things I must do at home. People coming to see me that I must see." Was there to be no counterinvitation? Apparently not.

Then Corey remembered that after they had left the hearing room and Seth Turner, the little man had hobbled away on his cane to huddle with a pair of soberly dressed, dark young men who seemed to have appeared from nowhere—they hadn't been in Lattner's hearing room—and who listened with keen attentiveness as he talked with them. They all looked faintly conspiratorial. No, not faintly—definitely. At the time he had gotten the impression that these were two of the "friends" Eloy counted on to bring him news in his semi-incapacitated state.

Apparently Eloy wasn't going to take Tom and him into his confidence on quite everything—not yet, at least. Corey had forgotten the confidential chat and the secret looks of the two young men as he and Tom went about the business of getting the former senator back in the buggy.

"Where shall I meet you, Tom, and when?" Corey had asked when he was settled in the driver's seat.

Did Tom Hendry blush then, as he had about the offer of a drink at the hearing? "Actually, Corey, I'd kind of hoped you could do without me for the rest of the day." Yes, he had been blushing. "There's a lady I'd like to spend some time with. Would you like me to see if she can find some company for you, too?"

"No, thanks, Tom. I'll be fine by myself. See you back at Mrs. Copeland's when you get there, then."

"To tell the truth, Corey, I might not get back there tonight at all."

It had hardly seemed the sort of prompting he should have needed to sit down and write his letter, but it certainly had worked out that way.

He then drove Eloy to the house in the Calle San Fidel, returned the buggy to the livery in Burro Alley, and walked back up Palace Avenue to the boardinghouse.

Now, with the letter to Lucy written and posted, the day's work had ended. He pulled his watch from his pocket. It was only three-thirty, and the rest of the afternoon promised to be interminable in its emptiness, with only a solitary dinner and an even more dismal evening at Mrs. Copeland's to follow. He almost envied Tom.

He knew what he could do. Here at the corner of San Francisco and Don Gaspar he was no more than a block and a half from the Territorial library, not as imposing by half as Gideon's at Tres Piedras, but perhaps improved and better stocked than when he had last been there—with Gideon— long before the war, in the August before he began his third year at Amherst. Should he bother? Why not? Books had always been his final refuge, hadn't they?

The foot traffic in the plaza was almost teeming, and wheeled vehicles—buggies, chaises, Studebaker wagons, and buckboards painted more gaily than the drab gray ones of

Chupadera County—surged through the dirt streets almost as madly as the chariots in *Ben Hur*. Perhaps Lew Wallace had watched frenzied scenes like this when he was writing his towering book there across the plaza in the Palacio, and Corey wondered if Governor Lew had found Santa Fe the bright, prideful place it seemed today. The capital wasn't a latter-day imperial Rome by any stretch of the imagination, but by God it looked as if it were trying its damnedest to become one.

The unlimited energy of Americans could still astonish foreign visitors as it had de Tocqueville. But so would have the energy of the other races who came to this land long before the Yankee traders and the soldiers and opportunists who followed in their wake. No railroads or coach lines crisscrossed the Territory when Coronado and his conquistadores nosed up from Compostela, no telegraph wires passed news across hundreds of miles of empty llano and mountain range, certainly no telephones or automobiles shrank those miles. And yet the Spaniards, in little more than a decade, seemed to have ferreted out every pueblo, every well, every tribe, and almost every band of nomads, brought them under merciless subjugation, and built a feudal empire on the backs of their reluctant subjects that prospered for three hundred years, more or less—until the hard, hungry men from the East in their turn took it for themselves. Perhaps it was the way things had to be. Perhaps what Eloy, Tom, and Corey were trying to do here was as hopeless a task as trying to stem the heavy tide of history with a foot-high dike made of sugar.

Gideon had said some things that day at the library, of which Corey had total recall. The rush to the Pacific was over now, he had said, had been for nearly fifty years. Now that the nation was engaged in backfilling the gouged-out places the rush had brought about, it was absolutely vital that the weak and alienated didn't get buried alive, either by accident or intent. Where could the country find the guardians who would keep such interments from taking place? There had been the first strong hint from the older man that Corey could—and should—become such a guardian. "My steward-ship has but a short time to run, Corey, in the larger scheme of things."

And he had said something else that August day which had burned its way into Corey's thoughts. "Glorious story, the westward expansion of our nation, Corey. Still, I wonder. Has it been an unalloyed blessing for us? Perhaps our country in the process has done irreparable damage to its psyche—or, much worse, to its very soul. Americans, with a continent to occupy and tame, have come to believe that all things are possible to them, and that the possible is always right. We have never learned to compromise."

They had talked a lot about much less grandiose ideas, too, about Corey's dreams for himself, his life in college. They had talked about Apaches. They always had in those days. Gideon hadn't been sentimental about Indians, they weren't Rousseau's "noble savages" to him; they were people, much like any other, to the man from Tres Piedras, and like any people were entitled to fair play, friendship, and recognition of their human dignity.

So wise, so reasonable, so gentle without weakness was Gideon Bainbridge that day. The memory was bittersweet. Corey had realized in the warm, quiet shadows of the library just how much he had missed in life by having a father such as the first Corey Lane—and how much more by later having none at all.

But what had happened to that particular Gideon? What had happened in the ten years since that day the man Corey himself had told Tom was "the best friend the Mescaleros ever had," a man whom wise little Eloy Montoya had char-acterized as "a fine man, more capable than I ever was"? He couldn't be—on the record of his words and deeds over the years—simply bent on vengeance as was maimed, embittered Horace Lattner, and he certainly, as Tom had pointed out, wasn't in this sordid conspiracy for the pittance it might produce. He must have some dark, hidden agenda peculiarly his own.

Perhaps—this was a wild leap of the imagination, but careful ones had produced no answers—Gideon Bainbridge, proud warrior that he once had been, now chafed, like Richard III, at this "fat, piping time of peace. . . ."

But Richard Crookback had been a monster.

"Do you by any chance have a book by Josiah Gregg called *Commerce of the Prairies*, miss?" he inquired of a pretty girl at the front desk in the library. For a moment, from the way she looked at him, he thought she might know him from somewhere, but decided no, it couldn't be. There appeared to be no one else in the building save an elderly Spanish man wielding a broom in silent but fussy care in the entrance corridor behind him.

"Yes, sir." She smiled. "But we don't have it just 'by chance.' It's an important book. Let me see if it's out on loan." She flipped back the top of a wooden box in front of her and riffled through file cards. "It's in, unless someone has swiped it. You'll find it in stack number three, way over on the left near the windows."

"Thank you. Is there a place to sit and read back there?"

"No, but you can take your book to the reading room." She turned and pointed back behind her. "You've picked a good time. We get almost no visitors on a Friday afternoon."

It was exactly what he wanted: a good book and a quiet place, a home away from home. If the young woman would make the impossible possible and let him camp here overnight he might even have her dig out the ancient stuff by Najera and sink into it to his heart's content. He had never looked at the original of the *Relaciones*, and starting nearer the beginning of things might be wise.

It was a little too dark for reading in the reading room as

he found it, and he put the Gregg book on the massive table and went to the window. Opening the shutters let in a shaft of light that gleamed like a bar of gold against the white walls. In Lincoln Street the bustle of afternoon Santa Fe was maintaining its manic pace, but the thick adobe walls held all but the loudest sounds at bay. Bliss, or close to it. He returned to the table, pulled out a Spanish chair with wooden arms carved like parentheses, and settled into it. *All right, Josiah Gregg . . . .*

But he found he couldn't read. He fixed his eyes to the page, but his gaze kept drifting upward. Memories.

"Corey."

He turned and looked straight into the eyes of Gideon Bainbridge.

"I heard you were in town and I thought you surely would come to see me," Gideon said. "When you didn't, I knew you would eventually show up here. Mary Jane has been watching for you. I told her you wouldn't be difficult to identify. Told her just to be on the lookout for the handsomest young man she would see this week. She sent Pablito for me." Corey's face must have signaled something. Gideon put up a hand as if to silence him. "It wasn't spying, Corey, just friendship."

"Hello, Gideon."

It had taken something in the way of, he couldn't claim courage, no, but of determination to utter the greeting. He had half feared he wouldn't find his voice, wasn't at all sure he had even after he heard it. It seemed the voice of a stranger. The "Gideon" had sounded warm and welcoming. Why now of all times? The last, the very last, thing he should want with this man now was anything approaching intimacy. They had become enemies, hadn't they? even if Gideon didn't know it yet.

"May I sit down?" Gideon topped his head toward a chair across the oaken table from where Corey sat. "I do think we should talk, or I should, at any rate."

Corey would have sworn he had remained as motionless, as stiff and rigid, as the crude wooden *santo* of San Sebastian that hung on the wall by the window. He must have given some tiny sign; Gideon moved around the end of the table, pulled out the chair—a twin of the one Corey was in—and seated himself. There would have been no way this man with the most impeccable manners of anyone in Corey's memory would have joined him at this table without what he took to be clear and unmistakable permission.

Gideon folded his hands in front of him, and the diamond on his left one caught the rays of the sun streaming through the window. He looked golden, his face not just aristocratic, but noble. Corey felt his throat constrict; something very close to a sob was building there. He swallowed it down, terrified that he might already have made a sound.

He became aware that the reading room held an odor he hadn't noticed until now, one that at almost any other time would have been a pleasant one. It was a smell of age and mustiness, of cracked old leather bindings and brittle paper, of glue that had dried so deeply one touch would puff it away to dust. In the arid New Mexico air it was a faint smell, not like the sometimes heavy, pungent odor of such places in the East. And it was packaged in more silence here in the Territory, too, than it had been in even the quietest libraries he had known in Boston or New York. Even so, it had turned the air to an essence of wormwood.

But now a sigh from Gideon broke the silence.

"We are involved in something neither of us wanted, aren't we, Corey?"

Even with the sun still coming through the window the light had grown dim. Gideon's golden face had darkened.

"I beg of you to stay out of this. There are forces at work here that you can't possibly cope with. Someone will get hurt."

"People have already been hurt, Gideon. Some have been killed. It has to stop."

"You can't stop it."

"I can try." He closed the book in front of him. "More to the point, you can stop it."

"No, I can't." Gideon stood up. "I tried to stop it years ago, and I couldn't."

Gideon rose, turned, and left the reading room.

As he did, whatever innocence might have been left to Corey Lane went with him.

14

"We're to pick up Eloy, meet Jim at the coach station, and the four of us will go to Seth Turner's hotel for dinner. Otero's secretary said the governor will see us first thing Monday, according to Eloy." Tom Hendry shook his head, in some sort of admiration, it seemed. "Eloy Montoya reaches everywhere. We're damned lucky to have him on our side, but I guess you've come to that conclusion yourself. I suppose we could have gotten Otero's ear without him, but I doubt if too many people manage that if Eloy sets his mind *against* them.

"Oh, one other thing. Jim didn't say who it was in his telegram, but it seems he's got another senator lined up. I suspect it's McLellan of Orogrande. McLellan's got some heft with Migeul Otero, too. We stand in a fair way to make a damned impressive delegation. Shouldn't be too hard to toss a handful of sand in Sierra's gearbox now. Slow things down a lot, and with luck stop it cold."

It was Saturday afternoon and Corey's first sight of Tom since he had driven Eloy back to Calle San Fidel. The slight anger he had felt all morning at the reporter's seeming abandonment of him—coupled with the dark uneasiness brought on by his talk with Gideon—had faded with the discovery that Tom hadn't spent the entire twenty-four hours indulging himself with his lady friend. Yes, the troubling slight anger was gone, but the uneasiness lingered. Tom's next words didn't dispel it, either.

"You didn't let that conscience of yours get in the way and tell Gideon what you found at Tres Piedras, did you?"

"Didn't come anywhere near it, Tom. I'm sure he knows already that we've tumbled to his involvement with Sierra in spite of the fact that there's no proof, no trail, but I'm sure he believes *you* did all the detective work. Oh, I suppose he's gotten a report from Kessler on my visit to San Isidro by now and has put two and two together and come up with five instead of four. He knows every move we've made here in Santa Fe, too. Not surprising."

"No, it isn't. I'm glad you kept buttoned up. Lattner's formidable enough, but Gideon . . . he's as resourceful as Eloy, any day—as powerful, too."

Of course, just about everything he had told Tom would appear as a wild surmise to anyone who had heard his talk yesterday with Gideon. He and Gideon hadn't mentioned even one specific detail of the terrible sequence of events on the reservation or what Corey had found at Tres Piedras, and yet . . .

They had come to a total understanding. To a point.

Gideon knew everything Corey knew, and he knew how Corey knew it, despite what Corey had just told Tom.

What Corey didn't know, had no understanding of whatsoever, was that last remark. *I tried to stop it years ago, and I couldn't.* He couldn't shake it from his mind. And he couldn't shake from his mind's eye the picture of Gideon just before he turned and left the reading room, the look of ineffable sadness on his face.

"Let's get moving," he said.

They hired a buckboard at the livery this time; Jim would have luggage. Corey hoped the stiffer-sprung small wagon wouldn't be too hard on Eloy. It was noisier than the buggy, and on the drive to the Calle San Fidel he and Tom didn't talk, giving him more than enough time and silence to think through the conversation with Gideon for the twentieth time since yesterday afternoon, the conversation that had been as short and swift as sudden death. It brought the same result. *Nada*, Eloy would say—if and when he told the Concho man all that was said in the reading room as it darkened. Tom might say, *Horseshit!* Well, it had either been somewhere between the two or it had transcended everything about this sea of troubles. All he knew was that it was bidding fair to cracking his heart in two, no matter what the outcome of the meeting with Governor Otero Monday morning.

That, at least, was looking more promising by the minute. From his demeanor, Tom Hendry thought so. Why didn't Corey feel more elation?

The two young Hispanic men he had seen yesterday were waiting with Eloy at the house on Calle San Fidel, but after an introduction too hurried for Corey to catch their last names, they left on foot.

"Two of your *compadres*, Eloy?" Tom said.

"Ernesto Vigil, the tall one, is the governor's secretary. The other, Javier Cruz, speaks unofficially for most of the Latinos in Tierra Amarilla, at least the farmers like my own people in the Rio Concho. He may be important to us, although at the moment I don't think we need concern ourselves too much."

Tom looked at Corey as if to say, *See?* and turned back to the Concho man. "It does look good, doesn't it?"

"*Sí.* But we must be very, very careful. Little overlooked

things have a way of complicating matters in this strange town." He had by this time hoisted himself into the buckboard with what was surely a tortured effort.

"Señor Lane," he said, "I would be grateful if you would tell me at least some of the things which passed between you and Señor Bainbridge yesterday."

A day ago Corey might have been surprised that Eloy knew of his meeting with Gideon. Eloy had called Santa Fe a strange town. It was indeed, but it was losing its capacity to astonish Corey insofar as keeping secrets was concerned.

"There wasn't much, sir. It was almost nothing."

"Did he speak of San Isidro?"

"No, sir."

Tom touched the whip to the horse and the buckboard rattled off.

At the coach stop Tom left the two of them and went next door to the Western Union office to check for messages. Corey wondered if Eloy would continue with his questions about the conversation with Gideon, but Eloy had dropped his chin to his chest and appeared to nap. Corey wished he could himself. He had known nights of sounder and more restful sleep than that at Copeland House after the talk in the library reading room and the tasteless supper he had found at a hole-in-the-wall café on the west side of the plaza, a place grandly named La Posada de los Árboles but no more Spanish than O'Brien's Saloon down by the railroad tracks, and certainly not an inn as the name implied. His stomach had complained intermittently through the largely sleepless night. It was still complaining, but now more because he hadn't felt up to Mrs. Copeland's punctual breakfast and had done little more than pick at the edges of the lunch he had shared with Tom. Perhaps when Jim arrived his appetite would arrive as well. He wasn't betting on it.

I tried to stop it years ago, and I couldn't.

* * *

It was a gray Jim McPherson who stepped down from the Albuquerque coach, and the grayness wasn't accumulated road dust.

"This is going to sound funny, but I'm sorry you brought Eloy with you," he said as Corey shook hands with him and Tom wrestled with his luggage. With his free hand the publisher pointed to the Concho man waving from where he sat in the buckboard, fifty yards away. "We three have to talk, preferably before we see anyone else."

"What's up, Jim?"

"Last night a raiding party came down out of the Mescalero and tried to set fire to Sierra Development's operation in San Isidro. Matt Kessler somehow drove them off before they could burn him out. Seven or eight riders. The people in the village who caught sight of them swear they were Apaches."

"Harold!" Corey said.

"Seems so."

"The damn fool!" Tom said. "We had this thing all but whipped, Jim."

"I gathered that from your wire." Jim nodded toward the telegraph office. "Speaking of wires, I held up filing a report until I could talk to you two. It should break here within the hour, though." He fell silent, then looked toward Eloy again.

There's more, Corey thought. "Jim, was anybody hurt?"

"That's the absolute worst of it, except for the fact that someone has to tell *him*." He started to point to Eloy, but dropped his hand to his side. "As the raiding party left town they took some random shots at some of the homes. A six-year-old boy was killed when he came out of his house to see the excitement. His name was Pepe—Pepe Montoya. He was Eloy's grandnephew."

15

Ana Bishop looked from Corey to Lucy and back again. This was hardly the tough, energetic woman he had known half his life. She looked drawn, defeated, subdued in a way he had never thought to see her.

"All right," she said. "Harold will never forgive me, but with all that's happened I guess I'll have to tell you now, but only if you both promise you won't tell Sam Naaki."

Corey raised his right hand as if he were taking an oath.

"You know I don't have to promise, Mama," Lucy said.

Ana went on. "Harold's got a camp about three miles northeast of Uncle Pete's old place, just south of the upper canyon of Sinuoso Creek. It's hard to find, even harder to actually get into, but Lucy will know the way in when she gets there."

"I will?" Lucy said.

"Yes. I used to take Harold there to pick berries when he was little, before Tony came back to us, and then we took you along too, until you were eight or nine. There's a double waterfall right below the canyon entrance."

"I remember. We called it *sash bituudeya'*." She turned to Corey and added, "Big Bear Spring. That's high, rocky country, Corey, hideout country a long time ago. Most of a day's ride from here. We couldn't possibly make it before dark, even if we started now."

Lucy was coming with him? He would have to put his foot down pretty firmly about that, but something else occurred to him first.

"Ana. Is he alone up there?"

"No. He's got six others with him, just youngsters—children is more like it. I think the oldest is Joe Ditsa's nephew John. He's only nineteen, maybe not quite that, and Chino Walksnice can't be seventeen yet."

"And they're armed?"

"What boy up here in the Mescalero timber isn't? They're all hunters when they're not in school." She turned and looked out the window as if she had been caught red-handed at something. It was that same old trick of hers, an ordinarily effective end to any conversation not under her complete control. She was acting as if she knew she had spilled a few beans that could take instant root and sprout trouble for her, and she was determined now not to spill any more. Well, he couldn't let her get away with it this time.

"You've seen Harold since the night Tom and I spent here, haven't you, Ana?"

She winced, realizing she had been outmaneuvered. "Once. He slipped in past Sam Naaki's men on Friday. He brought us those two horses in the corral to replace the ones he took. Didn't say where he got them, but he wouldn't have left them here if he thought it might bring trouble for me and Lucy." Her laugh had a bitter, slightly hysterical ring to it, but it was the only laughter he had heard since he arrived. "He came at lunchtime, when Lucy was at school. It was the only time Sam's scouts weren't on the lookout. At night he never would have made it."

"Couldn't you get him to stay here—forget whatever nonsense he's been dreaming about up there?"

"I tried. Harold is only listening to himself these days."

Friday. Harold had been here at noon on the day of the attack on San Isidro. Corey, Ana, and Lucy hadn't talked nearly enough about that particular insanity yet. The two women must have gotten all they wanted about the raid from Sam Naaki. He wondered if Harold had told Ana of his intentions before the fact, but perhaps he had better not ask her, not directly. There was nothing to be gained by forcing her to lie to him, but damn it, he *would* protest the idea of Lucy being put in even more danger out on that high mountain trail with him than she had been in here at Cow Camp Creek with her mother, with Kessler probably gearing up to storm the reservation after the raid.

"I want you and Lucy to move down to the X-Bar-7, Ana. And I'm going up to Big Bear Spring alone."

"You can't! It would be dangerous. Besides, you'd never find the place."

"Make me a map. And what do you mean, dangerous? Harold's my brother. Why don't I just take Sam Naaki instead and let Lucy stay here with you?"

"No!" A look of terror blanched the dark face. "Sam would try to bring him in. I think that would drive Harold right over the edge."

"Maybe he's already over the edge, Ana. It would probably be better in the long run if Sam did bring him in. Let's talk about that raid on San Isidro."

"What's there to talk about? It's done."

"Sure, it's done. That isn't all that's done. Do you suppose Harold has any idea what his rashness might have cost us?" He hadn't told the two Bishop women that the dead boy was

Eloy's grandnephew. "All right, I won't take Sam. But I sure
do want to go alone."

Lucy broke in. "I think Mama's right, Corey. Those boys
with Harold know me. I don't think any of them know you.
They will be pretty jumpy after a week up there persuading
themselves that they're Apache warriors again. If they see a
white man they don't recognize, they're apt to do something
crazy. You had better let me go in first."

"You'll *have* to take Lucy," Ana said.

He was beaten. "All right, I'll take Lucy with me only if
you'll go down and stay with Virgie."

For a moment he expected refusal, but Ana finally agreed.

Lucy smiled at him. "It's settled, then. We can leave at first
light, Corey. I'll take care of provisions and bedrolls. You look
after the horses."

Bedrolls? It gave him an odd turn, but of course they
would have to stay overnight in Harold's stronghold at this
Big Bear Spring, wherever it was.

Sam Naaki dropped by after supper and Corey decided
that on balance it was a good thing he had. Without a re-
minder that the police chief was keeping a watch, he and
Lucy might have gotten careless when they set out for Big
Bear Spring in the morning and be followed, but it saddened
him that he had to lie to the likable Apache lawman. The lie
came pretty quickly, the first moment they were alone after
Ana had fixed coffee.

Sam looked over the rim of the mug he had lifted to his
mouth. "You going looking for Harold, Corey?

"Wouldn't know where to look, Sam." True, as far as it
went.

"Ana ain't told you where he's holed up, then?"

"Does she know?"

"Sure. He'd never keep it from his mother. I know he's
been here to see her. Those new ponies in her corral didn't

get there by themselves. He sure snookered me. I was busy guarding her and Lucy from white men like you asked me. Didn't know I was supposed to look out for him, too. Not then, anyways."

"And now?"

"The council's hopping mad. Those kids he's got with him rode out of their backyards with their families' best riding stock, not to mention the guns and food they took. And now, with the raid on San Isidro, they want Harold and the rest of them young locos pretty bad. They think it's the only way they can keep the reservation out of trouble." He fell silent. "You'll let me know if Ana decides to let us in on things, won't you?"

"Sure, Sam." His stomach turned queasy.

"Good. Now, you want to let me in on anything else you know? All the things you learned up in Santa Fe, for instance."

Corey ran through everything that had happened in the capital. From Sam's look he could see the policeman didn't understand some of the words he had to use to describe the events at the hearing, but it was plain that the Mescalero, unschooled but no ignorant primitive, caught the full meaning of even some of the more obscure details. He only interrupted Corey once, to tell him that he knew Eloy Montoya. "He used to come up here when he was a senator. The council let him attend their meetings. I was there sometimes myself. Don't think he liked Apaches much, not the few Red Paint People living with us Mescaleros, anyway, but he never said so, and he did do some good things for the reservation up there in Santa Fe."

"Did you know that someone got killed in that raid? A six-year-old boy."

Sam made a little noise Corey could only have called a mournful growl. He shook his head like a great bear. "That's not good for Harold and his young friends. The whites will never forgive that. They never have forgiven killings from thirty, forty years ago, back when we was at war. You better talk Ana into telling me where they are, Corey. If they come in on their own it won't go as hard for them, and if I find them it will be the same as them coming in on their own. Maybe now that you and Montoya are on the same side it will help some, too."

"Don't count on that. The boy who died was his nephew's son."

Naaki's brown face paled, but all he said was, "How long you staying up here?"

"Just until tomorrow morning. I'm taking Ana and Lucy down to the X-Bar-7 until things get a little safer." Another lie. Corey felt less than pleased with himself and the way he had snaked his way through this talk.

"Good idea," Sam said.

They shook hands as they parted. It had been an even more wearing conversation than the ones Corey had suffered through with Ana and Harold these past few agonizing, scary weeks. Would his next talk with "brother Harold" be any better? He couldn't even think about one with Ana. As he expected, she avoided him through the rest of the late afternoon and evening, pleading an upset stomach and going to her room while Lucy fixed supper. He might have called her to account on this, except that he was overjoyed at finally being alone with the young woman who had occupied his mind on the trip back to Chupadera County and the Mescalero almost to the exclusion of all their troubles.

They embraced without a word once Ana disappeared, and indeed didn't speak at all until their evening meal was over.

"Your letter came to the school this morning, Corey," she said after he had carried dishes to the sink for her and helped her as she washed them. "You didn't doubt for a moment that I feel the same way you do, did you? Of course I love you. I've loved you for longer than you can imagine. I had almost given up hope that you might someday feel the same way. I thought I was always going to be your little sister."

He almost laughed. Hadn't he feared himself that she looked on him only as a brother? Then a sharp pain shot through him. Once before he had lamented the unfairness of it: that he couldn't recklessly spend every penny of his carefully hoarded emotional capital solely on the two of them and the discovery they had made. His lament was doubly infused with gall now. Some similar regret must have come her way.

"But I suppose," she said, "that we'll have to try to forget about us a little, at least until this is all behind us."

He would have raged, but he knew he could never rage when she was with him.

Instead, he talked.

At first, suffused with a happiness that almost drove his despondency into hiding, he only half heard the things he was saying: another rehearsal of everything that had happened in the capital, but with more emphasis than he would have expected on his meeting with Gideon.

"I didn't know Gideon there in the library, Lucy. There was something almost demonic about him. It wasn't exactly the things he said—he didn't really say much—it was the way he said them. When I think back to the Gideon we knew as kids up here on the Mescalero, I—" He spread his hands palms up in a gesture of frustration.

"You're right, Corey. Up here we always thought that, next to you and your mother, Gideon Bainbridge was just about the best friend we had in Chupadera County."

"All the work he and I did together led me to believe that, too."

"People change. Perhaps he has lived alone too long."

"I don't think it's that simple." There was a sound like a drawn-out sob from the bedroom Lucy shared with her mother. In his preoccupation with Lucy he had forgotten how small the Bishop home was. "We'd better hold it down. We're disturbing Ana."

"Yes. She hasn't slept well since Harold left." She stood up, crossed to where Corey sat, and took his face in her hands. "I do love you, Corey Lane." She kissed him. It was a gentler kiss than the one that night at the side of the corral, but it held the same promise. "I'm going to turn in now. We've got a long, hard day tomorrow."

Corey found he, too, had difficulty sleeping, even without a full moon lighting Harold's room as it had that other night. He got up, pulled on his trousers, stuffed his feet in his boots, and went outside as quietly as he could. It was a bright, crystal night, cloudless, in some ways more brilliant than if there had been a moon to wash away the nearby stars. No breeze stirred the trees at the far north edge of the meadow. The forest and the mountain were holding their breath. Something seemed pent up, held back. Pete Jandeezi's *gah'n* at work? Whatever. It was all at distinct odds with the turmoil he had felt for—how long now? The days were running into each other like the tail end of a herd of cattle when a stampede turns to milling at a river or a cliff.

Thinking of cattle—would all this dangerous business be put to rest before Virgie started her roundup down at the X-Bar-7 and the drive to Corona on which so much depended every season? She surely couldn't risk running a herd through the basin with Apaches riding point and flank, not with the sentiments Corey had found in Black Springs when he came down from Santa Fe, worn to the bone with fatigue and worry over what decision Eloy Montoya would come to while Corey looked for Harold, as Tom and Jim had agreed he must. The mood in the Chupadera town was ugly—worse, openly threatening. Harold's ridiculous raid had pumped life into old terrors.

He had gotten his horse from old man Kelly's livery stable

and had gone to the bar and grill of the Sacramento House to get a bite before starting for the X-Bar-7. The barroom was crowded, but he found a table near the front door and ordered a ham sandwich and a beer from waiter Bernardo Baca, intending to wolf it down and be on his way after glancing through the copy of the *Chupadera County News* he had picked off a stack in the lobby.

Sheriff Orrin Langley was holding court at the long bar served by Benjy Jameson, his fat belly creased by the edge of the bar as he leaned his great weight against it. The sheriff was twisting an empty shot glass at eye level, pointedly waiting for one of his listeners to buy.

"It won't be like the old days, of course," Langley declaimed. "We can't just ride up there and burn them out and hang a half dozen or so. But you can bet your ass that when we serve the warrants I got in the office for Bishop and them John Does he's got with him, old Geronimo will have a lot of new company up there at Fort Sill. Don't suppose Santa Fe or Washington will let us pack every one of their relatives up and ship them out the way we should, but we'll get the young bucks who did it, the ones who helped them, and any of the other red devils who even *thought* of helping them. Women and kids, too."

Ana at Fort Sill? Lucy locked away from him forever?

A nasty, satisfied rumble from Langley's listeners seemed to underline his words, and then the man next to him (Corey saw that it was Jimmy Lee Trafton, who owned Black Springs Feed & Seed Company at Frontera and the tracks) said to the bartender, "Buy the sheriff a drink, Benjy, and I'll stand the house a round." Bottles skated up and down the bar. Corey shook his head when Bernardo hurried one toward him. He didn't worry that his refusing the offered drink might cause a problem; none of the mob around Langley seemed to have noticed him.

Trafton was speaking again. "Gents. I think a toast to Matt Kessler is on order."

A chorus of "You bet!" "Amen to that!" "Here's to good old Matt!" and other similar cries came from the men at the bar, and several of them raised their glasses toward the back of the room.

Matt Kessler sat at a table in the far corner.

He raised his own glass to his well-wishers, but his eyes fastened on Corey. He swung his glass toward him, and gave it a little lift.

Corey had company on the ride from Black Springs to the X-Bar-7. It didn't take much imagination to figure out that after he left the Sacramento and stopped by the offices of the *News* to see if any messages had come down from Jim or Tom in the capital, Kessler must have found a rider to follow him. His watcher made no attempt to hide his intent, but he didn't come close, certainly not close enough for Corey to identify him, and he gave up the surveillance when Corey rode through the ranch gate that carried his father's big old sign, X-BAR-7—LANE.

But he, or a twin hired by Kessler, was back on the job the next morning when Corey left for the Mescalero.

Corey took the long way around up to the reservation, planning to travel the Concho Valley all the way to San Isidro before swinging back toward Cow Camp Creek. Again the other horse just plodded along a quarter of a mile in back of him, its rider making no attempt to close the gap. Clearly the man behind him was under some kind of restraint—for now. There had been plenty of secluded places along this trail for him to have made a move, if that was his intention. Still, it was the first time since all this grim business began that Corey wished for even a brief moment that he was riding armed. The surveillance wasn't frightening, but it was nerve-wracking, as of course it was meant to be. Corey wouldn't have believed Kessler capable of such subtlety. Thinking it over, he still didn't believe it. This was Gideon at work.

Only once did the other rider narrow the distance between them, pushing his mount noticeably faster when Corey reached the turnoff that led to the river and Kessler's Sierra layout. As much as Corey wanted to see for himself what damage Harold and his raiders might have done to the compound, it would be tempting fate to no good purpose were he to go in for the look-around he wanted; Kessler would now have the place under some kind of guard, and Corey would be hemmed in front and back. It was too important that he get to the Bishops, see Ana and Lucy, possibly Sam, and, without fail, Harold.

When he reached the little church at the northwestern edge of the village he discovered something else, something that made him forget his escort completely for a while.

Twenty or twenty-five people were gathered in the churchyard around a priest in a white chasuble: uncovered men whose faces were set like stone, women who had draped black shawls around their heads. Four of the men were lowering a small coffin into the ground. They were burying Pepe Montoya.

Corey lifted his own hat from his head, then turned his horse toward the trail up the mountain.

At the rocks that marked the Chupadera-Mescalero line—Gideon's map and its "Area at issue" notwithstanding—he turned off the trail into a thicket of scrub oak and waited for the man who was following him. After five minutes it became apparent that the other rider wasn't going to maintain his pursuit onto the reservation proper. The wave of relief that swept over Corey only served to point out how extreme the tension had been that had dogged him since he left the corral of the X-Bar-7. It was a double relief; it seemed unlikely that Kessler had other riders up here in the timber if the one lone one behind him had been reluctant to enter it. Still, his heart floated high in his throat until he reached Cow Camp Creek and Lucy Bishop.

He hadn't mentioned the rider to her or Ana. With everything else plaguing him, he had forgotten him until tonight. He would have to keep a sharp lookout for him as well as Sam's men in the morning, though.

Across the meadow, miles away but seeming at his elbow, a coyote yelped fitfully, something half strangled and yet mocking in its cry. A sly marauder, probably playing games with a lion. No blood would spill, but the coyote would win. Coyotes always did. This new century wasn't the time for lions.

Lucy shook her head in dismay at the sight of the four gunnysacks placed by the front door. Ana must have risen an hour before the other two to have gotten them filled and ready.

"Mama," Lucy said. "We can't possibly carry this much food!"

"But those boys must be starving up there, Lucy. They're not real warriors. They're used to their mothers feeding them. Harold looked too thin when he was here on Friday."

"Harold's looked too thin for ten years, Mama."

Corey broke in. "If Sam's men see us packing all these provisions, Ana, they'll never believe for a second that we're just going down to the X-Bar-7."

"Well, I can take a little something to Virgie, can't I? That will look all right."

"One bag. That's all."

Ana didn't seem quite persuaded, pushing out her lower lip into what under other circumstances would have been a compelling pout, but she said no more as they left the house and mounted.

It was another bright blue day, darkened only for a second when Corey glanced down to his saddle boot and Tony's

Winchester as they moved out, Ana leading. Lucy had walked outside with him after breakfast and watched silently as he put the old rifle in the boot. Like him, she must have recognized the absurdity of him carrying a rifle for anything but hunting.

As Corey had expected, two tribal policemen were hunched over a small fire at the far edge of the meadow. They waved but gave no sign of offering an escort. Ana turned the lead horse toward the trail that led downward toward Agua Prieta Canyon and from there to the X-Bar-7. So far, so good.

The terrain they rode through after leaving the meadow and the edge of the forest was on the southwest side of the mountain, a rock-strewn barren for the most part, with only an occasional scraggly jack pine to break an almost limitless expanse of shale and galleta grass, hot enough now and not a place to be in another month. The top piñon line was still several hundred feet below them. This was the trail Victorio and the Red Paint People had taken out of the Mescalero on that last, fatal flight. Across the wide valley of the Rio Grande the Black Range, where the Mimbreño chief and his warriors and their families had gone to ground twenty-one years ago, was a long, low smudge on the horizon.

It was strange to ride with Ana Bishop without her chattering away at much the same clip as the horses' hooves were striking the hard, twisting trail, but despite several efforts on the part of Lucy to elicit a response of some minimal kind from her as they dropped rapidly toward the piñons, Ana didn't utter a sound until they reached the little crease in the talus where the beginnings of the Agua Prieta water bubbled out from under an overhanging ledge, and where they pulled up in the patchy shade of the first piñon, a mature tree whose branches had been tortured by half a century of basin winds. Without some relentless force such as that working on it, nothing much would have happened to the look of this gnarled old brute in the past thirty years.

Ana looked down to where Chupadera County stretched away toward the lava flow and the Jornada. "I can go down to your place just fine by myself from here, Corey. Are you sure Virgie will want to have me? I'm not good company these days."

"Want to have you? Don't be ridiculous, Ana. You're family to Virgie if anyone in this country is."

"I still think I should be going with the two of you."

"Well, you're not—and that's final."

Again the pout, but no comment. Lucy eased her horse toward her mother, leaned over, and kissed her.

They waited until Ana and her horse rounded a small shoulder of rock and were lost to view, then started back up the trail they had just come down. It was unlikely that Naaki's two men had followed them, but they couldn't have hidden themselves from view on this stark, open trail anyway.

The better part of a thousand feet below Cow Camp Creek, with Lucy now on the point, they began a long traverse that led them deep into the forest. In the next hour and a half they crossed two high, timbered ridges and by noon Corey estimated that they had gained back all the altitude they had lost in the descent to Agua Prieta Canyon and perhaps another quarter of a mile as well. It was cooler up here, and although he kept a careful watch for any other riders, the late morning was an unalloyed delight—for him, anyway.

They stopped for lunch by a noisy mountain freshet where a grassy bank leaned out over the water, the edges near the trees dotted with moss campion.

While Corey tied off the two horses Lucy stepped down to the little rivulet and scooped water into her cupped hands, splashing her face and then running her wet fingers through her black hair.

Lunch was just sandwiches and water from the stream, but

it seemed nectar and ambrosia. When they finished they gazed at each other across the cloth she had spread. He reached over and took her hand.

"Yes, Corey," she said. "Yes, yes, *yes!*"

It was past five when they reached the double waterfall beneath Big Bear Spring.

"I think they've already seen us," Lucy said.

"What makes you think so?"

"You see that V in the rocks next to the right-hand branch of the falls? Someone would have been posted there as a lookout. If I remember right it's the only way anyone up there can look down this valley without climbing all the way to the top of the rocks, where they would be exposed, and they would *have* to keep a watch. You had better wait here while I go on ahead. Watch carefully where I turn. It's the only way in."

It made sense that he let her go first, but it didn't make him like it.

Lucy spurred her horse forward along the bank of the stream he guessed was upper Sinuoso Creek, reined it down into the stream bed to avoid a huge boulder that jutted over the bank, then up again and sharply to the right as she reached the foot of the twin falls, where she disappeared into a dense stand of juniper half hidden in a curtain of spray. She came in sight again fifty feet above the trees, hunched forward in the saddle as the horse gathered its hindquarters and bounded up a steep, rocky defile. Then, once more she was gone. He could find his way up the slope himself now, but Ana had been right. He never would have discovered this entrance without Lucy. Whatever other foolishness Harold might be guilty of, he had chosen the hideout for his little band with care. Even Sam Naaki, for all his keen abilities, wouldn't find them, even by accident. A rider would never turn into those dripping junipers on a lucky guess.

As Corey waited he tried not to think of what had happened after lunch. Lucy and he would face serious business in the next few hours and nothing else should be allowed to interfere. It was no use. For all that beset him he was the most fortunate man alive. He wanted to shout it through the canyon, tell the world. Virgie had to know—and Jim. He caught himself. In his heady excitement he had almost thought Gideon. Some things died hard.

Then his wait was over.

A figure had appeared at the top of the rocks. It wasn't Lucy or Harold, but one of Harold's young band. He was dressed in the old way, rifle cradled in his arms, and the dying sun had caught him full on. The short hairs at the back of Corey's neck bristled, but not from fear. The boy looked absolutely marvelous, a throwback to another time, of course, but a splendid throwback.

He waved Corey forward.

16

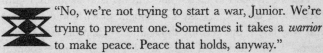"No, we're not trying to start a war, Junior. We're trying to prevent one. Sometimes it takes a *warrior* to make peace. Peace that holds, anyway."

"Hell of a way to go about it, Harold," Corey said. "You've got enough guns and ammo and blasting powder cached up here to outfit a company of infantry and a platoon of engineers. Where in God's name did you get it all?" It didn't seem that any of it had come from Kessler's place; there had been no hint of theft in the wire service report Jim had filed and that he had read in the office of the *News*.

"Here and there." Harold looked damned proud of himself and his absurd command here in this war camp *ranchería*. It probably accounted for the easy way he had taken the news that Ana had told them where he was. "You'd be surprised at the good stuff folks either throw away or leave lying around, Corey. How is Mama, Lucy?"

"As well as can be expected. Corey persuaded her to go to the X-Bar-7 and stay with his mother until things get better."

"Good idea. Thanks, Junior. Now, let me see if we can't free up a couple of wickiups. It's too late for you two to start back down tonight."

"One wickiup will be enough, Harold," Lucy said.

It was as if a horse had kicked Corey. He looked at Lucy. Her head was high and her gaze frank. He turned to Harold, forcing himself to seek his eyes; any brotherly objections would have to be faced sooner or later.

Harold looked as jolted by Lucy's calm statement as Corey doubtless did himself, but then his mouth curved into an even bigger smile than any they had seen since they arrived. "Well, I'll be . . . so that's the way it is. Does Mama know?"

"She doesn't know everything, but then Corey and I didn't know everything ourselves until . . ." Her blush turned her even more beautiful. "I think she's guessed, though."

Harold stepped to Corey and threw his arms around him. "It's about time. Can't say I'd thought much about you two this way lately, but yes, it's about time." Then his face turned grim. "I don't think I'd make any big happy noises about it for a while, though. It wouldn't be a good idea to have Corey known as a squaw man down in Black Springs. Not until we're out of this mess, anyway. We'd better think about eating."

Harold's young men had given the three of them a wide berth till now, but as they all gathered at the fire and its cooking pots Harold introduced them.

The slim, wiry sentinel who had waved Corey into the camp from the top of the rock was the sixteen-year-old Chino Walksnice whom Ana had spoken of only yesterday. Somewhere between Corey and Harold in height, he had a hard, set face and a wolfish look about him that hinted that he didn't much trust white men. He did shake hands with Corey, but it was a surprisingly limp handshake, limp not from weakness but from some long-held distrust and wariness.

John Ditsa looked older than the nineteen Ana had reported him to be, as husky as Sam Naaki and with some of the Mescalero lawman's quiet confidence, too. Obviously John was Harold's second in command, if only because of the two extra years he had on the rest of them.

Corey didn't catch but one of the names of the other three who filed up to him at the fire, and that was the Kanseah youngster Pika, whose father's tiny *rancho* they had ridden past the day they found Pete Jandeezi's body—but it was clear that all of them came from the high timber country and belonged to the families whose land and possessions had been savaged in the weeks before and after Tony's death. But that made only five. Hadn't Ana said that Harold had six young men with him? If she was right, one of them was out of camp now.

A meal of gravel-hard beans and stringy charred beef that they washed down with absolutely poisonous coffee, made barely palatable by the addition of more canned milk than he could ever remember drinking at one sitting, left Corey wishing they had, after all, hauled Ana's gunnysacks along with them. Something like that must have occurred to Lucy, too; she made a wry face at him across the rim of her enameled tin cup. She was lovely in the dying light. He couldn't help thinking about that one wickiup. The bad food notwithstanding, this junket would have been a trip through paradise for him if only there hadn't been the prospect of incipient war facing them.

It turned chilly when the sun finally sank into the woods below the falls, and Corey was grateful when one of the boys stoked the fire to a brighter blaze after supper. One by one Harold's "warriors," whom Corey would have expected to share the warmth, drifted off to other parts of the encampment, whether in some show of stoicism or to give the three of them privacy he couldn't tell.

"I know you don't approve of what I'm up to with these kids, Junior," Harold said when they were alone, "but I know I'm right whenever I imagine how they would look and act as secondhand white men at Carlisle. I honest to God think I just might have restored something to them, no matter how this thing ends."

Something like that had struck Corey, too, when he had waited below the falls and Chino Walksnice had materialized at the top of the rocks and waved him in, and again when Harold had introduced Chino to him beside the fire. The boy had looked like an Apache prince, a young lion. Perhaps Corey's absorption with these people and their past (a past he had been led to by Gideon Bainbridge; he couldn't forget that) had left him with entirely too romantic a view of such things. He didn't dare be romantic now, for Harold's sake or his own. It was, as he had thought last night, no time for lions.

"My only problem with that, Harold, is that I don't think you're taking into account the other likely alternative to Carlisle. There's Fort Sill, too, or—a damn sight worse—a regular federal lockup like Leavenworth. The boys might escape that because of their age, but you wouldn't. I think you should turn yourself in. If you did, the authorities might be inclined to lenience."

"You're not serious."

"I sure as hell am. There are already warrants out for all of you down in Black Springs, warrants I'm sure will let them come up here to grab you. Probably the only reason Orrin Langley hasn't acted on them yet is because he's the laziest peace officer in the Territory."

"Well, you can just forget about me turning myself in. For Pete's sake, why should I? We haven't done one single thing against white law. I'll admit we've helped ourselves to some things up here on the Mescalero, and we'll gladly answer to the council for that when the time comes, but we haven't taken so much as a sack of beans from anyone in Chupadera County. We've just been guarding our people's homes. Any white man would do the same. Sure we've chased some intruders off, but we haven't fired a single shot in anger. All we've done was warn riders who had no business up here by firing in the air. Except for one time, we haven't set foot outside the reservation."

"It's that one time that's the rub."

"Why? Oh, I'll admit we must have *looked* pretty warlike when we rode to the Concho last weekend, but we didn't hurt anybody. What the hell have they issued warrants for?"

Was it possible that Harold was glossing over the death of Pepe? or that he didn't even know about it? Could be. His small band, unused to this kind of violence, couldn't have followed the flight of every bullet fired, and even the villagers of San Isidro had thought it an accident, if one that should be paid for. Perhaps he was just afraid to bring the child's death into a talk like this. It had to be done.

"Harold, did you know that the little boy who was killed was the grandnephew of the only man we can really count on in Santa Fe, Eloy Montoya?"

Harold looked stunned. "What are you talking about? What little boy? *We didn't kill anyone!*"

"You didn't know a child died in that raid?"

"What *raid*?" Harold's eyes had narrowed. It was hard to tell for sure if he was scared now or not, but of course he had to be.

"The one on Kessler's place in San Isidro. Friday night. When you rode to the Concho."

"Are you loco? We haven't been anywhere near San Isidro. We did ride up to the Martins' old place on the *upper* Concho late Friday to scare those homesteaders, but nobody got shot.

We didn't do any shooting at all that time. I give you my word as a brother, Corey."

"How did you know about the homesteaders?"

"We've been patrolling the whole boundary line and we found a couple of them wandering around up near Nogal Peak last Wednesday. Said they were looking over land a Mr. Kessler promised them would be theirs in a few weeks. It was kind of hard to talk with them. Their English isn't even as good as that of some of our old people. We frightened them pretty bad. That's when we decided a visit to their camp might scare them even more, maybe encourage them to pull up stakes."

Something burst in Corey's head. Harold was telling the truth, the whole truth.

And then, just as suddenly, the rest of it became obvious. Somebody who knew the Concho and all the ancient fears had come up with the idea of having riders hired by Sierra stage a counterfeit raid, and again he was reluctant to credit Kessler. Gideon again. It wouldn't have been any trick at all for white men to pose as Apaches at night and fool the villagers of San Isidro; the raid had occurred just after dark, and according to the *News* report only three sleepy-eyed people, four if Corey included poor dead Pepe, had made it out of their adobes in time to see the raiders ride out of town.

But now he must persuade Harold to do what in the end was the only thing that would square matters in Chupadera County.

"Your word is enough for me, Harold. I believe you. But I still think you should surrender yourself to Orrin Langley."

"And stand trial? Not on your life! Can you picture an Apache getting a straight roll of the dice in a Territorial court?"

No, Corey couldn't, but he could picture an all-out manhunt that wouldn't respect the boundaries of the Mescalero

and that could end in hardship and perhaps tragedy for a lot
of people. He looked for a tiny glimmer of hope.

"Harold, what time were you on the upper Concho?"

"Just before sundown. About eight-thirty, I guess."

"All seven of you?"

"Yes."

"Did those homesteaders get a good look at you?"

"Sure. That was the whole idea. That's why we rode up
there while it was still light."

There it was, the hope. "All right. They'll be your alibi.
You couldn't have made it down to San Isidro by nine-fifteen
when the raid took place."

"But would they say so?"

"You'll have to count on it. Damn it, Harold! Facing the
law is your only chance to clear yourself and your boys."

"I wouldn't count on *any* white man." He shook his head.
"I'm sorry, Corey. I didn't mean that. Either that or I don't
think of you as white. Why can't I answer in a Mescalero
court?"

Lucy came to Corey's rescue, such rescue as it was. She
rose from her seat by the fire, walked to her brother, and put
her hand on his shoulder. "San Isidro isn't on the reservation.
The whites would never give jurisdiction to an Indian court."
She turned to Corey. "Couldn't he turn himself in to Sam
Naaki and stay in arrest of some kind at tribal headquarters
in the custody of the agent, Corey? If we could get statements
from the homesteaders perhaps there wouldn't have to be a
trial."

"I would hope so, Lucy. The point is, what other realistic
choice is there? Harold and the boys could stay on the dodge
for a while, but with both the sheriff and Sam hunting for
them, there could only be one outcome in the long run. And
while some trigger-happy posse tracks them down, they would
only look more and more guilty to Chupadera County. As for
Harold turning himself in to Sam instead of Langley, maybe

that does make sense. It keeps him from being a fugitive—technically, at any rate."

Lucy hadn't taken her hand from Harold's shoulder. They could have been the Tony and Ana Bishop of twenty years ago. Corey hadn't yet met this family then, but he knew that this was what the two older ones must have been like as the white world tightened the nooses around the necks of the Red Paint People. Tony and Ana had made their choice. What was the right one for these two people he loved so much?

Not a sound had come from the younger members of the band sitting cross-legged and impassive barely within the light of the fire. How much had they heard of the talk?

I just might have restored something to them, Harold had said earlier. Yes, he just might have. Wherever these remarkable people belonged—if they belonged anywhere at all anymore—they surely didn't belong in a Bible class.

Somewhere in the distant rocks a lion coughed. Perhaps this one time it could win its game with the coyote.

"Let's turn in," Harold said. "I'll think about everything you've said, Corey. You'll get my answer in the morning."

The wickiup Harold made available to them was set apart from the three other shelters and looked far older than the others, years older, and larger, too. It must be Harold's now. Its relative isolation was probably due to the desire of some long-dead Apache leader to be apart from his warriors.

Corey and Lucy didn't speak as they put their bedrolls in it and placed their few personal things against the walls, but when they settled down next to each other and Corey took her in his arms, Lucy said, "Wait just a bit, Corey. There is something I must ask you. I wish I could see your face when you answer."

"What is it, Lucy?"

"What Harold said about your people perhaps thinking of you as a squaw man. Doesn't that bother you?"

"Good Lord, no!"

She was silent for a moment, then, "I know you're telling me the truth, and it's exactly what I thought you would say, but *shouldn't* it bother you?"

"Why?"

"Those people down there are your real life, have been and will be, forever."

"You're my real life."

"That's not you talking, Corey. That's love. Oh, I'm grateful. And I feel the same way. But is love enough?"

"Yes."

"I want to believe you. I guess I have to believe you."

Then they made love.

It wasn't the same as it had been on the bank of the stream under the noonday sun; that first fine frenzied time could never come again. It was different—not more or less, not better or worse—but different. It was a resplendent wonder. It always would be.

Just before breakfast Harold met Corey and Lucy at streamside above the falls, where they were drawing water for washing up.

"All right, Junior!" he said, shouting to make himself heard above the sound of the rapids. "Let's get back toward camp where we can hear each other."

They followed him back up the trail. He stopped at a dead-fall, sat down on it, and bent his head into his hands.

When he looked up at last, he said, "I'll do it your way. I'll come in. It's not quite settled with the rest, though. They're not sure. I'll go down to the agency and talk to Sam, and if I get anything like a fair shake out of Black Springs, I'll send for them."

To Corey, Harold looked as if he hadn't slept, or as if he had been beaten.

What had he done to Harold? Was any outcome worth it?

"When can we leave, Harold?"

"Right after breakfast. Before I change my mind." He stood up and moved up the trail away from them.

"Don't take yourself to task, Corey," Lucy said. "You're doing the only thing you can."

When they had cleaned out the wickiup, packed their gear, and filled their canteens, Lucy and Corey went to the remains of the fire for a last cup of coffee. He watched Harold embrace each of his young men, one by one. Chino Walksnice watched Corey. There were only four of them, one of them holding a horse for Harold. John Ditsa must have been posted to the V in the rocks as a lookout.

In the cold light of the early morning the group seemed changed. Their eyes were still puffed with the last of the night's sleep, and the shirts and leggings they wore were soiled and wrinkled. They must have looked as shabby last night, but not to eyes that were seeking something else, something from the wild free days of the Mimbreños who had haunted these mountains and forests and deserts in Corey's father's time. Now, overnight, these young men had grown old before their time.

Harold mounted and signaled to Corey, but before he and Lucy could swing up into their saddles the sound of another horse coming up the trail echoed off the rocks.

It was another young Apache, one Corey hadn't seen before. He looked like he had made a long, hard ride. He steered his horse straight for Harold.

The boy talked earnestly with Harold, and when he had finished Harold walked his pony to where Lucy and Corey waited.

"There's a little hitch. It wouldn't be smart for us to try for the agency to turn me in to Sam. Chato, there, says there are three different bunches of armed riders, white men, on all the trails that lead toward tribal headquarters, maybe thirty men in all. What do you think now, Corey?"

"Black Springs, I guess. Yes, in the long pull we've got to wind up there, anyway." Would Harold change his mind?

"We'll have to go down through Gideon's place," Harold said. He set the spurs to his mount. "Let's ride!"

17

———

Harold led the way down the defile and out through the spray-clouded junipers. At the spot where Corey had waited for the signal to come into camp the day before, Harold reined up, turned in the saddle, and waved toward the V in the rock. Lucy turned and waved, too. Perhaps their vision was keener than his, and perhaps they had a different kind of sight, but when Corey looked up he couldn't detect a sign of anything but stone.

"Will they stay there, Harold, or will they go on home now?"

"They'll stay. They'll stay until they see me or hear from me. If you're right about their names not being on the warrants yet, this is the best place for them. As you've pointed out, they are just kids. I think they'd willingly charge a Gatling gun, but they're not quite that brave when it comes to explaining what they've been up to with me to their mothers and fathers." He laughed.

It surprised Corey that it was such a hearty laugh. Harold was taking this trip to surrender very well now that they were actually under way and committed to it. He looked considerably clearer and brighter than he had at the rapids before breakfast and later at the deadfall, looked certainly cheerful and almost blithe. Maybe Corey could persuade himself that he wasn't forcing his Mimbreño friend on this excursion. Bad enough that it had to be done at all; it would have been impossibly painful if Harold were facing this with the dread Corey had more or less expected him to show.

"Will they be all right?" Corey asked.

"Sure. They don't have to nose out of there for a thing. They've got food for two or three weeks. This thing should be cleared up by then—one way or the other. And sure as hell, nobody who doesn't know the way into that camp can find it. Could you before yesterday?"

"No. It's a good camp."

"John will keep them from straying. He's a tougher leader than I am."

Now, even more surprisingly, Corey laughed himself. "Forgive me, Harold, but from everything I've heard, your people don't have the reputation of being exactly amenable to discipline. Didn't small bands of the Red Paint People change war chiefs every hour on the hour?"

"Well, yeah. I'll admit that's the way it *was*. But you white devils have had us in one kind of school or the other for a couple of generations now. You were too clever to teach us *everything* you know, but you were pretty firm about our taking orders. We're so good at it now, that if we were to fight all those wars over again, I think we'd win."

It was like the banter that had passed between them for most of a dozen years, and in spite of himself Corey began to permit himself to think that things might turn out well. A satisfied little laugh from Lucy reinforced the idea.

They made good time, taking a series of interconnected little pathways through the trees and scrub that looked more like game trails than genuine thoroughfares, and before noon they had crossed the high ridge that separated the Arroyo Sinuoso from the Concho and were well into Chupadera County. They hadn't spoken about the danger of running into the parties of riders Chato had reported, but Corey felt that every mile they moved down out of the timber and toward the distant grassy *lomas* east of Black Springs, the safer they would be—at least until they reached the town itself.

He would discuss the strategy of dealing with any threat there when they stopped for lunch, would tell Harold of his plan that they ride pell-mell for the sheriff's office from the edge of town and arrive there before any deputy of Orrin's could stop them and claim they *weren't* coming in. Harold's facing the law had to be seen by the authorities as an entirely voluntary move.

There had been one good sign at the start of this journey. Harold had apparently recognized, without Corey's prompting, the wisdom, the absolute imperative, of not going armed. Just before they left camp he had pulled his rifle from his saddle boot and handed it to Chino Walksnice.

One thing, in spite of all the times he had hunted these uplands with Gideon—Gideon again—Corey knew he was thoroughly lost, and said so when they stopped for lunch in a clearing in a thick growth of ponderosa.

"We're on the Tres Piedras," Harold said. "The back road to the house is just over that rise."

Corey looked through the big trees and across the valley at Cuchillo Peak, and the shape of the mountain from here restored his bearings once again. The rise Harold had pointed to was where he had been the day the hailstorm had hit him, back when Gideon was still one of the three best friends he had in Chupadera County.

They finished lunch and mounted. As they reached the rise and could look down to where the road to Gideon's wound around a bluff fifty feet below them, Lucy pulled her horse up short.

"I'm sorry," she said. "I left the saddlebag the lunch was in. I won't be a moment." She turned and rode back down toward the little clearing where they had eaten.

As they sat their horses, Harold, whose unexpected high spirits seemed to have gone in hiding again now that they were looking down on Gideon's back ranch road, suddenly exploded, "I just can't get it through my thick skull. *Why*, Corey? He has *everything*! Why should he want the little bit we've got? Does he hate us that much? And if he does, how did he keep it hidden from us all these years?"

Corey had no answer for him, but even if he had one, he wouldn't have had time to give it. A group of horsemen appeared on the road, heading up toward the high timber country. A quick count made it a dozen. They weren't even at a lope, but they were moving fast. These men weren't cowhands today. The highest pastures of Tres Piedras were far behind them. They looked like men on a mission. Corey held his breath, praying silently that none of them would look up and see him and Harold.

Matt Kessler was out in front.

Before Corey could let his breath loose again, they were out of sight.

"Close," Harold said. "I'll never complain again when women hold things up."

When Lucy rejoined them, neither of them mentioned the vanished riders, and they started down the rise toward the road.

Black Springs in the middle of the week was half asleep and almost deserted; the only genuine activity was a gang of boys playing baseball in a vacant lot next to Bill Shipley's blacksmith's shop. A few women, shoppers, strolled the wooden sidewalks under the store porticos on Estancia Street, and a drunk staggered out of the Red Bull Saloon.

"They must have deputized the whole damned town and sent them after me," Harold said.

The peace and quiet was exactly what Corey should have expected, and it should have reassured him, but strangely it didn't. It felt faintly as if they were in some other time and were riding into an ambush, but after a bad moment he persuaded himself that that was nonsense. This town, for all its shortcomings, was civilization—wasn't it?

At the Chupadera County sheriff's office only Will Turley was on duty, with his feet up on Orrin Langley's desk and a copy of the *Police Gazette* in his hands. Will was decent enough, if as lazy as his boss and not as bright. After an off-hand but cordial hello to Corey he stared at Harold and Lucy. From his curious but clearly uncomprehending look it was obvious he had little or no idea what his three visitors had in mind, particularly since two of them were Indians.

"This is Harold Bishop, Will," Corey said. "He's turning himself in on that warrant Orrin has."

"Turning himself in? Warrant?" His face had now gone completely blank.

"Harold is wanted for that attack on Sierra Development Company in San Isidro the other night."

"Oh, yeah." Will's nod was a bureaucrat's nod. Then his eyes widened and his feet hit the floor. "Oh, *yeah*. Oh, my God!" He swallowed hard. "Can't you come back in the morning, Corey? Orrin ain't here."

It would have been laughable to Corey if it hadn't been so serious and so fraught with danger for Harold. It was laughable enough for Harold to snicker a little. "That's it, Corey. Let's get out of here," he said. The little imp was actually enjoying this. Perhaps he didn't grasp the deadly peril facing him if he left the sheriff's office now. Corey leaned over the desk.

"*No* we can't come back in the morning, Will. Pay attention. This is important. You can take his surrender as well as Orrin could. He's in your custody now. Lock him up or whatever it is you're supposed to do with wanted men. I want to get to Judge Farrell's office before it closes and see about him setting bail."

"Gee, Corey . . ." Will was almost pleading. "I don't rightly know what I should do. Look, Orrin's over at the Sacramento bar. Let me just race over there and haul him back. There's coffee there on the stove, and help yourself to the magazines and stuff." He came from behind the desk and started for the door. Corey began a protest, but Will's nervousness lent the deputy sheriff unsuspected speed, and he was outside and gone before Corey could say a word.

Harold's snicker became a full-blown laugh. He walked to the desk and picked up a metal ring holding at least a dozen large keys. He pointed to a plate with half-eaten food still smeared on it next to where the keys had been. "How did you people ever beat us, Junior? This town is guarded by a stale enchilada." He moved to the woodstove. "Either of you want coffee? It's cold enough for a hot day like this. Wonder how they brewed it. This stove hasn't seen a stick of firewood since May."

Harold's high good humor was amazingly contagious. "I suppose they ordered it from Carmen's, across the plaza," Corey said. "Carmi's coffee isn't too good even when it's hot."

So far this was going far better than he dared hope. He realize now that he had unconsciously feared that when they got close to town, and push came to shove, Harold might get second thoughts and bolt. He was instead having the time of his life. Brother or not, he was a hard man to fathom, his shifts of mood as capricious and quick to change as the weather of early April.

Lucy's face had become a mask. She, at least, didn't think

this affair a lark, but she certainly didn't show any signs of panic now that they were right down to cases. Strong people, both of them, as strong and tough as Ana and Tony.

"I'd better go out to the horses and bring in the things you'll need tonight, Harold," Lucy said.

Before she could start for the door, the huge stomach of Orrin Langley was pushing its way through.

The sheriff merely glanced at them as he moved to a cabinet behind the desk, picked up a gun belt, and strapped it on. He pulled the weapon from the holster, checked the chambers, and put it back again. He looked like he must have been bellied up at the Sacramento bar all afternoon. His eyes were red, and the wax had gone from his mustache. He was drunk, sure enough, but drunk in the way some big men get, not staggered or unsteady, but heavy, stolid.

"What's this all about, Lane?" he said when he turned back toward them.

"This is Harold Bishop, Orrin."

Harold broke in. "I think I'd better talk for myself, Corey. I'm here to surrender, Sheriff Langley."

Will had followed the sheriff through the door, and now Langley spoke to him. "Deputy Turley," he said. "Round up all the auxiliary deputies who ain't up in the hills looking for this . . . man, and have them report here pronto. I want a double guard on the jail tonight. Get going!" When Will had scuttled out, Langley turned back to Harold. "Get your ass over to this desk, Bishop. That's right, move . . . hold it right there . . . that's close enough. Now, bend over and put your hands on the desk and spread your legs, and don't so much as twitch or even blink until I say so, savvy?"

He moved around the desk and began a search of Harold, starting with his upper body. His hands seemed strangely intimate, insinuating. Harold flinched at their touch, and Corey was glad he couldn't see his face, and then he flinched himself at a soft sob from Lucy.

"Sheriff! He isn't armed. You can take my word for it."

"Your word's just fine, Lane, but I'll damned well see for myself. This hombre ain't a white man. For all I know he's got a holdout or a knife tucked away somewheres." His hands moved roughly down Harold's legs as he spoke. Then he straightened up. Harold looked no bigger than a child in front of him. "All right, now, bucko, let's just march you back to the lockup."

Harold stepped away from the desk. His face had gone pale. Langley took him by the arm and steered him toward a gaping door at the back of the office. In a matter of seconds the clang of iron echoed through the building.

It was probably the sight of Lucy that made Judge Terence Farrell's secretary, Helen Hollis, so nervous, and Corey reflected that it was well within the realm of possibility that she had lived all her life in Black Springs, less than forty miles from the Mescalero, without once confronting an Apache, certainly not a woman.

"I'm sorry," she said. "His Honor has gone for the day. He won't be back until nine tomorrow morning."

"Can we go to the judge's home, Helen?"

"I sure wouldn't if I were you, Mr. Lane, particularly if you need something from him. He's a bearcat when his afternoon nap's interrupted, and an absolute fury if he's disturbed at supper."

Actually, the delay wasn't a catastrophe; Harold would have to remain overnight in Orrin Langley's lockup in any event, and Corey could be at Farrell's chambers bright and early. Even if Corey had been able to get the judge to set bail this late in the day, there would have been the matter of waiting until morning for the bank to open to get the money. Still, there was no defense against the fleeting sense of ambush that had assailed Corey as they rode into town and which came again now, stronger.

And it didn't abate when he and Lucy arrived at the *Chupadera County News*.

They walked into Jim McPherson's office with Corey hoping to find a different atmosphere from the one they had left behind them at the sheriff's, but not too hopeful that they would.

His low expectations were justified. Jim and Tom had come down from the capital on the afternoon coach with news, all of it bad.

"The governor canceled today's meeting, Corey," Jim said. "He was all for it until the word reached him about the raid on San Isidro, and then he came under heavy pressure from Spanish-speakers from all over the Territory. He's gotten some pretty sharp questions from Washington, too. Lattner seems about ready to ram those bills through his committee again. In the present mood, they'll pass this time."

Corey had one paramount question he feared the answer to, but it had to be asked, "What about Eloy?"

"Don't know. We haven't seen him or heard from him since Tom drove him home last Saturday after we told him about Pepe. I wouldn't be too surprised to learn we've lost him. Our only real hope is that he won't actually fight us. That, of course, would be the end."

Corey turned to Tom. "Did Eloy say anything that gave you a clue?"

"He didn't say anything at *all*. The poor little guy was like a man in a trance, and damned close to collapse. Thank God those two young men he relies on so much—Vigil and Cruz—were waiting for us at his house. I sure didn't know how to cope with him myself. He didn't even look at me when we said good-bye."

Corey looked at Lucy, thinking he had perhaps made a mistake bringing her here. For all her contact with the white world, this had to be strange, bad country for her, particularly coming right after the near disastrous outcome at the sheriff's office, and with one bludgeoning of bad news after the other it was getting worse.

"There's one ray of hope," he said then, speaking to Jim and Tom, but with his words above all meant to cushion the shock his doubts might bring for her. He told them about Harold's denial of any responsibility for the San Isidro business and of Harold's possible alibi. "If we can get those immigrants on the upper Concho to testify on his behalf, perhaps we can turn the governor's thinking around—and Eloy's, too. Trouble is, those people camped up there have had their wits scared out of them—and by Harold and his boys—and Harold says they can scarcely speak English. And you both know how juries are hereabouts about outsiders. Terence Farrell's only marginally more open-minded. Their testimony would have to be strong and clear to carry any weight."

Tom stood up so fast the chair he had been sitting in fell over behind him.

"Hey!" he said. "Padre Stan!"

"Over at San Jose? What about him?" Jim asked.

"You know him, don't you, Jim?"

"Father Strelski? Not well. He deals with the girls when he brings the church announcements in."

"Well, I got pretty clubby with him when we ran those features on *los viejos de San Jose*, that series Ellen helped me with on the early history of the parish and *la iglesia*. Father Stan is more than just a dedicated priest, he's a damned decent man. *His* English isn't too hot, either, nor is his Spanish. It always tickled me that the archdiocese would assign a Polack padre to our Catholics. Might be a blessing now. I'll bet the good padre would give his right arm to relax into his own lingo for a while. He might be able to shape those settlers up and see them through this thing as witnesses for Harold."

"Great, Tom!" Jim said. "Why don't you get over to his church and see him, and then the two of you hightail it for the upper Concho soon as you can, if he'll go. If he hesitates, come and get me. The *News* has been a good deal of help to San Jose over the years. Maybe you could get one or more potential witnesses down here by tomorrow afternoon. We'll pay their expenses and something for their time. If they back Harold's story, it should at the very least affect the size of the bond Terence sets."

Tom groaned, but agreed to go. The newsman didn't relish the thought of that long ride up the valley. Corey wondered if the priest was any more comfortable on horseback than Tom was.

When Tom left, Jim turned to Corey. "Are you two going out to the X-Bar-7 now?"

"No, Jim. I want to be here first thing in the morning. I thought we'd go on over to the Sacramento and get a couple of rooms for the night."

"Corey!" Jim's tone was mildly chastening. He turned to Lucy. "Forgive me, Miss Bishop, my young friend here seems to be forgetting something, something that has to be faced even if it hurts."

"Yes, he is, Mr. McPherson. And please don't apologize." She looked at Corey. "The Sacramento would never rent a room to an Indian, Corey."

Again that feeling of ambush came. Yes, he had forgotten. He could only hope he wasn't getting careless about other things as well.

Jim had left his desk and stepped to the door. "Let me see if Ellen can put you up, Miss Bishop. She's Tom's assistant and our ladies page editor." He stepped out into the newsróom.

"Corey," Lucy said, "I want you to know something. No matter how this turns out, and I'm not at all persuaded it will turn out well, I've seen and heard things today that make me almost happy. As long as there are men like you, Mr. McPherson, and Mr. Hendry, there's hope for all of us in this country."

Ellen Stafford, not much older than Lucy, was delighted to have her as an overnight guest. She looked from one to the other of them and it was plain she knew how matters stood between them, and she seemed delighted about that, too, assuming that proprietary air some women have when they find themselves in the presence of new love. Ellen was a pretty girl and had been good company a couple of times at dinner before the war.

"I'll take the two of you over there now, if Simon Legree here"—she nodded toward Jim—"will let me play hooky. My ladies page is locked in the frame and ready to go to bed, Jim."

Jim harrumphed and then smiled at all three of them. "She's a passing fair cook, Corey, or rather, her mother is. Ellen steals the recipes the subscribers send in before she prints them and gives them to Mrs. Stafford. *Vaya con Dios*, Ellen—all of you."

The Stafford place where Ellen lived with her widowed mother, sister-in-law of Findlay Stafford who owned the general store on the plaza, was a white frame cottage with a picket fence, much like the one Corey had boarded in during the two years he attended the Black Springs school as a child. It sparkled in the waning sun. As he had at Tres Piedras, he wondered what kind of home he and Lucy could eventually make at the X-Bar-7. Perhaps he could get a clue when they moved there tomorrow night, with Harold coming with them—he hoped.

After he brought Lucy's gear to the door he took the three horses to Kelly's to be fed and put up in stalls overnight and then booked himself a room at the Sacramento. He laid out the last fresh linen in his saddlebag, shaved, took a bath, fretted a little about putting on the same shirt and trousers he had lived in for three days, and went downstairs to the bar, intending to have one quick drink before going to the Staffords' for the dinner Mrs. Stafford had promised Lucy, Ellen, and him.

As it had been with the town, in midweek the bar was virtually empty. Bernardo Baca pulled out a chair for Corey at the same table he had sat in the day he came down from Santa Fe, but he shook his head and went to the long bar.

"You're not busy, Benjy," he said to the bartender when he served him.

"Place is a morgue," Benjy said. "Damned town is emptied out, what with everybody up in the mountains looking for that Indian. Suppose they'll come pounding back in now that Orrin's got him in the lockup."

So the news was out. It was what he might have expected.

But Benjy's remark had alerted him to something else. If the frustrated, probably sorely disappointed riders now combing the timberlands and high arroyos of the northwestern Mescalero came back to Black Springs tonight or tomorrow it might complicate the task of getting Harold out on bail and tucking him away at the X-Bar-7 while Tom and Father Stan brought corroborating witnesses down from the upper Concho.

Was that where the nagging feeling of ambush had come from? It well could be.

But there was something missing from this equation which no shifting of emotional decimal points could bring back into balance. Corey could easily carry his love for Lucy past several exponential powers, could do the same for his different love for her brother and her mother. He could feel sympathy for all the unfortunates such as Pepe Montoya and Pete Jandeezi who had been sucked into this vortex of greed and power, even feel sympathy for himself at the losses he had suffered: that of his own tranquillity, won in a lifetime of struggles to free himself from a legacy of shame; and the loss of Gideon Bainbridge's friendship.

The thing that was missing was anger. A tempest should

have raged inside him long before now. Why hadn't it? Was there some deadly deficiency at the heart of him?

He lifted the glass of whiskey to his lips.

Outside the Sacramento a clatter of noise arose that for a second he thought was gunfire.

He put the whiskey down untouched, left the bar, and walked through the door leading to the veranda.

Across Estancia Street Gideon's Duryea was shuddering to a stop.

Gideon looked over at Corey, stepped down from the driver's seat, and without a sign or signal disappeared inside his office.

Ambush?

18

"They've apparently been coming in since dawn, Corey," Jim said. "I don't know how the word got up the valley so fast. There's no telegraph office in San Isidro, of course, and as far as I know not a single telephone."

Small groups of silent men in the familiar white cotton trousers and shirts of Rio Concho farmers were scattered across the patch of what passed for lawn in front of the Chupadera County courthouse. Corey counted them from where he and Jim stood by the steps. Twenty-two. Three more now crossed Frontera Street and joined the others. Most wore black armbands. Yes, there were three or four he was sure he had seen at Pepe's funeral.

Jim nodded toward the sheriff's office and jail next door. "The only good thing is that they're here instead of over there. Looks like they're just waiting for court to convene. They're good people—not much given to violence—and I don't think they would try to take Harold out of that cell or cause some other trouble, but you never know. I'm glad you were able to persuade Lucy to stay at Ellen's."

"It wasn't easy."

"Have you seen Harold this morning?"

"No," Corey said. "Orrin wouldn't let me near him. He quoted county policy about visiting hours. I couldn't very well argue the point. Couldn't get to Farrell yesterday, either. It's pure hell to be in the dark about things—worse not to be able to do anything. You don't suppose he'll order Harold held without bond, do you, Jim?"

"He could very well do just that. Our tiny Irish judge has always been a strict law and order man, and he hasn't been overturned on appeal in a coon's age. Makes him a shade cocky. About all we've got to impress him with is the fact that Harold came in voluntarily. That should convince him that the young man won't run if he's out on bail—particularly if he paroles him in your custody. Farrell *is* fair."

"Shouldn't I start looking us up a lawyer?"

"I wouldn't just yet. Terence will probably *tell* Harold he should have one, but secretly he'll be pleased that there won't be anyone holding things up by screaming 'objection!' on behalf of the defendant, not at a bond hearing, anyway. But if Harold comes to trial—God forbid—he'll sure need a lawyer. A good one."

"Well, I don't really know of any really good lawyer in town except—"

"Go ahead, say it, Corey—Gideon. Trouble is, I don't, either."

Far down the street Corey could see the Duryea, parked where it had been the night before, in front of Gideon's office. It had been there first thing in the morning, when Corey left the Sacramento for breakfast with Ellen, her mother, and Lucy. Gideon must have spent the night at the hotel, too, possibly right down the hall from him.

Some of the farmers on the courthouse grass had begun to stir. A buggy was rolling down Frontera Street toward them and was attracting the attention of almost everyone in the crowd, and when it stopped a few of them hemmed it in.

"It's Terence," Jim said. "Let the Concho men have him first, Corey. We'll see if we can't have our word with him in chambers. People still haven't learned that he just doesn't listen when they collar him outside strict working hours, or anywhere away from his office."

"I found that out yesterday. Will he believe us about Harold not being involved in the San Isidro raid?"

"Might. But Tom and Padre Stan are simply going to have to produce some testimony that comes under the rules of evidence. If I know Terence he'll insist on an appearance by those immigrants, not just a deposition. We might even hear from them as early as this afternoon. Keep your fingers crossed." Jim searched Corey's face. "There's another statement every bit as important as any we're likely to get from those hopeful homesteaders, Corey. Yours. You're going to have to pull out all the stops with Terence when we see him. You can't hold back. It's time now to name Gideon and reveal his part in all this—and everything else you know. Our only chance will be in chambers. Terence won't admit hearsay in the bond hearing or indictment—if one comes. But he can't simply ignore what you have to say. Take some heart from the fact that I'll be listening as a newspaperman. Nothing will be off the record."

Terence Farrell had alighted from his buggy and was making his way up the sidewalk to the courthouse steps. The farmers who had talked to him at the street now moved away from him. His face was already set, judicial, but it was the only thing about him that made him look like a jurist. His rounded shoulders and stumpy legs made his gnomelike body look even smaller than it was. He didn't look nearly as tough as his reputation, certainly not as tough as the gnarled hickory walking stick he carried.

He merely squinted recognition at Jim and Corey as he reached them. He didn't speak, but as his foot hit the first of the steps, he stopped and bent over to tie his shoe. He didn't look at either of them now, but his voice drifted up to them like light wind in dried grass. "All right, Lane. No! Don't say anything. Don't even look like I'm talking to you now. Helen came by my house at breakfast and told me you wanted to see me yesterday. Give me five minutes to check my desk and then come in. Use the back door to the courthouse. And you, McPherson, get the sour look off your kisser. You can come, too."

"How did you know I had a sour look, Terence?"

"I've got eyes in the back of my head. Besides, I never saw a Scotsman look any other way."

Corey and Jim waited for a moment and then walked as casually as they could to the alley between the courthouse and the jail, with Corey wishing they had time for one more attempt to see Harold. Once in the alley and out of sight of the men on the lawn, they fairly sprinted for the back of the county building and found the rear door, reaching it just as someone inside unlocked and opened it.

Farrell was waiting for them, his chin not much above the top of the huge old colonial Spanish desk he sat behind. He had a cigar going, and he pushed a humidor toward Jim and Corey. The cigar didn't smell like Gideon's Havanas, but at least it didn't poison the air as did the ones Corey remembered from the Senate hearing. Corey declined and Jim reminded the judge that he didn't smoke at all.

"Sorry about that hush-hush hocus-pocus out there," Farrell said, "but there's some tricky things about this business with that Indian Orrin's holding. I know you want me to set his bond at two bits or less so you can spring him, but I wonder if you *really* want him out. Hold it, now. I can see you're both ready to jump me, but I got reasons for wondering. Take a look at this. This was stuck in my door some time during the night." He handed Corey a piece of paper that looked like a bill of lading or an invoice form. "Turn it over."

There was a penciled scrawl on the other side. It read:

Keep that red devil under lock and key, judge. He will die if you don't. Others might die with him. Let's give him a fair trial and then hang the sonofabitch.
                                        —A friend of the court.

Corey's first thought was Kessler, but the handwriting bore no resemblance to that in the note he had read on the office door at the compound in San Isidro, and besides, hadn't he seen Kessler heading into the timber just yesterday, after lunch? Unless the man had gotten back out of the mountains during the night—highly unlikely, considering the purposeful way he and his posse or whatever it was were riding toward the Mescalero—there was no way he could have learned of Harold's coming in or had time to plant this message. Corey turned the paper back to the printed side. It was a blank order form, headed "Carib Tobacco Limited, 231 Ponchartrain Road, New Orleans, Louisiana."

Now he almost choked on the fumes from Farrell's smoke. The little judge waved the hand with the cigar, thinning the cloud in front of him a bit.

"At first," Farrell said, "I thought it might have come from one of them *campesinos* out there, on account of that youngster who died—but there ain't no way any of those people, provided they can write English at all, could have written anything like that. This is from some anglo. I don't put much stock in anonymous letters, and I'd sort of like to call the writer's bluff, but it sure wouldn't be good for your friend if I was wrong. Let McPherson see it, Lane."

Corey handed the note to Jim. The publisher would make

the same connection Corey had. Something was wrong here. Gideon hadn't used his regular, elegant hand in the note, but he must have known the printed matter would identify the author to anyone who knew him. This was appalling careless-ness for a man like Gideon. When Jim finished reading it he turned it over as Corey had. Then he glanced sharply at Farrell. "Corey has some things to tell you, Terence. I don't know how much weight you'll give them when it comes to your setting bail, but all of it will be germane in the long run."

"All right, Lane," Farrell said. "Spill it."

It was beginning to get automatic, this recital of the things which had happened up on the Mescalero, and of the ulti-mate responsibility for them, but in spite of that Corey felt uneasy. In the staid, orderly office it all seemed improbable, bordering on fantasy. Farrell half disappeared in a wreath of smoke during the telling, waved it away again when Corey had finished.

"I'm supposed to be shocked, ain't I, young Mr. Lane?" Farrell said. "Well, I ain't. Hard to be precise about what constitutes wrongdoing in a country as big as this, one that didn't have any law at all not too damned long ago. Now, don't get your asses in an uproar. I only said it was hard, not impossible. But you two better damned well trot out your wit-nesses. Whether we had laws fifty years ago or not, we do have them now. Now—while your Apache friend is certainly entitled to be out on bail pending further legal developments, the one thing I *ain't* going to do today is hold a bond hear-ing. I think he's as safe as he's going to be right where he's at. When all them riders come down out of the hills, and I reckon that will be this afternoon at the latest—on account of the news will be out that Orrin's got him—we'll sort of take their temperature. *Then* we'll decide if it's safe for Bishop to be out and about."

Corey's heart fell into a sick stomach. Harold would have

to be told, and Corey would have to tell him. "Judge Farrell, Sheriff Langley hasn't let me see his prisoner."

"That I can fix, and will." He reached for a piece of paper on the corner of the desk, dipped a pen in an inkwell, and scribbled something. "Take this and get out of here. And leave the way you came in. I'm going to get a bite at Carmi's and then head home. I don't want to be bothered by any more of this today."

Outside, Jim said, "I'm going back to the office. I want to find out what, if anything, is happening up in Santa Fe."

Terence Farrell had emerged from the front door of the courthouse and was walking toward Carmen's across the plaza.

Corey headed for the entrance to the jail.

"The food's terrible, but otherwise they've treated me all right. Langley was at me for a couple of hours trying to get me to give him a confession, but other than that they've left me strictly alone."

"Did you tell him where you and your boys were when the raid on San Isidro occurred?" Corey asked.

"No. Thought I'd better save that for the judge."

"Good. It might be nice to know something the other side doesn't know, just once."

It was clear that Harold was trying to wear a bright countenance, but behind the smile Corey could see the ravages the night had left. "When can you get me out of here, Junior?"

"There's a little problem, Harold. Judge Farrell won't hold a hearing on your bail today." Would it be wise to worry Harold with just why the little judge had balked? As Corey pondered the question Harold said something that made him realize he simply had to tell him of Farrell's fears.

"Well, maybe I should just walk out of here. I sure could have last night. That cell door was as wide open all night long as you found it a minute ago when you came in. Nobody was in Langley's office, either. If they want me so bad they sure ought to take better care of me. I would have left, except that I had no idea where I might find you and Lucy." The insouciant Mimbreño imp was back again. Hadn't he figured out what was going on here?

Corey's blood stopped running, but his mind raced like the wind back across the years. Mangas! . . . and countless other prisoners killed in custody. They wanted Harold to make a try for freedom. The story would be the age-old one: Shot while trying to escape.

Now the first anger Corey had known since all this began finally came, inundating him like the flow of molten rock in the *malpais* so many centuries ago, stopping his breath as surely as if he had been choked. For all the anguish of it, he felt pumped up and, for the first time, strong.

He had to get Harold out of here before tonight— somehow. The judge had been pretty final, and he wasn't by any indication the type to change his mind easily or to have it changed for him. To do that they would have to hear from the Rio Concho.

He gave Harold all the bad news then, pressing on him the absolute imperative of not making any foolish moves. "Don't play games with Orrin or his people, Harold. Get that smile off your face. There's far too much at stake here for you to indulge yourself by showing off."

"All right, Junior. I'll be good, but it won't be easy."

"Promise?"

"Yeah."

Corey closed the barred door to the cell when he left, avoiding Harold's eyes as he did it. A key was in the cell door lock. Sure, left there deliberately. He turned it, again avoiding Harold's eyes.

He dropped the key on the desk in front of Langley.

"You keep my friend back there locked up and as safe as

if he were in God's pocket, Orrin," he said. "If anything happens to him, I'll kill you."

He couldn't believe he had said it; he *could* believe he meant it.

The gross, heavy-lidded sheriff was wedged into the wooden swivel chair behind the desk. He seemed to flinch a little and managed a vacuous smile, but he said nothing as Corey stalked out into Frontera Street.

The Duryea hadn't moved.

At the office of the *News* Corey found that Lucy had come to work with Ellen Stafford, but she wasn't with the newspaperwoman at the moment.

"I begged her to stay with my mother," Ellen said, "but she insisted. She wants to be near where things affecting her brother are happening. I sure can understand. Lord, but she's a lovely girl, Corey. I should be jealous, but I'm not."

"Thank you, Ellen. Where is she now?"

"In Jim's office. They've had a long talk."

"Is Jim still with her?"

"No. He left about ten minutes ago, after he got a telephone call. He was pretty excited about something, but he didn't tell anyone what it was."

Had Tom and the padre come back down the valley with news, and was Jim on his way to meet them, perhaps at Farrell's chambers? Not likely. Farrell wasn't there now. Corey had been right next door and, with all the sheriff's office and jail windows wide open, would have seen them or heard something. Besides, there had been a telephone call. There couldn't have been one from the Concho, as Jim had pointed out earlier.

Curious as Corey was, it would have to wait; he wanted to see Lucy first, even though it meant telling her Harold would in all likelihood have to spend one more night in jail.

Ellen had set Lucy up on the divan under the windows

with a copy of *Godey's Lady's Book*. Lucy looked up when Corey entered the office, dropped the magazine, and rose and moved toward him in something like the magical way she had risen to the saddle the night he had ridden to the school to get her. She folded herself into his arms.

"I know it's only been two hours, Corey, but it seems forever."

"For me, too."

Without leaving his arms she leaned away from him and studied his face. "The news isn't good, is it?" she said.

"No, it isn't." He told her everything then, not only the things he knew, but those he felt as well. She took it well, or seemed to. He only knew that in the long run this was the way it had to be between the two of them, nothing held back, nothing hidden, nothing guarded.

When he finished she said, "Thank you, Corey. It's better for me to know what we're up against." She put her hand to his cheek. "You look tired."

"I am—a little. But there will be no rest for a while, for any of us. The first and perhaps the only thing we can hope for at the moment is a good result from Tom's trip up the Concho with Father Strelski."

"Can I see Harold?"

"I would rather get him out before you do. Then, if Judge Farrell has to bind him over—and, even with favorable testimony from the immigrants, he may have to—we can wait things out at the X-Bar-7."

"We've got to get news to Mama, Corey. She doesn't even know yet that Harold's left his hideout."

Corey certainly didn't relish that, but Lucy was right.

He was on the point of calling Ellen to see if she could send someone out to the ranch with a message when Jim exploded through the office door.

"We've got our first real break in a week, Corey!"

"Tom and the padre are back?"

"Not yet. This is every bit as big, tough. An hour ago I got a telephone call from Eloy Montoya. If you had worries about where he stood, forget them. He's with us all the way! We shouldn't have doubted him for a second. More important at the moment, though, is that he sent this down on the coach from Santa Fe." He held up a large, pebble-grained envelope sealed at the flap with wax, broke it open, and extracted a smaller one he handed to Corey. "Read this! I already know what it says."

On the face of the smaller envelope someone had typed:

Fair Copy of a Letter
from Mr. Matthew Kessler to Senator Horace Lattner.
Dated Fourteenth Day of June, A.D. 1900.
Made by María Elena Vargas.

Corey opened the envelope. He glanced at Lucy before he unfolded the two sheets inside. She was impassive. Perhaps she didn't realized how much the rededication of Eloy Montoya meant. Small wonder. With Harold still in jail, nothing else truly mattered yet.

The letter, too, was typed. He read it aloud.

Dear Senator:

I done everything just like you said. I've got my people from Chicago all ready to move into the Mescalero timber just as soon as your committee asks Washington for them new laws. What with them "Indians" hitting San Isidro last night we got the greasers about ready to back us, too.

Our "friend" here in Chupadera County says he knows what you been up against with Turner, McPherson, Montoya, and Lane. He says that you know where the votes are to turn things our way and what they will cost. He also says he will come up with all the cash you need.

Matthew Kessler

When Corey finished reading, Jim spoke up. "The original was in Kessler's hand and was signed."

"Kessler's hand? How does Eloy know that?" The big block K on Kessler he had seen on the door in the San Isidro compound loomed in his mind.

"He somehow found copies of reports Kessler made to Santa Fe when he was under contract to Fort Stanton as a sutler some time back."

"Where is the original now?" Corey asked.

"Still in Horace Lattner's files. At the moment only Eloy, you and I, Lucy here, of course, and the two people responsible for us getting a look at it know this copy has come into our possession."

"How did it?"

"Do you remember those young friends of Eloy's?"

"Yes. Vigil and Cruz, wasn't it?"

"María Elena Vargas is Javier Cruz's married sister. She works in Horace Lattner's office in the capital. She knew her brother had an interest in Lattner's Senate committee's proceedings. Fine young woman. This will cost her her job, of course."

Something still seemed wrong. This astonishing letter should have brought elation, a sense of triumph. Instead, there came the same nagging feeling of ambush Corey had felt since Harold, Lucy, and he had ridden into Black Springs yesterday.

"Jim . . ." he started, "why would Kessler put anything as absolutely damning as this in writing? He's not the most astute of the people involved, but even he must have known there was the strong possibility that the wrong eyes would see it, as they have. More to the point, why would Gideon let him send this letter?"

"Lots of reasons. Gideon obviously didn't want to be seen anywhere near Lattner himself while all this was going on, and he needed Kessler at the compound to make the raid look good. I suppose, too, that Gideon felt that it was safe in Lattner's hands. Probably, too, he thought that if it ever did come to light in any public way, everything would be over and done with. Hey! You don't look nearly as happy as this should make you, Corey. Don't look a gift horse in the mouth."

"I won't. Are we free to use this any way we'd like?"

"Yes. It will be a matter of record tomorrow morning, after Eloy delivers another copy to Governor Otero. We've got to get to Farrell pronto. This might be all it takes to get Harold out, but it wouldn't hurt a bit if Tom and the padre brought in their witnesses as well."

Then Corey realized what was troubling him. Even if Gideon hadn't written the letter himself, it carried his signal, the same signal of desperation the note to Farrell carried. When a man like Gideon Bainbridge found himself in any kind of fix, he didn't fold, only became more dangerous. He must certainly have divined that sooner or later Sierra's plan would fail. Perhaps he didn't care. Perhaps this was *his* plan.

Something else. Corey knew where he ultimately had to turn the rage he had felt when he left Harold and Orrin Langley. The prospect paralyzed him.

"I suppose we've won, Jim," he said, "but only in Santa Fe. We haven't won where Gideon is concerned."

"No. It doesn't make up for Tony's death—or Pete Jandeezi's. But at least we can get Harold free."

"Farrell left the courthouse a little while ago. We've got to find him and get a writ."

"You heard what he said. We're not to bother him any more today."

Corey felt a welcome surge of the same anger that had come over him in Langley's jail. "We can't let that stop us. Let's collar him and get Harold out now!"

Corey, with Jim and Lucy on his heels, found Farrell still at Carmen's.

The judge didn't even look up from his meal when Corey walked to his table, but with his face deep in a bowel of *posole* spoke instead to the graying cook and proprietress of the *cocina*.

"Goddamn it, Carmi! You know I ain't to be pestered when I'm eating. Tell these good folk I'm through working for the day. Give them coffee or whatever they want and put it on my tab, but keep them away from me."

Corey didn't see the smiles and winks that passed between Carmi and Jim as he took a step closer to the judge's table. He dropped the copy of Kessler's letter in front of him.

"Read this, *Your Honor!*" Even in Cuba Corey had never given an order with quite such a bite in it. Farrell looked up at him, and his tiny eyes narrowed until they almost closed. He bent his head to his food again, but after only one more spoonful pulled his napkin from under his chin, wiped his firm, small mouth, reached for the letter, and pulled his glasses from the breast pocket of his coat.

"You sound like an echo from the past, young Mr. Lane. I don't suppose you'll care much for this, but just for a second there I thought you were your old man come to life."

19

The dinner Ellen Stafford's mother gave in the little white house on Stanton Street turned almost festive after Lucy, Jim, and Corey arrived with Harold. That it didn't quite echo with joyous triumph for Corey, though, was perhaps due to his memory of how close they had already been to victory in Santa Fe a week earlier only to suffer a bitter setback, and perhaps to the fact that they hadn't yet heard from Tom or Padre Stan. Jim had left word at the *News* about where they would be, and Corey kept listening for a knock at the door. None came.

Farrell, as Corey and Jim had hoped, had issued a release order for Harold, but in a keen display of annoyance hauled him right across the alley to the courthouse for a hearing that bound him over for trial in another week. Lucy went with them, drawing stares from the few Concho men who had apparently eaten bagged lunches on the lawn and from the Black Springs folk who had come to the courthouse throughout the day out of curiosity. The looks of the cotton-clad farmers were noncommittal, but there was discernible animosity here and there among the anglos. Most of the onlookers followed them into Terence Farrell's courtroom. Some grumbled at his decision.

"Until the county prosecutor drops the charges, Mr. Bishop, you're still under indictment," the judge had said when he made his ruling. "The stuff Mr. Lane and Mr. McPherson brought in is evidence, but it ain't proof. I will turn you loose on your own recognizance provided your friend Mr. Lane will keep tabs on you. Now, don't you run and hide, or this court will get mighty vexed, and when it's vexed it's something to be reckoned with." Corey breathed a sigh of relief that the judge's pique hadn't mounted to animosity when they all but dragged him from Carmen's restaurant.

Harold's behavior in front of Farrell had been impeccable, and Corey, who had feared that the satisfaction of getting out of Orrin Langley's hands might have brought on an attack of flippancy, was grateful.

Once out of the courthouse, though, Harold caused a fuss by announcing that he would leave first thing in the morning for the hideout at Big Bear Spring.

"Harold!" Lucy chided him. "You'd be getting Corey in trouble, never mind yourself."

"I only want to see how John and Chino and the others are doing."

"Don't mess with me, *brother*," Corey said. "You're coming to the X-Bar-7 with Lucy and me."

"All right, all right. I had no intention of running away."

"It would look like running to Judge Farrell, though," Corey said.

"When will we go to your mother's, then?"

"We'll leave soon after supper as seems decent. It will be after dark when we get there, but I don't think it wise to spend any nights in Black Springs that aren't absolutely necessary."

Jim brought a bottle of wine to the Staffords' and Corey carved the roast Mrs. Stafford served. The lady of the house had seen troubles in her time, too, Corey remembered. Her late husband, Granby, older brother of Findlay Stafford, who owned the general store, had been the first Corey Lane's implacable foe in Black Springs. He had outlived Corey's father, but his last years had been dismal, empty ones. The two Stafford women were gracious ladies, and Corey would never have known of the rift between his and Ellen's fathers if his research into the great raid of '79, and his subsequent questioning of Jim, hadn't led him to it. It had been Granby who had brought the charges against Corey, Senior that had led to his exile with Victorio.

Corey wondered why he was remembering all this. He should have been celebrating, if decorously, as the others were.

For a few minutes after dinner Ellen played the piano, and as he turned pages for her, he mused again about the kind of home Lucy and he could eventually make. He caught her eyes once, and it seemed to him that much the same thoughts must be running through her head.

When the little recital was done, Corey excused himself and went to Kelly's for the horses and to check the Winchester out of old man Kelly's locked storage room. When he returned, Lucy and Harold were waiting for him on the veranda of the cottage with Jim and the Staffords.

The good-byes were brief. Ellen promised to come someday soon to the reservation and visit Lucy's school. "There might be a good article in it for my page," she said. "And you, Lucy—please do come down to Black Springs once in a while. I'd like to get to know you better." Suddenly Ellen turned red. "I'm sorry, Lucy. Forgive me. I simply wasn't thinking. I know coming into town would always be awkward for you." There it was again. It always brought nausea, even coming so gently from someone as decent as Ellen Stafford was.

Corey was still strangely uneasy. The thoughts of ambush hadn't quite left him, but he had to stop running scared. Harold was free. The trial next week would be a mere formality, whether Tom brought results down from the upper Concho or not. Sierra Development Company's grab for the Mescalero timber was now a thing of the past. Eloy Montoya, whose goodwill Corey had desired so devoutly for reasons quite above and beyond the particular considerations they had faced in the past weeks, had rallied to them and helped them thwart their enemies. Perhaps Gideon as a problem would fade as quickly and completely.

Soon he could turn his thoughts solely on Lucy and him— and their life together.

He brought himself up short. It was all too easy. He had forgotten there was far more at stake here than a few thousand board feet of lumber. Had he been conveniently pushing away the deaths of Tony, Pete—and Pepe?

No deus ex machina would settle those dark matters.

Although his first plan had been to leave for the X-Bar-7 immediately after Harold's release, he had agreed to go to the Staffords' for dinner readily enough when Jim relayed Ellen's invitation. Leaving town after supper meant there would be fewer townspeople about to watch the three of them ride out of Black Springs, and as they traveled toward the plaza it seemed at first as if he had made the prudent choice; Stanton Street was empty. But when they reached the corner at Frontera he found the intersection uncommonly crowded for the twilight hour. Men, women, and children crowded the sides of the dirt street leading to the plaza, and instead of wandering in the several helter-skelter directions of ordinary groups of pedestrians, they seemed to be moving in one steady flow toward the center of the town. As they guided their animals through the gathering knots of walkers, it soon became apparent that far from becoming objects of curiosity as Corey had feared they might, no one was paying them the slightest attention.

"Something's up," Harold said.

"Sure looks like it," Corey said. "You and Lucy wait here for a bit while I check it out." He urged his horse forward in the stream of people, whose pace seemed to quicken as they neared the courthouse, and he began to catch bits and pieces of conversation above his animal's hoofbeats and the almost surflike sounds of the boots and high-buttoned shoes rising from the caliche.

"You reckon it's over, then?"

"I expect so. They won't have no more stomach for it up there."

"It's the last time any number of them been in town since '79."

"All of them? Every last one of them red . . ." The last speaker's voice trailed away from him.

Then, far across the plaza as he neared it, Corey saw Kessler, mounted and out in front of another rider, the two of them just nosing in from Estancia Street. They led a pack train of six horses, all loaded.

For a moment it was as if Corey were back in that first time he had seen the Sierra man, the day he had ridden to the rocks and had been stopped by Harold. Kessler was dressed the same; the freight train moved at the same deliberate, plodding pace.

Except . . .

Except that the beasts of burden Corey looked at now with eyes that seemed almost wrenched from their sockets weren't mules but horses, and the bundles lashed to their backs weren't provisions or boxes of supplies or surveyors' instruments.

They were bodies.

Apaches. Young Apaches. He saw stocky John Ditsa and tiny, foxlike Chato, and the three whose names he never caught—and he saw Chino. He saw blood, dried and caked on the *tl'aakal* kirtles.

The bodies moved and heaved from the exertions of the horses in a grim counterfeit of life.

20

"The plaza is mobbed, and I don't like the look of things," he told Lucy and Harold when he returned to them. "We'll take Hidalgo Street to Mesquite Alley and go out of town the back way."

"What's going on up there?" Harold asked.

Corey's stomach rebelled, but he somehow managed to control it. "Couldn't tell. Too many people milling around. Probably there to protest your release. We'll play it safe." He could see the Mimbreño's curiosity was building rapidly, and he threw in another hook. "We shouldn't hang around here, anyway. We've got to get to the X-Bar-7 and put Ana's mind at ease about everything. She's probably frantic by now. I don't want her getting restless and taking off for Cow Camp Creek again." At least it wasn't another lie.

"I guess you're right, as usual," Harold said.

Good. The mention of Ana had turned the trick. From the look of Lucy perhaps he had satisfied her, too, and in ten minutes they were out of town and back on the south road to the X-Bar-7 that cut through the gentle, grassy swales below Sierra Blanca. Twice Corey almost told them what he had seen in that terrible moment in the plaza, and twice he fought the impulse off. He had to get Harold to the ranch before he told him. With Ana, Lucy, and Virgie to help him, and with nightfall and distance helping, too, there might be some small possibility of controlling his friend—in the short run. Long term, there was no chance at all. The only thing he could hope for was that when Harold learned what had happened and turned wild, there might be something he could help Harold do about Kessler that would both square with the law and satisfy the lust for vengeance that would doubtless build to a fire storm in the Mimbreño.

By the time they rode past the faint old trace that led up to the mesa where Corey's father had died, the sun had gone down and the tops of the San Andres west of the *malpais* were a purple sawtooth against a still, orange sky. Even with the turmoil surging through him he couldn't help but marvel, as he had since childhood, at the strange habits of light in this awesome, lonely country. A thin blanket of cloud stretched clear across the Ojos Negros Basin, from near the western slope of the great white mountain to the Black Range hidden in the distance beyond the unseen river, and the last rays of the sun beat against that blanket and angled down again to the immense pastures on either side of them. The rangeland was incandescent, even though no direct sunlight touched it.

They were on X-Bar-7 land now, and it brought Corey a little comfort. He needed every bit he could find now, would need much more later on.

The day that had begun so well had turned disastrous, heartbreaking. They had come so close to a decent resolution of this sad affair, even closer today than last week in the capital. If only Eloy's message had arrived a mere twenty-four hours earlier, Harold wouldn't have spent that one humiliating and by all odds hazardous night in Orrin Langley's jail, and Kessler would not have had a warrant to take with him to the mountains on his mission of murder. Without knowing any of the details beyond what little he had learned from the conversations he overheard at the edge of the crowd after the pack train with its grisly cargo had crossed the plaza to the jail, Corey knew in his heart that that was exactly what had gone on up at Big Bear Spring—murder. Harold's youngsters must have been taken completely by surprise, probably in sleep. The best mountain men in the county couldn't have gotten into the hideout if a lookout had been posted, as one would certainly have been during the daylight hours.

But how had Kessler and his butchers found their way into the encampment even knowing where it was, and even if Harold's tiny band had left the rocky overlook unguarded? The juniper thicket was as secret a doorway as he had ever seen.

Had one of the boys, Chato perhaps, who appeared to have been Harold's regular messenger, talked to someone? Who could he have talked to who would have told Kessler, and even if he had, wouldn't Sam Naaki, too, have learned of their whereabouts and gotten there well ahead of the Sierra man and his deadly posse?

It didn't really matter. The young Apaches were dead, all of them.

In the long run, Harold was dead, too.

Corey didn't know how it would come about or how long it would take, but he knew it to be as inevitable as that dying sun coming up again tomorrow morning.

After clearing town he had let Harold take the lead, with Lucy riding between the two of them, and now he studied the bobbing back of Harold Bishop.

Harold was singing. This friend, this brother, was the very essence of life—free, happy, lusty, unfettered life, life as anyone had every right to expect in this magnificent country. In any just and orderly universe he would stay that way.

But the harrowing events of the past three weeks had now thoroughly persuaded Corey Lane that there was only a minimum of justice to be had, and precious little order. The rest was chaos.

Farrell had said there were laws in the Territory now. Maybe the little judge actually believed it. But there weren't real laws; there were rules, codes, yes, and habits, but not laws. There could be no laws that counted as long as men like Gideon strode this land. Some other kind of man was needed before there ever could be laws.

Virgie, holding a lantern, met them at the door with Ana, who flew to her children, trying to embrace both of them at once.

There was something frantic in Virgie's eyes, and she nodded toward the end of the *portál*. Corey took the lantern from her, set it on the tiled floor, and moved to where she had nodded.

"Sam Naaki was here late this afternoon, Corey," Virgie said. "He told me about the massacre at Big Bear Spring."

"How did he find out?"

"One of his men spotted the posse moving up Sinuoso Creek near sundown yesterday. By the time he got the word to Sam it was dark. They heard a lot of firing, but they couldn't tell where from. They picked them up again this morning coming down out of the canyon—with the dead boys."

"Does Ana know?"

"Yes."

"She'll tell Harold?"

"Doesn't he know?"

"No." Corey told her of the scene in the Black Springs plaza and his decision to reach home before he broke the news to either Lucy or Harold. "See if you can persuade Ana to keep it to herself for just a bit longer. She must know as well as we do the effect it would have on him."

"Corey," Virgie said. "There's something else Sam told me. On the pretense that they were looking for Harold with that warrant for his arrest, Kessler split five men off from the posse and sent them to Cow Camp Creek. They burned Ana's house. Sam tried to stop them, but he only had one of his men with him. They wounded Sam's deputy and Sam was pretty badly beaten. He could hardly make it down here, but he was determined to see you and he thought you were here. I've put him up in the bunkhouse."

Yes, they had fooled Sam and his men, all right. Even the things Corey did well turned out badly. His friends could use a better friend.

"I have to tell Harold. I'll wait until morning, but I have to tell him."

"I suppose you do, Corey. Once we get the Bishops moved in I'll go down and tell Sam to be sure to stay out of sight until tomorrow."

She put her hand on his shoulder and squeezed it, then moved back to where the Bishops were still greeting each other.

"Mrs. Lane," he heard Harold say, "thanks for looking after Ana. Now—please talk that son of yours into letting us go home."

21

Corey arose before any of the others the next morning. He went to the gun racks in the study and gathered all the weapons stacked there, even the old percussion firearms left over from Grandfather Jason's time, including the Colt revolving rifle Mike Calico had fought with at Apache Pass, and of course Tony's Winchester, which had been a troubling companion to Corey these past few days.

It took three trips to cart them all to the tack room next to the bunkhouse. A sleepy-eyed Luís Mendoza, Virgie's head wrangler, roused from slumber and, still trying to button his trousers, helped Corey hide them in the tack room under a pile of steer hides and was sworn to secrecy. Corey had to count on Luís and the other hands to look after their own sidearms.

"One more thing, Luís," he said when they finished. "I want you to move all the working mounts to the small corral at the upper ranch. I don't want a riding horse even near the main house. Take the whole crew with you, and then check in with me tomorrow morning."

"All the horses, Corey?"

"Every last one of them. Sam Naaki's, too."

The wrangler looked baffled.

Corey didn't explain. It would take too long. Harold could leave the ranch, but he would have to go on foot, unarmed.

Corey looked in on Sam Naaki, but the lawman was still asleep, a bruised face turned sideways on a pillow Virgie had brought down from the main house.

Back in the house he fixed coffee, carried a cup to the sitting room, and settled into the couch facing the fireplace. It was still pitch dark, but he didn't light a lamp. The first rays of the sun would soon slant down from the top of high Cuchillo, bringing a day he didn't much care to see. More bad ones than good ones had dawned lately.

Moving and hiding the X-Bar-7's small arsenal had, of course, been an exercise in futility, but at least Corey felt as if he had done *something*. If Harold wanted a gun there were probably plenty up on the Mescalero that would be his for the asking, certainly any number from the families of the dead boys. Even Sam would be powerless to prevent his getting one. But at least Harold would have to hoof it to the reservation and no weapon would come from the X-Bar-7.

For that matter, if a man wanted to kill badly enough, he wouldn't feel he had to rely only on a Winchester or a Colt, Corey supposed. The lance hanging above the fireplace and just beginning to become visible in the first weak light would do very nicely, indeed *had* for someone a century and a half ago. The stains on the still wicked point weren't only rust. He himself didn't know the consuming lust for blood that some men knew, hadn't ever known it, even in Cuba. He could at least understand it now—the companion need for vengeance, anyway.

But he had to got his mind back on the nasty chore still facing him: telling Harold.

He would have to beg Harold—on his knees, if need be—to stand trial before Judge Farrell next week. There should be nothing for him to fear from that quarter, with all the information now in Farrell's hands or soon to be there. When the charges against him were dropped, Harold could take what revenge he could find *within* the framework of the law, not at odds with it. The way the land lay now, Kessler would never have to answer for the killings of John, Chino, and the others. *He* had acted within the law, even though his sole intent from the outset had been murder.

But the killing of Tony Bishop might still prove another matter. It was, of course, useless for Corey to wish now that he had appropriated the note from Kessler to Gideon which he had found in the library at Tres Piedras—together with Tony's journal. The letter Kessler had written to Horace Lattner, while damning enough to anyone who knew the matter from the inside out and convincing enough to bring about the release of Harold without bail, was still too ambiguous to be offered as evidence in Farrell's court or any other in the Territory. They needed more to bring Kessler, not to mention Gideon, to justice for the killings of Tony and Pete Jandeezi. That is, if Corey *wanted* to bring Gideon to justice.

With the aid of his friends in Santa Fe, Eloy Montoya had apparently built a fair to middling case for collusion, even conspiracy, between Sierra Development and the senators in the camp of Horace Lattner, but it loomed as more of a political matter than a full-blown indictable crime at this point, and even if the Concho man had somehow succeeded in thwarting Lattner—and with him Gideon—on the matter of the timberlands for the moment, it wouldn't be long before they, or others like them, began again. The predators were relentless. Corey knew that now. They hadn't been stopped, just checked. To stop them would require a continued effort over a long, long time, perhaps forever. It would mean that good men would have to stop doing nothing.

"Corey." It was Lucy. She was in a nightdress and robe of Virgie's. Her long hair was loose about her shoulders, framing her face in a new way, making her more lovely in the first light of the sun now coming through the high slit windows than he had ever seen her. But lovely as she was, the pain could not be hidden. She knew about Harold's boys; he could see it in her eyes.

"Did you sleep well?" he said after he had gotten to his feet and taken her in his arms.

"Hardly at all."

"I wish we could have been together."

"I do, too. I didn't know I could need someone so much."

"I wouldn't have cared what they all thought."

She smiled at him, then her face turned serious, dark and suddenly drawn. "Mama had a bad night, too."

"She told you, didn't she? About the boys, and about the house?"

"Yes."

"Will she tell Harold?"

"She's leaving that up to you, Corey. She knows what it will bring about, how crazy it will make him, and she doesn't want it to happen in yours and Virgie's home because of her."

"You should begin to think of this as your home, Lucy."

There was a soft, warm laugh, with perhaps just the slightest touch of rue in it. "Isn't it a bit early for that? You can't be thinking of me now. You have too much to do."

"It seems to me that everything I could possibly do I've already done, and I've done just about all of it wrong."

"That's not true, Corey."

He spread his hands. "Yes, it is. I haven't taken a strong enough stand on things with the one man I should have. I haven't known how to go about it. Or perhaps, to be more truthful, I lacked the courage."

"I don't believe that for a second! Being sensitive to the past and having a regard for old ties and loyalties isn't a lack of courage." She eased herself from his arms, turned away from him, and took a small, seemingly uncertain step toward the fireplace. He could see her slender back swell under the robe as she drew a breath. "When I said you have a lot to do, I was thinking of the talk Mr. McPherson and I had the other day before I went to Ellen's.

"He told me how many times he and Gideon have asked you to run for office in the Territory. You should, you know. It's more important than ever now. We—all of us, on and off the Mescalero—need people like you in Black Springs and Santa Fe."

"I don't think that's for me, Lucy. I just want to do my work—and be with you."

She started to say something and stopped. Like him, she must have heard other people stirring in the house, and he reached for her while he still had the chance. She came back to him for the embrace he offered, held him tightly, fiercely, as if she feared he might get away.

"I love you, Lucy. As soon as we get Harold out of this I want us to get married."

Again she was about to say something and stopped when the sound of footsteps echoed from the long hall leading to the bedrooms. They broke apart, but slowly, longingly.

It was Ana. From the look of her she had struggled through a tortured night. As with Lucy, her hair was unbound, but it didn't frame the same sort of face at all, except for the pain. Ana Bishop had become an old woman overnight. She went to Corey.

"We mustn't tell Harold about the boys and the house *at all*. It will fill him with too much hate."

Something inside him cried out, *Yes, yes, let it all go unsaid.*

"We can't *not* tell him, Ana. The hate would be turned on us when he found out."

"We can pretend we didn't know."

"Mama!" Lucy walked to her mother and took her in her arms. "You know we can't do that. Trust Corey." The older woman buried her face in her daughter's shoulder, lifted it at last.

"I trust him, Lucy. He's the only friend we have among the *ind'aa*."

She trusted him? A lot of good that had done her thus far. Oh, how he was tempted to heed her and not tell Harold, not until they went to town for trial, at least. It had to be done by that time, of course; ironically, Kessler would be a witness for the prosecution, and even if the immigrants testified on Harold's behalf, something he wasn't dead sure of yet, the whereabouts of the young men who were alleged to have made the raid on San Isidro would somehow become central to the whole affair. No, the idea of keeping the young Mimbreño in the dark was patently absurd. The hands here at the X-Bar-7, and indeed every rider in the basin, must know all about it by now. The news must have reached the remotest corner of the Mescalero, too, and Harold Bishop could be the only soul in Chupadera County still living in ignorance about what had happened two nights ago at Big Bear Spring.

Ana was saying, "I know you're both right. But Corey will have to tell him. I can't."

"I'll tell him," he said. "Right after breakfast."

That much was settled. But there was still the central mystery that had plagued Corey since he had seen Kessler's pack train of death in the Black Springs plaza. "Ana. Aside from Harold and his boys, did anyone but Lucy, you, and me know about Harold's hideout? Sam, or any of the boys' families?"

She stared at him for a moment and then began shaking her head, the movement slow at first, but then increasing in speed until her features were almost a blur. Finally she stopped, and then the sobs came, sobs so powerful they shook both women when Lucy took Ana in her arms again.

Had she broken? Had that great strength at last deserted her?

Corey was grateful he didn't have time to consider that too deeply when Virgie entered the sitting room.

She looked at the two Bishops with a face showing the same helplessness his must be showing. Then she turned to Corey. "Harold was still sound asleep when I passed his room."

"I'm not surprised. I don't believe he got a wink while Orrin had him in that cell."

"María is fixing breakfast. There's nothing we can do this morning that can't be done better if we get some food inside us."

At the sound of Virgie's voice Ana had regained a small measure of composure, but she shook her head again. "I couldn't eat anything, Virgie."

"You can sit and watch us, then," Virgie said. "We're going to eat in the dining room, and we're going to do it right. We're not going to give in to any of this. We'll let Harold sleep as long as he likes. María might even be persuaded to give him his breakfast in bed. She always had a soft spot for him while he was growing up."

It was as if her words had restored sanity. They trooped into the dining room where a smiling María Gonzales was setting the table. María, almost seventy now, had smiled through a lot of bad times at the X-Bar-7.

Virgie had meant it when she said they were going to do it right. The table was covered with the lace cloth she had bought in Florence on that trip abroad after the first Corey Lane's death, and María was laying out Grandmother Alicia's silver service that Corey couldn't remember seeing on this table since Jim McPherson's fiftieth birthday just before the war.

Virgie certainly had infallible instincts. Even Ana, despite her protests, ate a little bit of María's *huevos rancheros*, and Corey astonished himself by helping himself to seconds. María's coffee was immeasurably better, too, than the dark bitter brew he had made himself in the kitchen after the trip to the bunkhouse and the tack room, and while he didn't feel a whole lot better about what the day would ultimately bring, he could feel the first feeble pulses of survival. But he did want to get the telling of the tragedy to Harold over with.

When they finished breakfast he decided he had better get down to the bunkhouse and see to Sam Naaki.

"Never even heard of it before yesterday. The place was a Bishop family secret," Sam said when Corey asked him who might know about Big Bear Spring and the gateway to it. He was sitting up in the bunk, naked to the waist. Nothing looked broken, and he had assured Corey he was already on the mend, but Kessler's five riders had done a thorough job on him. "There ain't much game in that part of the reservation, and unless a Mescalero is in the lumber business, nothing takes him up that way. I looked the hideout over before I got called back to Cow Camp Creek when Kessler's men made their move on Ana's place. I never would have found it if they hadn't set fire to everything there, too, after they killed the *elchinnde*. The smoke led us into Harold's camp, but it still wasn't easy."

The policeman shuddered, but he wasn't shuddering from the welts and contusions Corey could see on his chest and shoulders. He must have been remembering what he had found at Big Bear Spring. And Sam hadn't even seen the worst of it, the dead boys themselves. "You better keep an eye on Harold, Corey," he said.

"I'm trying to do just that, Sam. He doesn't know about it yet, not the killings or about the house."

"Well, when you or somebody tells him, you better be

ready. He'll turn into one helluva loco Mimbreño. Hey! Maybe somebody better keep an eye on me when I'm up and around again. None of them kids was a relative of mine, but their folk are all good friends. Somebody sure better keep an eye on those families, too. If I was running things in Chupadera County I'd damned well put a big guard on that place of Kessler's at San Isidro. I don't think even the council can stop a war if them families start to get excited."

Corey brought Sam up to date on everything else and told him of hiding the guns and moving the horses out.

"Sorry about yours, Sam, but you're in no shape to ride out of here, anyway. Don't rush. Stay until you're absolutely fit again. We're going to need you before this is over."

"Tell me something, Corey. I thought Gideon Bainbridge was a friend. I worked for him a couple of seasons when I was a boy, and I swear by *Ussén* I never knew a better man, red, white, or Mexican. Why is he in on this?"

"I've asked myself the same thing a million times, Sam. There's been no answer, and it's driving me absolutely crazy. Maybe we read him wrong all along. I know damned well I did."

When he returned to the main house he found Virgie, Ana, and Lucy in the sitting room again.

"I won't need money, Virgie," Ana was saying. "We help each other up there, and I understand the council has enough in their safe we can borrow on to see us through rebuilding, and until I can sell the sawmill."

"Just count on staying here, then, until you can move in again. Will you build a new house at Cow Camp Creek?"

"I've got to think about that awhile."

"Well, until you decide, this is home. For all three of you. If Harold wants to, he can ride for the X-Bar-7 again. We've still a roundup facing us, you know, and we'll need riders."

Lucy was on the couch, and Corey seated himself beside her and took her hand in his. Virgie had seen it. Her face darkened. She surely had no misgivings about him and Lucy, had she? No, that was unthinkable.

He wanted to mull over the things that might be lurking behind that funny dark look a bit more, but Harold entered the sitting room.

"Good morning!"

He looked rested and fit and was smiling broadly.

"Have you had breakfast, Harold?" Virgie asked.

"Sure have. María hasn't lost her touch in the years since I worked here." He looked at each of them in turn. "You're sure a gloomy-looking bunch. I thought we got the world by the tail with a downhill drag yesterday. Somebody want to tell me what's gone wrong?"

"Sit down, Harold," Corey said. "There are some things I have to tell you."

He didn't take his eyes from Harold's face as he told him. The smile vanished quickly, of course, but nothing took its place. Corey might as well have been talking to the Chiricahua shield he could see out of the corner of his eye. Harold had slipped completely away from them, into one of those blank states Corey remembered all too well. When he finished he waited for what his friend had to say. It was a long wait.

Lucy took her hand from his. He had forgotten he had been holding it. Ana coughed. The tall clock in the corner of the sitting room sounded as if it were at the detonation point.

"Corey."

Even watching him, Corey hadn't seen Harold's lips move, but he heard him clearly enough. The coldness of the Mimbreño's voice was like an icicle plunged into his stomach. "How did Kessler know where the camp was and how to get into it? Only the boys, Ana, Lucy, and I knew about it. And *you*."

"Harold!"

"Did *you* tell them where we were, Corey? Was it your way

of making double sure that I turned myself in to Orrin Langley?"

"You can't possibly be thinking that. I'm your friend, your brother."

"No white man is my brother."

Corey could hear his own heart beating now, close to bursting, and the rage that had taken hold of him briefly only twice before took hold of him now and shook him. There was a focus to the rage this time. Gideon.

Gideon had a lot to answer for, and Corey vowed silently that sooner or later he would demand those answers.

Harold stood up. He took his eyes from Corey once to glance at the lance on the wall above the fireplace, and for the briefest of seconds Corey was sure Harold would go for the ancient weapon and come at him.

Then, with an anguished cry, Ana got to her feet and moved between her son and Corey.

"It wasn't Corey's fault, Harold," she said. "It was mine. I let someone know about Big Bear Spring."

Harold stared at her. Then he turned and left the sitting room. Ana looked at each of them as if begging something from them, and then raced after him.

As she ran she uttered a low, keening moan, the sound of someone in agony too deep for words.

22

 "How long has he been gone?" Jim McPherson asked.

"Three whole days."

"And no sign of him?"

"Not even a shadow. Virgie's had every hand at the X-Bar-7 out looking for him. They're riding day and night. Unless she calls off the hunt pretty quick, we won't have a roundup."

"Do you think he's still alive?"

"I expect so, Jim. Mimbreños are pretty good in the high desert. He sweet-talked María out of enough grub to get him up into the Mescalero."

"You were out on his trail, too, weren't you?"

"Still would be, but I thought I'd better come in here to tell Farrell, see if we can't get a postponement."

"Tom may already have helped matters there even before he went to Santa Fe. We've got those two immigrant witnesses housed in the storeroom at Kelly's, and Tom took a statement Padre Stan had them sign to Terence's chambers. He took a copy of it up to Santa Fe for Eloy to show Otero, too."

"Will the immigrants hold up under questioning?"

"I think so. They're scared, but they're decent men. Sad that by doing the right thing they'll ruin whatever chance they had to get the land Kessler promised them. I think their testimony will really count with Farrell. But we've eventually got to produce Harold."

They were having coffee together on the veranda of the Sacramento House, waiting for the coach bringing Eloy Montoya down from Santa Fe. Actually, neither of them had touched their coffee.

Eloy's telegram had been cryptic: "Will arrive with important news for Chupadera County. Please arrange a meeting with Terence Farrell." Jim had been excited, and uncommonly sanguine, when he showed the wire to Corey in his office. Jim's spirits weren't easily dimmed in any event, Corey had learned over the years, and of course the publisher hadn't witnessed any of the heartrending scenes at the X-Bar-7. Corey wasn't going to tell him just yet what he had heard and seen himself. The trauma of the morning he told Harold about the killing of his pathetic little band of "warriors," shattering as it was to Corey personally and everyone else at the ranch, would only be a troubling sideshow to what his three friends would play out here.

Across the street, the office of Gideon Bainbridge looked as empty as Corey knew it was. From Jim's report Gideon had left town, for Tres Piedras, probably, the same evening Kessler had ridden into town with his obscene pack train.

Sam Naaki had gotten word that new attacks had occurred on the reservation, even closer in to the agency than the earlier ones. Someone had killed fifteen head of cattle above Los Árboles, and for one horrifying afternoon snipers had kept the children at the Baptist Mission School, the same school Harold attended before Tony brought him to Virgie and the X-Bar-7, huddled under their desks. Fortunately, none of the youngsters had suffered a scratch, but the council had ordered the school closed for the summer a week early. Corey was glad Lucy's school had closed when it did. According to Sam, some of the Mescaleros thought the gunners, firing from hidden vantage points in the forest, were villagers from San Isidro, out to avenge Pepe's killing. Now privy to everything Corey knew, Sam was easy to persuade where the blame really lay, but, he had added glumly, "Don't make no never mind, Corey. They won't listen to a no-account Indian policeman like me. People are beginning to talk war. Sure, we'd lose, and sure, we know it, but . . ."

Corey's mind drifted back, against his will, to the rest of the day after he told Harold about what happened at Big Bear Spring and Cow Camp Creek, and after Ana had passionately if futilely taken the blame for the discovery of Harold's high mountain camp.

When Harold had left the sitting room with Ana chasing after him, her wail of pure torment gradually diminishing, the remaining three of them had sat stunned, hardly daring to look at each other, it seemed.

Corey had finally summoned up the will to speak. "What on earth did she mean, Lucy?" he asked. "Have you any idea who she could have told? Did Kessler get to her and force it out of her somehow?"

"I don't know, but I don't think so. I was with her all the time after Harold left the house, almost every minute, right up to when you and I put her on the Agua Prieta Trail, and then she came straight here."

He looked at Virgie, who shook her head. "No one came to see her here. I know that for a fact. She didn't even tell *me* about Harold being at Big Bear Spring, just that you and

Lucy were going to see him 'in the mountains.' She hardly left her room until the three of you arrived last night."

Mysteries bred mysteries. Ana now had locked herself in her room and admitted no one but María—to bring hot water for washing up and breakfast leftovers that were carted out again untouched—not even answering Lucy or Virgie when they tapped at her door and called to her. Corey didn't try himself. If she wouldn't heed the entreaties of the two women, she certainly wouldn't answer him. Besides, his first duty had been to keep a watch on Harold.

And he had tried, Lord knew he had tried.

Under other circumstances his surveillance of the Apache might have been comical. About ten o'clock Harold quit his room, where he had holed himself up in much the same fashion Ana had in hers. He must have left by the window. Corey had guarded the corridor from the sitting room, not seeing nearly so much of Lucy as he wished, and he didn't learn that Harold had gotten loose in the ranch compound until Virgie, after a trip to the bunkhouse to minister to Sam, reported that he was prowling the corral and outbuildings, obviously on a search for a horse, and a gun, too.

Corey had raced out into the yard just in time to see the Mimbreño round the corner of the farrier's shed, and he had sprinted for it, wisely, he thought, circling to the other side to intercept Harold, only to find thin air.

Corey caught sight of Harold next on the lip of the arroyo, flitting from cottonwood to cottonwood, but by the time Corey reached the trees and the edge of the narrow, serpentine gully, Harold was gone again. The Apache must have gone right down into the dry creek bed. When they first met they had already been too old to play hide-and-seek. They were playing it now with a vengeance, and, as Corey began to feel more and more as the morning wore on, in something like desperation.

He jumped down into the arroyo himself and began to explore it foot by foot. The gully varied from six to ten feet in depth and wound for almost half a mile in the general direction of Three Rivers, but on such an erratic course that corners and bends limited sight to sometimes no more than a dozen feet. The search took more than an hour.

Harold had thoroughly outsmarted him.

The time it had taken Corey to examine the arroyo was all Harold needed to get back up the slope to the kitchen side of the house, talk María out of a packet of food and a water jug, and start toward the foothills and the Agua Prieta Trail to the Mescalero. Lucy and Virgie, who were trying to coax Ana out of hiding, hadn't even known that he had outsmarted Corey and gone.

When Corey reached the fan-shaped runout of the arroyo and saw nothing in front of him but the alkali flats leading to the *malpais* and, beyond that, the forlorn peaks of the San Andres, he realized how cleverly he had been duped.

He ran most of the way back to the house and then on to the bunkhouse and the corral. It had turned ungodly hot. There wasn't a breath of air to carry away one drop of burning sweat.

It took him more than a minute of scanning the lower eastern pastures before he picked out Harold's figure, a speck, almost *nada*, against the staggering panorama of tilted rock and wasteland rising from the X-Bar-7 toward the massif of Sierra Blanca. He had the horrible feeling that the giant mountain with its double-domed head would suddenly heave and roll its uncounted billions of tons over his friend and bury him. Harold looked so tiny, so pitiful, so defenseless, but— even from a distance of considerably more than a mile—so manically determined.

There was absolutely no point in giving chase. With both of them on foot, and with the start Harold had, there was little chance of catching an Apache raised by Tony Bishop before he reached the timberline twenty miles away, even if Corey started right this second, without water or provisions.

He cursed his own abominable cleverness of the dark hour of the morning when it had seemed such genius to have Luís Mendoza move the horses to the upper ranch, ten miles to the north and east. The wrangler wouldn't even be checking back with him for further orders until the next morning, and then it would take another five or six hours for Luís to bring the hands and the remuda back. The ponderosas would have long since swallowed Harold up by then—if he lived.

Corey watched until the now inconsequential speck of matter that was Harold Bishop crested a distant *loma* and disappeared.

Utterly defeated, Corey returned to the house to find that Virgie and Lucy had finally lured Ana from her self-imposed seclusion.

"I have something to tell you, Corey. It's time now. I want Lucy and Virgie to hear it, too," Ana had said after he had hugged her and kissed her cheek.

Tell? Hadn't there been more than enough of telling? Telling had brought only misery to this day.

But he had listened, and as he listened it seemed as if Sierra Blanca actually did move from its ancient base, to crush not only Harold, but all the rest of them as well.

For three days, now, he had tried to rid his mind of what Ana told them, tried to block it away completely, pretend that he and Virgie, and above all, Lucy, had never heard it.

His only solace, and that would be short-lived if and when Harold returned, was that the young Mimbreño hadn't heard her. He had refused to listen to her when she followed him, wailing, to his room, and hadn't heard the second, more damning part of her confession—if confession was what it was.

Corey decided not to tell Jim, not now. The publisher had other things to think about, and while the things Ana told them had explained matters, they wouldn't help settle them. It was too late for that.

The coach swung into Frontera Street and thundered to the steps of the Sacramento House.

It must have been a grueling trip for Eloy. The gnarled Concho man who stepped from the coach after Tom Hendry was gray with fatigue, his arthritic body more twisted even than Corey remembered from Santa Fe, his legs barely supporting him. He was an improbable-looking deus ex machina come to rescue the earthbound mortals of Chupadera County.

"*Cómo están, amigos?*" he said when they had shaken hands all around. "Will Judge Farrell still see us today?"

"Yes, he will, Eloy," Jim said, "but wouldn't it be a good idea for you to take a short rest first? We've got you a room here at the Sacramento."

"*Gracias, pero no.* The matters we are concerned with have dragged out too long already. If I could just have a little something to eat and drink before we go over to the courthouse?"

Tom seemed even more ebullient than usual. As Jim helped Eloy up the stairs of the veranda, Corey collared him.

"You're in a dandy mood."

"Got reason to be. I think we're in the home stretch, Corey. Of course, we can't ease up on the whip just yet."

"What happened in Santa Fe?"

"I'd rather Eloy told you. He's the one who did it all."

"The god from the machine . . ."

"What's that, Corey?"

"Nothing, Tom."

The table at the front end of the barroom, where Corey had watched Orrin Langley and his cronies toast Matt Kessler on a day that now seemed ages ago, was empty, and Bernardo Baca was dispatched for a ham sandwich for Eloy.

The waiter seemed delighted at the chance to serve Eloy. It was heartening to see the esteem in which the former senator was still held in at least part of Black Springs.

If Corey had expected a sudden unburdening of news on the part of the little man, he didn't get it. Eloy nibbled at his sandwich in tiny, careful bites, but he ignored the glass of beer Bernardo set in front of him. He seemed lost in thought and not really with them while he ate. When he finished he wiped his mouth with his napkin almost daintily.

"Very well, amigos," he said at last. "Governor Otero saw us yesterday morning. He was very disturbed, of course, by everything we told him. He has decided that until this is over, Chupadera County will be governed by a special emergency commissioner. I am not sure he has made the right choice, but he has asked me to serve in that post." The note of sweet apology in his voice brought Corey as close to tears as he had been since his first sergeant had died in Cuba.

"Eloy!" Jim McPherson almost shouted. "I think Miguel Otero made the best choice he could possibly have made."

"But I am uncomfortable with this kind of authority, Jim. Miguel tells me that, among other things, I have the power to declare martial law."

"I don't think it's quite come to that yet, Eloy." Jim laughed, and so did Tom, but Corey felt something quake at the center of him, felt it again when Eloy turned his eyes on him. "Bring me completely up to date on everything, Señor Lane, *por favor*."

Again that strangely comforting formality, the slight distance Eloy maintained between them, a distance that permitted Corey to focus on the little man more sharply—and Eloy on him, of course.

He told Eloy of Harold's surrender, of the twilight horror of Kessler's entrance into the Black Springs plaza, and of Harold's most recent disappearance. He hit hardest on the culpability of someone other than Apaches for the raid on

San Isidro. Eloy believed him. Of course. He had been the first of them to read Kessler's letter. Good. It would save a defense Corey felt himself poorly equipped to make. He didn't tell Eloy any of the things which had come pouring out of Ana in the wake of Harold's exodus. But he did tell Eloy of his own fears for Harold when the young Apache was in Orrin Langley's custody.

"About Orrin, Corey," Tom broke in. "He's in this, too, although it will be kind of hard to prove, unless we find that he owns shares in Sierra. He was in on all the talks Kessler had with the Polacks. I've got a hunch his real interest was to make sure he had Gideon's support when he makes a run for Gideon's Senate seat this fall."

"*Gracias,* Tom." Eloy turned back to Jim and Corey. "Now it is time for us to see Judge Farrell."

"*Con respeto,* Your Honor," Eloy said. "The governor has no wish to interfere with the processes of your court."

"That's damned good!" Farrell snorted. "I don't let nobody interfere. The young man is going to have to appear here in two more days, and that's final. If Bishop ain't at the defendant's table when my bailiff calls court to order, there'll be no dismissal and no continuance, not even if the prosecutor moves for either. The Territory's ready to go to trial, and this Apache kid had better be ready, too. Now, what else have you got in mind, Mr. Commissioner?"

"Governor Otero would like you to issue an order removing Sheriff Langley from office."

"On what grounds?"

"For misfeasance—for . . . whatever you wish to call it, Judge Farrell. I will not lie to you, sir. Mostly it is for Governor Otero's pleasure." Eloy dropped his voice almost to a whisper. "*And mine.*" What power he had! The lowered voice carried even more weight than less.

"It's all right with me, Senator. Never much liked the no-account oaf, nohow, and if you—the governor, that is—want him out of there, he's out."

Of course, this was probably playing fast and loose with due process, but Corey, remembering that cell door left gaping, inviting Harold to run to certain death, wasn't inclined to put too fine a point on such considerations at the moment.

"There are two other matters we will need your help with, Judge Farrell," Eloy continued. "Governor Otero has also appointed a special prosecutor to begin an investigation in the capital. It is his intention to bring charges of conspiracy against a number of Territorial senators and others. Senator Horace Lattner is at the moment under house arrest." He reached inside his jacket and pulled out two envelopes and handed one across the desk to Farrell. "This is a letter from the governor asking you to issue a warrant for the arrest of Senator Gideon Bainbridge. He has already been suspended from his post as senator pending the outcome of the special prosecutor's findings."

"Gideon? You're joking."

"I assure you I am not, Judge Farrell."

"Exactly what is the charge?"

"Conspiracy—as with the others. Señor Bainbridge left a trail of money. Bank records in Santa Fe reveal that he has underwritten the entire operation of Sierra Development."

Terence Farrell looked at the envelope. He put his hand to his brow, pressed hard as if he had felt a sudden stab of pain, shrugged his bent shoulders, and then reached over and pulled the humidor of cigars toward him. When the others had refused his offer—Tom with obvious regret—and the smoke was alight, he leaned back in his swivel chair until Corey feared they might lose him to gravity, and gazed at the ceiling.

"Ain't you and Miguel Otero forgetting something, Mr. Montoya?" He leaned forward now, and Corey let go of the breath he had held. "You want me to have Gideon Bainbridge arrested, but you just took away my sheriff. Just who in tarnation is going to bring Gideon Bainbridge in? I don't need to remind you, do I, that it won't be no easy chore. Serving a warrant on him up at Tres Piedras will take a heap of doing. Do you honestly think we can find one man in Chupadera County—or ten—who will risk it?"

"*Sí, señor*. I do." Eloy placed the second envelope on Farrell's desk and tapped it with a crooked finger. "This is Governor Otero's appointment of an acting sheriff to serve until the elections in November. It bears the name of Señor Corey Lane."

23

Telling Orrin Langley to clean out his desk and leave the premises had been the easy part.

The fat lawman had looked almost relieved. Will Turley, however, had been the picture of fear until Corey told him he could stay on if he applied himself with a shade more rigor. Poor Will wasn't a bad sort and even with a loose rein should be able to handle the routine work. Corey, mindful that they had ridden with Kessler to Big Bear Spring, let Langley's other two regular deputies go and posted a help wanted sign in the window of the office. In twenty-four hours there had been no takers. Somehow word must have gotten out about the first task facing the new sheriff. He wrote, and had Will post at the end of his first shift, a letter to Kessler at San Isidro telling the Sierra man that he was no longer a deputy either.

What hadn't been easy, and didn't promise to become so, was thinking of himself as sheriff.

He had cried out *"No!"* as if stabbed when Eloy had said, "It bears the name of Señor Corey Lane," in that small, dulcet, but devastatingly authoritative voice. Certainly Corey had meant his refusal, meant it from the bottom of his soul, but perhaps even as he said it he also knew he could never make it stick.

And now, one of his very first tasks would be to arrest the man who had made the first suggestion that he serve in just such a job as this.

After his pronouncement Eloy hadn't said another word. But Jim and Tom, their eagerness and desire barely under control, had begun to hammer at Corey, and even Terence Farrell, while trying his damnedest to appear even more judicial, had pressed him to accept. He could have stood against their three insistent voices, but in the end the utter silence of Eloy Montoya, who kept those sad dark eyes fixed on him while the others did all the talking, had proved too much.

"I'm not usually one to give a lot of advice in situations like this," Farrell had said when Corey finally accepted—feeling he had bent his head to the ax of an executioner—"but I don't want you going after Gideon until I get Harold Bishop's trial out of the way. Your first order of business as the chief law enforcement officer of the county is to go out and get that Indian if he doesn't show day after tomorrow."

Corey's heart sank right to the heels of his boots at that.

The way matters stood, Harold was in all likelihood still harboring the suspicion that his white friend (was he still a friend?) had been the one who had led Kessler and his killers to the hideout, despite Ana's blurted claim that *she*, not Corey, had been at fault. The suspicion would only deepen now that that friend had to find Harold and bring him in. Corey's only comfort was that Lucy, at least, knew the truth.

He needed her now more than ever. Maybe she needed him now, too, in the light of the other, infinitely more harrowing things they had learned from Ana. He remembered how he had despaired of Lucy ever needing him that night he told her of Pete Jandeezi's death.

When they left Farrell's chambers, he had still been in shock, as numb and inert as the rocks in the nondescript garden ringing the band shell in the plaza.

With all the things the first Corey Lane had dealt with as sheriff, had he dealt with anything quite like this?

But brooding would solve nothing.

Work probably wouldn't, either, but it might keep Corey from thinking about things he didn't want to think about.

After the two sullen deputies he had dismissed turned in the guns the county owned and left the office, he began a thorough examination of his new surroundings.

In the lower left drawer of Orrin Langley's—no, *his*—desk, he found a half bottle of rye whiskey and dropped it into the wastebasket. He picked up the ring of keys holding the one he had used the day he locked Harold into his cell and hung it on a peg near the door leading to the jail.

He had to get back to the ranch tonight to let the people there know about what had happened today in Black Springs and to see if any of the hands had located Harold. Not much chance of that. If the Mimbreño had made it into the high forests it would take better trackers than the X-Bar-7 riders to run him down. Sam's men could do it, perhaps, if Sam were up there to direct them. He hadn't been quite ready to travel yet when Corey had left at daybreak. Maybe now.

But a room at the back of the office beckoned to him. He opened the door and looked inside. It was windowless and dark. He took a lamp from the table by the stove, lit it, and went into the vault or whatever it was.

It didn't take much looking to see why everyone he knew in Black Springs had commented on the slovenly work habits of Orrin Langley. The room was a mess; file cabinets bulged open, their contents stuffed no more tightly than loose piles of hay, and papers littered the floor of the room. He would have to set Will Turley to work in here.

He was about to close the door on what he was already calling in his mind the "village dump" when a wooden box shoved in the corner caught his eye. It, too, overflowed with papers of various kinds. When he stepped to it and held the lamp close he found it was an old ammunition box with a note tacked to the side. *Save for G.B.*, the note read. G.B.? Sure. Gideon Bainbridge.

He hauled the box out to the desk and choked when he blew the dust from it and it curled back against his face.

As he went through the papers in the box his eyes widened. There seemed to be letters to every Chupadera County sheriff in the past ten years, arrest records, all manner of documents, payrolls, even confessions extracted by means it was probably best not to speculate about. Gideon must have asked Orrin to save all this stuff for him, paid him, too, Gideon being Gideon. The scholarly pack rat at work again. It was another lode of treasure to be added to the ones already in the archives at Tres Piedras.

Strange to think that it was this lust for acquisition that had brought Corey to the realization that the man he had almost worshiped was responsible for most, if not all, of the tragic events visited on Chupadera County and the Mescalero. Corey might even have discounted the note from Kessler to Gideon he found in the Tres Piedras library. But he couldn't discount or explain away Gideon's possession of Tony Bishop's journal.

He went on with his study of the papers and records in the box.

There was a sheaf of letters dated from early February through March of 1892, all signed by Gideon and addressed to Amos Hurley, one of the sheriffs of Chupadera County between the time of Corey's father and that of Orrin Langley. From the first few letters it was a bit difficult sorting things out;

no copies had been made of Hurley's replies to Gideon—or none, at least, had been kept—but Gideon's correspondence all had to do with the case of a young Chiricahua living on the Mescalero. Corey now vaguely remembered the incident. Amos had arrested a seventeen-year-old Apache boy, only identified by his first name, Asa, for kidnapping a fifteen-year-old girl, also a Chiricahua, who had been working as a maid for a rancher named Tanner near Tularosa, and Gideon had been Asa's lawyer. He had somehow gotten the Indian youngster off with a suspended sentence despite some pretty damning evidence. Not so vague was Corey's memory of what Gideon had said when the trial was over.

"The territory's prosecutor is confusing Apache mores with our own, Corey. If the lady in the case had been working up on the reservation we probably never would have heard of this down here in the basin. You saw the girl. I suppose Asa did use more in the way of force than persuasion. But she accepted that. A warrior never uses the white man's methods of seduction. He wouldn't think it honorable. Is our way better? Most of the marriages in America today are the result of negotiation, some of it economic and a lot of it fairly sordid. I think sometimes that the Apache way is far more honest, certainly more natural, whether you accept Mr. Darwin's notions or reject them."

Gideon's remarks had seemed like merely the rhetorical rationale of a winning lawyer at the time. After the happenings at the X-Bar-7 the day Harold left, Corey knew them for the articles of faith they must have been.

Will Turley reported in again at four o'clock, carrying a bedroll. He would have to sleep here tonight, probably for a number of nights, if Corey couldn't find more men for the department soon. All Corey could hope for was that a crime wave wouldn't break out before he could extricate himself from this onerous appointment.

He stopped at Carmen's and had her fix a supper he could eat in the saddle, reclaimed his horse from Kelly's, and hit the south road. Something itched on his chest. It was the pin from the badge Farrell had insisted he take from Orrin. He smiled. At least he still hadn't strapped on the gun the fat man had handed over.

Another sunset ride to the X-Bar-7. There was no laughing, singing Harold this time—and no Lucy. There were, though, thoughts he could not keep away as successfully as he had kept them away the past few days.

Darkness had fallen when he rode through the ranch gate. As he topped the last rise before he reached the house and could see its lights, he reined up.

The scene in the sitting room four days earlier played itself out again in his mind.

"I have something to tell you, Corey," Ana had said. "It's time now. I want Virgie and Lucy to hear it, too."

She was sitting in his father's old chair at the side of the fireplace, and he had dropped onto the couch, exhausted from chasing Harold and drained emotionally as well. Ana looked even smaller than she was. The seat of the chair was too high for her, and her feet didn't touch the floor. Her brown hands were clasped and in her lap.

"As I told you all earlier, it is all my fault. The person who told Kessler about the hideout and how to get into it was Gideon."

"Mama!" Lucy gasped. "Gideon wasn't anywhere near Cow Camp Creek."

"He didn't have to come there. He's known about Big Bear Spring for twenty years, since before you were born, Lucy. That's what this is all about. It's why he had Tony killed and why he killed Uncle Pete." She looked just as Harold did in one of his silent moods, but she went right on talking. "And why Harold will be next. Gideon did it because of me."

She left the chair, inching herself forward until her feet

could touch and then pulling herself upright. She faced Lucy, her eyes troubled even more than they had been for weeks now, and a shadow passed across her face, replaced in an instant with the look of hard determination Corey had known since boyhood. Then she turned and looked up at the shield hanging above the fireplace.

"Twenty years ago, when we were all so sure Tony was dead, Gideon Bainbridge and I were lovers. We used to meet at Big Bear Spring. I built a wickiup for us there."

Lucy sought Corey's eyes. God in heaven! It must have been the same wickiup they had shared that night.

"Of course, I stopped the whole thing when Tony showed up on the Mescalero. I hardly even saw Gideon for the next sixteen years. Tony knew, though. Why he didn't cut off the end of my nose I will never know, but that was Tony.

"Gideon would have punished me that way if it had been the other way around. In spite of that big house and the fancy clothes and the way he lives and seems to think, he's more Apache than any of us, or at least more the way he thinks we are.

"Anyway, when I broke off our affair, I thought Gideon took it well, that he understood. He sure went on being a friend to the Mescalero people, from everything I heard about him. Once or twice he rode by where we lived near the agency, but he never actually came to our houses, not the first one, the one at the sawmill, or at Cow Camp Creek.

"I think I told you I took Harold and Lucy up to Big Bear Spring for berries when they were little. Once or twice Gideon was up there, riding, but he always left when we showed up. Of course, that's how Harold knew about the hideout and the way into it. Uncle Pete knew about it, too. Uncle Pete knew everything. Nothing moved up that way without him knowing. I think maybe he was going to tell you about Gideon and me when Gideon killed him. It probably killed him a little even before that when he thought about how he would be giving me away, but he must have figured it was the only way to save Harold."

She turned from the shield and looked at each of them in turn, as if making sure that they knew she desperately wanted them to hear every word.

"A year and a half ago, when I had really forgotten Gideon, and even Tony had forgotten him, and when I thought Gideon had at last forgotten *me*, he came back into my life. He began coming to Cow Camp Creek. I didn't know him, not this Gideon, anyway. He wrote me letters. I burned them before Tony saw them. Sometimes Gideon would find me when I walked to St. Joe's to see Lucy, or when I was coming back from the sawmill after taking lunch to Tony. Uncle Pete saw us together a lot. I don't know what he thought.

"It became a nightmare. I begged Gideon to stay away. Foolish as it sounds, I even threatened him.

"What it came down to was that he had some wild idea that he was going to *take* me. Take me the way a warrior takes a woman after battle. He spouted a lot of nonsense about how it was Apache custom for a warrior to marry the widow of the man he killed because he owed it to her for taking her man away from her. Said he would remove every man close to me if he had to so I wouldn't have a choice." The black eyes filled with tears. "Funny thing, though. This time he never once said he loved me the way he used to all those years ago.

"I never told Tony. I know I should have, but I was scared. He *had* forgotten about Gideon and me, I *know* he had."

It didn't sound as if she quite believed it.

"That's it," she said. "That's why all the killing started and how Gideon knew about Big Bear Spring. He knew where Harold would make his camp. Then he sent Kessler up there to kill Harold and get rid of *all* the men in my family. And even if he missed Harold at the hideout because Corey and Lucy got him out of there, he'll keep after him until he gets him." She looked straight at Corey then. "Find Harold, Corey. Find him so I can tell him it wasn't you. And find him before Gideon can get to him."

Her shoulders began to quiver, shook violently. Corey went to her, took her in his arms, and held her until she sobbed herself dry. Then he led her to the couch and sat her down alongside Lucy.

"Ana." He breathed her name as softly as he could, hoping he could keep his other words as low. "This tells us how, but it doesn't quite tell us why. It's hard for me to believe that a man like Gideon, a man who has spent a lifetime keeping himself under tight control, would suddenly, after all these years . . ." He felt almost criminal, but damn it, the doubts were there.

She had stared at her hands after she sat down, but then she looked up at him. There had been a snap or something in her eyes for just a second. "You don't believe me?" Then whatever it was he had seen was gone and the eyes went dead. "All right. I guess I'll have to tell you everything.

"A couple of years ago or so, Gideon was at Mescalero headquarters, checking some old records about something he told the tribal clerk he was working on with you. Somehow he found the record of Lucy's birth. The council tries to keep family stuff private, but he found it." She looked down again. "Lucy is just a little older than she thinks she is. She was born five months after Tony came to Mescalero. She is Gideon's daughter, Corey."

He couldn't run, and he couldn't hide. He would have to go into that house of sorrow and confusion. Lucy needed him.

24

"Sure, Corey, I'll go with you," Sam Naaki said. "I still got some aches and pains, but I can ride. Only one thing. What makes you think your people down in Black Springs will hold still for an Apache deputy?"

"I can't concern myself with that now, Sam. Will Turley's not a real lawman, and I don't have anyone else. I'm afraid I'm not going to find anyone else soon, either, at least no one who gives a tinker's dam about Harold Bishop."

"Tinker's what?"

"Never mind. It's a silly white man's saying."

"Yeah. We got them, too."

"Do you think he's still alive, Sam?"

"From what your riders tell me about where they looked without finding his body, I think he made it to the woods. I'm a Mescalero, but I got to admit that Red Paint men are maybe the toughest Apaches going."

"Get a good night's sleep. We'll saddle up and bust out of

here at first light. María will fix us grub for two days. Two days are all we have. We've got to get Harold before his trial is called."

"It will be two *good* days, anyway," the Mescalero policeman said. "I've never eaten better than the stuff María fixes here at the X-Bar-7. Why ain't you Lanes fat?"

Corey turned his horse over to Luís Mendoza and walked from the corral to the house, feeling a little guilty at pulling the wrangler away from his three-card monte game in the bunkhouse. It had always been a ranch rule that every rider, even the owner's son, unsaddled, watered, and brushed down his own mount, but Corey knew he was too bushed to do even a halfway decent job.

He had looked at the hands around the game being played on a blanket-covered suitcase and for a weak moment thought of asking all of them to join him in the morning. They were all good men and fine riders, but not one of them was an Apache, and try as they might, they would be useless in the high timber compared to Sam. Virgie's extra hands hired from the reservation wouldn't come down the mountain until late next week, just before roundup—if she could even muster a roundup now with the delays caused by that first fruitless search for Harold. Hell, the second one would most likely be as barren. She would miss Corey a lot less than she would Luís, Fernando, and the others at the makeshift gaming table.

Virgie must have heard him as he came through the front door. She motioned him into the sitting room. "Keep your voice low," she said. "I think Lucy and Ana have already gone to sleep. Any word in town about Harold?"

"No."

"I guess it was too much to hope that he would come in on his own. Any luck with a postponement?"

He shook his head. "How are they?" He had said "they," but from her slight smile she knew he meant Lucy.

"Bearing up. If I'm any judge, I think Ana probably feels better. This thing with Gideon has wormed at her for years, at least since he started in on her again. The worst part of it right now, of course, is the fact that I have the feeling deep down inside me that she never quite stopped loving him. Oh, I'm sure she loved Tony, too, but . . ."

Shrewd, understanding lady. She wouldn't report on Lucy, even though she knew his question was really about her. He would have to find out about Lucy for himself. It was as it should be.

The cooler desert air must have invaded the sitting room earlier than usual tonight, long before bedtime. María had started a small fire in the huge old fireplace. It looked ineffectual in that enormous cavern, rather like the efforts to resolve things he had made of late, but unlike him, the little blaze was getting the job done. It was warm. He hadn't removed the jacket he had put on when the dark came down on him during the long ride from town, but he did now.

Virgie stared at him as if her eyes were being ripped from their sockets. For a second he couldn't figure out what had brought about a scrutiny so intense he could feel it; then he knew.

He had forgotten the sheriff's badge Terence Farrell had pinned on him.

At last Virgie spoke. "I would have sworn it would make me physically ill to see that badge on a man named Corey Lane again. I'm surprised. It looks right."

He told her then about the arrival of Eloy Montoya and where things stood. "How does Jim feel about your becoming sheriff?"

"He approves, I guess. He wants me to stand for election in November. So does Tom."

She didn't say anything. She would never urge him as if he were still a child. But she smiled. Over her shoulder he saw a white-clad figure in the hallway.

It was Lucy. "Corey! I thought I heard your voice, but then I thought maybe I was dreaming."

Yes, she had been asleep. She hadn't slipped on the robe of Virgie's she had been wearing during the stay here at the X-Bar-7, and her body under the flimsy nightgown she had on was still warm from the bed she had left and warm from love and need, too. She pressed her whole body against his without hesitation or embarrassment, and her mouth sought his in a rage of hunger. Even so, her need was nothing compared to his.

Then, with a faint, hurt cry, she stepped away from him. Her hand moved swiftly to her right breast, stayed there for a second, and fell beside her. Where her hand had been, a tiny stain of red was spreading on the fabric of the nightgown.

He put his hand to his own chest. The badge had come unfastened and the pin pricked his palm.

"Oh, God, I'm sorry, Lucy!"

"Don't be sorry, Corey. Nothing you could do would ever really hurt me."

They slept together in his room. He would have wagered he would be too tired to make love, but he wasn't. It was every bit as wonderful as he remembered, and yet something about it was tinged tonight with something almost like desperation.

"We better go to my office first, Corey," Sam said as they rode out together the next morning. "Maybe somebody has spotted Harold or cut sign. If we're lucky he might even be there."

"I'm not counting on it, Sam. The man who left the X-Bar-7 five days ago was on a mission."

Up on the two best horses Luís could find for them, and trailing two other good ones, not packhorses but spare riding animals, they made good time, passing Blazer's Mill by ten-fifteen and reaching the agency well before eleven.

Sam went into the board-and-batting shed that was his office to check his messages, and Corey didn't even dismount as he waited for the Apache officer, who came out with a sober look.

"What's up, Sam?" Corey asked.

Sam shook his head as if he were trying to clear cobwebs away to think better.

"Nothing, Corey. Nothing for sure, anyway. But Nelson Tamwas way up near Deadman Lake claims he had a horse stolen last night. Nelson's said stuff like that before when his animals have died, hoping he can talk the council into paying him for them. Maybe we ought to suppose it's true, though. If it is, it ain't likely it was them raiders who been bothering us. It's a hell of a way from the timberlands they been working over, and from the way they been behaving they'd have shot Nelson's whole herd. By *Ussén*, Corey!—if it's Harold who lifted that pony, our little runt Mimbreño has done some hard traveling since he left your place."

"Anyone report any firearms missing?"

"No. But we can't figure he ain't latched on to one. The families of the dead boys have been watched pretty damn hard. Still, he could have slipped into one of their places without my people spotting him. He sure got by *me* when he came down from Big Bear Spring to see his mama."

"How far is it to Deadman Lake?"

"Ain't far, but what difference does it make? I don't figure we ought to head that way, anyhow. If it was Harold, he ain't anywhere near there now."

Corey felt stupid. He should have doped out for himself that Harold wouldn't stay in one place very long, and certainly no place where he had called attention to himself. Well, the fact that Sam had brains and just plain savvy wasn't the least of the reasons Corey wanted him along today.

"Got any ideas, Sam?"

"Well, my first idea is that you ought to get off that horse for a spell. Poor critter's earned a rest, even if you ain't as fat as you should be."

Corey slid from the saddle. By the time he had tied off the horse at Sam's hitch rail, the policeman was squatting in the dust and was scratching some lines into the caliche with a stick.

"Now, this ain't much of a map," he said over his shoulder, "but it'll have to do. Up here in this right-hand corner is Deadman Lake. Over here"—he poked the stick into the upper left of the square he had sketched out—"is San Isidro—and a little bit left of San Isidro is Tres Piedras. He's heading for one or both of them, ain't he?"

"Yes."

"Well, the trick is not in figuring out where he was or where he's heading so much as figuring out what he's thinking."

"How do we do that?"

"Men out to kill other men get to be pretty much alike, Corey. Start thinking of how *you'd* go about it."

"Don't know if I could do that. I've never wanted to kill anyone."

Sam grunted. "White men been pretty damned good at it. All right. I'll do Harold's thinking for us."

"Aren't we wasting time?"

"No. We got *time*. Keep looking at my map." He streaked two more lines into the caliche, both more or less leading from the spot he said was Deadman Lake to the hole he had gouged out as San Isidro. "Harold's problem is a little tough. From what you told me, he's got two men he wants to kill. Getting to them would be easy, except that he knows everybody and his brother up here is looking for him. He's got to get from here, Deadman Lake, to here, Kessler's place, or here at Gideon's. If he goes straight to Gideon's he has to go through too much of the reservation, so he's just got to go to San Isidro first. He's going to mosey along easy. He don't know that horse he's riding, and he ain't going to want it used up. That's why we have time. Unless he traveled last night, he's got three more miles to cover to the village than we have, and he's going to have to head way north and swing back in. Then he's going to lay up and rest his horse. He'll want to move fast when he finishes with Kessler. For all he knows, Gideon's got riders out looking for him, too. He'll want them to *think* he's coming from the Mescalero side. I think he's going to hole up in the scrub across Concho Creek from this Sierra place. I would. If we're waiting for him there, we got a good chance of catching him. 'Course this is all guesswork."

"It's better than anything I could come up with, Sam."

When Sam had said *I would*, it sounded more that he sometimes *had* done this. If not exactly this, something close enough that the difference didn't matter. He must be an unpleasant man to have on your trail if he didn't have the affection for you he had for Harold Bishop.

"There's one more thing, Corey," Sam said next. He pointed to Tony's Winchester jutting from the saddle holster on Corey's horse. "Ain't you got a handgun with you?"

"In my saddlebag."

"Strap it on, please."

"I'd rather not."

"I know that. But I'd as soon not ride with you if you ain't armed all the way. We might have to work in close."

"For Lord's sake! We won't need any kind of guns with Harold."

"Maybe not. Dig it out." There was no "please" this time.

Corey went to his horse and opened his saddlebag. He pulled out the gun belt and holster holding the Peacemaker Special that had been part of the pile of weapons Luís had helped him hide and that he had hauled back to the study in the days before he went to Black Springs to meet Jim, Tom, Terence Farrell, and that persuasive little man, Eloy Montoya. Virgie had handed it to him at the front door when he left this morning. The sight of Virgie holding the gun out to him with both her delicate hands was now perhaps his oddest memory of her since they had ridden with Grandmother Alicia through that frightening meadow filled with Apaches so many years ago. He'd known the revolver since he'd been a boy. It was the gun the first Corey Lane had carried the day he died.

Sam spoke again. "Have you got that warrant for Gideon you told me about last night?"

"Yes, but its postdated until after Harold's trial. I can't use it yet."

"White men!" The Indian didn't hide his disgust.

"Let's ride, Sam."

Yes, he was lucky to have Sam along. Three times on the ride to the Rio Concho the lawman jerked them off the trail into the rocks or patches of scrub and forest, and three times bands of armed men rode toward the Mescalero on the trail they had just come down. They sure weren't alone in their hunt for Harold. How the hell did Sam know those men were up ahead of them? Maybe he smelled them. Once, when the smallest group, only three men, passed the cover that sheltered Corey, Sam, and their four horses—it was hell's own time keeping animals, nervous from the sudden rough handling, quiet—the group brushed so close Corey could clearly see the Tres Piedras brand on the shoulder of the leader's pony.

But with all these men heading toward the timber and the reservation, was Sam right in what he thought Harold's plans to be? Or did all those other riders know something the two of them hadn't heard or hadn't guessed? Corey couldn't think about that now. He had put his trust in the stocky Mescalero lawman, and he couldn't extract it now.

They stopped for lunch about half a mile from San Isidro.

"Got to eat now," Sam said. "We might not have time to

be messing around with food after we cross the creek and get set for Harold."

Corey's appetite wasn't big, considering the late hour and all the efforts of the ride; he couldn't get his mind off the last lunch he had eaten in these precincts, when he had played eye games with little Pepe. Sam ate most of the food. Between bites of one of María's sandwiches the Mescalero pointed to the Peacemaker Special belted to Corey's waist.

"Hell of a looking gun. I know you ain't comfortable with it, and that kind of surprises me. I used to watch you and Harold practice your draws when you was kids. You were a good shot, too, I remember."

"That was play, Sam. I don't have much faith in my ability if it came down to the real thing." True enough. War in Cuba had been different, more of a set piece thing. You seldom saw your enemy. Corey had stood up well in Cuba, though, and he had finished the fighting with quiet pride in himself. He hadn't funked it.

He eased the Peacemaker from the holster and thrust it quickly back again. It was almost a match for the gun that Gideon Bainbridge once showed him how to use. Mike Calico had been Corey's first instructor with firearms, of course, but he had only been seven or eight when Mike had laughed at his misses with this same revolver down by the corral, and firing at tin can targets had been merely a game, a pastime like his butterfly net. When Gideon instructed him he was seventeen. He hadn't yet seen men killed, but by that time he had had a pretty good notion of how terrible it must be for both the victim *and* the shooter.

Corey remembered the day well. He hadn't thought of it in years, but it came back in sharp detail after Sam's talk about the sidearm he was wearing. The instruction had taken place near where he and Sam sat now and had been right after a lunch very much like this one, if a sight more sumptuous.

Corey had been compiling notes in the library at Tres Piedras that morning when Gideon appeared in the doorway.

"All work and no play makes Jack a dull boy, Corey," he said. "Take a ride with me. Juanita's packed a hamper for us and Pedro's fixed the fishing gear and a can of bait."

The remark about dull Jack notwithstanding, there had been a little work on the part of Gideon first. They had ridden to San Isidro to see an ancient bean farmer named Octavio Ramírez who had sent word to Gideon that he was getting a lot of heat from Santa Fe about some unpaid taxes he felt he didn't owe. Gideon wrote a letter for Octavio. Good Lord! It came to Corey now that the letter had been addressed to *Eloy Montoya*, still Chupadera senator then. Sure, he remembered Gideon telling Octavio that "the senator will set things right, *viejo*. Do not worry anymore." Gideon had refused the wrinkled *campesino's* offer of payment. "*Es nada*, Octavio, but if your chiles are good this season, *abuelo*," he had said, "Juanita would appreciate a few. At Tres Piedras we can't grow any as sweet as those of the upper Concho."

They had then headed from San Isidro to the Rio Ruidoso, setting their poles in the banks of the noisy mountain stream, paying scant attention to the bobbers as they feasted on quail, French rolls, and apricots, washed down with a lively, satisfying Mexican red.

After lunch and an only mildly disappointing harvest of speckled trout—considering their neglect of the fishing setup—the lesson with the gun began. How the subject had come up was the only part of the day that wasn't fleshed out now in Corey's memory. He only remembered Gideon unstrapping his gunbelt and handing it to him; Corey hadn't been armed himself. He had never gone into the timber with anything other than a rifle or a shotgun.

"No, no!" Gideon had protested at Corey's first draw. "Don't rush. You always have far more time than you think you have. Draw with deliberation. Merely *wipe* the weapon from the holster. Your enemy will always be at least as terrified as you are. Let *him* jerk *his* gun out. Ninety-nine times out of a hundred the adrenaline pumping through him will cause him to swing the weapon way too high. Good odds. *And don't aim.*"

"Don't aim?"

"Never. Not consciously. Just imagine the bullet is at the tip of a rod reaching from the muzzle of the gun to your opponent's chest. Lift your weapon and its imagined extension carefully and place the bullet on his heart. Then fire."

The empty wine bottle became the cowardly desperado "Dirty Dalton," and after a couple of near misses Corey shattered it. A dozen large pine cones fared no better as Gideon counted aloud while he drew and fired. "Two seconds, Corey," he said. "If you can fix on him and pull in two seconds or less, he's dead—even if he's managed to squeeze out a round himself. Bear in mind that it isn't speed or marksmanship that wins a gunfight. It comes down to a matter of will. You must truly want to kill." Then the master of Tres Piedras turned almost sheepish. "Don't know what prompted me to go into this, Corey. It's not as though this is a skill you will ever need. Not the way the world is becoming reconstituted in this day and age." He seemed to lose himself in thought for a moment, then, "Only one more thing. Never just hold a gun on anyone. When you point it at an enemy, always fire. You may never get another chance. Time comes into play here. Any delay, for whatever reason, is almost always fatal."

For a few weeks just about every tin can in the X-Bar-7's garbage bin "bit the dust." Harold had been amazed.

Sam was a swift eater, and in no time they were on the trail again.

Sam had been right about not hurrying. They were across the little *río* from the Sierra compound with time to spare, it seemed. Things looked quiet, ordinary, at Kessler's place.

From the cover of the cottonwoods that lined the north bank of the creek, as Sam called it, they even got glimpses from time to time of the burly Kessler himself, or somebody, at any rate, through the windows at the rear of the building.

"Yeah," Sam said. "He ain't watching this side. That's what Harold is counting on."

They switched their saddles to the horses they hadn't ridden yet, walked them well to one side of the cottonwood grove, and tethered them. They settled into a thicket of scrub oak that gave them a view up the slope Sam indicated Harold would in all likelihood come down. Their hiding place afforded them a good look at the rear of the compound, too.

"He might not come until tonight, Corey."

"But he'll come, won't he?" Corey was beginning to feel the confidence Sam had shown since the outset.

Sam growled. "I only hope he shows up before it's time to get at that X-Bar-7 grub again. I don't want the little *gusts'ile* spoiling supper."

Corey smiled in spite of himself. It was preposterous, but comforting, too, that Sam would think of food at a time like this and refer to Harold as a little chipmunk.

Yes, they had time. Too much time, in fact.

Lucy was beginning to appear in his mind's eye, and that was something he wanted to avoid at almost any cost. Cuba again. Perhaps it was mere coincidence, something peculiar to the company of riflemen he commanded, but it had seemed to him that the most recklessly efficient fighters in the three tropic actions he had seen had been men who had no restricting romantic ties back home. Censoring his company's mail had told him more than he wanted to know about them, and his recollection was that the more "in love" or more truly "married" a combat soldier was, the more he had to live for, the less value he was to his fellow soldiers. These men declared their love often enough in their letters home. Sadly, wanting to live *too* much was like carrying an extra field pack into battle.

The thicket formed a barrier to the light afternoon breezes stirring the leaves of the cottonwoods, and it was turning hot. Corey hadn't realized how hard he had been staring at the slope, scanning it from side to side mechanically, until the very *weight* of his vision caused his eyes to ache. He would have closed them, but he feared that despite the tension in him he might doze off at just the second Harold came in sight. That wouldn't do. They had to get him before he confronted Kessler.

A piñon jay fluttered down to a branch of one of the scrub oaks above his head, cocked an agate eye downward, and screamed off in protest. The noise jolted Corey. The jay landed in a cottonwood fifty feet away and squawked its indignation at them.

"Smart *kuushe*," Sam muttered. "We must stink by now."

There was almost an hour of silence, broken only by the wet rattle of the Rio Concho, and Corey was amazed to see that Sam, at least, napped. By God, *he* wouldn't!

Then he heard a door being opened and slammed somewhere in the compound. There was no back entrance to the building, so it had to be the glass-paneled door at the front he had peered through at the time of his last visit here.

When he turned his head in the general direction of the sound, he saw Kessler rounding the corner on the side where the shed holding the tools and supplies had been attached. The man was in his saddle tramp outfit again, but unlike the other time, he was armed. And his holster was tied off above the knee in the same way a professional gunfighter would wear one.

Corey moved to his knees from the sitting position he had been cramped in and raised his eyes just above a branch of the scrub. He could feel Sam do the same.

Was Kessler leaving? That might knock all their plans into

a cocked hat. But he shouldn't despair. Even if the Sierra man was leaving, Harold couldn't know about it. He would still come looking for Kessler.

And, no, Kessler wasn't leaving. He stretched his powerful arms over his head and leaned backward the way office workers sometimes do to get the kinks out after a long time bent over a desk. Then he fished a *cigarro* from the pocket of his shirt, lifted his boot and struck a match against the sole, and lit the smoke.

The same thoughts came again that had come on Corey's first trip here. Harold would be insane to tackle this killer in his own bailiwick. Even Sam might not be able to handle him here.

Kessler, the *cigarro* clamped between his teeth, was fumbling with the buttons on his pants. He had just come outside to relieve himself.

Corey relaxed a little. He looked at Sam. Sam was smiling and whispering something in Apache Corey only caught the last of. ". . . a goddamn little *chuu* for an *ind'aa* that big—"

The Mescalero lawman stopped talking. He cocked his head as the jay had. But he wasn't looking, he was listening.

Then—so faint above the noise of the Concho he could barely hear it—Corey caught what Sam's keen hearing had fastened on. Hoofbeats. A delicate but furious drumming.

It was plain Kessler didn't hear them. The sound was coming from the far side of the building, straight at the scrub oak thicket, not at Kessler. And maybe the stream of urine arching away from the big body and splattering on the rock-hard caliche covered the sound, too.

Harold Bishop, riding bareback on a small dun pony, rounded the corner away from Kessler at an all-out gallop.

Now Kessler heard. He turned. He still hadn't retrieved himself or buttoned up. His lower jaw dropped and the *cigarro* dangled from his mouth, stuck to his lower lip.

Harold lashed the dun pony with the free end of the reins.

His speed seemed to double. His right hand held something above his head. It looked like a club with something heavy at the end. It was a crude stone ax.

Kessler went for his gun, but he was way too late.

As Harold reached him, veering the horse a little to make room for the blow he leveled, he brought the ax down on Kessler's head.

The sickening, thick, squashy sound of it reached into Corey's stomach.

Harold and the pony swept on around the corner of the building Kessler had come from and were lost to sight. The Mimbreño never once looked back.

The jaw was squawking again.

"Goddamn it!" Sam yelled. "The little *chihende* shit outsmarted me. He must have ridden straight through the village. It was the one damn thing I didn't figure on. Most Apaches won't go through an *ind'aa* town if they can help it. Let's mount up and get our asses to Tres Piedras."

"Shouldn't we look at Kessler first? Maybe we—"

"No! He's as dead as them kids he killed. Let's move, Corey. By the time we reach the horses and cross the creek he'll have a good ten-minute start on us. And we don't ride like Harold Bishop, either."

25

They untethered all four horses, but left behind the two they had ridden first to the agency and then to San Isidro, and they jettisoned the rest of the food, the bedrolls, saddlebags, and feed.

It took time—not much, but it took time. It took even more to work their way back up the near side of the *río* to the crossing they had used to get into position to intercept Harold.

As they moved along the bank of the stream across from the compound, Corey took a last look at Matt Kessler's body. The crushed head lay in a pool of blood that had been sucked so quickly into the caliche it didn't even shine. Kessler had managed to draw his gun, but it lay unfired beside his outstretched hand.

Even as successful as Harold's sudden attack had been, Corey didn't need Sam to tell him that Harold could never take Gideon Bainbridge down with the makeshift stone-age weapon he had used to kill the man lying in the compound.

When they reached the San Isidro side villagers were swarming down the road. The villagers must have seen Harold streak through their town on his ride toward the compound, must have ducked for cover at the sight of an Apache riding bareback and brandishing a weapon right out of old settler yarns, and then emerged only when they thought it safe. They walked slowly, rather like a skirmish line in Cuba, and from what Corey could see as he and Sam reached the road through the trees where Pepe had disappeared that day, they each looked as nervous as a wary skirmisher, but were too consumed by curiosity to stop. How did they feel about Kessler? Had he been a brute in their eyes, too, or had he been *patrón* and provider? It was, after all, their village where it happened. Harold was an Apache, the ancient enemy. He had killed on their ground. Would they, like the grim hunters from Tres Piedras, eventually take up the chase for him when they found the body?

"Harold must have already reached Ghost Pass," Sam said when he and Corey turned their horses to the trail leading from San Isidro to Tres Piedras. "Maybe ten minutes ahead of us now."

They moved well, as fast as Corey had ever taken a horse through mountain country. Perhaps five minutes to Ghost Pass, a narrow cut in the Concho Ridge wall, and then into the forest. And yet—bright as the day was at five in the afternoon, and dry and firm as was the trail they traveled—it seemed to Corey that they were getting nowhere, as if they were riding through a muddy lowland *ciénaga* after a downpour.

He beat the flanks of his poor horse without mercy. Sam had taken the lead. The trail wasn't wide enough to pass Sam, or Corey would have—his mount seemed a shade the swifter animal—but he crowded dangerously close to the rump of the lawman's horse.

It didn't seem possible—with his eyes glued to Sam and the trail ahead of them, and with the constant effort needed to keep up this pace and guide his mount through narrow rocky passages, and with the desperate need to stop Harold—that he would be assailed by unwanted thoughts, thoughts he didn't want to think, but as they rode, and overhanging branches whipped his face until he felt flayed, the memories and thoughts came and came again.

Gideon. Was the man insane, or just obsessed? Was there enough difference between the two to make it matter? How many times had Corey ridden this very trail with him?

They passed near the aspen glade where Gideon had found Corey alone and almost in the grip of terror that autumn day when the elegant squire of Tres Piedras had allayed his unspoken fears of something stalking him and had led him out of the spookiness and yellow gloom and back to Harold.

Gideon must have divined the fear that had frozen him in that *gah'n*-haunted glade that afternoon, but they never spoke of it. For all his strength, there had been a gentleness about Gideon that day that calmed the young Corey Lane without once making him feel ashamed.

There had been years of other gentleness as well, gentleness that shaped him, made him whatever man he was today even more than Virgie and Jim McPherson had.

Jim, of course, had been Corey's first real friend. He had taught Corey a good deal of the language he worked with now. "Corey," he remembered Jim saying once. "Perhaps the finest work of art man has created is the English sentence." The publisher had laughed at himself when he said it. Blushed then. "Arrant pedantry, Corey." But he had been deadly earnest, too. More than any master at Hotchkiss or professor at college, Jim had taught him to write, but he had never dictated to Corey what he ought to write about. It was

Jim he had gone to for advice when growing up, not that Jim was too quick to give it, and Jim who had been his ally against Virgie the year his grades slipped so abysmally at Hotchkiss, Jim who had helped him wheedle out of her the new blazer he had wanted for a spring holiday lark in Boston. Jim had been a model of understated courage for him, too, a model without which he probably could never have made it through the war in Cuba.

An hour or an hour and a half into the ride Sam reined up his pony where beavers had dammed a small, slow-moving stream.

"Water!" he shouted back to Corey. "We can use some, and the horses need it bad." When Corey reined his animal toward the pond, Sam yelled again. "No! Ride over there on the left. Harold stopped here, too. You'll mess up the tracks he left, and I want to look at them. Let's get down and rest."

They slid from their saddles, and Corey took the reins of both horses and led them to the pond. It was a struggle to pull them away from the water when he figured they had drunk all they could tolerate.

Sam was peering down at the soft soil on the bank of the pond.

"Yeah. From the look of it, he was here for a spell. Kind of getting ready for the last run to Gideon's. By the time we leave here we'll have gained on him." He looked up at Corey. "He might have fooled me *once*, coming through San Isidro the way he did, but maybe I still know how he's thinking. Come and look for yourself if you want. I've seen all I need to see."

Corey led the horses to him and looked where Sam had looked. Yes, hoofprints, lots of them. He didn't have to be a tracker the likes of Sam to see that they were fresh. Made by an unshod pony. That accounted for the light sound of Harold's charge on Kessler. On the hard caliche of the Sierra compound, a horse with shoes would have rung the changes like a blacksmith on an anvil.

"Shouldn't we get back on the trail, Sam?"

"How long you figure this stop took us?"

"Two, maybe three minutes."

"Harold was here a lot longer than that. Take your time."

"We're still way behind him."

"Yeah, but he'll be taking the upper trail and then the back way in to Tres Piedras. That's half a mile longer, and a tougher climb than going straight up that nice graded road of Gideon's the way we will. He'll be leading his pony as much as he rides for a hell of a lot of it. He had to go that way. He can't let Gideon know he's coming. *We* don't care. It will be damn close, but we might be waiting for him in Gideon's front yard when he gets there. 'Course, it will be near on dark by then. Mount up."

In seconds it was as if they hadn't stopped at all.

The sun was below the tops of even the smaller ponderosas now, and when they came to a clear space it blinded them. The hammering of the hooves was drumming deep into Corey's head. Perhaps it could keep those unwanted thoughts away, or beat them down. Another low-hanging branch grabbed Sam's hat and sailed it back past Corey's ear. The Mescalero didn't even look back at it.

The thoughts came rushing back.

Virgie. She had shaped him, too. What Jim hadn't taught him, Virgie had. Coming back to the basin after the trip to Europe and the brief stay with the cousins in Kansas City must have taken far more courage than Corey had ever needed in the war. Running a ranch as big as the X-Bar-7— which nothing in Virgie's life as city girl, then as coddled wife, had prepared her for—made his running of the sheriff's office seem the play of children. And she had done it well. Small wonder she had only smiled when he told her that Jim wanted him to run for the office he now held temporarily because of Eloy Montoya's silent pressure. She had been telling him he could do it. She would never say he *should*.

She and Jim McPherson belonged together. What was wrong with them? As he had reminded himself so many times before, he knew.

There was one paramount thing Corey's mother had done for him. By persuading him to get close to Harold Bishop and become his friend, she had turned his fear of Apaches to the beginnings of understanding.

And Gideon Bainbridge had done even more.

He had turned that understanding first to liking, then to love.

He had persuaded Corey to take the words and the language Jim had given him and put that love in writing. All the present horror would never take that away.

Now Corey was riding armed to Gideon's home with a warrant for his arrest. It didn't matter that he couldn't use it yet. He would have to use it soon enough.

"Do you honestly think we can find one man in Chupadera County—or ten—who will risk it?" Terence Farrell had asked of Eloy.

"*Sí, señor.* I do," the Concho man had replied.

What had made Eloy so sure? The man whose name Otero had affixed to the temporary appointment wasn't sure by any means.

They reached a fork where one branch of the trail they were on turned up the mountain, and Sam called another halt.

"Here it is, *Naat'eje*—Eyebrow Trail."

This was where Harold would have to turn if Sam was right. The policeman leaned out from his saddle and stared hard at the ground. Then he nodded his satisfaction, and in another second they were under way again.

Corey had been on the Eyebrow, too, many times—with Gideon. It was little more than a shelf of rock for a mile or more. There was a wide place or two where a rider could turn back, but there was no turning off the trail. Harold Bishop wasn't turning back. Yes, they would gain precious minutes on him now by taking the lower, easier road. *Good work, Sam.*

With less than a hundred yards to go to reach the main road from Black Springs that led to the gate to Tres Piedras and an even better road, disaster struck.

A small gully crossed their path, and someone—one of Gideon's hands, most likely—had bridged it with half a dozen roughhewn planks, and as Sam lifted the reins and spurred his pony across, the planks parted and the pony's right foreleg plunged down between them. The frightened animal tried to get its hindquarters under its body, but as it did, Sam pitched from the saddle and fell heavily to the rocky bottom of the gully, the horse collapsing then on top of him.

"You have to shoot it, Corey," Sam said when Corey had dismounted and gotten to the gully. "The critter's *jade'* is busted. Shit! Maybe you better shoot me while you're at it. My leg's busted, too."

Corey tied his horse to a juniper at trailside, and pulled out the Peacemaker Special. Sam's horse was screaming, thrashing wildly with its head, its eyes great crazed white marbles, and when Corey took hold of the bridle he needed all his strength to hold the head still enough to make dead sure his shot would do the job.

As Sam had reminded him, he had fired the gun before, but he had never fired it at anything that lived. He pulled the trigger. The gun jumped away from the horse's head, and the roar echoed from the steep stony slope above them like a voice from hell.

"Ain't so hard to kill when you have to do it," Sam said. Then he bit his lip so hard Corey thought he surely would draw blood. It was clear he was in a lot of pain.

"What are we going to do about you, Sam?" Corey said.

"Can you pull yourself up enough so I can get you across my horse's back?"

"*We* ain't going to do one damn thing! *You* are going to Gideon's. Wait. You *can* pull me up where the ground is a little softer and a flash flood can't give me more than I can drink. And you can take the blanket off that horse. It's going to get cold tonight before you or somebody can come and get me. Don't waste any time trying to go easy on me, Corey. We'll have lost enough of it, anyway. Maybe every second we gained so far."

It did take several minutes to tug Sam to higher ground, slide his saddle under his head, and wrap him in the blanket. They didn't speak as Corey untied his horse, but as he put his foot in the stirrup, Sam chuckled.

"You will remember where you left me, won't you, Corey? Or should I draw you another map? What the hell am I laughing at? This ain't funny."

As Corey urged his horse down to the road he pulled his father's watch from his pocket. Eight twenty-two.

Corey didn't even look up at the fifteen- or twenty-foot-high wrought-iron sign that arched over the main gate of Tres Piedras, didn't so much as glance at the seven registered brands of Gideon Bainbridge worked into its intricate black pattern. He had seen every one of them dozens of times on cattle drives and at the Corona shipping pens.

As Sam had said, it was a nice graded road. Jim had remarked that Gideon had ordered it built to accommodate the Duryea. The automobile had left black oil stains on the fine white gravel, marks of its journeys in and out of Tres Piedras. Corey wondered if even Sam's gifts as a tracker would be able to tell him if the "car"—as a West Point major from Michigan he had served with in Cuba had insisted on calling an automobile—had gone in or out today, and whether it was more likely to be here than down in town.

It was almost dusk. Would Harold wait until after dark for what he had in mind? He didn't know the house and the compound at Tres Piedras nearly as well as Corey did, but he had made several visits there when they were young and would remember its general layout. Harold certainly would have a better chance with Gideon if he caught him sleeping.

Did Corey dare hope Harold had abandoned whatever plan he had to attack Gideon and had either holed up in the mountains again or, infinitely better, had ridden on down to the X-Bar-7 to see his mother and sister? He didn't know that Corey and Sam had seen him kill. Had the killing itself persuaded him of the mortal danger he would be putting himself in by going up against a truly deadly man like Gideon? Would common sense and the natural desire to live another day perhaps change his mind? Would he now know fear?

No. No to all of it. Harold would swell with confidence and purpose to match his rage after his success at San Isidro. The brief, heart-stopping glimpse Corey had gotten of Harold as he bore down on stupefied Matt Kessler had been of a man whose rage had carried him far beyond fear or even caution.

But these weren't the questions Corey should be considering now.

He had to worry about what Corey Lane would do when he and Gideon and the now completely savage Harold—yes, he had to think of Harold like that, even if it hurt—came together.

And he had a more immediate worry at the moment. He had to get up this road to Gideon's himself—undetected. It ran within eighty or a hundred feet of the Tres Piedras bunkhouse. Although it was getting dark, it still hadn't turned as chill as Sam had said it would. Would Tres Piedras riders still be lounging in the bunkhouse yard as he had seen them do so often on his visits here? Even if they weren't, some of the hands would be bound to be roaming between the bunkhouse and the other buildings. It was just about the hour when the day's last after-supper chores would be under way. If the hands were outside and spotted him, would they let him pass?

Corey could break through the fence somewhere this side of the bunkhouse, ride around it, and rejoin the road nearer the main house, but that would rob him of precious minutes. In the failing light there would also be the risk of having an accident in the broken country down the slopes, as Sam had. He had to chance it on a straight ride in.

Corey had the horse moving at a lope, and he reined it in a little to go by the bunkhouse with a minimum of noise and to keep it ready for a hard run if Gideon's men did spot him and come after him.

But there wasn't a soul outside the bunkhouse as he passed it. Gideon must have sent all his men out on the hunt for Harold.

What if they had already found Harold? What if Harold *didn't* come down out of the trees and rocks up ahead? How could Corey explain his own presence here?

He surely couldn't say that he had come to use the library, or to chat about old Mangas and his missing head or whether Cochise or Victorio had been the better Apache leader.

If Harold hadn't reached the big house by the time Corey did, though, he sure as hell would have to lift the knocker on the massive door and, when Pedro Chavez ushered him in to Gideon, tell him Harold was lying in ambush somewhere nearby. It was the only way. Somehow Corey would have to talk Gideon into letting *him* stand guard. He would have to tell him about Kessler and persuade him he was only there to bring Harold in on a charge of murder. He couldn't mention the warrant for Gideon himself now burning inside his vest. But what if Gideon already knew about it? He seemed to have known of everything else since all this began.

At least Corey had managed to keep at bay the thoughts he had feared most might assail him now. Thoughts of Lucy.

Don't let them come now. Think of Ana. Was that any better?

So many things were clear now. The matter of Ana's language, for one. The long, intimate association with Gideon must have made the difference. Corey wondered why he had never noticed before that when she spoke English she even used some of Gideon's words and turns of phrase. Not important now.

Two more minutes to ride. It was almost full dark now.

The road curved here, and one of the ponderosa groves blocked a view of the house from this far down, but light was flickering through the thick greenery, light fractured and diffused by the long needles of the mountain pines, faint light . . . but wait—light far too bright to come from just the lamps inside the house. The whole yard in front of Tres Piedras must be lit—with torches, maybe. Corey had once seen it flooded like that for a reception Gideon had given for the governor. But why now? And why this early on a late spring evening? Did Gideon have guests? If he did, that would really tear things up. Or perhaps the men Corey hadn't seen at the bunkhouse were up here instead.

Sure. Gideon had set a guard.

With that the case, Corey couldn't ride blithely up to the front door.

Quickly he decided to get off the road, tie the horse to a tree, and go through the woods on foot.

Inside the woods and dismounted, he found it had really gotten dark and his vision was cut to almost nothing. He had to move at a snail's pace, feeling each step with his boots before he put his weight down. Discovery now could be disastrous. Careful as he was, dead branches cracked under his boots, the noise deafening to ears more sensitive than he could ever remember them.

Then he heard something else and his heart froze. From somewhere ahead of him, where he was now certain the torches were, he heard something like the muffled sound of gunfire.

Shots? God in heaven! Had he gotten here too late?

He broke into a run, but after slamming heavily against a tree and then catching a boot in the roots of another and falling, he slowed again, but kept moving toward the light.

By the time he reached the last barrier of big trees and brushwood in front of Tres Piedras's sweeping lawn, Corey could see again. The grass ahead of him was a sea of brilliant green in the light of the torches he had expected. At the house the road widened to a parking apron. He swept his eye across the Tres Piedras compound, searching for where the shots had come from, and he saw the Duryea, its nose pointed back down the road, some distance away from the steps that led to the covered porch and perhaps a hundred yards from where he had stopped.

The engine was running, popping and banging, sounding like small-arms fire had in Cuba. The automobile's staccato firing had been the "shots" Corey had heard. He drew the first decent breath since he began his run.

But was Gideon leaving? If he was, maybe this tragic farce wouldn't have to be played out tonight. Surely Corey, or someone, one of the council's men or one of Sam's, someone who wouldn't be out merely to spill Harold's blood, would find the Mimbreño and bring him in. Harold would still be in deep, deep trouble, but at least he would be alive, and many strange things could happen in Terence Farrell's court, even relatively good things—and even to a Red Paint Apache charged with the murder of a white man. Corey had to believe it.

He had been wrong about one thing, and he was grateful that he had been.

There were no Tres Piedras riders up here. No armed guard had been posted. He couldn't see a soul. Sam had been right again. Time had worked *for* him, after all.

He began a careful examination of everything in front of him.

The torches weren't the only source of light. Oil lamps, half a dozen of them, sat on the broad top of the porch railing on either side of the stairway that led to the mahogany door, and there were lighted lamps in every window, two of them in the nearest large bay window of the living room where Corey had looked out over the Ojos Negros Basin during his last trip here, three more in the French doors at right angles to the window that opened from the library to the porch.

With this much brightness Tres Piedras must be visible from Black Springs—and from high in the hills behind it, from where Harold now must be looking at it.

Then Corey had a powerful feeling, almost a certainty, that his friend was no longer in the hills, but already just behind the house, or over on the left, more likely, where more ponderosas bordered the compound. A picture of him came to mind. Harold would be on foot. He couldn't risk the sound of a horse's footfalls when he started his last, irreversible, probably hopeless, stalk. He would be gripping his stone ax with the same right hand that slipped from the bat time after time when Corey had tried to teach him baseball one summer between years at Hotchkiss. At least it would curl with more confidence around the handle of the ax. His grip had been more than sure enough at San Isidro.

Then Corey knew an even more powerful, more certain feeling.

Gideon Bainbridge knew all this, knew as much as Corey did about Harold's final plan, maybe more. He would have at least come to the same conclusions to which Corey, with Sam's help, had come. He couldn't know, of course, of Kessler's death; it didn't matter. He would have done Harold's thinking for him just as Sam had, but with more swiftness, ease, and sureness.

He was a far more accomplished killer than the young Mimbreño was, had seen battle, was hardened to it.

But he, too, had been a beginner once at the killing business, had felt the same rage at some point in his early life that Harold was feeling now. He would remember. And he would know how to play Harold's rage to his advantage.

Nothing would turn Harold Bishop aside now, and Gideon knew it. Harold would run as unswervingly toward death as a blind brave bull in the final act of the *corrida*.

The bright light—and perhaps even the rattling Duryea—was a trap. How would it be sprung?

Then Corey saw Harold. On the left, as he had thought. He was moving from tree to tree as he had a few short days ago when he had eluded Corey in the arroyo.

But this time he didn't leap into a desert gully and slip away. He broke from the trees in a light-footed run, crossed the far lawn, making a dozen shadows in the light of the torches, shadows that all met at his slim running figure. He stopped, looked at the Duryea, then moved toward it.

My God! He thinks Gideon is hiding in it. It was part of the trap. Corey saw now that there was a sack or something propped in the front seat behind the steering lever.

Corey looked at the house. Nothing about the place had changed. The covered porch was still empty. Thank God! He had made it here in time to save his friend.

He left his cover in the line of trees and raced toward the dark form of Harold Bishop. He wanted to shout, thought better of it. It might alert Gideon or someone else inside. With any luck at all he could reach Harold and take him in before Gideon knew either one of them was there.

He was only fifty or sixty feet away from Harold before the Mimbreño heard him.

Harold turned.

"Corey—"

Then he looked past Corey, and his dark eyes went wide. His mouth opened.

Between the detonations of the Duryea Corey heard another, different cracking sound.

Harold shook once.

His knees buckled. He crumpled forward in the grass.

Corey turned to where the report of the pistol or rifle had seemed to come from, somewhere in or at the edge of the woods behind him.

Gideon Bainbridge was replacing a revolver in a holster tied off at the knee as Kessler's was.

Corey moved to Harold with all the speed he could and dropped to his knees beside him. The grass was wet from the first nighttime dew. Harold was on his face, and Corey rolled him over. The dark eyes looked sightless, but the lips were moving. Blood covered Harold's chest, and bubbles in it were catching the light just before they broke.

"Corey . . ." he rasped. Blood rising in his throat must already be choking him to death. He made another, weaker try, and Corey bent his head toward him. "It's up . . . to you . . . now—*k'is* . . . *i'ltse'* . . . *naagh*—" He didn't finish the word for "older brother."

He closed his eyes. The ax lay on the grass in front of him. Kessler's dried blood looked black in the yellow torchlight.

The blood on Harold's chest stopped bubbling.

The Duryea suddenly coughed its way into silence, too.

He would never remember getting to his feet.

Blind with rage?

No! He saw everything in front of him, saw it well. Gideon had crossed the wet lawn and had reached the house. The point from which he had fired couldn't have been a dozen feet from the trees in whose shelter Corey had hidden to watch the house. Gideon must have known he was there almost from the start—had heard him first as he crashed through the woods, then seen him and watched his every move.

Now Gideon was walking up the steps as casually as if he had just been out for a pleasant evening stroll.

At the top of the steps he reached over and took one of the lamps from its place on the railing of the porch.

"Gideon!"

Gideon turned.

"Yes, Corey? Is there something I can do for you?"

The cool, polished, courteous calm of the question set the blood to pounding in Corey's head.

"Do you know that I have been appointed sheriff of Chupadera County?" He was surprised at how low and steady he kept his voice. How innocent and reasonable it sounded. He was surprised, too, at how well he could hear the man on the porch and how well Gideon seemed to hear him, with all that expanse of lawn between them. Perhaps it was because the Duryea's noise had ceased. Their voices weren't raised a bit above the level they had ever used when they had worked together in the library.

"I heard talk to that effect. Congratulations. I'm very proud of you, son." Son? By God, he meant it!

"I'm placing you under arrest, Gideon."

Gideon looked puzzled, honestly puzzled. "What for, Corey?"

Corey pointed to Harold's body. "For murder."

"Oh, come, now. Murder? How can you possibly think that? That young Indian came here to kill me. And this isn't truly Chupadera County, anyway. This is Tres Piedras. I've never given anyone jurisdiction here."

"You're a lawyer, Gideon. You know well enough that jurisdiction isn't yours to give. This land is in Chupadera County, Territory of New Mexico. I'm the sheriff of this county, and I—" he swallowed hard, "have a warrant for your arrest on other matters, anyway." Would the lawyer in

Gideon make him show it and discover it wasn't valid yet? He tried to slow his breathing, which suddenly had gone a little wild.

Now something changed in Gideon's face, fully discernible even at this distance. His eyes had narrowed, but not enough to keep the torchlight from reflecting some sudden menace. The lamp was still in his left hand, but his right, which had hung quietly, almost primly at his side, made a nearly imperceptible brush of his holster.

"I wouldn't try to serve that warrant, Corey." The words found Corey's bowels.

There was nothing more to say.

Corey took a step toward the house.

The gun flashed into Gideon's right hand. The movement had been so efficient the lamp in his left didn't waver, and it took all the will Corey could muster not to reach for his own gun in reflex. Even if he managed to get it out before Gideon fired, he knew his chances of hitting Gideon from here were next to nothing. The markmanship Sam had praised was no match for that of the man in front of him. Corey stopped. Gideon was saying something.

"Don't! One of us will have to die."

"You're under arrest, Gideon." He took one more step.

Two flashes of fire erupted from the muzzle of Gideon's weapon.

Corey heard them splash in the grass beside his feet. He kept on moving.

"No!" Gideon had abandoned his cool, civil tone. "Please, Corey, *please!* Don't make me do it. You've meant too much to me."

Corey took another step.

The muzzle of the gun bloomed orange.

The shot took him full in the right shoulder and spun him halfway around. It was a second before the heat and pain began. There was no feeling in his hand. He might not be able to draw at all now, but he kept on walking. Another twenty feet and he could make a shot count if he wasn't dead by then.

Gideon's next shot ripped through his left thigh and took his leg out from under him. His face struck the wet grass hard. He pushed himself to his knees and began to crawl. He could feel blood gushing from his leg and a strange low drumming in his ears. Gideon's voice drifted to him from a million miles away.

"I told you in Sante Fe that I tried to stop it long ago and found I couldn't."

Corey's pants were soaking, but whether from the heavy dew or the blood that had spurted from him in seeming gallons, he couldn't tell. But Gideon only had one shot left. There had been one for Harold and four spent on him. If he could only crawl close enough before he lost all his strength, and if Gideon's last shot didn't kill him, he had a chance. But only if his right hand worked.

He made a few more feet or a thousand miles; he couldn't tell that, either. There was no point in going on. He was too weak to make it. He straightened up and nearly pitched to the grass again when dizziness and nausea seized him. He settled back on his heels. He reached for the Peacemaker Special and somehow dragged it from the holster.

He couldn't lift it.

The revolver Gideon held was perfectly aligned on the spot between Corey's eyes. When he fired that one remaining shot it wouldn't hurt as the shot through the leg had. It would be over before Corey took another breath.

Never just hold a gun on someone. When you point it at an enemy, always fire.

The gun didn't waver—but the expected flash didn't come.

Gideon Bainbridge lowered it as swiftly and surely as he had wiped it from the holster. Then he turned and took two stately, determined paces along the porch. He raised the lamp he still held and hurled it through the glass of the French doors of the library.

He gazed into the library, alight with an instant burst of flame, turned back, and came to the top of the steps again. He looked down at the revolver still in his hand, raised it again—put the muzzle in his mouth—and pulled the trigger.

The last thing Corey remembered before he tumbled into complete unconsciousness was the front of Tres Piedras masked by flame. The whole west wing that housed the library was ablaze. With a deafening roar the roof of the porch fell in just as he closed his eyes.

26

 "Señor Lane . . . Señor Lane!"

The voice broke through the hard shell of a dream.

He opened his eyes. Pedro Chavez stood in front of him. How did the little Mexican come to be here? The rest of the shell crumbled to shards. Gideon! He looked past Pedro, expecting to see the fire consuming the library, but there was no fire, no library, no house in front of him, and no Gideon—he was in a room somewhere, not sprawled on wet grass, but lying on a dry warm bed.

It was a small room, Spanish or Mexican. *Retablos*, their soft earth colors dim in the light barely seeping through drawn curtains, graced the walls, and a shelf straight ahead of him where he had looked for the fire held carved wooden *santos*.

Pedro was holding a glass of cloudy brown liquid toward him.

"I am sorry to wake you, Señor Lane, but you must drink this," he said. "*Es uno de los remedios de mi esposa.* Juanita says it makes the blood. You will need to make *mucha sangre, señor.* You have lost so much." He held the glass to Corey's lips.

Corey was too weak to protest, scarcely strong enough to sip, but he did. The drink was bitter. When he swallowed the last of it, he said, "Where am I, Pedro?"

"*En nuestra casa.* Juanita's house and mine. She stopped the bleeding and cleaned out the wounds, and when the fever came she took care of you all night, but you are better a little, cooler, *sí,* and now Juanita sleeps."

Yes, he remembered the little house Gideon had built for the couple a dozen years ago, close to Tres Piedras, but discreetly tucked away in the ponderosas, out of sight. There had been plenty of room for them with Gideon in his huge, rambling house. He must have been courting loneliness for longer than anybody knew.

"How did I come to be here, Pedro?"

"When Juanita and I saw the fire last night, we ran to *la casa grande.* We could not get close to it. The heat, *señor.* We found you in the yard." He looked away. "We found Harold, too." Yes, he had known Harold Bishop as a boy. "We didn't find Señor Gideon, though. He must not have escaped the fire.

What must Pedro and Juanita have thought last night, and what must they be thinking now? They would know he hadn't received these wounds fighting a fire, with a revolver in his hand and with a dead Apache next to him.

Where *was* his father's gun? No matter. He didn't need it now, and he didn't much care if he never saw it again.

Something stabbed at him. "Sam!" he cried.

"Sam, *señor?*"

"Sam Naaki, the Mescalero officer. He's hurt, too. Bad. And he's alone."

"We found no one there but you and Harold, Señor Lane.

Tell me where Señor Naaki is, and we will go and get him. If he is hurt, he will need Juanita, *también*."

It was a week before Corey could even think of returning to the X-Bar-7, two days at Pedro and Juanita's, five more in Black Springs. He had wanted to go straight home from Tres Piedras, but the ride Pedro gave him into town in the buckboard—with Pedro protesting weakly that he still wasn't fit to travel—had taken a heavy toll. Jim got him into a room at the Sacramento House and Dr. Colvin came to see him twice a day.

"You're a lucky man the Chavez woman was there, Corey," the doctor said. "The hole in your thigh is just a flesh wound, but it's as big as Bronco Canyon, and it sure leaked a lot of blood. If she hadn't stopped the bleeding, you'd be pushing up daisies now. Thanks to her your wounds are healing nicely. I think you'll want to keep your arm in a sling for a month or so, but you should walk in another two weeks."

He railed at "another two weeks." He had to walk, and he had to ride. He wanted to go to the X-Bar-7 and see Lucy *now*.

But he knew the medical man was right. Or was he unknowingly glad he couldn't get up and go to her? He wanted her badly enough, but he dreaded seeing her—and Ana, too. Someone had to tell them about Harold, and it should be him. He pinned Jim down about it his third day at the Sacramento.

"What have you told them at the X-Bar-7 about what happened at Tres Piedras, Jim?"

"Nothing, really. Just that there had been some trouble at Tres Piedras and that Gideon is dead. They know you're hurt, but not how bad. I'm going out there again in a day or two."

"Don't scare them, Jim. I'm doing fine. And don't tell them

about Harold. I'll do that. Just get Lucy and Virgie to come and see me—Ana, too. I'll tell them then."

He didn't see Jim the next day, but the following day the publisher dropped in with Tom.

They didn't talk about Gideon or about the investigation up in Sante Fe. They didn't speak of Harold's death, either. Instead, the two newspapermen bent every word toward that damned election in the fall. Would Corey make the run? Corey shook his head. He hoped he meant it.

Tom stayed behind when Jim left, and then he did discuss the happenings in the capital. He told Corey Eloy's investigation was sure to result in the arrest of Horace Lattner and four others on half a dozen charges, including obstruction of justice, accepting bribes, and conspiracy. "Sure feel sorry for them Polacks Lattner and Kessler enticed to the upper Concho. They would make good citizens here in the Territory, but they're talking of heading back to Illinois. Jim has some idea that they could be granted some Tres Piedras land, since the state is bound to get it, but that could take years, even though Gideon had no heirs."

No heirs? What about. . .

He decided he had better hold his tongue until he talked to *both* the Bishop women.

Tom went on. "Jim will keep trying, though. You know how stubborn he is, Corey. He's already hired a lawyer up in Sante Fe to work with Eloy on presenting the proposition to the Territorial government and in Washington, and he's bought food and grain and had it wagoned up to the immigrants' camp, along with a ton of candy for their kids."

It shamed Corey a little. Here was Jim, who had done so much over the years for his community and his country, and just for other *people*, all kinds of people—stirring himself to action on behalf of some he didn't even know; and here was Corey Lane, who wouldn't do the one thing everyone seemed to agree might make things better here for friends and neighbors.

Eloy had gone back to Sante Fe, and it was too much to expect that the former senator would make yet another trip down the valley before Corey left for the X-Bar-7. In a way, he was glad. He knew that if Eloy were here, he would turn that persuasive silence on him again about standing for election in November. Added to Tom's pleas, and to Jim's, Eloy's silence might prove too much to hold out against. Tom, just before leaving, had piled it on again, too, about what a "great thing it would be for Chupadera County if you'd get into public life."

By the time Virgie came to see him, his fifth day at the Sacramento, he had been half carried down to the dining room by Bernardo and a busboy for his dinner for a couple of nights. To his surprise and disappointment, Virgie came alone. They sat in the lobby in the easy chairs near the front.

"Lucy?" he asked.

"Tell me how you are first," she said. She seemed uncomfortable.

"Not bad. I got good care. First from Juanita, and now here in Black Springs." He tried to look into her eyes, but she kept her gaze away from him. "You're stalling, Virgie. Where's Lucy? Why hasn't she been to see me?"

"Jim lied to you, Corey—a little. Lucy and Ana and I have known everything since the day Pedro brought you down to Black Springs. Please don't think too badly about Jim. He wanted you to mend a little before—"

"That doesn't answer my question."

"I know it doesn't." Now her eyes met his. It was the honest look he had always gotten from her, strangely missing for a few seconds there. "I was about to lie to you, too, Corey."

"Forget that. You know about Harold, then?"

"Yes."

"And Lucy and Ana know as well?"

She said nothing. Her lower lip was quivering.

Suddenly he felt as burned out inside as the great house at Tres Piedras had looked from his litter in the buckboard the day Pedro had brought him to town.

"Something's wrong!" he said. "How *is* Lucy?"

She still held her eyes steady on his. "I can't honestly say, Corey. She's not at the X-Bar-7 now."

"They've gone back up to the Mescalero?"

"No." The steady eyes suddenly brimmed with tears. She opened her handbag, took out a handkerchief, and dabbed at them. Then she reached in the bag again and pulled out an envelope. It was one that matched the X-Bar-7's stationery. "She left this for you, Corey."

When he took the envelope from her, his hand trembled with far more violence than had her lip. He tore it open.

My dearest love—

By the time Virgie brings this to you and you read it, Ana and I will have reached Fort Sill.

We have kin there, as, of course, did Tony. The council has found a teaching position for me there, and Ana and I will be all right.

I can truly do something for my people at Fort Sill. Some of the children there have no idea what being an Apache means, other than that white people hate them.

It is so hard to tell you how much I love you, and say good-bye at the same time.

Even harder to tell you I can never marry you.

That's not to say I don't want to. I do. I just cannot.

I have known for a long time that marriage between us was never truly meant to be, but I was too much in love with you to face the truth.

Please believe me that this has nothing to do with

Harold's death or the fact that I am Gideon's daughter. I will accept both those things in time.

It was the dinner at Ellen Stafford's that finally made me see why we weren't meant to be together. When I watched you sit with her at the piano, I realized that hers is the kind of home in which you belong.

The good people in Black Springs and Chupadera County are counting on you, Corey.

Running for sheriff will, or should, be only the start. That start would never happen if you took an Indian wife. Things are better between our two peoples now, but some things haven't changed enough. Maybe they won't even in our lifetimes, although we can hope and pray and, above all, do what little we can to change the bad things, each in our own way. Your way should be clear to you.

Please stand for election in November. Do it for me, I beg you. Or else all this is wasted.

Even if I stayed, I would not marry you. Oh, I think I would be your *kah*, your mistress. That would not be good for you, either, as a public man, nor for me as a woman, but I know I wouldn't be able to stop myself. That is why I must go away.

Forgive me for writing all this, and not coming in to tell you face to face. I would weaken at the sight of you, and *never* tell you then.

I will never forget you, Corey. Please try to keep one small good memory of me.

I love you with all my *jeh*, and I will love you until *dahitsaah*.

—Lucy

I love you with all my heart, and I will love you until death.

"When did they leave?" he asked when he finally looked at Virgie.

"Two days ago. Luís drove them in to town to catch the train."

He looked out through the glass doors of the Sacramento House. She must have rolled right down the street outside while he lay like a slug in that dismal second-floor front room. He should have felt something. He should have known she was close by. When you're in love you're supposed to *sense* these things.

"You know what's in this letter, Virgie?" He kept on staring at the street.

"Yes. I tried to talk her out of it, of course. She wouldn't listen, and she made me promise not to tell. I had to respect her wishes, Corey."

"I know you did."

Across the street the sign on the *portál* of the adobe office building was swinging a little in the afternoon breeze: GIDEON BAINBRIDGE—ATTORNEY.

He turned back.

"I've just decided something."

"What?" she said.

"I'm going to run for sheriff in November."

In spite of some vestigial pain in her eyes, Virgie turned radiant. "I'm glad! I'm truly glad, Corey. I never thought I would be, but I am."

She suddenly looked a little different from any way he could ever remember her looking. She looked free. Yes, free!

"Now . . ." he said, "I want you to do something for me. And for yourself."

"What's that?"

"I want you to say yes to Jim McPherson the next time he asks you to marry him." He laughed. It wasn't a big laugh, but it was the only one he had had in a long, long time. "My guess is that he will ask you again in about thirty minutes, when the paper's been put to bed and he comes here and finds you with me. He asks you every time he sees you, doesn't he?"

She sat straight up, her mouth open. "I might just do that. Yes, I very well might!"

"Not 'might.' Do it, Virgie! The poor devil's waited long enough."

27

Corey had been back at the X-Bar-7 for a week. Dr. Colvin had been too pessimistic. Corey was not only walking well, but he found he could drop his right arm from the sling for two or three hours at a time without too much pain in his shoulder.

When Jim had helped Luís Mendoza load him in the ranch buckboard, he had pressed on Corey a packet of material for him to study before the campaign began in earnest in September. The publisher had seen to his petitions and had gone to the courthouse with him when he filed. He was a happy man.

"Your mother hasn't said yes to me yet, Corey. But she let slip a maybe. Do you know how far that means I've come?"

It made it easier that the shoulder didn't keep him from working. The house, with Virgie riding in the high eastern pastures looking after her roundup crew most of the daylight hours, on these, the longest days of the year, was empty from sunup until sundown, save for María, who had never been much of a talker at any point in her nearly three score years and ten.

One of Sam's men rode down from the Mescalero.

"Sam said I should look you over and go back and tell him how you are," the Apache said.

"How is *he*?"

"Bad-tempered. Driving us loco. He don't like them crutches, and he says that plaster stuff they put on his leg itches.

Corey's forced idleness and solitude gave him plenty of time to write. And he did. Some of the work he turned out was passable.

Of course it was a little tougher getting on with it, knowing he could never again go to Gideon's when he hit a snag. Maybe his career as a historian would come to a full stop soon—and maybe, if he could win the election this fall, by no means a certainty, he could somehow find fulfillment in the sheriffing business. He damned well had to.

But he would never give up on the history, not if it took him until *dahitsaah*.

Well, he never *had* believed he could keep Lucy out of his mind, even for a moment.

On his eighth day back, sitting on the patio with his manuscript for a change from the study, he saw a buckboard pulled by two sorry animals that weren't X-Bar-7 stock coming up the ranch road. There were two people in it. He put his work down and went through the gate in the patio wall to the front of the house to see who they were.

It was Pedro and Juanita Chavez.

"I forgot to give you this when you left our house, Señor Lane." Pedro held out a bulky object wrapped in heavy muslin.

It was the Peacemaker Special. He almost said no, he

didn't want it, but then he decided that if Virgie had freed herself from the ghost that rode this range so long, so, damn it, could he.

"*Gracias*, Pedro," he said. After all, he would need a gun of some kind if he won his new job permanently.

Pedro looked embarrassed. Corey knew he hadn't forgotten the revolver that day. He had hidden it the night he found it and had kept it hidden until he was absolutely sure of his wounded, surely delirious guest. These old people had in all likelihood been scared to death of him, but Juanita, with her husband's help, had nursed him back to life without any hesitation.

Then Corey's heart went out to the little ex-majordomo and his lady for quite another reason. The buckboard was piled with their belongings: the *retablos*, pots and pans, bedding, the melancholy-looking *santos*, boxes by the dozen. With Gideon gone, they had no stomach any longer for the little house he had built for them.

"Do you need a job, Pedro?" he asked. "I'm sure we could find something for the two of you here at the X-Bar-7. María isn't getting any younger."

"*No, no, no, señor! Pero gracias.* Juanita and I have an *hijo* in Alamogordo. Antonio wishes us to live with him *ahora*. He says *his* children need *los abuelos*."

"Didn't know you had grandchildren. I'm happy for you."

Pedro began to turn the buckboard. "*Adiós*, Señor Lane."

"*Vaya con Dios, familia Chavez.*" He waved good-bye.

Pedro shook the reins of his team; then he suddenly pulled them in. He set the lever brake and left the seat.

"*Dios!*" he cried. "I have become a *viejo estupido*. I have forgotten something else—twice." He went to the rear and lifted out two heavily taped boxes. "Señor Gideon brought these to our shed the night before the fire and said that if anything happened to him we were to bring them to you. When you were so bad at our *casa* I forgot them."

"What's in them, Pedro?"

"I do not know, *señor*! Señor Gideon said they were for you alone to see." He sounded scandalized. As if Pedro Chavez, majordomo of Tres Piedras, would ever question in any respect the orders of his *patrón*!

Corey waited until they were half a mile down the road before he carted the boxes to the study to open them.

The smaller box was the size of a letter box and not heavy, but the other was bulky and carried a bit of weight. His shoulder was giving him fits by the time he placed them on the desk.

He opened the smaller one first—and found Tony Bishop's journal. Gideon hadn't destroyed it, after all.

He waited a few minutes for his pulse to slow again before he tackled the other box.

The inside of it was jammed with wadded-up copies of the *Chupadera County News*. Someone had packed it seven years ago. The newspapers were all dated 1893. He pulled the packing out.

Grinning up at him, faintly yellow and shot through with hairline cracks, was a massive human skull.

AUTHOR'S NOTE

 Some of the characters mentioned in this story were real people in the Territory of New Mexico before or at the turn of the century.

Miguel Otero occupied *el palacio de los gobernadores* in Santa Fe in 1900, and Mangas Coloradas, "Red Sleeves," was real, as were many of the other great Apache chiefs Corey struggled to write about.

The story of the giant Mimbreño warrior's death at Fort Craig is true, so far as the record shows. His outsized head was hacked off after he was killed, and his skull was used on the lecture circuits of the East by the phrenologist Orson Squire Fowler, also real, who told his audiences, among other things, that Mangas was "almost as intelligent as a white man because of his apparently great brain weight, unusual among the inferior races."

When Fowler died in 1887, the skull disappeared, as Corey Lane discovered.

Was the skull Pedro Chavez delivered to Corey the genuine article? Did Corey believe it was?

The author can't answer those two questions.

The descendants of the Red Paint People still want Mangas's head returned, but no one has ever reported finding it.

His spirit, in the Apache view, cannot rest until his skull is back with the rest of him.

The author thinks that Corey probably could never have been entirely sure the one in his possession was that of Mangas. Not having proof, he would have been reluctant to claim it was and to give it to the Mimbreños. The author can't believe the Corey Lane he knows would deprive his friends of this sacred object if he knew for sure.

N.Z.

MORE FROM NORMAN ZOLLINGER

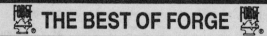

THE BEST OF FORGE

❑ 55052-8	LITERARY REFLECTIONS *James Michener*	$5.99 Canada $6.99	
❑ 52046-7	A MEMBER OF THE FAMILY *Nick Vasile*	$5.99 Canada $6.99	
❑ 52288-5	WINNER TAKE ALL *Sean Flannery*	$5.99 Canada $6.99	
❑ 58193-8	PATH OF THE SUN *Al Dempsey*	$4.99 Canada $5.99	
❑ 51380-0	WHEN SHE WAS BAD *Ron Faust*	$5.99 Canada $6.99	
❑ 52145-5	ZERO COUPON *Paul Erdman*	$5.99 Canada $6.99	

Buy them at your local bookstore or use this handy coupon:
Clip and mail this page with your order.

Publishers Book and Audio Mailing Service
P.O. Box 120159, Staten Island, NY 10312-0004

Please send me the book(s) I have checked above. I am enclosing $ _____
(Please add $1.50 for the first book, and $.50 for each additional book to cover
postage and handling. Send check or money order only— no CODs.)

Name_____

Address_____

City_____State / Zip_____

Please allow six weeks for delivery. Prices subject to change without notice.